THE FOREIGNER'S TALE

THE FOREIGNER'S TALE

A Novel

By John Scott Brinkerhoff

Book Design & Production: Columbus Publishing Lab
www.ColumbusPublishingLab.com

LCCN: 2018963084
Paperback ISBN: 978-1-63337-235-1
Hardback ISBN: 978-1-63337-236-8

Printed in the United States of America
1 3 5 7 9 10 8 6 4 2

This book was written for the three youngest

of the wonderful women in my life.

Long may they reign.

Vastland Sea

WELLAN

Blue Mountains

MAURISIA

Broom Island

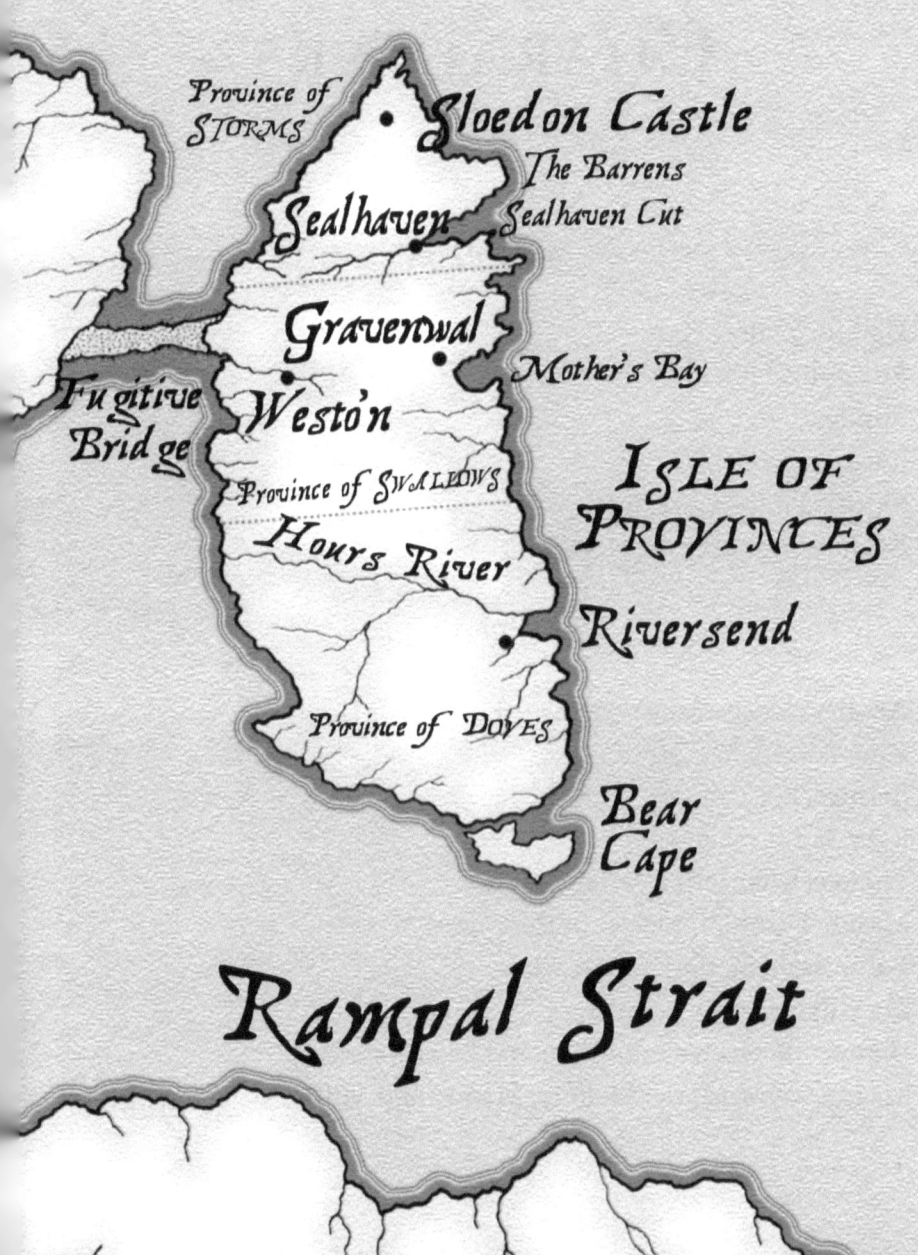

Norwall

Province of
STORMS · Sloedon Castle
The Barrens
Sealhaven Sealhaven Cut

Gravenwal
Weston Mother's Bay

Fugitive ISLE OF
Bridge Province of SWALLOWS PROVINCES

Hours River
Riversend

Province of DOVES

Bear
Cape

Rampal Strait

PRINCIPAL CHARACTERS

MAURISIA

Harald, a village boy
Edvar, his father
Sundor, a hunter
Jovar, a competitor
Sigrit, Harald's girlfriend
Paulus, one of the interlopers

GRAVENWALL

Anelie, Queen of the Province of Swallows
King Allred, her father
Bernice, her mother
Rory, her brother
Thomas Chancellor, family advisor
Master Turnbolt, Master of the Guard
Tutor Sashem, the castle teacher
Ma Guen, Celia's seamstress
Hanna, Ma Guen's foundling and Anelie's friend
Madge, Myra, Marie, Melody, Mandy and Millie, Ma Guen's girls

Baron Alfred, her uncle (Sloedon Castle)
Bernice, her aunt (Sloedon Castle)
Harald Stonearm, marauder from Maurisia, usurper of Gravenwall

ON THE LIONFISH AND THE ROAD TO GRAVENWALL

Passage Master Penwyn, captain
Captain Kepper, Captain of the *Lionfish*
Dogman, a traveler aka The Foreigner
Fogbow, a Bear Dog
Rollie Roundtree, a wagon wheel entrepreneur
Mister Starling, an enchanter

RIVERSEND

Mister Carpenter, a shipwright
Benjamin, his son
Marya, his daughter
Mother, a baker and mother of Benjamin and Marya
Mistress Nearly, the local schoolteacher
Harbor Master Twining, ship traffic manager
Micah, his son
Brother Gerome, leader of Brotherhood of Penitents
Lorr Burnside, Doves sea guardsman
Rand, his nephew
Darwen Avellone, Special Counsel to the Sovereign Lord and Lady
Captain Treer, skipper of the *Red Moon*

THE BLEAK SHOALS

Brother Moutin, who gave a cloak to Benjamin
Brother Tom, helped Benjamin at the wheel
Brother Caril, part-time helmsman
Brother Enoch, a fisherman
Umjuno, leader of the Tulak

THE GYLGOVANS

Wulfkin, name given to Benjamin by Kinish
Kinish, captain of the *Abbe Glen*
Snod, a villager
Rogie, a shipmate
Porcee, a shipmate
Rowen, a Broom Island expatriate
Leeni, Kinish's wife
Abbe, their daughter

RED CLIFFS

Lord Tryon Freehold, Sovereign Lord of Rampal, Indus, and the Isle of Provinces
Lady Freehold, Tryon's wife
Princess Lilea, their daughter
Princess Sofia, their daughter

Book One

A Year Of Songs And Light

Chapter One

HARALD

And so it was that in the Seventh Year of Peace, when the milk trees shed their blossoms in the fresh spring breezes which trailed them like drifts of snow across the green, green hills of the Province of Swallows, that King Harald Stonearm declared a celebration to be inaugurated in early summer and marked by a storytelling competition planned to last until the milk trees once again shed their brilliant blooms one year hence. The winner, to be decided by Harald himself and judged by his level of amusement, would be granted 20 hectares of prime farming land and one bull, not too old. The contest was to be held in the amphitheater on the morning side of Castle Gravenwall so everyone who cared to listen could enjoy the game. When cold weather or rain arrived, the proceedings would be moved indoors and as many locals as could be safely accommodated would be admitted into Gravenwall's Great Hall.

King Harald, as might be assumed from his pleasure in the art, was no stranger to storytelling himself, having spent a middling share of his childhood in Maurisia (a cold, isolated wilderness far from where he sat now) gathering tales from among the rough, fur-bundled kinsmen of his clan as they escaped through flights of embellishment the fitful winds and broken, brooding skies out-side their smoky longhouses. Harald enjoyed the telling as much as the tale, noting that inspiration often seemed to come from an idle beard-stroke or ear tug accompanied by a playful light in the speaker's eyes that did not come from the fidgeting flames of the communal fire. Sometimes he heard a muffled chuckle from the shadows where the women were tending babies, if there were any at the time, or stitching hides or grinding bread grains between two curved stones.

The stories, quite logically, came from the labors of their lives, as certain clans contributed certain skills to the community at large. Harald's clan, most having been born with an impatience for the tedious work of weaving the tough strands of climbing vines or tanning, and born without the artistic sensibilities for construc-tion, adornment or tool-making, were hunters. They were greatly respected for their knowledge of the vast surrounding forests and their skill in navigating them, an expertise accumulated over many generations and passed along from the old to the young. As a re-sult, Harald began his schooling among the towering trees and del-icate ground cover at a very early age. He was first taught plant and shrub identification, a simple and suitable subject for a child even though one could spend a lifetime on such things. His education in the local greenery was both for the purpose of learning which ani-mals or birds favored which plants, and which plants would either sustain or poison the hunter. That curled and clotted patch of tree moss? A bear has scratched its back against it. That lovely cluster of bright, blue berries? Taste them, and you'll be squatting in the weeds for hours.

So time passed for Harald, stalking the woodlands with his father Edvar during the day and listening to strange tales in the evening. The weaver Danolf once told of putting the finishing touches on an intricately knotted design for an entrance mat when, as he prepared to sew the last stitches, a fearsome spirit appeared, wavering like smoke before him, warning him that some designs possessed magical powers and to complete them would condemn the entire village to be swallowed up whole into a maw of fire and molten stone. Thereafter, one could always spot Danolf's work by distinctive tufts of loose fibers at the corners, knotted below their unfinished ends.

But it was those who left the sight of the villagers who always had the best tales to tell. The hunters, the plant and egg gatherers, the woodsmen and the fishers of the cold black lake that lay among the trees beyond their clearing were the ones who knew of giant stags with fangs the length of a man's hand, and cackling bird spirits which would pluck out the eyes of anyone who looked directly at them, and darting sprites of the forest floor which no one could ever quite see no matter how hard they looked, and the King of the Trees, which continually moved from place to place so that it could never be found except by the forest creatures under its benevolent rule.

Some storytellers were better than others. Some spoke haltingly or corrected themselves or added details in hindsight, and Harald noticed in those sees how quickly inattention set in among the listeners. Others, however, recreated their adventures so clearly that everyone was involved in the moment; everyone felt the hot breath of monsters and the fear of a breaking twig in the darkness. When these people spoke, Harald saw an audience locked to the speaker's words, all activity suspended, as if spellbound.

Danolf was hesitant, uncomfortable being the center of attention. Harald's father, Edvar, and Ror, the best fisherman in the village, were compelling. Sundor, Edvar's favorite hunting companion, never told a story at all, preferring to sit at the edge of the firelight with his brightened eyes shifting back and forth between speaker and listeners with a strange air of expectancy. Harald envied the speakers upon whom all eyes were riveted, the ones who with only their voice and illustrating hands led the imaginations of others wherever they wanted them to go. He envied that skill because it represented power.

Even at an early age, Harald also recognized that the best tellers had a stature that set them above the rest. Had Ror really driven off the water snake with barbed tentacles and a mouth big enough to swallow every unattended child whole? No matter if he had or had not, everyone believed he could. This was a truth Harald felt more than thought.

His father possessed such power. In fact, one of Harald's favorite stories was of a place his father spoke of one winter evening. He told a tale of hunting boar with Sundor, and spearing an animal that under normal circumstances would have dropped dead on the spot, but in this case was especially large and furious. It fled into the deep forest, and Edvar and Sundor chased its blood trail farther and farther until they were in a part of the woods they had never seen before. Day followed day. They heard the boar once in a while, just ahead, crashing through the undergrowth, and continued to be led along by bright red spots and smears of boar's blood. The trees were unfamiliar. The birds shrieked at them. Frantic rustlings erupted in the thick ground cover beside and ahead of them, causing the exotic, brilliant blossoms of strange plants to sway in the shadows. Neither man could believe how the boar had survived this long, or gone this far, but here they were, days beyond the farthest they had ever traveled before. Then, as they had just decided to turn around and follow the blood trail backward, Sundor saw shifting light ahead. They crept forward slowly, spear and bow upraised.

The light grew brighter, but dimmed and flared in an uneven

rhythm. They kept advancing toward a screen of ferns higher than their heads, its delicate leaves becoming translucent and then dark green in the rising and falling light. They parted the stalks and stared in wonder.

They had come to the end of a forest they did not know had an end. Ahead of them was a vast plain of chest-high grass that rippled and flowed in the wind like the surface of the lake near their village. Overhead was a dome of blue sky clotted with great white clouds the size of longhouses, and as these passed in front of the blazing sun they dimmed the light and turned the sea of grass to purple and blue. In the distance, impossibly far away, was a wall of mountains with brilliant white caps, though neither Edvar nor Sundor really knew what they were.

The world was silent.

Frightened, they dared not step into the grass, having no idea what to expect once they left the safety of the trees. The blood trail did not go there, either, which meant that the wounded boar was behind them now. Nervously they watched the grass ahead and listened to the woods behind.

A gust of wind came with the next shadow. It flattened the grass. Sundor pointed.

Ahead, between them and the far mountains was a large, dark object atop thick curved legs. It was immense. Both Sundor and Edvar recognized its shape instantly. They were gazing at a spider bigger and darker than any imagination could conjure. It remained motionless, though the men knew it had seen them. When the wind passed and the grasses stood up again to hide the spider, both men turned and quickly backtracked.

Day followed day, until they returned to their familiar forest and their hearts calmed again. Fortunately they managed to kill two small boars on the way back, so they did not return empty- handed.

Harald was entranced by that tale. Though Edvar's voice was soft and his modulation less exaggerated than some, he made the story so vivid that it sent a shiver down Harald's neck.

Harald sometimes practiced using his voice and hands as he repeated sections of stories he had heard previously, but only when alone in a shady glen beyond the last longhouse at the edge of the village. He dared not try it in front of anyone else, because he had no story of his own to tell, and would rather be carried off by Ror's water snake than be laughed at. But there, in the cool breeze and mottled shade, he felt places where he had never been take shape, and creatures he had never seen come to life. He put great trees where he wanted them, and caused the sun to rise or the clouds to mob the moon when he wished. He made the great earth turn within his hands.

He felt the first stirrings of power.

By the time Harald was eleven years old, he had learned enough to find his way home after short forays into the woods and was a reliable enough plant gatherer to contribute to the family table as well as the village emergency food cache. He had also learned what animals and birds lived around him, where and when they moved on their feeding or migratory rounds, where they slept and found water, and what they ate. Edvar was pleased that Harald never resisted his instruction in order to play, but rather found play in the instruction. Edvar also liked the way Harald moved in the woods, keeping his weight on his rear foot while lightly putting down his lead foot, gently brushing aside dry sticks or leaves if need be, before moving himself forward. The motion was oddly bird-like, but very nearly silent. Harald had become so adept in this technique that he could move along fairly quickly without making a sound any louder than the wind stirring dry stalks. Edvar sensed that Harald was born to be a hunter, even though he was only hunting wild carrots at the moment.

How he would actually spend his life in the village would be determined within the next circle of seasons or two, because now his serious schooling was to begin.

At the beginning of his twelfth birth season, he and fourteen other children his age were brought together into a single group, boys and girls together. They had also been studying various skills from their parents up to that point, but now they would all be taught something about everything. For the village to flourish in good times and bad, every person had to do whatever work they were best suited for, and here was where such decisions were made.

The children of course already knew each other, but on the first day of lessons together they still gathered into two separate clusters. And as boys will do, Harald and his acquaintances decided among themselves who would be best at certain things before the first adult word was uttered to them. They had concluded that Lohin would be the best at eating, Piri the best at peeing the farthest and Garal the best at sleeping the longest before they were told to be quiet and herded off to a cooking lesson.

The girls were bored, most being familiar with this instruction already, and the boys were fidgety, knowing that in the grand scheme of things the females would cook for them for the rest of their lives anyway except for the occasional fire-seared rabbit on a long outing. Harald, however, was eager to learn all he could for reasons he could not name. He simply felt compelled to know as much as possible about how certain ingredients combined to create different consistencies and tastes, what roots and leaves were best for creating the largest quantities of soups and stews, and how long to boil or heat various items for the most nourishment and best flavor. His interest was so strong and such a rewarding novelty that the women instructing the group were soon focusing most of their attention on Harald while enjoying themselves immensely. In a way, the student became the teacher, for in the midst of this lively exercise the women began revealing their own ingenious, proprietary little secrets to each other as they disclosed them to the boy.

The next lesson swung the group to the other end of the spectrum as they were taught how to skin, dress, and harvest particular organs of several different kinds of animals, birds, and fish. In this, most of the boys were already somewhat knowledgeable and the girls were notably squeamish. Harald was already adept at skinning smaller creatures, so when a lovely young girl named Sigrit, whom he had noticed from time to time about the village, started her practice on a dead hare, he gently guided her hand and said, "No. Like this." She glanced at him quickly several times and seemed to enjoy the light touch of his hand, but said nothing.

The boy who appeared to be Harald's closest rival in intelligence and nascent skill was taller then him, quiet, and watchful. His name was Jovar, and he too glanced up as Harald helped instruct Sigrit, though Harald never noticed.

They alternated between cooking and skinning for several days, and Harald's interest in the alchemy of the cooking pot never flagged. Sigrit, however, proved to be quite timid when it came to ripping the hides off various creatures, recoiling at the sound of the pelt leaving the flesh. Harald was puzzled by her reaction, but merely shrugged it off as he perfected his own skills. It seemed to him that as most of the boys were content to let the women manage the cooking, the girls were content to let the boys, Harald in particular, handle the dismemberment of the game because that was the way it had always been. The notion of so little change made Harald feel uneasy and restless.

After the elders concluded that at least the fundamentals of cooking, dressing game, and managing pelts had been adequately covered, they moved the children along to lessons in sewing the hides into clothing and the care of hunting tools.

Their knives, spears, bows, and arrows were made of the bone, stone, vines, and wood that surrounded them. These had to be fashioned and honed with patience and delicacy. Harald much preferred the next phase of the process, the actual hunting and tracking, but applied himself as diligently as he was able to mastering the maintenance of the edges and points, knowing that his own dinner or perhaps his life would depend on it. Sigrit, he noticed, considered the whole thing a chore and a bore, another skill to be left to the hands of men.

The first day, as they practiced stitching small hides together with gut thread, Harald pinched two edges together and started his thorn needle through. A hand softly touched his.

"No," Sigrit said. "Like this."

She scraped a thin band free of fur at the edge of each pelt and overlaid them, then had Harald stitch them through a seam as thin as the cut of a fingernail. He saw the sense of it.

"It will not let water in," she said.

"Nor scrape my own hide."

They made small items that would not waste fur if they were incorrect: a glove, a small pouch for extra arrow string, a baby's shoe. Harald learned his needlework well. The elders noticed.

The elders also noticed that Harald and Sigrit would make a fine couple when they came of wedding age in their fifteenth birth seasons. They were handsome children, looked comfortable together, and their skills complemented each other well. Other matches among the children were more difficult to envision, as they did not seem to gravitate to each other as easily as these two did. In Harald and Sigrit, however, they saw the future of the village.

As for encouraging the children to pursue their strengths, it was clear to all when the first round of lessons was completed that the best hunters among them were Jovar and Harald. Of the two, Harald was the better tracker and skinner, but Jovar was physically stronger and a better marksman. The two were neither friends nor rivals, because each respected the other's abilities. They were cordial and cooperative, but guarded. Even at the age of twelve, they both knew they would never in their lifetimes grow any closer than they were then. This development was of little concern to anyone, for as long as Jovar and Harald weren't vengeful or openly critical of each other, the village would prosper.

But Harald differed from Jovar in one profound respect that would eventually affect his entire community.

One cool day with a dark, bruised sky overhead, Sigrit came upon Harald at the edge of the village, standing at the head of the Lake Path. He was outfitted with a food pouch, his skinning knife, a short spear, and hide gloves. Sigrit found this amusing and smiled at him.

"My goodness, why are you dressed like that?" she asked.

Harald looked at her coldly.

"I'm going to the lake."

Her smile washed away, though, truth be told, it was due more to the severity of Harald's glance than concern for what he was doing. "By yourself? Alone? The water snake will get you."

"It can try."

"Why do want to tempt it? Everyone will be angry with you if you get eaten. I will be angry too."

Harald studied her face. "You will? Why?"

"Because you are a good hunter and the village needs you."

He nodded with a fleeting expression of disappointment and looked away.

"The village has my father, and Sundor, and Jovar. The snake must be killed for everyone to be safe. I'm going to do it."

"By the time you see it, it will be too late. It will eat you."

"I know how to fight it," Harald said confidently. "I've learned about snakes in the forest." An idea occurred to him. He glanced back toward Sigrit. "Do you want to go with me?"

Sigrit drew back, shocked by the thought.

"No, no. I'd be too afraid. I could never do that."

"Afraid of what? You don't know if there really is a water snake."

"Ror said there was. So there is. And it will eat you. And you are being selfish."

Harald nodded again, only this time there was glint of contempt in his eyes.

"If it is there, it should be killed. I'll try to be back before dark. Don't tell anyone I've gone to the lake. Just say I'm out hunting for mushrooms. If one of the elders appears, the snake will not come out."

"If someone asks me, I must—"

"Just tell them I'm hunting mushrooms," Harald interrupted. "If I'm not back by morning, then you can tell them where I really went." He looked sternly at her. "Don't fail me, Sigrit."

"Yes, Harald."

Her meekness surprised him, but he had seen the same reaction in his own mother from time to time, when Edvar was firm about something.

Feeling far more fearful than he appeared, Harald walked briskly down the path into the dimness of the trees, glancing back once to see Sigrit standing motionless, watching him go.

The way was cool and still. Harald heard insects clicking and humming in the thick foliage beside him, but they did not pester him. He recalled the name of each slender vine and bright bloom he passed, and paused once to gather a handful of meal nuts from a low-hanging branch. Chewing on the firm, earthy nutmeat and surrounded by the woods he knew so well, his anxiety relaxed. He felt comfortable and at peace.

After he had walked a mile or so, he saw light ahead at the end of the trail. He quietly asked the forest spirits to look after him and not stray too far from his side. Then he cautiously stepped away from the shadows onto the lake's shore, a long band of small stones that curved into distant trees.

The surface of the lake rippled slightly in the breeze. Overhead, a cold sun occasionally dimmed behind great cliffs of cloud. Even though the lake water was black and deep, it was clear enough for Harald to see glints of silver far below as schools of fish lazily made their rounds.

Harald found a long stick and jammed it into the rocky beach at an angle. He took off his tunic and hung it on the end of the stick, where it swayed on the passing breaths of wind. He reasoned that the snake would be drawn to the tunic first while he waited motionless nearby. When it came to explore the tunic's scent with its flickering tongue, he would slice it off. Without its tongue to guide it, the snake would have a much harder time locating him, and the advantage would be his. The trickiest part of the operation would be cutting off the tongue before the snake sensed him coming. Here his practiced quickness would be his greatest weapon.

He sat in a shadow a few yards from the bait with his skinning knife in hand and the short spear at his side. His eyes searched the lapping water while he imagined a huge scaled head rising from the lake, its tongue flickering this way and that searching for prey, and its jaws yawning open like the mouth of a foul, final cave.

But somehow, Harald knew there was no snake. He suspected the tale was a way to keep the village children away from the deep water unless someone older was there to watch them. And, as the peaceful morning wore on and the great white clouds drifted slowly by and the birds chattered from the edge of the forest, he became more certain he was right. After all, how could there be monsters in a place so serene?

He tossed stones into the water. He piled them up into columns, and then knocked them down. He walked the beach to the edge of the trees. He dragged a smooth log onto the stones and sat on it to eat his lunch from the food pouch. He took a nap in the sun. Then, as the shadows began to advance across the shore, he put on his tunic, used the stake for a walking stick, and went home.

Edvar and Sundor were waiting for him. His father was leaning against a tree at the end of the path with his arms folded over his chest, just out of sight of the last longhouse, and Sundor was sitting easily on his heels, poking the dirt with the butt of a spear. Harald could see from his father's attitude that he was not angry.

"So. You went to the lake alone," Edvar said.

"Sigrit told you, didn't she?"

"I commanded her to tell us. She was wise enough not to refuse. She said you went with a purpose."

"Yes. To kill the snake."

"Did you?"

"No. It never came. There is no snake."

"Oh, there are snakes, Harald. Never doubt that. But do you know why the snake you went to kill did not come?"

"Because it does not exist."

"Because you went there to kill it. The snake favors unwary

14

children, Harald. You have grown too bold to suit it."

Harald considered this doubtfully, frowning.

His father smiled. "You were brave to seek it out, Harald. You will make a good leader for this village."

Sundor stood and laid a hand on Harald's shoulder, then slapped him lightly on the back.

Without speaking another word, the three of them walked back into the village.

* * *

The summers were short in Maurisia. After a few weeks of mild temperatures and sunlight and white clouds, the air chilled and the sky lowered once again. The sun, when it showed itself at all, shrank to the size of a button, as if backing away from the snow and cold that seemed to creep through the forest.

But there was never a best season for the hunters.

There were certainly more and fatter animals and birds out and about foraging among the leaves and berries during the brief summer, but that was also when the cover was thickest and did more to hide them, and the hiss of wind in the leaves helped mask the sounds of their movement. The hunters had to rely on patience and knowledge to find them.

There were fewer animals and birds around during the winter since some crawled into their dens for a long sleep or traveled to warmer places, and the creatures that continued to search for food were smaller, quicker, and scrawnier, but more exposed and easier to track.

Harald continued to hone his skills under the guidance of Edvar and Sundor, and quite often with Jovar as part of their group. And he continued to find himself in the company of Sigrit as it became obvious to both of them that their respective families intended for them to marry one day. It was mostly for this reason that when she once mentioned how flattered she was that Harald had asked her to go with him to find the water snake, he did not tell her that he had intended for her to be his bait.

Once, twice, summer came and went, and the village boys grew a bit taller and stronger and their voices changed, and the girls grew taller and began developing interesting curves under their soft hide tunics. Sigrit seemed more beautiful by the day and Harald noticed a new, thrilling directness in the way she looked at him. Nevertheless, he was often bored when they were together. He knew that the plans were for them to be married before the first snows came. He saw the life ahead very clearly, each of them falling squarely into the separate worlds of their parents. He would hunt, trap, skin, and bring home the food. Sigrit would gather greens and berries, cook, sew, and have babies. Together they would tan and stretch the hides, and sharpen tools. In time, each would pass along what they knew to their own and other village children, and then they would gradually relinquish their roles to age, and die. That is, if he wasn't gored, mauled, or poisoned in the meantime, and if Sigrit did not expire during childbirth.

As far as life in the village went, the most exciting things to happen during the past seasons were that Garal was terribly stung by bees and a small tree fell on the elder Azreh's longhouse. After Garal recovered from his fever and Azreh was talked out of going off in a rage to find and cut down the King of Trees, everything returned to normal.

Thus, as the fourteenth summer of his life was beginning to fade, Harald went to Sundor with a request.

"Take me to where the forest ends, Sundor."

Sundor studied Harald's face with seriousness.

"Why do you want to go?"

"I want to see it."

"What makes you think *I* want to go? The spider is there. I saw it too."

"Is it not too big to come into the woods?"

Sundor rubbed his chin, thinking about this. "Yes. I believe it is."

"Then we will stay in the trees."

"We would have to tell your father."

"Of course."

"He might say no."

"Not if I convince him that we will be safe." Harald smiled. "As I just convinced you."

Sundor laughed. "So you did."

Edvar was not happy with the idea. His eyes narrowed in the dimness of the house where he was honing spear points.

"The end of the world is far from here," Edvar said. "Whom will I hunt with while you are gone?"

"Jovar is a fine hunter. A better hunter than I am," Harald said.

"No, he's not. You sense far more and have more courage. And I have hunted with Sundor for half my life. Jovar is a good young man, but no match for either of you."

"We will travel as quickly as we can, Father. I just want to see what you saw so I can tell your story my own way. I want to see what you saw before responsibilities keep me here forever."

"What if you come across trouble on the way? A bear? A huge boar?"

"By now the bears are fat and sleepy. And you said I was a good hunter. Sundor and I together can handle the biggest boar in the world if we should happen upon one."

Edvar continued grumbling. "I saw the spider with my own eyes, Harald. It is not a thing to treat lightly."

"We will stay in the trees. It is too large to come into the trees. I promised Sundor we would stay back."

Sundor, who as usual was shifting his attention back and forth between the speakers, nodded in agreement.

Edvar looked grimly at Sundor.

"Do you remember the way? It was many days, as I recall."

Sundor nodded. "I remember things that will guide us. In winter or summer, they will be the same."

Edvar closed his eyes briefly. When he opened them, he gazed sadly at Harald.

"I have never been able to be angry at you, Harald. I have never been able to say no to you. All I have been able to do is fear for you, and fear losing you. Remember that along the way. I won't rest well until you come back. Move quickly."

Delighted, Harald jumped to his feet and grasped his father's shoulders. "We will. We will be home before long. Thank you. And when I return, we will sit by the fire, and I will tell everyone the story."

He and Sundor spent the rest of the day arming and provisioning for the journey. When Harald was satisfied that they had packed well enough to be prepared, but would still be able to move swiftly, he went into the forest and hunted until dark, coming home with a pouch full of rabbits and several fat grouse. He presented these to Edvar as his contribution to the village cooking pot during his absence.

In the morning, before the sun had risen high enough to cast much more light than a murky grayness through the trees, Sundor and Harald hugged their families, promised a quick return, and loped away into the dimness.

Because they were not hunting but merely traveling as fast as they could, they ran at a light-footed trot, making enough noise to warn away the animals ahead of them, but not noisily enough to draw the attention of bigger beasts. It was a pace they could maintain for hours at a time, but not so fast that they couldn't avoid or overcome a sudden obstacle or change of route.

Sundor ran ahead of Harald, his bright eyes continually cataloging trees, stones, hills, ravines, creeks and ponds, recalling the landmarks he and Edvar passed long ago.

When darkness began to fall, they found a suitably open spot in which to build a small fire. Sundor hardly spoke at all, being a firm believer that people as a rule talked far too much while contributing very little. To him, the gift of speech was to be used sparingly and with a specific purpose—to tell a tale or to plan or warn or offer direction. Idle conversation and joking were a waste of time and energy.

When they finished eating, Sundor stabbed a stick into the ground, draped a length of vine-cloth over it and slept under its cover. Harald had brought a light mat to sleep on, covering his head with a flap of cloth sewn into his tunic. Both slept lightly, resting while still being alert to every unusual sound.

Day followed day.

Harald gathered sights into his memory around which to build his story. A far away whisper turned into a lovely, arcing waterfall that cast droplets like rain onto a carpet of flowering lily pads. A magnificent stag stood atop a stone outcropping fearlessly watching them pass. Along a clear section of sunlit trail, the forest sprites shook the trees to shower them with a blizzard of bright yellow leaves.

Harald had never felt so awake in his life.

At the end of the fourth day of running, as they sat by the fire eating strips of dried and peppered rabbit meat, Sundor said, "Tomorrow, we will be there." His eyes never left his rabbit jerky.

The words electrified Harald. He had been so immersed in the journey that he had given little thought to the goal. Now it was upon him. They were near the edge of the world. Near the spider. Near the grasslands that moved like a sea. He felt a shivering mixture of fear, sadness, and excitement. Before the sun set again, he would have gone as far as he could go.

Sundor said nothing more. He belched once, and then shifted about into his sleeping position.

Harald's night passed fitfully. He would doze off, then remember that soon he would be seeing something remarkable, something fearsome, something only two people form his village had ever witnessed before. His eyes were wide open when the blackness around him paled slightly, and Sundor snorted, arose, and made water at the edge of their clearing.

After a few bites of dried rabbit and a few swallows of water from their water skins, Harald and Sundor found themselves in enough light to move on. At first they moved slowly, straining to see in the gloom, but as the dimness brightened they once again began to trot. Harald's breath was soon labored in his excitement and he felt light-headed a couple of times, but eventually he calmed himself and resumed his steady, ground-covering lope.

The sun was overhead and the forest floor was dappled with shifting medallions of leaf shadow and golden light when Sundor stopped, crouched, and pointed ahead. Harald saw that in the distance, a much brighter light shone between the tall, straight tree trunks. Harald smiled and urged Sundor on.

They moved more slowly and quietly now, since their objective was in sight. Harald held his spear with both hands, moving brush and branches aside with the shaft, watching tensely for any gigantic shadow that might suddenly dim the bright light ahead.

They never expected to see other men instead.

The brush hissed loudly around them as four tall men with weapons abruptly surrounded them. Sundor and Harald were so surprised they froze in place, their eyes wide and jaws slack with shock.

The men were bearded and wore shimmering tunics made of a substance Sundor and Harald had never seen before. Their legs were covered with the hairless hide of some animal that must have been larger than any the two hunters had ever felled. Two of the men held spears tipped with a shiny, sharp point that was not bone or stone, and the two others aimed long, shining blades at them with both hands.

Harald reacted first, unthinking. He lunged with his spear at the man nearest him, who quickly swung his own long blade and effortlessly sliced Harald's spear shaft in two. As the point of his weapon fell away, Harald realized that his hands had barely felt the blow.

They could do little else but look from man to man and wait. Harald stared at the man before him, who gazed back sympathetically through one eye. Where the other should have been was only a small knot of scar tissue between two long, ragged, thinner scars above and below.

From outside the circle, a fifth man approached. This one was taller than the others and walked with the easy stride of a commanding elder. He had a long, thin face and glistening black hair that hung to his shoulders.

"What in the world have we here?" he smiled.

Harald and Sundor did not understand a word.

"Almighty One," the man said, looking his prisoners up and down. "Bog people, Paulus. How on earth did bog people spread so far?"

"P'raps they was brought here," the one-eyed man answered.

"But why just a few? Why not all? They are of little more use than squirrels." He looked into the forest behind the hunters and pointed, bringing his eyes back to Harald's. "From whence did you come, Bog Boy? There? Back there?"

Harald knew his meaning. He nodded. The tall man's eyebrows lifted in surprise. "What? A smart Bog Boy? How can this be, Paulus? Something must be amiss in the natural world. Perhaps we should seek out the rest of his kind. Perhaps we have discovered something freakish here that will bring us some measure of respectability at long last."

The one-eyed man glanced quickly at the tall man. "There'd be nothing to steal, sire. Look at 'em. They's starvelings in the skins of deer and hare. Not even iron in their tools; naught but wood and bone. There'd be no point to it."

The tall man stared at Paulus for a moment. "I will decide what has a point and what does not."

Paulus nodded sharply. "Aye."

The tall man looked again into the gloom of the trees. "But you are probably right, Paulus. These two seem to be provisioned. Perhaps they have come far. I do not wish to go far. I wish to remove my weary ass from this dull place as soon as possible."

Paulus nodded again. "Aye."

"I wouldn't think our pursuers are still behind us. It has been ten days. Boredom alone should have driven them back, as boredom will now drive us forward. Prepare the horses, Richter."

One of the four, a short man clotted with muscle, nodded and scuttled off toward the bright light beyond.

The tall man looked coldly at Sundor. "I don't like this one. Kill him."

Sundor and Harald both knew from the tall man's attitude and tone what he had said, and they both reacted at once. Harald dove for the short, pointed end of his spear on the ground and Sundor leaped toward the tall man with his spear. The tall man jumped back as a sword blade suddenly emerged from Sundor's chest. Paulus struck Harald over the head with his own spear shaft, knocking him senseless.

Sundor's body thumped softly to the ground. The tall man pulled the sword from Sundor's body, and cleaned the blade with a handful of leaves. Sundor twitched, gasped, and stopped breathing.

The tall man looked at Harald lying still. "Leave the Bog Boy," he said. "He's a child. Perhaps he will be able to find his way home. If not, it will be no great loss."

In a fog sparking with bright white flashes of light, Harald heard their footsteps receding through the leaves and brush. He did not trust himself to move until the flashing lights faded and were replaced by a headache that pulsed with every beat of his heart. He raised his head slowly and looked about for any trace of the men, but saw only the corpse of Sundor nearby, the slick cape of blood on his back already abuzz with insects. Harald rose to his knees, paused as a wave of nausea rolled through him, and then stood.

Once upright, he did not know what to do next.

The sensible action would be to immediately retreat as quietly as possible along the trail that would eventually lead him back to the village. But in his addled mind he also thought that to come so far to see the end of the world and turn back mere yards from that vision would be foolish. Besides, he could not take Sundor home again, and would not leave him unattended, so he would have to stay long enough to find a suitable resting place for his father's most loyal friend.

Harald took a few wobbly steps toward the light at the edge of the forest, emboldened by the knowledge that since the men had allowed him to live once, they would not likely kill him if he were discovered again. As he neared the perimeter of the woods, his steps became more confident and steady, and his strength returned, though his head still throbbed.

He heard unfamiliar sounds from the light, shuffling and snorting and clinking. He crouched and crept forward. He carefully parted the thick ferns that masked the brightness beyond.

He could not believe what he saw.

The men were climbing atop big, four-legged beasts with long necks and thick bodies and small, tapered heads. Packs and bundles were tied to the animals and hung on either side. Once they had climbed onto the animals' backs, the men tugged on short ropes and the beasts calmly carried them away through the river of grass toward a distant wall of blue, snow-topped stone.

Harald was entranced. How he would love to return to his village aboard one of those animals. That story would be told for-ever. But it was a fleeting thought; his attention was more direct-ed toward what the spider would do when the five men and their animals wandered across its lair. It was true that to get here at all, they had to have safely crossed once, but perhaps the spider was hunting elsewhere.

The wind ruffled the plain. The birds remained silent, holding their song until they were certain danger was gone. Harald felt the heat of the sun on his face from the field ahead.

Then he saw the spider, its squat body dark and forbidding atop thick, angled legs.

It waited patiently for the riders, who seemed either not to notice it or not to care. As Harald held his breath, the riders calmly passed the spider, which did not move an inch, and disappeared into the long, undulating grass.

As Harald watched, the spider never blinked, never breathed, never stirred.

A thought settled across his mind.

As there was no sea snake, perhaps there was no spider either. He didn't know what it was, but it was nothing alive. His fear ebbed, and the throb in his head lessened.

He turned away from the warmth of the field to the cool shadows of the forest. Sundor had to be buried. Harald shooed the insects way from Sundor's wounds and covered the bloodstains with dry leaves. Then he walked through the woods in widening circles until he found an abandoned bear den. As the light slowly dulled to the gold-speckled shade of afternoon, he dragged Sundor into the small cave and laid him on his back with his spear and bow beside him. He took Sundor's water skin to a small, trickling stream and filled it, then placed that by his side, too. After putting what little food he had left in Sundor's pouch, Harald sat quietly beside him for a few moments, remembering the man as he was alive. He patted Sundor on the shoulder.

"Food and water for the journey, good friend. There was no need for you to leave us. No need at all. Father will look to his side every day from now on and feel his loss anew each time. He will never forget you, nor, I think, ever forgive me."

It was then, while listening to his own voice and words, that Harald realized he had come to a decision. As he laid Sundor to rest, he had decided to find the riders. He had decided to see what measure of revenge he could exact. He knew it would be easy to bring down the animals they were riding, leaving them to wander on foot, but he didn't want to do that. The tall man would be much more difficult to deal with atop his animal, but it was the tall man who had killed Sundor.

Once he had struck a blow in Sundor's memory, he would go back home.

After he sealed the entrance to Sundor's resting place with stones and fallen logs, Harald took the time to find a long, strong stick that he fashioned into a crude spear by sharpening it to a point with his skinning knife. He gathered some mushrooms and berries and dug up a couple of wild potatoes for his food pouch. Then, feeling prepared for at least a two-day journey in the grassland, he walked to the edge of the forest.

With a deep breath and a wary eye on the hulking shape ahead of him, Harald stepped into the whispering plain. He felt a thrill up his spine at the touch of the tall, feathery grass on his bare arms. His heart beat quickly. The trail the riders had left was so clear that he found he could run over it more easily than he could run through the woods.

As he neared the spider, he slowed and crouched, willing himself into the hunting steps that made no sound, and held the spear with both hands. He slowly approached one of the spider's giant legs, sniffing the air to see if it smelled of life.

But the creature was made of stone.

He jabbed the leg with his spear and flakes of multi-colored rock fell loose. He picked them up, smelled them, tasted them, and rubbed them between his fingers. They looked like tree bark and splinters of wood, but were most definitely stone.

He looked up and walked all around the huge shape. It seemed to be what was left of a gigantic tree whose roots had been exposed. He had seen the same sort of thing along the bank of the lake, where water had washed away the dirt and left roots dangling. Perhaps the grassland had been a wide river that tore away the earth around this massive structure. Perhaps this was the true King of Trees. He explored the ground under the grass and found more and more of the petrified tree trunk, which had probably broken and fallen long before his own people had arrived in the forest.

Harald smiled and filled a pocket with a handful of the splinters. They would be part of a good story for the village.

He looked up. The breeze was growing stronger, signaling the coming of evening. The grasses hissed around him. Clouds above sent shadows fleeing over the surface of the plain. The trail ahead was clear and straight. His fear was gone.

Bending to keep his head below the top of the grass, he started jogging toward the far, blue mountains.

* * *

Harald caught up with the riders by late afternoon of the following day.

By then he had come to the edge of the grassland, which bordered a wide moraine of boulders and smooth stones in what Harald presumed to be the bed of a long-dry river. The riders, apparently preferring an open view of their surroundings to the greater comfort of the grass, were setting up camp on the gravel, their steps crunching and clattering as they moved about.

Harald watched them, lying concealed by the grass. Because men were merely animals on two legs, he studied them as he would any others, noting the strengths and weaknesses of their location and movements as well as those of his own position. Even he could not move soundlessly over the loose stones, so approaching them with stealth would be nearly impossible. He would have to find another way to get close to them.

"Bog Boy," he whispered to himself, mimicking the words he did not understand but feeling the contempt in them. And that contempt gave him an insight.

He lay patiently as the light turned golden and the shadows of the men grew longer. The riders sat upon wadded blankets as comfortably as they could, gathered around a small fire which burned in a shallow pit they had formed by moving aside rocks. They ate and drank in utter silence. Harald joined them in his cover, nibbling on a handful of berries and sipping from his water skin.

Presently one of the men picked up his short sword, glanced quickly at his companions and walked toward the grass. Harald watched him step a few feet into the covering plain and squat. Harald listened and from the sounds he heard envisioned the rider first stabbing the sword into the ground next to him, doing his business, then tearing loose a handful of grass to wipe himself.

As he watched the man return to the circle of riders, Harald knew what he was going to do if the opportunity arose again. When gloom had settled, Harald crept forward and retrieved a hand-sized stone, pulling it with him back into the grass.

After a second night of sleeping in the whispering prairie, during which he imagined himself as a hummingbird skimming in and out of sleep, resting but always alert, Harald rolled onto his stomach at the first hint of daylight and watched the camp.

It was some time before the first man stirred, groaning and climbing to his feet in stages. The others awoke at the sound, and all struggled through the pain of raising themselves from their rocky beds. The first up poked the fire and added a handful of sticks from a pile they had built nearby. There was grumbling and short, guttural words spoken back and forth among them. The tall man laughed once, a brief bark in the gray silence.

Then one of the men stood, grasped a long sword lying near him and walked stiffly toward the plain.

. Harald, holding the rock in his hand, wriggled along a path that would intercept him. When the rider had stuck the sword into the ground and dropped his trousers, Harald quickly lunged and slammed the stone against the man's temple, dropping him without a sound. Harald took the sword in both hands, pulled it free, and took a deep breath. The sword, as he expected, was heavier than any weapon he'd ever held. He would use its weight and his own youth to his advantage, but what he was about to do was still very risky. He closed his eyes, summoning courage from the added weight of Sundor's death.

He lugged the long sword beside him out of the shelter of the prairie and onto the moraine. The sword clanged and clattered and the rocks slid beneath his feet. He was making so much noise it was almost painful to his ears. He kept his eyes on the camp as he pulled the sword along.

The tall man stood first, slowly rising from his crouch near the fire, and a smile spread across his face as Harald struggled toward him. The others rose warily.

"My, my, my," the tall man said with a chuckle. "Bog Boy has followed us, Paulus. I believe he means to hurt us, too, from the look of it." Then he laughed out loud.

As Harald drew closer and closer, the sword blade ringing loud in his ears, the tall man put his hands on his hips and shook his head in amazement.

Harald said, "I saw no mercy in your eyes when you killed Sundor. Do you see any mercy in mine?"

"What did he say?" the tall man asked. "Bog Boy growls like a man, Paulus, but I have no earthly notion of what it means." Then he spoke to Harald, with a nod toward the sword, "That seems to be far too heavy for you, Bog Boy. Would you thrash my ankles, perhaps? Damage a foot? Cause me pain that way?"

Harald dropped the sword and suddenly sprang into the air, his quickness and strength carrying him alongside and past the tall man. Harald landed in a crouch, his skinning knife firmly gripped in his fist, looking quickly from man to man for a threat from the other riders. Not one moved. Mouths agape, they instead stared at the tall man, who stood wide-eyed, his hand over his throat as a flood of crimson flowed over his chest. The tall man's mouth worked, but only a bubbling sound emerged from between the fingers at his neck. He dropped to his knees, and all saw a sleepy distance come to his eyes as his blood flowed down into the stones, a brilliant new stream where a river used to run.

The tall man fell.

Harald shifted from side to side, expecting the men to come for him. But they did not. Paulus merely looked at him with astonishment.

"Bog Boy," Harald sneered.

Paulus smiled. "Young p'raps, Bog p'raps, but that wasn't no work of a boy." His good eye looked down at the tall man's body and the scar in his ruined eye twitched. "Never did like this one much, in truth."

The squat man who had been called Richter lifted a chin toward Harald. "What do we do with 'im? What if he means to kill us, each one?"

There came a clatter at the edge of the prairie as a man lurched out of the grass onto the riverbed, rubbing the side of his head.

Paulus thoughtfully stroked his bearded chin with one hand.

"I believe he meant harm to none save this 'un. Elstwise, Mister Richter, you'd be holdin' your breakfast basket in your hands right now. No, methinks it's done in its entirety." He studied Harald for a moment, and continued talking softly, as if to himself. "That was clever, his ruse. We could use cleverness with us lot. Sneaky. Fast. A good hand with an edge." He appeared to come to a conclusion, and opened his hands as if making an offering.

"Come with us? Will you join us?" He fashioned a sort of sign language, pointing toward Harald, patting both hands on his own chest, pointing at one of the animals, and then gesturing toward the high, blue mountains.

Harald watched him suspiciously.

Paulus tried again. "You. Ride with us. Over the mountains."

Harald followed Paulus's signs to himself, the huge, restless animals, and the looming, sheer walls of stone. Understanding opened within him like a blossom, a shivery commingling of fear, wonderment, excitement, and sadness. He looked at each of the men in turn and saw no duplicity in their eyes. They stood calmly, weapons in their sheaths and scabbards. The one-eyed man, Paulus, grew more animated as he warmed to the idea of Harald joining them.

Thoughts and feelings swirled within Harald. The idea of riding atop one of the big, shuffling beasts was fearsome, but thrilling. What a tale he could tell after attempting that feat! His excitement was suddenly blunted by a reserve of distrust, however, with the image of Sundor being run through still fresh in his mind. Yet that reserve was slowly being eroded by Paulus's guileless joy. The man was nearly dancing, and Harald felt the peculiar warmth that leads laughter to the throat.

Then there were the mountains. Going beyond them meant leaving the forest behind, leaving the village, his father and mother, his friends, and Sigrit, who was to be his wife the very next season. He had come much farther than anyone in the village ever had. He already had tales enough for a lifetime. When he and Sundor did not return, they would worry, then grieve, and then go on, never knowing that he, beloved by some, still breathed. If he returned, the story for which he would always be remembered would be the death of Sundor.

What extraordinary things lay on the other side of those walls? If that was the place from which came the heavy iron blades and shifting animals, what other miracles would there be? The thought of such an adventure took his breath away.

Then he decided. He would go for just a little while. He would join the riders for a few days, and see where they drifted. He would mark the way back in his mind. He would be the hummingbird in sleep with his knife in hand until he felt he could trust them. He would see, hear, smell, taste and touch everything he could so he could carry his journey back to the evening fires and the rapt attention of everyone in the village.

He turned to the one-eyed man and nodded sharply once, and pointed toward the mountains. Paulus happily clapped his hands.

"Mr. Richter, fetch him my horse."

Paulus removed some skins and weapons from his horse and transferred them to what Harald discovered was the tall man's horse after Paulus pulled some items from its saddle and tossed them dismissively onto the dead man's back.

"Mr. Richter, help the lad up and teach him as best you can while us others mound a cairn."

So Harald was boosted aboard the horse, a broad-backed grayling with bored eyes, and felt the dizzying insecurity of sudden height as well as the startling power of the beast beneath him. Richter led the horse to and fro, both horse and man clattering clumsily over the stones, showing Harald how to work the reins. During this brief and half-hearted tutorial, Paulus and the other men piled stones over the tall man's body. When that was accomplished, Paulus stood, panting slightly, and dusted off his hands.

"Well, then, there's that. Now we've far to go, and no plan if them that nosed us here is still over there. Suspense causes the bowels distress, so let's move on."

They mounted and formed a column with the horses moving carefully over the rocks. Harald rode tensely behind Paulus, gripping the reins and saddle horn with a grip that would gradually lessen as he became more comfortable traveling this way.

At the point where the moraine seemed to suddenly dive into a swath of sand that led to the lifting foothills of the mountains, Harald turned in his saddle to look beyond the riders behind him at the forest that was his home. The tree line looked much smaller now, ribbon-like and unimpressive. He imagined all those he knew and loved standing side by side in the shadows, unsmiling, watching him go.

"I will come back," he said aloud. "I will come back."

* * *

Twenty years later, Harald Stonearm sat astride a giant, muscular warhorse he called Typhoon, a word he had heard among a group of bandits and free lances with whom he roamed the windy coast of a land far to the west. Some of those bandits were among his small army this day, as he gazed down from the top of a sweeping hill across meadows and swales at the gray bulk that was the castle Gravenwall.

He leaned on the pommel of his saddle, resting on an elbow above one of the tapered slate gauntlets he wore to protect his lower arms from the blow of a cudgel or the edge of a parrying blade. They had become his identity, and over the years since he crossed through the deeply hidden snowy pass through the blue mountains, the snug, cord-bound pieces of stone had protected him from both many times.

Harald had proved an invaluable resource for the riders in the early days before Paulus and Richter and several others fell along the way. He had often found food where the others saw none, and his hunting skills had brought meat to the camps in what seemed like impossibly barren country. He had also used these skills as the foundation for becoming a sly and fearsome fighter in whose shadow other men, adept at both murder and theft, were willing to follow. Thus, Harald had gradually assembled a lean, hard army of horsemen who had plundered the broad lands of the north and west for many years. Their reputation now flew ahead of them like falcons so that whenever they reached a settlement it was either abandoned or bristling with resistance. And so far, resistance had never succeeded.

Harald now looked down upon a town and castle flurrying with activity. He watched them for a time to take their measure, feeling lulled by the cool breeze that washed over him and caused the pennants about him to hiss and snap. Typhoon shifted restlessly from hoof to hoof.

"Some mean to fight," he said to no one in particular. "But only in token resistance. Few will die today."

Harald looked up and took in the vast, green land around him. As far as he could see lay a patchwork of emerald squares stitched together by seams of dark, shimmering trees. Within some of the fields were small settlements, herds of animals, or dots of houses with wisps of smoke trailing from their chimneys.

"I like this place," he sighed. "And I am tired of wandering."

He turned Typhoon toward the men massed behind him.

"Some may stand against us," he said loudly. "But not many and not for long. These people do not seem to be warriors and I see no army assembled, so we have not been led into a trap as we expected. It appears that Master Turnbolt has kept his word, such as it is.

"We have all come a long and hard way, and the road will be no easier from now on. I propose to stay awhile. I propose that here the stone ceases to roll. This seems a fruitful and quiet spot, one we can easily defend. Once we have it, any who do not care to settle here until boredom spurs us on may go forth on their own." He did not expect any to leave. They were all too far from their homes to return.

Harald turned Typhoon back toward Gravenwall. Figures scurried along the ramparts. Wagons and columns of people carrying bundles or pushing barrows ahead of them hurried toward the castle gate.

"So this is Gravenwall, Darien?"

"Yes, Harald," a tall, lean soldier nearby said. "In the Province of Swallows."

Harald smiled. "Swallows, of course. Fast, agile little fellows. There would be many in such country. Did you know they line their nests with the feathers of other birds, Darien?"

"Never have noticed."

"Well, they do. And so shall we, of many different feathers as we are."

He shook his head slowly at the columns of refugees coursing along the roads like blood through veins.

"Look at them. Rushing to find safety in what they don't realize is the least safe place to be. Curious, are they not, Darien? People?"

"Yes, Harald," Darien said, glancing quickly at the man next to him. "Curious indeed."

The breeze lifted. The battle flags cracked. Horses shifted and snorted behind him. Harald felt a delicious, joyful calm come over him.

"We will walk down, men. There is no need to hurry on this day."

In the glorious autumn sunshine, he spurred Typhoon forward.

Chapter Two

THE BLUE QUEEN

The south tower was almost complete. Madam Anelie, Queen of the Provinces of Storms, Swallows and Doves, deftly placed another massive stone astride the seam of two below it, and then carefully applied mortar to seal it tight. Behind the tower, the sky was pink and bluish gray. A new day was dawning on the far side of the hills beyond Gravenwall.

She laid the paintbrush on a palette beside her and sat back in her chair, losing herself for a moment in the memory she was bringing to earthly form. In the painting, a sweet late-summer morning was dawning, but the air against her cheeks was cold and damp. In the painting, swallows darted and dipped, and evoked breezes sighing with the low coo of mourning doves, but in her ears was the boom and wash of churning surf. She gazed at the Province of Swallows, but she lived in the Province of Storms.

Other such paintings leaned against the stone walls of her spacious tower quarters in Sloedon Castle, the dark, squat bulk of which sat atop a forbidding cliff known as Bitter Foreland. The pictures were all of Gravenwall from various angles and in different seasons of the year. Those who had occasion to visit her expressed surprise and delight at how very lifelike and evocative the images were. Even Baron Alfred and Baroness Bernice, her gracious and loving hosts, never failed to compliment her skills, despite the rather limited range of subject matter. She had been painting them for nearly seven years.

Nearly seven years in exile, and she still could not accept what had happened.

She had lost Gravenwall and the Province of Swallows with a speed and finality that still caused her dizziness and tremors when she thought about it. Although she had been made aware that Harald Stonearm was approaching, his army seemed to rise up out of the ground. With breathless fear complicating the simple tasks of buckling her breastplate and knife belt, she found Thomas Chancellor, her court advisor, suddenly beside her, also short of breath and white-faced with alarm. His trembling hand lightly touched her arm.

"Your Majesty, we must leave now, right now. Your guards will not fight."

She was stunned into stillness, so Thomas hurried on.

"There is a plot against you in motion, Your Highness. The guards will not fight."

She believed him. She knew why, and knew it was true. In her mind she saw the dark, expressionless face of Turnbolt, Master of the Guard, and realized that, in an eyeblink, he had beaten her.

"How could this happen? How could I not know anything of it?" she snapped.

"Your Highness, Master Turnbolt is giving us a little time to flee and that is why we are not now in chains," Chancellor fairly gasped. "Moments, seconds only, perhaps. I have just now dispatched a rider to prepare Baron Alfred for your arrival at Sloedon. Horses for six await at the lower gate."

"How did this happen, Thomas? How?" She stared into his eyes. He was frightened. Yet the real question on her mind and unspoken was, "Why is it that you know, and not I?"

"Ponder these questions in freedom, Your Highness, and not in the dungeons, I beg you!" Chancellor tugged her sleeve toward the door. Castle attendants scurried in the hallway, fearful and weeping. "Come, come, please. We must go now! I will explain what I know on the way."

She felt as if she were sleepwalking as she followed Chancellor down the Siege Stairs, a long flight of dark, winding steps within the castle walls, to the lower gate, a small emergency exit near the vegetable gardens. There she found a wagon and a short column of horses that shuffled nervously in the shadows. Most carried her last loyal soldiers, and one bore her beloved handmaiden Hanna, whose eyes were glistening with tears. In the gloom of the covered wagon Anelie could see Hanna's mother Guen weeping quietly, her face in her hands. Anelie and Chancellor climbed atop their own mounts, and with a last disbelieving backward glance, she was torn away from Gravenwall.

Sloedon was the only place to go, of course. It was the castle of her late father's brother, and was in an almost impregnable situation on the wild coast of Storms, far, far to the north where cold clouds lumbered over a gnashing sea. Anelie would be safe there for as long as she cared to stay, but she also knew that the Baron Alfred would not commit his army to retaking Gravenwall. The journey was too far, the odds too long, the costs too high. Because her own guards had deserted her, she knew that she was not a queen going afar to regroup, but a queen going into exile.

After two weeks of arduous travel, the small party slogged into the gated maw of Sloedon with a sleeting tempest behind them, and passed under the pitying gaze of armed guards whose vivid red capes cracked like whips in the wind.

Once in her quarters, bathed and dressed in soft, warm woolen robes, she wept often for two days, partly from the pain of loss, and partly in gratitude for kindnesses shown. Her uncle Alfred and his wife Bernice did their best to buoy her spirits by behaving as if her visit was the happiest affair Sloedon had experienced in years, and holding modest feasts accompanied by musicians and tumblers for several days. But the feasts had to end someday, and she had to find a way not to insult her hosts' graciousness with an uncompromising gloom.

One day, while walking the ramparts in a blustering, chilly breeze, she vowed never to forget Gravenwall, or Swallows, or the peaceful, industrious people she had left behind.

That was the day she began to paint, and she realized that by doing so she was painting from fresh recollection to keep alive memories for her future, preserving the rough, sun-warmed stones she could still feel under her hand before the tricks of time and distance could turn them into uncertain mirages.

What those old, worn walls concealed, however, would always remain clear in her mind, vivid with life and color and sound and scents. And Rory.

Anelie was the first child of King Allred and his wife Celia. She was told years later that her arrival was met with a festival and the cheers of a happy, curious crowd gathered on the green outside Gravenwall. Inside the castle, she was swaddled in the softest skins and rocked to sleep to the music and songs of the court musicians, comprised of a lute player, lap harpist and finger drummer. Many songs were written about her in those first few months, but Celia's favorite was sung when Anelie was old enough to gaze at the wonders of her new world. She seemed to study everything she saw, and her eyes were a startling blue, but (the lute player sang) a blue "the color of no summer sky that ever held the sun, no sea that ever touched the shore, no flower that ever bloomed beside the door."

There was no need to accuse her parents of indulgence, for Anelie was a quiet, mannerly child of notable intelligence. By the time she was two years old, Celia had already introduced her to Tutor Sashem, the tall, impossibly thin young man who would be her personal teacher until she was of marrying age. The instruction at that point was no more than Tutor Sashem telling her simple stories in his lilting baritone voice and then asking questions about what she had heard. The stories always contained numbers and common objects (a goblet, a ball, a candle) that he would magically produce from the deep pockets of his worn green robe with a sly smile as he repeated its name.

Tutor Sashem found spiritual reward in serving hungry minds. He had studied and later taught at one of the first universities in Savony, a very progressive city at the foot of the picturesque Albion Mountains across the Sea of Caprice, and delighted in the marvelous vagaries of thought and creation as well as in the strange beauty of unalterable fact. And just as he absorbed every bit of what was known then, he expected his students to be held equally as rapt. It was not always so, and his disappointment was visible when he found himself facing utter disinterest or inflexible skepticism. In these cases, he doted on the more eager of his students while reinforcing fundamentals for those less quick.

"Write what you know of the Battle of Rusting Vale," he might say, "but in the form of a letter from a commander to his family."

Thus, the more stolid would relate the basics they had been taught — the date, armies involved, strategies developed, casualties, and so forth—while the more imaginative would be moved to embellish the facts with wind and clouds, the treachery of the great rough swale, and the mad screech and roar of battle. All would be correct, and Tutor Sashem would feel he had fulfilled his duty.

He had been engaged by King Allred to teach the simpler points of agronomy and bookkeeping to the farmers and their offspring of Westo'n, an energetic and successful village near Gravenwall. On occasion, Tutor Sashem received a summons to the castle, where he would be called upon to instruct or merely entertain the children of visiting dignitaries. He was paid well and enjoyed the diversion.

When he was first given charge of Princess Anelie's schooling, he felt a tremor of dread. The responsibility was great, and he knew that his performance would be judged more harshly than usual, but his fears vanished during his first hour with the girl. Tutor Sashem was utterly charmed by the child, and excited by the brightness in those extraordinary blue eyes. In his idle hours, he found himself continually re-mapping her education, getting further ahead of himself at times than he should have. As he returned to Westo'n after these sessions, he devised lesson plans for Anelie that would introduce her to some of the natural aspects of the land outside Gravenwall. At meals, he often smiled to think of amusing lessons he could give using peas and beans and bits of carrots. As he blew out the flame of the guttering lamp before sleeping, he eagerly envisioned a long bridge of study that reached into Anelie's adulthood.

For her part, Anelie absorbed her lessons with surprising ease. While she seemed to be distractedly playing with things, humming and tossing her head from side to side, she was actually arranging objects in orders of color, or numbers, or shapes. Tutor Sashem sometimes startled her by suddenly clapping his hands together with undisguised joy.

Then Rory was born.

He was the son King Allred had wished for all along, the male heir to Gravenwall and the Provinces of Storms, Swallows and Doves. Now four years old, Anelie was confused and a little frightened by the commotion Rory's arrival caused — there was so much noise, music, cheering, bells ringing, celebration and laughter. She was picked up and comforted with big smiles and the singsong question, "You have a baby brother! Aren't you happy?" She wasn't sure about that, of course. She could only survey the wild joy with her wide blue eyes and feel in her heart that things had changed.

Not long afterward, Tutor Sashem was summoned by the king.

"Tutor Sashem, we thank you for your efforts with our little princess," King Allred said. "Your skills are admirable and much appreciated by us. But now that there is a male heir, Anelie no longer requires your instruction. You will be summoned, of course, when Prince Rory is old enough to begin lessons, but Anelie will now be introduced to teachings more suited to women."

Tutor Sashem's knees weakened, and he struggled not to weep at the waste in what he had heard.

"Your Majesty, perhaps once in a while, a lesson now and then. She is so bright..."

"We appreciate your devotion, Tutor. But no. Rory will benefit more from the knowledge you can give than Anelie. Knowledge allows wise and long rule, where force can rule only as long as strength holds out. I wish for Rory to rule wisely and long. Anelie will find her own place within Gravenwall."

Tutor Sashem closed his eyes in despair and nodded slowly. "Yes, Your Majesty," he fairly whispered. "Of course. May I say goodbye to the child?"

"Certainly," Allred said kindly. "She adores you. Certainly you may."

They met in the lessons room, with its long obelisks of sunlight on the wooden floor, light that embraced the tables and chairs and books and boards of learning. Dust motes danced in the air. A cool breeze sighed through open windows and half-open doors. As guards looked fixedly ahead, Tutor Sashem knelt before Anelie with brimming eyes.

"Dear girl," he said. "I have no fear that you will take away the meaning of whatever lessons you happen upon. My anguish is that I cannot be your guide. The way of the world says I must leave you on your own, and I am so very, very sorry for it."

Tears spilled over, and Anelie, watching him seriously through her brilliant blue eyes, reached out and touched a droplet with her finger. Tutor Sashem grasped and kissed her tiny hand, then stood and rushed away.

That was how Anelie came to be among Ma Guen's girls.

Ma Guen was Queen Celia's seamstress. She was a largish, sturdy woman with big hands and strong fingers suited to the work of manipulating and stitching heavy cloth. She had a perpetual smile on her lips, long white braids coiled atop her head, and seven daughters.

Ma Guen was a native of Swallows, and spent most of her life in the little farming hamlet of Nodding Elms. At the age of sixteen she married and moved from her birth home to her Mister's house three lots down the lane, where, it seemed to many others, she and the Mister enthusiastically entered into the business of raising rabbits, chickens and children. Six girls were all born within twelve months of each other, an experience some thought would be the poor woman's undoing, but Guen was one of those rare beings to whom having babies was no more bother than twisting a knee. The

Mister, however, appeared to grow wearier with each new arrival, and spent progressively more time in his gardens and potting shed.

Then serendipity paid a visit.

On a crisp, foggy fall morning, the Mister entered his cottage carrying a child wrapped in a blanket. He trudged to where Ma Guen was brushing the girls' hair; they were all lined up with their backs to their mother, each stepping aside when she declared them done.

The Mister held out the bundle to her. "Not enough we got a 'erd ourselfs, there's ones leaving strays besides. Found this'n right near the front stoop."

Ma Guen took the child and guessed it was about six months old. The infant lay quietly without complaint, even though the blanket was damp from the morning air. The child looked into Guen's eyes, unsmiling but unafraid.

"Ho, goodness be served, could hit be?"

Ma Guen quickly peeked into the baby's diaper. She looked up at the Mister, smiled, and shrugged her shoulders. The child was a girl.

The Mister sighed heavily, shook his head, and trudged back outside.

The baby quietly cooed what sounded like "Mum," and smiled. Ma Guen's heart responded.

"Yes, love," she smiled. "I will be Mum."

The foundling became just one more of Ma Guen's little ones. Ma Guen did not even put forth an effort to find out whose child it really was, because, knowing for certain it was no child from anywhere around her village, she believed that if it was unwanted enough to leave in someone's yard, then giving it back would wrong the child even more. The girl was unusual, though, Ma Guen had to admit, in ways she could not quite put her finger on. The child looked different somehow, and was quiet, cheerful, and alert to everything around her. She also appeared well fed and well cared for, prompting Guen to wonder why such a lovely creature was abandoned at all. But Guen had little time in her hectic world to ponder anything for long, and despite her efforts to never show favoritism, she felt her heart lifted most by the foundling. Since the girl was different, she received a name that would always mark her as different from her own daughters Madge, Myra, Marie, Melody, Mandy and Millie. Ma Guen named the foundling Hanna.

One day in Hanna's third year, King Allred was charging about the countryside on a boar hunt with a group of his friends. As they thundered past Nodding Elms, one of the horses kicked up a large missile of mud at the center of which was an egg-shaped rock, and both of which struck the Mister square in the head as he was tending his radish beds. He pitched over dead on the spot.

When King Allred heard about this terrible accident, he and the queen personally visited the widow, who cried, "What am hi s'posed to do now, y' Majesties, my dear 'usband kilt by a clod?"

The king was moved to promise a monthly stipend and the loan of a gardener to help her muddle through. Queen Celia, noting the volume, imagination, and excellent handiwork displayed by the seven little girls' clothing, had another thought. She needed a good seamstress, she said, and if Guen would like the job, it was hers. She and her children would have to leave Nodding Elms, however, and move into Gravenwall.

The older girls jumped up and down clapping their hands and squealing, "Can we, Ma? Say yes, Ma! Please, Ma!"

So Ma Guen and her daughters and a few possessions were carted off to Gravenwall by a team of wagons and royal guardsmen. They were housed in what used to be a large, square, well-lit storeroom near the south ramparts. The floor was dusty and rough, so Celia ordered that a thick grass mat be put down and then covered with a carpet. Beds for eight were lined up along one wall with benches and a big plank table installed to serve as both a work surface for Ma Guen and a dining table for meals.

For the first time the girls had room to play and chase each other around. And in this new, spacious environment with its cushy floor, they soon demonstrated an astonishing proclivity for tumbling.

While Ma Guen stitched away, the girls ran and flipped and bounced and jumped and rolled with tireless devotion, their eyes sparkling in faces flushed and damp. They were so persistent that Ma Guen began coaching them from her working chair, inventing different routines for them to practice. All this commotion delighted Ma Guen, who chuckled quietly while her thick fingers gathered and stitched, gathered and stitched.

Hanna was not gifted in the tumbling arts. As she grew, she could most often be found standing off to the side watching her sisters bound about, sometimes timidly attempting a clumsy tumble herself. The others included her in their playing by occasionally having her kneel down on all fours to give them something to jump over one after another in a close order torrent of little bodies.

By the time Hanna was five years old, she was calling out some of the various routines and clapping her hands like a metronome to help with the girls' timing. Being a source of order seemed to delight her far more than the exercise itself.

It was one day during a Chainstitch drill (in which the girls would tumble over a wooden bench, run in a looping path to an imaginary line on the floor, then do a series of short tumbles back and forth over the line) that Anelie was presented to Ma Guen and her girls by a senior guard of the queen. The room stilled instantly when the guard entered, looked sternly about, then turned and left the princess standing awkwardly by the door while the others stared at her in wonder.

A messenger had informed Ma Guen the day before that Anelie was now to be in her charge during the days. Anelie would rejoin her family in the late afternoon for supper and the evening, when she would be close to her brother Rory, whom she would one day serve. Ma Guen's task was to entertain Anelie and teach her the secrets of her trade, not so that Anelie would become a seamstress, for that was below her station, but so that Anelie would know enough about it to confidently praise or correct the work of others.

Ma Guen left her sewing chair, went to Anelie and bowed to the girl, who seemed quite intimidated by the group of panting, sweaty children before her. Ma Guen turned to the others.

"Girls, this his Princess Hanelie. She'll be our newest friend from now." They all bowed in unison. "Now, Your 'Ighness, let me introduce the girls." Ma Guen pointed to each girl in turn, who either nodded or curtsied as her name was called. "This is Madge, Myra, Marie, Melody, Mandy, Millie and 'Anna."

Anelie had already singled out Hanna as being different from the rest, and spoke to her first.

"Hello, Anna."

"No, no, no," Ma Guen chuckled. "Not Anna, '*Anna*!"

Anelie looked confused. The girls started laughing, obviously familiar with their mother's game.

"'Ello, Anna," Anelie said.

"No, no, no, you 'aven't got hit," Ma Guen said. "Ello, 'Anna, Ello, 'Anna!"

The girls were laughing loudly now.

"'Ello, Hanalie!" they shouted. "'Ello, Hanalie!"

Anelie smiled. "Hello, Hanna!" she cried.

The girls cheered and clapped, Ma Guen, laughing said, "Girls, show Hanalie your stitches, hey?"

The girls suddenly ran away and formed a line on the far side

47

of the room. Hanna took a place near the line, shouted, "Chain-stitch!" and began clapping her hands in rhythm.

After the girls had leapt and tumbled through the Bowstitch, Featherstitch, and madly flipped through the Backstitch, Ma Guen called a halt to the exercising to quiet the group before lunch, which was always followed by nap time.

This became Anelie's life during the days.

Rory was her life from those hours on.

The first time her parents gently led her to the squirming baby, she simply stared at it. Its eyes were closed, and its skinny arms and legs seemed to poke the air rather than pedal or wave. Then, as the days passed, Rory opened his eyes and seemed to look into some deep place in Anelie's heart. It was a sensation beyond her knowledge, but it stirred when Rory kicked and smiled and reached out to touch her whenever she was nearby. She could not take her eyes off him, and was thrilled by the feel of his tiny hands grasping her fingers. Anelie had to be ordered away from his side for bedtime. But even then, Celia was sometimes awakened by the sound of Anelie dragging her covers across the bedchamber floor to a place beside Rory's cradle. Celia would wait a few minutes, rise to make certain Anelie was properly bundled against the cold, then return to bed. She could hear the truth in their breathing, as only mothers can—neither child ever slept as soundly or dreamt as deeply apart as they did when they were together.

As the years passed and the girls grew, they became ever more expert at their tumbling disciplines until even Ma Guen was dazzled by their intricate choreography and cat-quick gracefulness. Hanna developed into an imaginative and observant director who was responsible for most of the more creative routines in their repertoire, and could see when any of the tumblers was even mere inches out of place.

As Hanna spent more time with the girls as their chief choreographer, Anelie took over the duties of calling out the presentations and marking time. Though Anelie exhibited some talent for these gymnastics, her mother considered it a bit too far beneath her station to pursue full time. Anelie did not protest, because she knew in her heart that she had neither the dedication nor the strength for it that the other girls had. She was content with her small role, and greatly respected Hanna's gifts for guidance.

The guards who accompanied Anelie to Ma Guen's great chamber each morning gradually started staying longer before they left, intently watching the girls practice and often shaking their heads and smiling with wonder as the athletes spun and twisted and soared high into the air, only to land light as feathers. Allred and Celia overheard the guards talking about these antics and requested a performance one fortnight hence.

There was great excitement among the tumblers, of course, for it was their first formal recital. Ma Guen added some colorful flourishes to the girls' outfits for the occasion, and it was decided that Anelie would be the orchestrator of the demonstration. She and Hanna worked out an order, and the girls rehearsed with more energy than usual.

Finally, the grand day arrived. The king and queen arrived with young Rory, and were shown to comfortable seats against the wall beside the door for the best view of the floor. This was the first time Rory had been allowed to visit Ma Guen's quarters, and he was thrilled to finally see where and with whom his big sister spent her days.

For dramatic effect, the girls were all seated cross-legged on the floor facing the far wall. When the guests were situated, Ma Guen raised her arms as if lifting them in offering, and the girls all stood, turned to their left, and marched around the room with Anelie in the lead.

Rory bounced with delight in his seat and pointed.

"Mother! Anelie! Look, it's Anelie!" He laughed and clapped his hands together.

The girls solemnly marched in front of their guests, turned to face them, and curtsied in practiced unison. Then they straightened, turned to their left again and continued marching to the point at which they had begun. Anelie kept marching four paces beyond where the others stopped. She turned, shouted, "Basting stitch!" and clapped her hands to set the pace. The girls skipped into action.

Although the girls were quite nervous, they had executed their parts so many times that they performed flawlessly, and the event was a huge success. The king and queen were amazed and utterly enchanted, having had no idea this sort of thing was going on in their own household. Allred was particularly pleased to see his daughter directing the show, as she would one day be called upon to do the same with the Gravenwall servant staff when Rory was king and had taken a wife.

Allred and Celia were so impressed, in fact, that Ma Guen's fabulous tumbling daughters immediately came to their minds as the centerpiece of entertainment for the impending visit of royal guests from Sloedon Castle in the Province of Storms. The First Family of Sloedon was bringing their daughter Bernice to meet Allred's brother Alfred for the purpose of a marriage of opportunity. Alfred was Gravenwall's Master of the Guard, and known to possess a keen military mind as well as a gift for leadership and training. Storms' aging ruler, Roland, felt it necessary to have such skill close to the seat of power to better defend Bernice when she gained possession of Sloedon and Storms upon Roland's death. Because of Alfred's station, Sloedon would become a baronial house, and in return pledged its arms, treasure and assistance to Gravenwall any time they were called for.

The visit (lasting a month in the high season) was a bright, noisy, happy affair. Roland and his wife and daughter were more than content to spend their days strolling Gravenwall's grounds and riding through the countryside, glorying in the sunshine and warm breezes that were so markedly different from the brooding skies and the raw wind of storms. Evenings were given over to feasts, endless supplies of elderberry wine, music by the court musicians, and puppet plays.

The troths were given after Bernice and Alfred had spent considerable time together discussing likes and dislikes, plans for the future, and politics. The wedding was announced for the last week of Bernice's visit (although the preparations had already been made, for it was far easier to call things off than to hastily arrange them), with a second celebration to be held at Sloedon after the newly united couple arrived back home.

Before the ceremony, however, Alfred was treated to a rowdy party in the guards' barracks, where he formally conferred the title of Master of the Guard to his second in command, a stern, highly capable soldier named Vas Turnbolt. His appointment was no surprise to anyone, however, since the transfer had been submitted for consideration and approved in advance by King Allred, Celia, and their chief court advisor, Thomas Chancellor. The gathering was ribald, boisterous and noisy, with only one injury reported, that being to a soldier who leapt from a table into the arms of comrades who weren't aware they were supposed to catch him. Regarding the condition of his legion on the following morning, King Allred grumbled that on that particular day a herd of cattle could have captured the castle.

The wedding day dawned clear, sunny and cool, as if that were a planned part of the proceedings. Services were held in the Prayer Hall, which was gloriously illuminated by shafts and fans of sunlight. The Most Reverent Sire Cleaves presided, calling long and loudly for favor from The One Lord, grantor of the first breath of becoming, progenitor of all that sighs or cries, author of all that flows or takes root, artist of all that bears texture or tint, etcetera, etcetera, etcetera. When arms were joined and vessels were raised to seal the union, doves and swallows were released in the Prayer Hall, and everyone present was dazzled by the flashing brilliance of the fluttering birds as they wheeled through the shafts of golden light. To all eyes, it looked as though the sunlight itself had shattered to pieces.

To commemorate the occasion, King Allred and Celia staged a monumental feast that included a number of randomly chosen citizens, who were at first quite uncertain of their manners in such illustrious company, but wound up enjoying themselves immensely. After the banquet, King Allred stood, called for attention, and announced that a very special presentation by Ma Guen's extraordinary tumblers was next on the agenda.

Ma Guen had prepared for the honored occasion by dyeing cloth in six different vivid hues and creating costumes for the girls that made them resemble brightly colored rolling balls when they tumbled. Anelie, again the director, was outfitted as a wizard and directed the routines with a baton, which she slapped loudly against a wooden replica of a crystal ball for cadence instead of clapping her hands as she usually did.

Hanna, behind the scenes, also modified the program a bit by adding a few new drills to the stitching routines. Of those creations, "Muffins and Jam" and "Pigs, Porridge, Pie" were great crowd favorites. The audience of royalty and hoi polloi were for a few moments joined in common delight.

"Oh, ha! Lookit them darlings go!"

"Bravo! Bravo! Well done!"

The show was a huge success, and earned a personal visit from King Allred and Celia, who, still smiling and flushed with amusement, clasped each girl's hands in their own one by one, but embraced Anelie with great pride and affection.

In the days that followed, and in fact even after Alfred and Bernice had departed on the long journey north toward Storms, the citizens of Swallows who had witnessed the performance were still chattering excitedly about it to those who had missed it. Soon, curiosity had spread to every corner of Swallows.

One day King Allred granted an audience to one Servus Mogren, a short, round person who was, by his own description, an entertainment entrepreneur. For an hour he outlined a plan to take the tumbling act to the people of Swallows in a series of tent shows, which would also feature three young men from Redbud Forest who were particularly adept at rope climbing stunts.

"Can you envision it, Your Highness — delights and amazements from earth to the air! A living history of human athletic prowess ascending to the firmament!"

A nominal fee would be charged, of course (but certainly not one to create the merest hardship on the country people), a portion of which Mogren would retain for operating expenses and the remainder of which would go into the King's provincial general fund.

Throughout his presentation, Mogren never ceased smiling, and continued to do so as Allred considered the plan, tapping his lips lightly with a forefinger.

"I see no fault in it, Servus Mogren. The people work hard. They deserve amusement. And it always serves our interests to have Gravenwall well thought of."

Mogren nodded at each point, his smile fixed as a carving on stone.

"I permit the six tumblers to go. Anelie must stay, naturally, as must Hanna, who is Anelie's closest distraction. Ma Guen will decide whether to go with her girls or stay. I hope and rather think she will stay. If Hanna has new inventions for the troupe they can be delivered by courier, I should think. That seems like a workable arrangement. Proceed with Thomas Chancellor on the specifics, which I will then review and seal."

That was how Ma Guen's girls became "Ma Guen's Tumblers of Rare Grace and Surpassing Skill."

The girls were excited to suddenly be professionals in the pursuit they so enjoyed, but there were many tears shed in the days leading up to their departure. Servus Mogren's own daughter proved to be an enthusiastic and capable director under Hanna's training, and the girls liked her. Means for regular communication were established, as were terms of time off for visits home.

Leave-taking was more difficult than any had expected it to be. Even Celia felt warm tears on her cheeks as the girls waved good-bye from their brightly colored wagon as it trundled away into the moist, green morning, leaving behind, for three at least, days quieter, emptier, and more melancholy than all the ones before.

Ma Guen, however, was not one to stay glum for long.

While she and the girls occupied the big, empty room alone, Ma Guen cheerfully made up games and invented things for them to do. The girls played their own version of broomball, running about with whisk brooms and a ball of yarn encased in silk, created and performed one-act plays, and challenged each other in guessing games. Ma Guen also got them more involved in her own work, giving them simple stitching and darning tasks to do.

One morning, Anelie was unusually subdued. Hanna could not interest her in broomball or even a crab race down the length of the room.

"Speak what's hon your mind, Princess," Ma Guen finally said, then chuckled. "Before you worry hus lot."

"Majesty Mum talks of moving us out of here," Anelie said softly.

"Moving hus?" Ma Guen chuckled unconvincingly. "But the girls will 'ave nowhere to sleep hon visits 'ome, with their beds hall gone."

"She said she would find places for them, their visits being only occasional. You and Hanna would have smaller quarters of your own."

Ma Guen looked around the room that had become her home, at the row of beds that still gave her the comfort of her girls even though they were not there. "Hi can't leave," she said softly, more to herself than to anyone else.

Anelie knew Ma Guen would gratefully do whatever she was told and make the best of it, but she also knew she would lose part of her spirit when she did. She could not bear the thought of Ma Guen being wounded so.

"I will tell Majesty Mum she cannot do it," Anelie suddenly said firmly. "I will not let her. I am a princess, after all."

Hanna touched Anelie's arm.

"If Your Highness pleases, that would only force her to move us. She will not be told what to do, especially not by her daughter."

Anelie regarded Hanna with curiosity.

"What would you do, then?"

Hanna looked around the room. "Make use of the space. Benefit the queen."

Hanna thought for a few minutes, staring up at the light behind the windows up above her.

"This is a room made for playing and sleeping. Could we not entertain six or eight Swallows children for a day? Ones too young to work in the fields but old enough to be underfoot? You and I could lead them in games and tumbling, and they could nap for a while in the beds after they've had their midday broth and bread."

Hanna looked from Anelie to Ma Guen, who was brightening at the idea of little ones rolling all around the room again, like old times.

"The people of Swallows might be even more industrious in gratitude for the queen's benevolence," Hanna continued. "The queen would not have to rearrange any other quarters in Gravenwall. She is also securing the loyalty of her future subjects while they are children."

Hanna looked at Anelie.

"And the queen would not have to wonder what to do with you while Rory is being groomed for the throne."

Anelie smiled ruefully. "Certainly, there is that."

"You would not suggest this last to her, of course," Hanna said quietly. "The thought will come to the queen on its own."

Anelie studied Hanna's face. "You are very clever, Hanna. I will suggest it all to Majesty Mum at supper tonight."

"Then let's practice what you will say, so that every argument your Majesty Mum might have is answered before she can speak it."

"Cleverer still."

"No, Princess, not cleverness. Calculation."

As they had decided beforehand, Anelie did not approach the subject until her mother again mentioned moving Ma Guen. Then Anelie, performing the role of someone idly thinking out loud, presented their scheme and how it would be carried out, concluding with the specific benefits to all concerned. Both king and queen stared at their daughter with more attention than they ever had before. Both considered her proposal in silence, each stealing glances at the other as they ate, and by supper's end resolved to do it.

Messengers were sent out, and, as might be expected, the first day class consisted of six children from nearby Westo'n. Anelie and Hanna involved the youngsters in tumbling and marching drills and broomball games. After their bread and broth lunch, Ma Guen told stories as she sewed until she saw heads begin to nod. Then the children were sent to bed for a nap.

The Gravenwall day classes were a big success, and soon there was a waiting list, which Hanna managed. Some requests came from as far away as Bald Knob two days away, from farmers or drovers wanting someplace to park their young ones while they sold and bought goods at the Gravenwall markets. The children had fun and learned a thing or two, and the parents appreciated at least one mouth being fed for free. Ma Guen was energized by the return of children running and shouting about the room, and, as Hanna had predicted, Queen Celia was rescued from having to figure out what to do with Anelie.

For Hanna and Anelie, the arrangement also came with an unexpected benefit: nap time for the children became free time for them.

At first they timidly explored other rooms along the hallway from Ma Guen's former storeroom. There was a smaller chamber full of unused or damaged chairs and tables, all draped in cobwebs that moved like the surface of a calm sea when the door was opened, and there was a saddle room, and a cask room that smelled sharply of wood and spirits.

As time went on and they grew bolder, the girls might be seen anywhere in Gravenwall.

They played hide-and-go-seek in the Great Hall with its huge paintings, velvet bunting, and fireplace so big a man could walk into it without ducking his head. They visited the laundry, enjoyed treats in the galley where the pots steamed and bubbled and game birds hung from hooks over a long wooden table, and they peeked into the apartments of everyone from cooks to ministers. They tiptoed past the throne room, where Hanna would never be allowed to go, stood in silence in the majestic light of the Prayer Hall, and avoided the heavy iron door that opened the way down to the dungeons, even though no one had been imprisoned there in a lifetime.

From the long, narrow windows of the upper hallways of Gravenwall they could look down on the outside lawns and inside courtyard below. The courtyard was a quadrangle fronting a number of other chambers, into and out of which soldiers walked, marched, or muscled kegs and crates and other stores. It was a gray, rough looking place that looked particularly somber when the rain fell. It was on one of these rainy days that the girls saw young Rory cross the courtyard with two guards. He was greeted by Master Turnbolt, who first bowed to the prince, then smiled as he affectionately patted the boy's shoulder before leading him into one of the chambers.

Hanna could tell from a quick glance that Anelie was stung by what she had seen.

"One day we'll go have a look," Anelie said. "We'll see what goes on down there."

"Do you really think we should?"

"Quite," Anelie said firmly. "I am princess of Gravenwall. Who will deny me?"

More than a week passed before Anelie could summon the courage to enter the courtyard. Hanna reluctantly followed.

They peered into a storeroom where kegs of various sizes sat in the gloom and the walls were hung with strange looking iron tools. Another chamber from which a rhythmic pounding came held a variety of saddles on sawhorses, a number of reins and belts hanging from hooks on the walls, and a leather worker working with a hammer and punch who, startled by the sudden appearance of the girls' faces, stopped in mid-swing and stared openmouthed at them. They scurried into a passageway that smelled of horse manure and hay and knew it led to the stables and pasture outside the castle walls. A soldier walked past them, turning and walking backward as he stared, before rounding the far end of the wall.

As they followed the quad, Hanna was relieved to see that they were approaching the way they came in. They halted once more, stopping in the doorway to what they immediately knew was the armory. In a scene Hanna would never forget she saw a big, muscular man standing shirtless before a forge, his reddened skin shining with sweat under a leather apron. Beside him was Master Turnbolt studying the blade of a sword.

When he saw the girls, his look of profound surprise melted into narrowed eyes and a grim smile. He bowed his head slightly, never taking his eyes off Anelie.

"Well, well. Are we just out and about, or does Your Highness have a purpose?"

Anelie's voice sounded meeker than she intended. "Just looking, Master Turnbolt."

"Just looking," Turnbolt repeated. "Then what you see is a place of weapons and armor, Your Highness. Sharp steel, bludgeons and mail; the tools and salvation of soldiers."

A thought seemed to cross his mind. He approached Anelie, holding the sword out to her.

"Perhaps your highness would like to examine this latest effort by Youri, here?"

Anelie reached for the sword. Her fingers trembled as they grasped the cold hilt. When Turnbolt released it, the sword's extraordinary weight ripped the hilt from her hands and the sword thudded on the dirt floor at her feet.

Turnbolt continued as if she were holding it.

"I believe the pommel and blade are ideally suited, and thus the balance is nearly exceptional. The fuller could be a bit deeper and the back a bit narrower, but altogether a nice effort, don't you agree?"

Anelie did not speak, and could only endure Turnbolt's sneering smile.

"Let's see how it handles, shall we?" he hissed.

Turnbolt picked up the sword and walked toward a thick, scarred, upright log the size of an ancient tree trunk. Without breaking stride, he cocked the sword to one side and swung it with terrific force at the log. The sudden shock of violent sound made Hanna and Anelie jump backward, each clutching for the other.

Turnbolt worked the blade out of the deep cut it had made and theatrically studied it.

"It seems adequate. A solid impact to the hands, but comforting. No vibration. No uneasiness in the grip. Would Your Highness care to try it?"

Anelie's face grew hot. She shook her head slowly, her lips compressed.

"No? Hmm. Then perhaps I'll give it to your brother. When Prince Rory is your age, I expect he will be able to hew this log in half."

The girls turned to leave, and Turnbolt held up a hand.

"Thank you for visiting, Your Highness. We are honored. But as you can surely see, this is no place for girls."

Anelie was quiet for days afterward. Hanna could see storms of anger cross her features, followed sometimes by the start of tears, but she didn't say a thing. She waited for the mood to wear itself out or for a distraction to appear.

As it turned out, Rory provided it.

One evening after supper, Rory and Anelie were playing a

game of stones, sitting cross-legged in the well of a tall window overlooking the rolling western lawns. Their father and mother were both elsewhere, and the guard at the door was dozing off behind his spear. With a conspiratorial grin on his face, Rory tugged at Anelie's sleeve.

"Majesty Mum and Father showed me a secret," he whispered. "Want to see?"

"What secret?"

"A secret door and some steps. They call it 'Siege Stairs.' Want to see?"

"Siege Stairs? What are they for?"

"So I can get away if someone bad comes. I'll show you."

Anelie followed Rory, frowning. That her own parents had told Rory about an escape route to save his life and hadn't told her was not lost on her. Would people never stop wounding her?

Rory went to a large tapestry of a hunt scene at the end of the room and pulled its edge away from the wall, revealing a doorway only a little larger than they were. Delighted to have his sister's full attention, he beckoned her under the tapestry while he quietly opened the door.

The passage on the other side was dark, narrow, and cool. A musty breeze stirred the air. The only light seeped in through small ports cut through the thick walls to the outside and disguised by the ends of hollowed logs. After their eyes adjusted to the dimness, Rory led Anelie down the hall to a winding, narrow stairway. As they went down, their hands were chilled from touching the cold, slick stones.

At the bottom of the steps was another door, and this one opened onto the late-day light, a small courtyard, and the vegetable gardens. Beyond the gardens, nearly invisible, was an entrance to a path through dense woods, presumably, thought Anelie, to conceal a run toward open country until the escapees were well away from the castle. It was so well disguised that had Rory not pointed it out, she never would have seen it.

Rory was thrilled to have shared his secret. Laughing, clapping his hands, he goaded Anelie into a game of chase until the sunlight softened and the doves began to coo.

When they made their way back upstairs and stopped beside the little doorway to their chamber, Anelie saw that the passageway continued on.

"Where does it go?" she whispered.

Rory shrugged, suddenly serious. He obviously didn't want to find out where it went, and tugged at Anelie to come back inside.

That night as she lay awake listening to her brother's measured breathing, she imagined the pale pools of light on the stones in the gloom that led away into darkness. Her heart quickened to think about it: a secret passageway. And she didn't know where it led.

Several days passed before Anelie had an opportunity to revisit her secret. One evening her mother and father took Rory along to an informal meeting of little importance in the cabinet room, just to introduce the prince to how the advisory process worked. Attending was the executive administrator of Westo'n along with Thomas Chancellor, the royals' official counsel, and the subject was a public works proposal of some kind.

Thus Anelie found herself alone for a couple of hours. She would have liked having Hanna along but knew that Hanna, as common stock, could never set foot inside their chambers without it costing her, at best, banishment to the wolf-riddled forests of the Somber Dells. As soon as enough time had passed to accommodate a hasty return for some forgotten item, Anelie lit a bedside lantern, shielded it with her body as she slipped behind the tapestry, and stepped through the narrow doorway.

Her heart beat quickly and her skin became pebbled with goosebumps in the chilly draft. As her eyes slowly adjusted to the dimness around the lantern's glow, she looked to her left, into the unknown space opposite the way to the Siege Stairs. She walked slowly through the faint pools of light on the floor, counting her steps as she went in case she had to make her way back to the chamber door in the dark.

At ninety paces, she came to a short flight of stone steps leading down. The air smelled of ashes and cold smoke. She descended, and the lantern light revealed a tall, very narrow door to her left. She pressed it and it gave a little, telling her that instead of a dead-bolt lock, the door was probably held by a latch lock. She pulled a stout splinter from the edge of the doorway, and set the lantern down well away from the opening. She poked the splinter through the seam, and lifted the latch.

As the door opened, she knew exactly where she was. The entryway was part of the wide, wooden molding alongside the huge fireplace in the Great Hall. She surveyed the dim, empty room and the great blocks of shadow that were the long tables and chairs. The discovery delighted her, because this was how she could get Hanna into the secret corridor with her.

She retrieved the lantern, closed the door and latched it, and went back to the royal apartments by the main hallway, passing under the watchful, curious eyes of the guards. Once inside, she closed and locked the door behind the tapestry, and waited for her family to return.

The next day in Ma Guen's quarters, she excitedly told Hanna all about her discovery. They decided to use their free time that day to see where the passageway went, and could hardly wait until the town children finished their noon meal and went to bed for a nap.

Ma Guen looked suspiciously at the excitement in their faces as they rushed up to her for permission to leave. She nodded, and off they went at a run.

After a careful look around the Great Hall, listening for the echo of clinking silver or the swish of a hem against the stone floor that would mean someone was there in the gloom, they each swiped a candle lantern from the end table and slipped through the doorway beside the fireplace.

Once in the corridor, they lit the candles. Hanna was shivering from both the chill air and fear, and Anelie's eyes glittered with excitement in the guttering light.

"This way," Anelie whispered. "I haven't been down this way yet."

And she led them away from the Great Hall into the murkiness beyond, each stepping into their own trembling cloaks of light. Anelie softly counted their steps out loud. They saw no other entrances, only slick, stone walls to their sides and draperies of cobwebs above them. The hallway turned to the right. Here the darkness ahead was complete, save for two faint traces of light at floor level. They hesitated. Anelie took Hanna's hand and they stepped forward.

When they came to the first pale patch of light on the floor, Anelie knelt down and peered into its source. She found herself looking through a vent grate the size of a window into the library room. She stood again, not recognizing what that meant, and they continued on. At ten paces from the grate in front of her, she heard a voice and froze in surprise.

"Tutor Sashem!" she whispered.

They hurried ahead and Anelie peered through the grate. Through the tight weave of iron bars she saw Tutor Sashem pacing slowly in front of young Rory, having him recite the typical number of soldiers in the legions of various other countries. Seeing that room and hearing his voice again brought the start of tears to her eyes. She sat down and snuggled into the opening to listen for a while. Hanna remained quiet, knowing Anelie would explain everything when she was ready to, and she listened too. Having had lessons in little more than household chores, she was intrigued by what other, completely different things there were to know.

When the candles had burned down by a quarter, Anelie wiped her cheeks and rose to her feet, knowing she would be back again. She would learn what Rory learned, at least in part. She would resume her lessons after all.

As the seasons came and went and came again, Anelie was indirectly schooled in rudimentary mathematics, simple diplomacy, law, the nuances of military strategy applied to specific situations, the basics of agronomy, and what to look for in a good horse. They might not have been subjects she would have chosen given a say, but she embraced them nonetheless, content with the sound of Tutor Sashem's voice and the challenge of learning new things.

Hanna sat beside Anelie whenever Ma Guen didn't have something else for her to do. In the mornings before the guest children arrived for their play days, the two of them quizzed each other in whispers about the subjects of the day before. They discovered that even though they could only overhear the parts of lessons that fell within their free time, Tutor Sashem had a habit of summarizing his previous lessons for Rory, which filled in some of the blanks for the girls quite nicely. Hanna and Anelie called themselves "the mice in the wall," and made certain to leave no evidence of having been in the corridor that might lead to their getting shut out.

The game was made possible because no one paid much attention to Anelie. The routine of leaving her in Ma Guen's care during the day and returning her to the royal chambers for the evenings suited everyone, so it continued without a second thought. Even the subject of marriage was casual. Since she was not to inherit the throne, there was no pressure to form a suitable alliance, and since she was still a princess, an appropriate mate was not likely to be found among the shopkeepers, farmers, and animal husbands of Swallows. Thus, while there was a determination not to let her get past the age of twenty unmarried, the subject of who she would marry was, for the most part, left to fate.

Meanwhile, Rory became the favorite of the Legion of the Guards. The boy was an eager combatant, a fearless horseman, and comfortable in the company of soldiers. Even when barely in his teens, he often preferred whiling away his time in the barracks rather than in the family chambers. He enjoyed the banter of the guards and was entranced by the tales of past battles. Vas Turnbolt was particularly fond of him, and often commented on what a fine king Rory would make, a king like his father, whom the Legion of Guards could and would confidently follow into fire and chaos.

Anelie sometimes saw her brother, no longer so little, in the courtyard working with light sword or shield or horse under Turnbolt's guidance and felt a deep ache in her heart. He was slipping away from her now, and though they would always be very close, a distance between them would grow as their roles in Gravenwall drew them apart. Already she could bring tears to her eyes thinking about him as a feverishly playful child. The time when she was the most precious thing in his world seemed to have gone in a hundred blinks of an eye.

That is why, when the unforeseeable, the unthinkable, the unholy happened, she was certain she would die.

His foot missed the stirrup, that was all. In the space of three heartbeats he was mounted, then tumbling, then dead on the ground. It was inconceivable that so quickly, so simply the world could be sundered.

Though Turnbolt had nothing to do with the accident, he offered his life to King Allred, but both men were so stricken with grief that Allred could only command an embrace. Celia seemed to turn into an old woman overnight, her eyes lusterless, her hands suddenly skeletal and trembling. She would enfold Anelie in her arms when Anelie wept, but there was no strength or feeling in the holding. That she could not be cherished more even now crushed Anelie beyond words. Even Hanna, now more than ever her salvation, could not console her.

Appropriately the sky lowered the day they buried Rory and a misty rain fell every day for a month.

Everything changed. A listless King Allred ordered Anelie back into Tutor Sashem's care because now it seemed that Anelie would be next to rule. Allred and Celia considered themselves too old to attempt having another son, not because they couldn't, but for the child's safety — they would likely die before a son was old enough to capably and fairly command. Discussions began about whom it would be most advantageous for Anelie to marry.

Tutor Sashem was delighted to have her back as his student, but saddened by the circumstances. At their first meeting she softly told him about her years as a "mouse in the wall," which surprised him greatly.

"Had you but told me, I would have made the lessons more interesting for you," he said. He covered his face with his long, thin fingers. "Oh, how much time has been lost!"

But just as the sun cannot be made to repeat a glorious day, the enchanted classroom they once had also passed. There was little joy in Anelie, and he frequently found her distracted or suddenly tearful. She often did not do her lesson work, and sometimes snapped angrily at him when he pressed her to do more. Tutor Sashem became more watchful and wary, but she knew he loved her still.

Hanna grieved too, but her grief was over the loss of her closest friend. For many years she and Anelie had been as close as sisters, spending every day together. Now she and Ma Guen handled the children alone, and Hanna spent her free time gazing out the chamber window at the rolling hills outside.

Allred and Celia found the end of their sorrow in the cold blackness of The Dorhills Lake, where they often sought solace in the gentle rocking of the royal boat nearly out of sight of land, sole occupants of a peacefully lapping, creaking infinity. Their craft capsized in a fierce and sudden spring windstorm six months after Rory's funeral. They and their oarsmen were lost, along with two guards who jumped into the water from shore attempting to save them.

Thus, a day before her eighteenth birthday, with a heart heavy as a stone and cheeks wet with tears, and as bells tolled mournfully throughout the land, Anelie became Queen of the Province of Swallows.

The immensity of her loss struck her hardest when she entered the family apartments. The silence of the furniture, the cups and bowls and spoons that remained unmoved, even the emptiness of the shadows all converged on her, sending her to her knees in grief. Though she loved them all, the memory of Rory's laughing face tortured her most.

Thus, her first order of business was to drastically change her quarters.

The main bed was moved to face in the opposite direction even though the morning light would fall across her face, and the mattress was replaced. She had Ma Guen make new bedcovers for her, and the beds in which she and Rory had slept were dismantled and stored. Tall candelabras were stood in the darker corners to make the room seem bigger and warmer. Servants were told to leave nothing but a pitcher of water and a few goblets on the dining table.

Then, at least, she could enter the rooms without feeling shattered and abandoned, for whether she liked it or not, she had to change to meet the changes in her life.

Her first official meeting was with Thomas Chancellor, who entered the Gravenwall conference chambers bowing over steepled fingers. Anelie had seen him occasionally in the past, but had never met him, for her previous role in the scheme of things did not require it. She noticed immediately that even when Chancellor smiled his intentionally reassuring smile, his eyes seemed detached from it, his emotions, his gaze moving objectively over the features of Anelie's face as if he were reading a letter.

"You served my father well, Thomas Chancellor," she said, willing herself to echo the way she had heard her parents speak to their staff members. "If you do not wish to serve me, you have only to say so and you are released with my blessings and rewards."

"I would not hear of it, Your Majesty," Chancellor responded. "I serve the family, and always will, if allowed to."

"Thank you. Your guidance will be very important to me, and I am grateful for your loyalty."

"Equally grateful to serve," he murmured. His eyes then met hers. "There are some matters that require your attention, of course, and they in turn require a meeting with your ministers. Should I arrange it?"

Anelie sighed. "Yes. We must do that, I suppose."

Chancellor regarded her for a second, and bowed his head again. "If I may be so forward, Your Highness, as to offer some cautionary advice, if Your Majesty pleases."

"Go ahead."

"I speak only because of the novelty of your position, Your Majesty, and certainly not as any sort of criticism, which Your Highness's exceptional bearing has already demonstrated is unwarranted in every way."

"Go ahead."

His emotionless eyes met hers again. "Always doubt in private, Your Majesty, and command in public. If a judgment is asked for that you are not prepared to make, defer it until we can discuss the issue. And never apologize."

"Even if I am wrong?"

"Even if you are wrong. Learn from it, certainly, but never apologize."

She nodded slowly. "Thank you, Thomas. And do arrange a meeting with the ministers for the day after tomorrow."

As she gradually assumed the often-tedious duties of chief administrator, she surprised many with her confidence and calm, neither of which she truly felt, but was able to project by continually repeating in her mind the words, *Doubt in private, command in public.*

Through these meetings, she became aware of the astonishing number of considerations involved in managing the people and businesses of Swallows, balancing political relationships with other provinces and monarchies, and directing the affairs of Gravenwall itself. She also quickly learned the twin needs of delegating responsibility and watching the delegates to make sure they didn't overstep their authority.

But by far her thorniest and most dangerous issue was dealing with Vas Turnbolt.

She managed to avoid him for some time with a busy schedule of conferences and information sessions, but one day Turnbolt demanded her attention in a message carried by Thomas Chancellor.

Chancellor was at her side when Turnbolt approached the conference table, bowed, and said, "Thank you for taking the time to see me," then, with a barely concealed sneer, "Your Majesty."

She felt his contempt and also felt anger sting her cheeks, but kept her voice level. "What can we do for you, Master Turnbolt?"

"Since you are the monarch of Gravenwall in the tragic absence of King Allred, Queen Celia and the beloved Prince Rory, it is your duty to design the deployment of the Legion of Guards for the defense of Swallows. Your Highness."

The words came down on her like lashes, but were not insolent enough to have Turnbolt arrested. She needed Turnbolt, and he knew it. Yet she had to find a way to stand up to him or risk losing whatever respect she was slowly gathering.

Though her eyes burned with anger, she refused to avert them from his, and refused to be shaken by his thin, mocking smile.

"I welcome that charge, Master Turnbolt, since it concerns the well-being of all the truly honest, hardworking, and dutiful citizens of Swallows. I will have your orders in two days."

Turnbolt's smile twitched and his eyes narrowed. He seemed to be thinking, searching for words. Anelie could feel Chancellor's eyes on her.

Before Turnbolt could respond, she said quietly, "Did I also say you were dismissed?"

Turnbolt's long, thin face grew even paler than it normally was and he swallowed hard. He barely tilted his head, turned quickly, and stalked out of the room.

After the door closed, she sagged in her chair, leaning her elbows on the table in front of her.

"I fear you have made an enemy, Your Majesty," Chancellor said softly.

"He was an enemy when he walked through the door, Thomas. Now we must make him a subject. What answer do you suggest I give to his request?"

"I would suggest that you adopt the deployment scheme that your father designed. Nothing has changed in the province to require a drastic change. No riots, no banditry, no rebellions."

Anelie studied Chancellor's face for a moment. "Keep things as they are, then? For those reasons?"

"Yes, Your Majesty. Despite some apparent friction between you at the time, I believe Master Turnbolt will respect such common sense. I believe any alteration will appear to be change simply for change's sake, and will worsen matters." He paused. "Supposing that Your Majesty is aware of what alterations to recommend."

There it was, she thought. Anelie resisted a rueful smile. Turnbolt's words suddenly sounded in her mind: "This is no place for girls." It appeared that most around her were certain Rory would naturally know what to do, but she, just as certainly, would not.

"Thank you, Thomas," she said. "I will give your advice some thought. Are we done with meetings today? If so, I am tired and want to rest."

"Certainly, Your Majesty," Chancellor said uneasily, detecting a change in the tone of her voice. "I will await your summons." He bowed his head quickly and left the room.

Once the room was empty, she allowed the misgivings coiled within her to spool out. She was alone, uncertain, and new at this. Why should anyone have faith in her judgment? Faith had to be earned. And yet, sound judgment required equally sound counsel.

At the moment, there was only one person in her world she could trust for a truly objective opinion. That person was Hanna.

Even thinking her name comforted Anelie. Things had changed, however, and the simple act of seeing Hanna again had become infinitely more complicated. How would it appear to Thomas Chancellor, Master Turnbolt, the soldiers, the common folk within Gravenwall, if the new queen were huddling with her girlhood friend? Appearances are also politics, Anelie thought. She had to be circumspect.

"Guard?"

There was a shuffling outside and a voice called back through the door.

"Yes, Your Majesty?"

"Summon the seamstress. There's work to be done."

"Yes, Your Majesty."

Anelie went to her desk, drew a small piece of paper to her, and wrote upon it, *Mouse in the wall.*

A short while later the guard rapped on the door.

"The seamstress, Your Majesty."

"Enter, then."

The door swung open and Ma Guen hesitantly came into the room. She nervously curtsied and bowed as Anelie coolly regarded her, aware that the guard was watching. She waved the guard away, and the door closed.

Anelie rushed to Ma Guen and embraced her, confusing the old woman even more. Anelie put a finger to her lips and led Ma Guen by the hand toward the back of the chamber.

"Several new gowns are required, seamstress. Three for everyday use and two for formal affairs," she said in full voice, then whispered, "It's so good to see you, Ma Guen. Are you well? Are you comfortable?"

Ma Guen nodded slowly.

Anelie pressed the paper into Ma Guen's hand and closed the old woman's fingers around it. "Take this to Hanna. She'll understand. It's urgent." Then she straightened and firmly said, "You already know my size and preferences. I wish to review your work at each interval of progress. You may begin immediately."

"Yes, Your Majesty," Ma Guen murmured.

Anelie again embraced her, and then walked her to the door, whispering, "I will see you soon, I promise. "

"Guard?" Anelie called.

The door opened, and Ma Guen shuffled out.

Anelie returned to her desk, leaned back in her chair, and closed her eyes. Her thoughts whirled in the spark-streaked dimness, a cavalcade of questions, possibilities, causes and effects. She also felt the fear of responsibility. The people of Swallows were now hers to nurture and defend. The implications of the sudden changes in her life went far beyond her predicament with Chancellor and Turnbolt, but they were inextricably linked. She had to successfully resolve these predicaments in order to effectively carry out her responsibilities to the gentle souls of Swallows.

She had no idea how long she had been wrestling with these thoughts, or even if she had momentarily dozed off, but she was startled by a timid knock on the door behind the tapestry on the far wall.

Hanna was in the dim hallway. Anelie joined her there to assure that they wouldn't be heard. As Ma Guen had done, Hanna curtsied and bowed her head. And as Anelie had done with Ma Guen, Anelie embraced her friend.

"Hanna, I need you," she whispered.

In the cool passageway, Anelie recounted the challenge put to her by Turnbolt, and Chancellor's recommendation for defenses to continue as they were. Pacing, wringing her hands, Anelie softly voiced her concerns and doubts. Hanna listened intently.

"What would you do, Hanna? I have never been a soldier, I have never been in battle, I have never commanded an army into motion."

"No, Your Majesty," Hanna said. "But as you yourself wrote to me, you have been a mouse in the wall."

Anelie stared at her.

"Think back, Your Majesty. Remember Rory's lessons. Do you recall Tutor Sashem's threat assessment lessons last year? When he drew the map?"

Anelie was forming her memories into thoughts.

"The map, yes." She began to recite. "The severity of Storms protects Swallows by land from the north. Any threat from the Artrean Continent can only come by ship across the Eastern Ocean. Aggressors from the south, through the Province of Doves, must enter the Rampal Strait, which is patrolled by Rampal, our strongest ally. That leaves the west."

"Do you remember the only real threat Tutor Sashem recognized?"

"Yes," Anelie said. "He mentioned an army of bandits marauding their way across Welland for years. Harald of Maurisia."

"Yes. And there's only one path Harald or anyone else can possibly take into Swallows without ships, if he dared to try it at all?"

"The Fugitive Bridge," Anelie nodded.

Every twelve hours, when the tide was low, a strand of sand-covered flat rock ten wagons wide appeared, forming a bridge between the eastern coast of Welland and the western coast of Swallows that only the most desperate would attempt crossing. The route was long, treacherous and allowed for little rest before the cold waters of the Vastland Sea closed over it to join the Northern Ocean. Even if the passage was made safely, a stout net wall blocked the way into Swallows. A small army moving quickly could reach and breach it, however, and the western defenses had long been undermanned.

Anelie looked at Hanna. "But we have nothing. Why would Harald try it?"

"To hide," Hanna said. "If he is being pursued, and he likely is, he might attempt to cross. His pursuers most certainly won't."

"Our defenses are focused on the east, toward Artrea. We should shift more forces to block Fugitive Bridge, just to be safe."

"You have your answer, Your Majesty," Hanna smiled. "It makes more sense now than before. We don't know where Harald of Maurisia is."

Anelie sighed with relief. She saw that if she had spent less time tangled up in her problem and more time seeking a solution, she possibly could have reasoned it out for herself. There were lessons for her here. She vowed to learn them. And one of those lessons was that she needed Hanna's presence.

She embraced Hanna again.

"Thank you, Hanna. Here's what I want you to do. Meet me here, exactly as you just did, every second day at midday, when the children are sleeping. I will make things more comfortable for us, and we will talk about the things that confront Swallows."

"I would be honored. It will make me happy to see you so much more often, Your Majesty, and I will pass on to you what I hear around me."

When Anelie returned to her chambers, she felt stronger, more confident, and more relaxed than she had in some time. She felt for the first time that she could, indeed, be a queen. She had someone she could trust. A friend. A confidante. A mouse in the wall.

✳   ✳   ✳

Two days later, Anelie entered the conference room purposely late. Both Thomas Chancellor and Master Turnbolt were standing, of course, being as yet unbidden to sit, and bowed as she approached them.

She sat and motioned toward the two chairs before her. Turnbolt was grinding his teeth, she noticed, as her peripheral vision detected the flexing and relaxing of his jaw muscles. Chancellor merely looked uncomfortable.

"Gentlemen," she said. "We are here to discuss, among some other minor bits of business, the defensive scheme for Swallows, rightly requested by Master Turnbolt.

"The province has been quiet. There seem to be no imminent threats from our continental neighbors to the east. Is that correct? Mr. Chancellor?"

"Yes, Your Majesty. That, to my knowledge, is correct."

"Master Turnbolt?"

"I have heard nothing to the contrary, Your Majesty."

"What is the latest intelligence we have on this Harald of Maurisia, who has been plundering in Welland for so long? Where is he now?" She looked at Turnbolt.

Turnbolt shifted in his chair, a slight widening of his eyes betraying his surprise that she knew anything at all about Stonearm. The look quickly passed, however, and was replaced by his usual insolence.

"Of course Her Majesty would have heard her father discussing this bandit in the past," he said smoothly. "Stonearm moves slowly. The last we heard, he was bargaining his way through Ostragard, near the Central Steppes of Welland."

"Among the Seven Tribes. Yes, he would have to do that," she said coldly, her eyes never leaving Turnbolt. "And my father never discussed military matters in front of me or his queen. Do not ever presume to know the source of my words again, Master Turnbolt, but concern yourself more with what keeps you useful to Gravenwall. What defensive scheme do we have in place now?" She stated this last, leaving no doubt that she knew the answer.

Turnbolt was pale. "The Cornerstone Defense."

"Yes. And how long has it been in place?"

"Precisely, I do not know. Years. Many years. It is a sound defensive position for a variety of situations, Your Majesty."

"True. But it defends situations, as you call them, of eastern origins. We just discussed such a situation in Welland, to our west. Would the Cornerstone Defense be the best option for us should Harald of Maurisia decide — or more likely be compelled — to move quickly out of Welland?"

A sheen of sweat formed above Turnbolt's brows. "With proper warning — "

"Do we have informants in Harald's army?"

"No, Your Majesty."

"Then from where would our warning come?" She did not wait for Turnbolt to answer. "No, Master Turnbolt. A defense should be in place to give Swallows the best chance should this outlaw show up unannounced. What would you recommend that defense be?" Again, she made it clear that she already knew the answer.

Turnbolt's breathing was strained, which in turn strained his voice.

"To counter a direct, large assault from Welland, I would choose the Sand Wall Defense, Your Majesty, to bulk up the garrison at Fugitive Bridge."

"Wonderful," Anelie smiled. "So would I. You can begin to redeploy your troops as soon as possible, Master Turnbolt. Please keep me informed as you do so."

She glanced at Chancellor, who was staring at her, breathing through an open mouth. His face was every bit as pale as Turnbolt's. He quickly shifted his eyes to documents in his lap.

"Do you agree, Mr. Chancellor?"

"I do, Your Majesty. I do, yes," he mumbled.

"Fine, then. What else is there to go over, Mr. Chancellor? And does any of it require us to detain Master Turnbolt any longer?"

"No, Your Majesty." Chancellor looked at the papers and feebly waved a hand in the air. "What remains is minor…public works…a question of ownership…matters such as that."

"Then Master Turnbolt can turn his attention to more important things."

Turnbolt rose slowly, bowed, and whispered, "Your Majesty."

The door closed behind Turnbolt. From the hallway came a muffled thump, and the door guard yelped. Anelie smiled.

Chancellor was again staring, as if he did not recognize her. In spite of what she considered an obnoxious imperiousness she would much prefer not to exercise, Anelie felt more comfortable in her new role.

"You appear doubtful, Mr. Chancellor. Is there something you wish to say?"

Chancellor stammered. "Master Turnbolt, Your Majesty was, that was harsh treatment, Your Highness, it seems to me…"

"Mr. Chancellor," she said. "If I am to have an enemy nearby, I want there to be no mistake that it is mutual."

* * *

Anelie carefully washed her paintbrushes, testing the suppleness of the bundled rabbit's hairs as they dried to remove any stiffness that might remain. The light was growing dimmer in her chambers, signaling that another day was waning even though the sky had been choked with clouds since dawn. She lined up her brushes on the windowsill, and moved about the room lighting lanterns. She smiled. The rich, golden lantern light in the evenings was what warmed her soul the most.

Gravenwall was so long ago. Everything was so long ago.

A year after she had settled into Sloedon Castle, word had come from Swallows that Turnbolt had been put aboard a ship bound for the Faradays, and then set adrift in a small boat under the burning sun of the Southern Ocean. The messenger said rumor had Harald of Maurisia telling Turnbolt as he tied his arms behind his back that a man who would betray his queen with such ease would likely betray him as well at some point, and he'd rather not be bothered by doubt.

The messenger also mentioned that Harald seemed to be a good ruler. Stern but fair, he appeared to wish no one any harm.

These were two thoughts that gave her some comfort in her exile. While her scalding anger had subsided, her bitterness had not. And at the heart of it was a perpetual longing to go home. Though her family was gone, their voices remained in the vaulted halls, in the wind-stirred summer trees, among the stones in the coursing brook. She ached to hear them again.

There was a soft knock at the door.

"Madam Queen?"

She sighed.

"Come in, Thomas."

Chapter Three

CHANCELLOR

Chancellor entered the chamber with his head bowed and a thick sheaf of documents held tightly against his chest as if they were a shield. Since he was never to show his back to Madam Queen, he fumbled for the edge of the door with his free hand and closed it with his heel.

As he made his way forward to Madam Queen's conference table, he studiously avoided looking at the portraits of Gravenwall lined up against the chamber walls. Years ago he had gazed at each of them mournfully as they left the easel, and Anelie had asked him, "Would you like one, Thomas?" And he had answered quietly, "Thank you, no, Your Highness. I am haunted enough as it is."

His long journey from "Mr. Chancellor" to "Thomas" had reached its conclusion with a confession made in the chilly evening shadows at Sloedon, but began in the heat of a summer afternoon in Gravenwall several weeks after Anelie's decision to adopt the Sandwall Defense.

Thomas Chancellor had been walking purposefully along Gravenwall's west portico, his thoughts temporarily distracted by the delicious feeling of time and again passing from the heat of sunlight into the cool shadows cast by the columns, when he nearly ran directly into Master Turnbolt, who was leaning against the wall with a bemused smirk on his lips.

"Good afternoon, Mr. Chancellor. You know, in battle such preoccupation would likely get you killed."

Chancellor's cheeks flamed. This man always made him feel suddenly weak. "I assure you, Master Turnbolt, that if there were a battle raging here I would not be preoccupied by shadows," he said testily.

"Of course not. You would be running for your life." Turnbolt regarded Chancellor for a moment, and then said, "Mr. Chancellor, would you do me the honor of joining me for a chat in the command room?"

Chancellor was instantly wary. "Well, I do have an appointment…"

"It won't take long. We'll enjoy a cool drink on this warm day."

Chancellor saw no possibility of refusal in Turnbolt's unsmiling eyes.

"Yes, of course."

The sweat Chancellor felt on his face and under his tunic was not from heat, and it chilled him as they walked down the dim, cool hallway of the officer's barracks. His eyes caught quick glimpses of perfectly kept cells, and from one the fleeting image of a cold, hard stare from a man folding a shirt. Turnbolt said nothing as they walked, but when they reached the command chamber he abruptly snapped, "Beer," to the guard alongside the door.

The room was as tidy as the cells Chancellor had passed, and on one wall was a large map. On it he saw the provinces and the edges of the countries nearby across the seas and bays. This was a position map, not one of the world.

Turnbolt noisily pulled a chair away from a table and sat down on it, laying one booted leg up on the tabletop in front of him. He motioned his guest into a chair across from him, and sat staring at Chancellor for what seemed to Thomas an excruciatingly long time, until the guard arrived with two steins of beer, placed them on the table, then closed the door behind him as he left.

"Mr. Chancellor, we have a delicate matter to discuss." Turnbolt shrugged, and continued as if talking to himself in a singsong voice. "Well, actually, not to discuss since you'll find very few options in it for you. Nevertheless..."

Thomas saw that this was Turnbolt's idea of humor. Turnbolt's cold gaze locked onto Chancellor's eyes.

"Mr. Chancellor, I have deployed my troops in the Sandwall Defense as commanded by our Majesty, who surprised me, incidentally, with her awareness of the situation." He smiled humorlessly. "Now you wouldn't have had anything to do with that, would you?"

"Military matters are not the concern of counselors. And Her Majesty spoke the truth when she said her father did not discuss troop matters in front of her. Only Rory. I've no idea where she heard of these things."

"Tutor Sashem, perhaps?"

"My lady was not included in lessons until recently, Master Turnbolt."

"Hmm. Curious," Turnbolt lightly slapped the table. "But the 'how' of it doesn't interest me all that much at the moment. As I was saying, the Sandwall Defense has been implemented. And I also took the liberty of dispatching three riders to Welland across the Fugitive Bridge for the purpose of discovering the actual whereabouts of Harald Stonearm's forces. Two riders made it across, and one of them located Harald. Do you know what happened then?"

Chancellor had no idea, but his stomach lurched with alarm. He shook his head, more in tremor than response.

"Stonearm was given a letter. In it he read that if the letter is returned to me with his mark on it, I will know that he agrees to my proposal and may approach Gravenwall without resistance."

In spite of himself, Chancellor's eyes widened in disbelief. "Without resistance? You would give up Her Majesty and Gravenwall without a fight?"

"Her Majesty, yes. But not Gravenwall. Stonearm has been struggling among the Seven Tribes. They are all mad as fleas and would set upon each other over a scrap of meat. A stranger trying to work his way through their country would find it exhausting just to stay alive. Stonearm must be very clever and very strong indeed to have come so far. My proposal is to offer him safe haven in Swallows, with dominion over half the province. I will remain in Gravenwall. " Turnbolt chuckled. "Come there, Mr. Chancellor. You look as if you've swallowed a burr."

"But...what if Stonearm decides to take Swallows on his own terms?"

"Her Majesty knows of the Sandwall Defense. Harald Stonearm does not."

"You have that much confidence in the defense, Master Turnbolt? Against so hardened an army?"

"Sandwall is a ferocious bear trap, Mr. Chancellor. It was designed to more than equalize the efforts of a smaller force against a larger one. Yes, I have confidence in it."

Chancellor's gaze darted about as if he were looking for something. "But...what if Stonearm returns the letter, then decides to take Gravenwall when he's here? What will stop him if he's within our defenses?"

Turnbolt shrugged. "Then we will have to fight, won't we? But think about it, Mr. Chancellor. Inside our defenses, he would be surrounded. Why would he deliberately put his men in such a disadvantageous position if he intended to fight? It would be a terrible battle of attrition, and for what? An unfamiliar province with an unknown population? No, he's smarter than that."

"But if mutiny is your aim, why do you risk so much? Why court Stonearm at all? I don't understand! This is treason!"

"Study your history, Mr. Chancellor. Swallows has always maintained a force large enough to defend Swallows, but not large enough to command it, particularly with an aroused citizenry. There are former soldiers among our countrymen, after all. The presence of two armies, especially if one of them is the dreaded Harald Stonearm's, will give us an inert population."

"Why are you doing this? Do you despise Her Majesty so much?"

Turnbolt leaned forward. "Yes," he hissed. "I will have Gravenwall. My allegiance was to King Allred first, Prince Rory second. It was never to some milk-skinned little girl who can barely ride a horse."

Chancellor thought he might faint from the force of such blasphemy. While he may not have complete confidence in Her Majesty's military acumen, he was still in service to the family. With his heart quaking, he whispered, "What of the queen, Master Turnbolt? Would you harm her?"

Turnbolt brightened. "I'm glad you asked me that, Mr. Chancellor, for now we come to your role in the whole affair."

Chancellor's eyes rose abruptly to meet Turnbolt's.

"Come now, Mr. Chancellor. It must have occurred to you to wonder why I'm telling you all this now, when you could rush right out, warn the queen and allow her to marshal the few soldiers in Gravenwall who would fight for her.

"When Stonearm arrives, you will gather the queen and her staff and leave Swallows. She will go to her uncle in Storms. You will remain with her as my eyes in Sloedon. You will discreetly send me news of everything Her Majesty says and does while she's there. If there is any sign of her attempting to assemble a force, I will know about it—from you—long before the first horse is saddled and…" He paused with a smile. "…do something about it."

Chancellor tried to muster conviction, but his question arrived as a croak. "And if I refuse?"

"The queen will die the moment Stonearm arrives. As will you." Turnbolt waited a few seconds for his words to sink in. "I do not want that, Mr. Chancellor. I really do not. It would be a public relations nightmare, as you can imagine. It would involve endless placating among the people of Swallows, for which I have little patience. Lives would no doubt be lost. It would be a great bother to me. I do not wish to be bothered."

"What if Stonearm does not agree? What will you do then?" But Chancellor's spinning mind knew that he already had, or Turnbolt would not be telling him any of this. There would be no point in it.

Turnbolt withdrew a letter from his boot top and laid it on the table.

"He is on his way."

Chancellor's shoulders sagged in resignation. "So. That is it then." He could, however, still warn the queen. Perhaps she could act swiftly enough to turn the troops against Turnbolt. Perhaps she could act covertly enough that Turnbolt wouldn't know what she was doing. But if Turnbolt found out, he would be forced to act against her. In trying to aid the queen, Chancellor might very well be gravely endangering her. Which would she prefer? Which was right?

As if reading his mind, Turnbolt said, "The clockworks turn on loyalty, don't they? Yours, mine, the guards, the militia. Each affects each." Turnbolt smiled cheerfully. "Now here is something we can discuss after all. What is loyalty to you, Mr. Chancellor?"

"To stand by the family I serve against all odds."

"And that is judged by most as noble, indeed. But I contend

that there are two types of loyalty. There is the loyalty of faith, which you have just professed, and there is the loyalty of obedience. The loyalty of faith is founded upon the unseen, upon ideals and emotions, upon duty and love, if you will.

"Then there is the loyalty of obedience. This is loyalty based on the consequences of failure. It is the loyalty I command, Mr. Chancellor. Do you believe in a Great Creator?"

Chancellor had been watching and listening to Turnbolt as one would regard a serpent. The question startled him out of his trance.

"I do. Yes."

"Most people do, I've come to learn. Yours and theirs is a loyalty of faith, Mr. Chancellor. You have never seen this Great Creator, nor felt his lash split your skin if you disobey his rules of order. Most of my soldiers believe in the Great Creator, too. Some are quite ardent about it particularly before a battle. However, they can often be seen drinking and gambling and engaging in the most shocking behavior when freed from responsibility. I would suspect that the Great Creator disapproves of such carryings-on. Mostly it is forgotten, but occasionally some beg forgiveness, knowing it will be granted with enough groveling. A fortnight later, there they are again, wallowing in drink and flesh.

"Yet if I tell them not to engage in such behavior, they will not. They may grumble and pout, but they will not. Curious, isn't it? Do you know why this is?"

Turnbolt leaned forward with a menacing joy in his eyes.

"Because they have not seen what a wrathful Creator will do to them. They can only try to imagine it. They have, on the other hand, seen what a wrathful Turnbolt will do to them. They know there will be consequences, and that in this world the author of those consequences will arrive in their doorway as surely as rivers run downhill."

Turnbolt relaxed again, sitting back with a sigh.

"That will explain why, despite your loyalty of faith in the queen, you will serve me in Sloedon, Mr. Chancellor. I have a very long reach and a short attention span. If reports do not arrive in a timely manner, there will be consequences. But you are a very bright man, and I feel I'm needlessly belaboring the point."

Chancellor found his voice, meek as it sounded. "Faith in something is everything," he said, as if trying to convince himself. "In salvation or the innate goodness of the heart or the eventual passing of pain. Faith in something is everything to life."

Turnbolt smiled. "You can have faith in me, Mr. Chancellor."

His smile suddenly widened in surprise.

"Mr. Chancellor! We've hardly touched our beer!"

Through the following weeks, Chancellor's burden nearly buckled him. His breathing became strained, his skin paled, and he spent much of his time in his own chambers dithering among stacks of parchments. Anelie remarked on his appearance several times, wondering aloud if Chancellor was ill and in need of a visit to the alchemist.

For his part, Thomas wondered if this was how it felt to await the imminent arrival of death—to feel friendless, freighted with guilt, and fearful of retribution—and decided it could not be. Death, at least, would mean an end to it all, the thought of which carried a muted joy of its own. When his resolution arrived, it would only mark the beginning of his trials.

Many times he found himself mapping the repercussions of telling the queen all he knew, of warning her and plotting a response with her. Thomas did not care much about what Turnbolt might do to him if he found out he had gone to Anelie, but he did quake at the thought of what Turnbolt might do to the queen. He always concluded that the risk was too great to take, and continued his otherworldly existence, a sort of sleepwalking in which he would find himself dropping off to sleep in the daylight and unable to close his eyes in the darkness.

How long he remained in this state he would never really know or indeed have a need to know. But one morning he abruptly awoke to the diamond-bright light of panic when Turnbolt was suddenly at his side saying, "He's here. You have two hours to make an escape. And remember…you are my eyes in Sloedon."

He bolted into action, dispatching a messenger to Sloedon and then rushing Ma Guen and Hanna and a few faithful retainers to the assembly point while Turnbolt ordered certain of Anelie's most devoted guards to leave his ranks and go with the queen. Chancellor would always remember those hours more vividly than any other hours of his life. The shock and dismay, the bewilderment and fear directed back toward him as he executed a plan he'd visualized a hundred times before but now could scarcely believe was happening.

But what he would remember forever was the searing pain of the confusion, hurt and disbelief in her eyes as she said, "How could this happen? How?" while both of them knew he had betrayed her. What else? The bitterness of her tears as their small party left Gravenwall for the cover of the forest, all looking up at the impossibly long line of horsemen atop a far hill, their pennants fluttering in the wind.

Then came the long, grim march to the north.

They hurried for the first two days until they came to realize they did not have to. No one was pursuing them. They were too small a group to pose a counter-threat. The countryside was calm, since word had not yet spread through traveling merchants, journeymen and brigands that Gravenwall had fallen. The queen's sudden presence in the villages was cause for a hasty celebration, with the surprised and delighted townspeople apologizing for the lack of proper hospitality. The entourage was fed and housed as lavishly as her subjects could muster in the few hours they had. Anelie was often moved to tears by their devotion, because they did not yet know that she had failed them.

As the days passed, the air grew colder, and they sometimes found themselves hunching against snow squalls and bursts of cutting wind. The villages became farther and farther apart, were more primitive, and the villagers, now far from anyone's dominion, were suspicious and occasionally hostile. Little comfort was found in these wilds. The guards were edgy, and the group found it more advisable to camp at night than try to find any shelter in the rough settlements. At midday Anelie sent scouts ahead to find the most protected sites in the empty, windblown plains.

One afternoon, amid moving shafts of sunlight that escaped through jagged cracks in a leaden sky, her scouts came back with three riders from Castle Sloedon. They were hard, weathered men who had been waiting for Anelie for days, and their purpose in intercepting the caravan was to guide them through Sloedon's formidable, natural southern defense: The Barrens.

By now all of them were exhausted, filthy, and cold. Ma Guen felt herself near perishing, and Hanna spent much of her time trying to make the woman comfortable in their little wagon. Anelie and Chancellor had barely spoken since they set out from Gravenwall, and Chancellor's guilt weighed on him far more than the wind, rain or snow. Only the soldiers seemed to be faring well, with their hardships serving only to make them more alert and eager to face some enemy, they cared not who. Thus, when the party started out early the next morning and arrived at the top of a long, gradual rise, the sight before them nearly broke their spirits.

The Barrens stretched ahead to infinity, an endless flat sea of wind-battered brown grass scarred by treacherous rills, sinkholes and expanses of swamp. The sky seemed to hover directly above it like a vast, descending weight. In the space between earth and the sooty, roiling firmament, clouds of snow blew one way, then another.

The riders from Sloedon turned to the group, studying their faces.

"No fear, all," one growled. "There's ways through it. Just follow in our tracks and you'll be well."

This they did for three miserable days. The Sloedon riders led them on a winding path that ended each day at a well-used campsite where they started fires and distributed water and fur robes from storehouses that resembled giant cairns built of thick, flat stone. One evening as he stared into the flames of the campfire, Chancellor overheard Anelie ask one of the Sloedon men what was to keep an invader from following the same trails to these established camps.

"There's water under all out there, moving day and night," the guide said. "The breaks change season to season, sometimes day to day. You have to know how to read the grassland or you'll founder and drown." The guide's voice became softer and gentler. "You've no worries, Madam Queen. You're safe here."

In the weakening light of the third day, they slowly entered the castle grounds with Ma Guen weeping quietly in the wagon and Anelie trying to keep her bearing under the pitying gaze of the sentries. After that was bliss. After that was warmth, hot water, food, wine, and soft beds to sleep in. After that were weeks of kindness and comfort.

And after that, Chancellor could bear his guilt no longer. He had decided on the journey that he could not serve Turnbolt, that he would serve only Queen Anelie, and that he would tell her all he knew even though it meant, as Turnbolt had said, that someday the author of consequences would be standing in his doorway, and it all would come to an end.

One afternoon Thomas Chancellor begged Anelie's attention for a few moments, and under her hard gaze made his confession. He began with his misplaced doubt in her abilities to rule, which apparently contributed to Turnbolt's belief that Chancellor could be easily molded to his own intentions. He recounted Turnbolt's ultimatum, and his orders to keep him informed of everything Anelie did and said at Sloedon. He said he had been forced to betray his queen then, but would not willingly do so now, even if it meant being slain by one or the other of them.

Throughout his often-halting monologue, Anelie's eyes and features gradually softened. When he was finished and sat with his head bowed in misery, she spoke.

"I understand that you were protecting my life, and how difficult it must have been to remain silent. I also understand that Master Turnbolt is a force difficult to resist. You were left with few alternatives, and I no longer bear you any ill will for what happened. Now you must understand that your role as my advisor has ended. I cannot afford to have you as my chief counselor. Instead, I would prefer you be my court organizer." At this she smiled ruefully and said in an aside to herself, "Such court as I have. You will schedule whatever meetings I might have, bring me correspondence, transcribe letters, and keep me informed of the well-being of all those who came from Gravenwall with us. Is that acceptable? Thomas?"

He heard it. Thomas, not Mr. Chancellor. Thomas, the old family friend, one of her late father's cronies. He nodded. "Yes, Your Majesty. I am grateful to serve you in any way I can." His thoughts continued in silence: *For as long as I am allowed to live, that is.*

"Madam Queen, Thomas," she reminded him. "Or Your Highness. I am just a guest in the house of the King and Queen of Storms."

"Of course, Madam Queen."

So ended one career, and another less taxing one began. Chancellor went about his tasks dutifully and meticulously, but always with a worm of fear in his stomach that one of Turnbolt's men would arrive to assassinate him. With the arrival and departure of every journeyman messenger or free lance who could be hired to carry messages from Storms to Swallows and other provinces, not one bearing a letter from Chancellor to Turnbolt, Thomas felt his doom moving closer.

One day, nearly a year after they had left Gravenwall, Chancellor happened to be crossing the courtyard when a lone rider was admitted. Thomas was near one of Anelie's loyalists standing guard duty.

"That's Goran," the guard said, and nodded toward the rider. "Served beside him back when."

Thomas felt a chill envelop him. So, he thought, the long arm of Turnbolt had finally found him. He hurried back to his chambers to write his final note to the queen.

Some time later, as the light was beginning to fail and he was near the end of his notes, there was a knock at his door.

"Madam Queen summons you," a voice said.

Trembling, he went to Anelie's quarters. Both she and the rider turned toward him as he entered.

"News from Gravenwall, Thomas," Anelie said. "News that might interest you."

Then the rider told the story of Harald's arrival at Gravenwall. He spoke of the tense first weeks, as Turnbolt's guards and Stonearm's soldiers mingled distrustfully and sometimes clashed. No one was killed, but there were a few broken bones, and the wounded almost always were guards. One morning all of them, both soldiers and guards, were assembled in Gravenwall's central compound. Stonearm marched out with a phalanx of armed soldiers.

He announced, the rider said, that he and Master Turnbolt were parting company. Harald could and would never trust a man who would connive against his own queen, particularly since she was the blood daughter of a man to whom he had sworn allegiance, so Turnbolt was going on a journey not of his own choosing.

"Who among you stands with him?" Harald asked. "Who will join Master Turnbolt?"

Even though there was great suspicion, about twenty men stepped forward. Harald nodded approvingly.

"Good, good. Thank you." He turned to the soldiers at his side. "Arrest them," he said. "The rest of you I invite to join our cheerful band. You will be paid as well as the rest, and work no harder than the rest. However, as you might expect, you will immediately become carrion if you plot or raise a hand against any of us. Those who decide not to stay may return home. You will have some time to think it over. Say, one hour."

The twenty had been quickly surrounded and disarmed, the rider said. Over the next few weeks, in bits and pieces, the rider learned that they were imprisoned, while Turnbolt was put aboard a merchant ship bound for the Faraday Islands. The captain was paid handsomely to set Turnbolt adrift in an open boat somewhere in the Southern Ocean. Once it was certain that Turnbolt and his most loyal men could not reunite, Stonearm hired the guards who chose to join him and sent the others on their way.

Thomas felt relief seeping through him, warm and welcome. He thanked the queen for being courteous enough to let him hear the news first hand. He backed out of the queen's quarters bowing and repeating his gratitude, and returned to his own rooms, where he lay upon his bed and repeated in his mind what he had heard the rider say.

Then he slipped into the deepest dreamless sleep he had experienced in a long, long time.

Chancellor laid the sheaf of documents on the table and waited for a signal from Anelie to seat himself. She sat across from him, her hands folded in her lap. There were the faintest traces of amusement around her lips and eyes. She enjoyed these catch-up sessions. At Gravenwall they would carry much more gravity, but here? Exercising the propriety of court between a queen without a throne and a powerless counselor? Sometimes she had to concentrate on not laughing out loud.

Chancellor picked through the parchments, even though they had been organized a number of times already.

"The king and queen of Highmont send their most sincere, although obviously much belated, best wishes for Your Highness's birthday," Chancellor began, and carefully turned and set the document before Anelie.

"News has come that Prince Bethel was unhorsed during a boar hunt and gored to death. Shall I prepare your condolences?"

"Yes, please do," Anelie said.

"Baron Jorma of Rockham, Welland, is sending a wagonload of his highly regarded wine to her highness as a pledge of his esteem and support," Chancellor read. "It will be a mixed lot of dry and fruity whites and chewy reds which King Jorma prays is acceptable to Her Highness. His vineyards are finally producing at pre-Harald Stonearm levels and quality, a remarkable achievement since, as Your Highness might recall, Stonearm burned and trampled it all to the ground ten years ago."

Anelie raised her eyebrows in approval. "Wonderful. Our hosts will be delighted. Prepare my sincere gratitude for both his marvelous gift and his invaluable support."

"Yes, ma'am," Chancellor nodded, making a notation on a page beside the stack of letters. He picked up another sheet.

"The Fiftieth Earl of March begs his highness to entertain the thought of considering his son Roland as a possible suitor for Her Highness's affections. Roland is an accomplished astronomer and quite clean of person. Should this be an attractive thought to Her Highness, perhaps a meeting can be arranged during the next equinox."

Anelie was smiling now. "Thank the most thoughtful Earl for us, but for the time being solitude suits Her Highness best, even though she is aware that she might well be making a most regrettable mistake."

"Yes, ma'am," said Chancellor, making his notations. That he was not smiling at all brought Anelie close to bursting. She looked at the walls to quell the laughter nudging her throat.

Chancellor raised another page.

"News comes from Swallows that Harald Stonearm is hosting a storytelling competition throughout the coming summer with grants and gifts as prizes. All are welcome, and an air of celebration is promised. Details are within, over which Her Highness may linger at her leisure." Chancellor laid the page in front of Anelie.

"A storytelling contest?" She slowly shook her head. "He must be a popular pretender."

"I have heard that said, Your Highness. But I have also heard it said that Her Highness is grievously missed, even after these many years."

Anelie's buoyant mood dissolved. She let her sight rest on her most recently completed painting of Gravenwall, *her* Gravenwall, in warmer and happier times.

Chancellor laid a sealed parchment in front of Anelie. "A personal note to Her Highness from Hempton in Swallows." He did not open or read personal letters to his queen.

There was a soft knock at the door.

"Your door guard, Madam Queen," a voice on the other side said.

"You may enter," Anelie said.

The guard stepped into the doorway, but no farther.

"I am instructed to inform Your Highness that two riders with a monstrous dog have approached Sloedon. They were intercepted on the cliff trail."

Despite knowing that Turnbolt was long gone, Chancellor felt a bolt of fear at the news. He licked his lips nervously.

"They request an audience with Madam Queen," the guard said. Then, after a short pause, "And Miss Hanna."

Chapter Four

THE PASSAGE MASTER

Passage Master Penwyn (who was also the ship's cook, doctor and spiritual counselor when required) awakened in his tiny cabin aboard the ferry vessel *Lionfish* during the Hour of Regrets (that melancholy time of troubling dreams or contemplative wakefulness just before dawn's first faint glow) as he had nearly every day of his life. He took a few seconds to assess the degree of stiffness in his joints before moving to leave the comfort of his berth.

His dream was still vivid in his mind and was often of the same kind, with interesting variations from time to time. He was due on watch, but had to retrieve something from his cabin. The ship was huge and bustling with people. He anxiously went from deck to deck searching for his cabin, but could not remember exactly which one it was. He smiled to himself. From where do these thoughts come, and what do they mean? And so clear — sometimes as palpable as his waking life. There was certainly no getting lost on *Lionfish*.

His existence was such by choice. He could have worked and whiled his time away to his present respectable age on land in a town or on a farm, but he preferred the continual motion of the sea under him, a motion that seemed like the breathing of a far greater, more powerful life than his own. He felt calmed and embraced by it.

He inched himself upright and lit the lantern beside his bed. Light jumped about the close bulkheads and ceiling. He stood, opened the door, and with the lantern in one hand and his night bucket in the other stepped into the companionway. After briefly setting down the bucket to close the door, he set off toward the midship ladders leading to the deck. At this hour, no one else was yet stirring below.

Topside, he smiled again. The chilly breeze was damp and rich with the scents of the sea, and he heard the wing-rustle and squawks of the night fishers working the windward waters. Above, thin, streaky clouds drifted between him and a firmament brilliant with vast smears of stars. Here the Stork Constellation, there the Sea Eagle and Fish, above the horizon the Huntsman and his Horse. Ship's timbers creaked under his feet. There was a wonderful vibrancy in the waking day. How Penwyn loved this world.

A shadow a bit darker than the sky behind it approached.

"Good morning, Penwyn."

"Good morning, Cap'n. Pleasant one, although with some iffiness to it."

Captain Kepper grunted in agreement and passed by. The captain was up and around far earlier than most of the crew, even in port, checking lines and rigging and sails and hitches that really didn't need to be checked at all. Penwyn had been working with Captain Kepper nearly half his life. Most of the time each man knew what the other would say and do before it was said and done. They had shared many a meal together discussing business and improvements and needs for the ship, and had relived a thousand moments over stronger drink than tea, and yet they knew that when the time came to part ways, each would, without remorse, live out the rest of his life without ever seeing the other again.

"I'll have tea and biscuits brought," Kepper called over his shoulder, as he always did.

Penwyn emptied his bucket over the side, rinsed it in the barrel of sea water on deck, secured its lid and set the bucket alongside it, where he would retrieve it before going below decks again that evening.

Following the pool of lantern light just ahead of his steps, Penwyn walked down the gangway to shore, then across the wharf to a small wooden shed, his passage office. At the sound of his unlocking the door, a small chorus of bleating, grunting and cackling arose from behind the building.

"Yes, yes, I'm coming, children. Patience, patience."

The noise did not abate throughout the time he entered the office, straightened up a desk that he had straightened up before he left it the day before, filled several pails with different meals and grains, and opened the back door that led to two different pens. One was for animals to be ferried from Sealhaven in the Province of Storms, where *Lionfish* was now docked, to Mother's Bay in the Province of Swallows, three days of sailing away, and the other was set aside for livestock offered as payment for a passage when no currency was had. The payment pen was, at the moment, empty, so Penwyn had only the one to tend. He chatted pleasantly with the few animals in the ferry pen as he fed and watered them and tidied up their straw.

"You'll be lucky ones, I think, my friends, " he said, "and have a smooth journey. I could tell you of a time a terrible storm set upon us and every man was down sick and every creature terrified and crying out, but I won't as it might upset you needlessly, but it seemed the bottom was coming to the top and the top was bound for the bottom and the sky was being pulled down with it. Yes. So."

By the time Penwyn was finished with the feeding, it was time for his own, as a crewmate cheerfully arrived knocking at the door with a plate of tea and biscuits. Penwyn sat atop his stool, opened the double shutters in front of him, and slowly munched on his biscuits (just made and slightly sweet, exactly the way he liked them) and sipped his tea, watching the world in front of him slowly take shape in the fading darkness. Across from him was a passenger terminal, really just a small shelter open at one end to protect people from the frequent provincial rain showers until they could board. The wharf gleamed with a sheen of spray and dew. Tall trees loomed behind it all. Lanterns floated along the railing of *Lionfish*, carried by a crew now stirring to duty, for today was sailing day, with the anchor to be raised by midmorning.

The passengers began arriving in this first, gray light. A prosperous-looking, portly man and his wife, he holding her elbow as they walked carefully over the wet planks, went directly to the shelter, having paid for their passage the day before. Not long afterward, a tall farmer, whose animals were now snuffling contentedly behind the office, arrived alone and approached Penwyn's office.

"'Ower m'animals, eh?"

"Fine, sir, as you are most welcome to see for yourself. I've only just fed them, haven't I?"

The farmer strolled around the shed to the pen, no doubt, Penwyn thought, counting the stock to make sure none somehow disappeared into Captain Kepper's barn. Satisfied, the man nodded to Penwyn as he left, and crossed the wharf, where he stood outside the shelter with his arms folded across his chest.

As the light grew fuller, six more pre-paid customers arrived and stood in self-conscious little groups awaiting the signal to board. Penwyn was beginning to think it might be a rather lean passage when a family of three walked toward the office, followed by a man with a muscular black and white dog at his side and a walking stick that would have also fairly passed as a cudgel in his right hand.

Penwyn greeted the family, a nervous-looking lot, the mother and father flanking a wide-eyed child of about twelve years.

"Hallo, hallo, welcome to the *Lionfish*. It's a fine day for a sail, is it not?"

"Well, yes, we hope so," the father said. "None of us has ever been on a ship before, but we must go to Swallows to settle some affairs, you see, or we probably wouldn't be going at all, you see, if my uncle had not died after falling from a window in Barnside, you see, as the idea of being on a ship, out there on all that water, does not attract us at all, any of us, not even the boy, you see."

Penwyn was staring at the man.

"Have no fear, sir. It will be a pleasant passage, as you'll see. Three days of pleasant weather and good company, as you'll discover, sir. Now, will that be an inside cabin, or a berth in the common hall?"

"An inside cabin, if you please. We can't really afford it, but I expect to be reimbursed from my uncle's affairs, and we would prefer to be together in a secure cabin for our first voyage, comfortable and together, you see, playing simple games and nibbling crackers which we have brought with us to pass the time, quite a bit of time, I hear, three days. Will there be people to see to us from time to time, do you know?"

Penwyn smiled pleasantly.

"Yes, I do know, and there will be crew about at all hours, sir, to see to your needs and appetite. Have no fear of that, sir. An inside cabin for three it is then."

Penwyn drew up the passage parchment, thinking, *Ah, the next to last cabin sold. If the Dogman behind them buys one too, they'll have a profitable journey after all.*

"You say the weather will be fair, then?" the father said, licking his lips nervously.

"Yes, sir, easy all the way, as far as can be told," Penwyn said, counting the man's coins with pleasure. "The seas grow calmer the closer one gets to Swallows in every case, sir. "

"Good, good, you see, it's the first ship journey, for any of us. We discussed it, you know, whether to go by land or ship, but a month overland to Swallows, a whole month, whereas only three days by sea, well, there wasn't much more to discuss, really, except for the expense, and the part about being on water for even that long, three days, for our first time, any of us."

"So you said," Penwyn remarked, hurrying to finish up. "The crew will make every effort to see to your comfort, sir." He handed the parchment out the window. The family moved aside, so closely bunched together they nearly stumbled over each other.

The Dogman stepped up. Penwyn got a better look at him now. He was a young man with a foreigner's face—prominent cheekbones, dark brown eyes and a strong jaw. A thin white scar curved from the corner of one eye to the top of his upper lip. He was wearing a hooded cloak of a type Penwyn knew to be stout against both wind and water. A quick glance told Penwyn that beneath the cloak, easily reached through long, hemmed vents in its sides, was at least one knife or short sword, and most likely two, one on each side. On his back was a medium-sized deerskin pack with what looked like a roll of oiled sailcloth tied on top of it. The Dogman was smiling slightly.

"You should have told them the truth," he said.

Penwyn's eyebrows lifted in surprise. "What truth might that be, sir?"

"That tomorrow the sea will be big, but easy. All day. And wet fog."

"Really, now. Who told you that?"

"The smell of the water. The birds." He circled a finger in the air. "The wind."

"Spent much time on the water, have you, son?"

"Yes."

Penwyn glanced down at the black and white dog, which was staring at him intently without blinking or moving a muscle. Penwyn became unsettled.

"So, then, young man, you're interested in passage to Mother's Bay?"

"Yes."

"Cabin or common hall?"

"On deck, if you please."

Penwyn looked up. "On deck? Then you must not have much faith in the heavy weather you foretell. The wet and waves and all." He was curious now. Not even soldiers stayed on deck for the two nights.

"The dog and I are more at ease on deck. What is the fare, please?"

"Well, young fellow, we have an inside cabin fare and a common hall fare and a livestock transportation fare and a cargo fare and a midpoint departure fare, but we don't have a deck passage fare, as no one has ever asked for one."

"Then charge me for space in the common hall and I'll choose my place on deck, one that won't hinder watch or crew." The Dogman was amused. "Would that suit you, Passage Master?"

"Certainly, yes, that will do nicely as you will then be free to take provenance in the common hall, and shelter, if you change your mind."

The Dogman passed coins through the window, delivering them into Penwyn's upturned hand. Local currency, Penwyn noted, no treasure. He expected treasure from this one. As he set about drawing up the common hall parchment, he said, "Are you attending the fair at Gravenwall, by chance, while you are in

Swallows? The king there, Harald Stonearm, has arranged for quite a large fair this summer. Many people have already gone over. Not so many today, however, but I expect quite a number more in a few weeks' time. A full ship, perhaps, now wouldn't that be nice?"

"I might attend," The Dogman said.

"Ah, so the fair is not your principal business, then, eh? Visiting relatives, by chance?" Penwyn chuckled. "A dog show, perhaps?"

Silence. Penwyn handed the parchment through the window. Now both dog and man were staring at him, the man as if to ask, "Why do you want to know?" or perhaps Penwyn was only imagining that intent. Penwyn suddenly felt nervous.

"Thank you," The Dogman said, and both he and the animal turned away to take up a place by themselves up-wharf of the passage house. Penwyn blew out a breath of air in relief, then made himself busy to keep his attention elsewhere. It was nearly time for the tethering and crating of the livestock anyway, so he took one last, quick look at the winding path to the wharf, and seeing no one approaching, straightened up his desk, pursed the fares, and closed his shutters.

As he stepped out the side door, he saw the two ship's stock handlers approaching. Once the animals were below decks and their inevitable, frightened emissions swept and scrubbed from gangway and deck, the passengers would be called to board.

Penwyn looked up at the sky. The clouds were thickening and shifting. The night fishers had not yet roosted, and the gulls were listless, preferring to huddle in sandy thickets beneath the trees than bicker over fish scraps and careless crabs. He noticed the family, the first-time travelers, all watching the ship rock gently beside the dock, and felt the sharp edge of guilt.

The Dogman was right. Something was coming.

* * *

Lionfish left Sealhaven under half-sail in the midmorning, as planned, so that the ship could make its way through Sealhaven Harbor in the best light. Once the anchor was hauled, Penwyn took up his favorite embarkation spot at the bow, where he would stand with his hands behind his back and the wind in his face until they reached the open water of the Sea of Caprice. On this day, however, Penwyn found himself in the company of the first-time family, all three of whom seemed bound together and all of whom huddled against the rail beside him. The father was smiling.

"My, my, this is breathtaking," he said loudly, looking all about him, from the rippling green water ahead to the land slipping past to starboard. "Well, this isn't so bad, is it? It's exciting, really. I understand why so many young men take to ships."

Penwyn, hearing the Dogman's accusation in his thoughts, said, "Open water is up ahead, sir, through that gap. It gets a bit more lively after that. I would recommend that you be seated by then so as not to stumble."

Penwyn saw the boy staring up at him uncertainly, and it brought a pang to his heart. It would have been a different life for him to have had a child, a son to teach, an eager ear for his stories.

"If you stay on deck, son," he said, "you'll see a remarkable sight as we reach the harbor's mouth. It's a pleasant enough ride to get there, and not long."

They all stayed, each looking ahead, their eyes taking in all they could of this extraordinary adventure of theirs. Penwyn could imagine them already describing it to their friends with the slightly smug merriment of survivors, and it brought to mind something a fellow sailor had told him long ago—that a tourist never really leaves home, but the true traveler never expects to return.

As the gap ahead grew nearer and wider, the sea beyond it took on an ominous darkness. Penwyn turned his face to the boy. "Listen, now, boy," he said, smiling. "Listen hard."

They all did, mother, father and son, their faces grown ruddy from the wind and their eyes bright with anticipation. The father reacted first, cocking his head. Then the boy.

"I heard a dog, Father," the first words the boy had spoken. Penwyn was disappointed; the boy's voice seemed as shrill as a seagull's call.

Lionfish plowed resolutely on, and the sound of full-throated barks grew louder and more tumultuous. Soon they saw hundreds of huge, sleek seals sprawled atop the boulders and rocky beaches on both sides of the ship, and their barking was so loud and insistent that the family, laughing at each other, covered their ears. Penwyn smiled at them, trying to imagine himself as part of such a group.

"Sealhaven Cut," Penwyn shouted, but they didn't hear him. He turned his gaze back to the sea ahead. The water was choppy. The clouds were low and dark. The wind took on a sharpening chill and strength. The ship, once clear of the gap, began to buck and slap down against the waves. As the din of the seals faded, the family became alarmed, hanging on to the bow rail and each other. It was time for Penwyn to make his rounds of the common hall and galley, seeing to passengers and crew. For once he had an able cook on board, but his cook's assistant and server was a dullard and needed watching.

"Best go to your cabin now," Penwyn said over the wind. "Make yourselves comfortable, won't you? Hot broth and bread will be served soon. Let me lead you to the ladders. I'm going that way myself."

"Thank you so much," the father said, already groping his way along the rope-lined rail.

Penwyn's sea legs carried him easily to the midship hatch, where he stood waiting for the family to uncertainly inch its way to him. He opened the hatch and grasped the arm of each in turn, guiding them to the handrails inside as they bumped from side to side on the rocking deck.

As Penwyn himself was stepping over the threshold, he glanced up and saw that the foreigner and his dog now occupied his place at the bow. The man was standing as if grown from the deck, one hand inside a pocket of his cloak and the other holding the walking stick, his body moving easily with the ship as it climbed and cleared the waves. He was looking straight ahead, watching something Penwyn could not see.

* * *

As expected, it was not long before some of the passengers became seasick and Penwyn went about making them as comfortable as he was able to, dispensing, along with buckets, his own formulation of herbal tea to calm their stomachs and a clear pine balm for their upper lips to help freshen the air they breathed. The family was overtaken only minutes after they reached their cabin, and following his first visit, Penwyn left them alone in their collective misery. After tending to the ill, he helped his crewmates serve bread, broth and beer to the more seasoned fares.

To accomplish his chores took Penwyn until midafternoon, as *Lionfish* entered the narrow, frothing Sundered Strait, a potentially treacherous piece of wild water between a hulking chain of rocks and the Storms coast that Captain Kepper always preferred to traverse with a clear view. Penwyn's final task before his hour off-duty preceding preparations for the evening meal was to check in with Captain Kepper, whom he found anxiously studying the waves form the tiny watch house. Penwyn recited to the captain a summary of the passengers, the sick, conditions in the galley, and the state of the livestock on board.

"Did you say we had a deck passenger?" Kepper asked, his eyes never leaving the sea.

"Yes, sir. A young fellow with a dog. He seems familiar with sailing."

"Does he have any valuables he might lose by staying on deck, do you think?"

Penwyn knew that this meant any coin Penwyn might be able to filch during the night.

"He paid with local coin, but seems poor. Regardless, it would seem to me unwise to arouse either dog or man."

Kepper grunted. "He's armed, then."

"He is, and seems experienced."

"Pity," Kepper remarked softly.

"Until supper, then," Penwyn said, and backed out of the watch house.

He always spent this hour alone at the bow, but today he would be sharing that space with the Dogman. Under normal circumstances it would have peeved him to find someone else up there, but as he made his way forward he found himself anticipating the moment.

"Hallo there, Dogman," he said cheerfully.

Dogman glanced at him and smiled. "Hallo yourself."

"What you see there is the Sundered Strait, made when a land bridge was broken during a terrible storm a good many years ago. Saves times on the voyage, compared to what it takes going around it, I can tell you, two days at least, as I recall. By the way, I beg your pardon for calling you Dogman. It seems disrespectful. What is the proper name by which I might address you?"

The man shrugged. "That one is good enough. Dogman."

Penwyn squinted at him curiously. "Really, now? Then Dogman it is. And I am called Penwyn. How about your companion, there? Does it have a name?"

"No. He knows my voice and I know his. That's all."

Penwyn looked at the dog, which was again staring him.

"You say you know his voice. It is a hunting dog, then."

"Yes. A Bear Dog."

"Hmm. Seems like it ought to have a name. I've never heard of a dog that had no name."

Dogman laughed. "Then you may name him."

"I couldn't presume…"

"It's no bother. You've already named me, and he won't listen to you anyway. Name him. What does he look like to you?"

Penwyn noted that the dog's ink-black fur was tinged with blue and brown and in the sea light seemed to possess an aura, a ghostly, iridescence that pulsed as the wind stirred it.

"That fur, when the light hits it. That glow. It looks like a fogbow."

"Fogbow it is, then," Dogman said, and looked ahead again, pensive. "The name is more appropriate than you know."

"Have you been this way before, Dogman?"

"No. Not this passage."

"Well, it's quite spectacular, really. Beyond the Strait we come to The Boulders, which aren't really boulders at all but a group of roundish islands no one could live on. We will pass them in the night, but there is no fear of grounding because the current though the strait carries all ships straight and true well shy of them. Tomorrow morning in the light we'll pass Eden Isle, kept by a church, which I know well. When I was a boy, I worked there as a pruner, tending to the shape and blooms of the sentinel bushes and fruit bearers, both trees and hardy plants. Hard work, that, pruning. It makes the hands ache and your fingers cramp to your palms, like this."

Penwyn clamped the two middle fingers of one hand against his palm.

"It's mostly hand work, you see, and you'd sometimes have to pry the fingers up to slip a tool handle under them, see, if you had to use one, and then, pop, down they go again." He chuckled. "Ah, hard work, and cold sometimes too, oh yes. I worked for room and board on the island, a spare life, but comfortable enough. Do you know anything of pruning, Dogman?"

He shook his head "no."

"It's an art, I believe, and rewarding overall. The artistry comes in the years between the maiden tree and cropping tree with the fruit bearers, oh yes. Done right, the cropping tree delivers wonderful harvests that command a premium market price. I studied them, each species already in the ground and the new ones as well. Studied them, and worked mostly alone.

"But one day Captain Kepper came ashore in a tender. He was a young man then, too, newly in ownership of *Lionfish*. He asked me in that voice of his, 'Boy? Do you want employ on a merchant ship? My cook's mate has died on me,' he says, 'and good for that, too, because it was from tasting a mushroom stew he was going to feed me and my crew. I pay well,' says Kepper, 'and I don't beat anyone unless it's deserved. Yes or no?'

"For some strange reason, I liked the man, and agreed to join him. I had no home to leave, unless it was Eden Isle, because it was my Ma indentured me to the pruning job in the first place, at the tender age of nine, it was. And I did miss Eden Isle. I fretted over my lovely trees; were they being cared for properly? Eden Isle. Interesting place. Do you how it came to be?"

Again Dogman shook his head "no," but with an indulgent smile on his lips.

"Oh, it is a whole island made a garden by a rich ship owner named Mr. Florynoyle, a devout man, too. He collected plants and trees from all the strange and far-off places his ships journeyed, and planted them there, on Eden Isle. Blackwood trees from Vreeland, Poisonberries from the Cloudlands, Nutfigs from the Spice Islands. Ah, it is a lovely place everyone should see before they die.

"Mr. Florynoyle was a kind man and treated me well, yes, and said I was a free man when I was fifteen, but where was I to go?

"So I said yes to Captain Kepper when he came, and I've been on *Lionfish* ever since, I have. For many years we bought and sold what you might call disputed cargo in the Southern Ocean, from south Welland to the Faradays. We did well on the money, until Captain Kepper grew tired of the constant harrying by thieves and brigands and lying homelanders. He said to me, 'Penwyn? Let's you and I seek calmer waters. A freighting business, perhaps. People and pigs and crates of common goods not worth the trouble for anyone to steal. There might be money in that, too.' There happened to be a need for such a service between Storms and Swallows, and from Swallows down to Riversend, because of the way the land is. Indeed, there was a rough trade in operation already, which Captain Kepper assumed with both threats and treasure. "

Penwyn finally fell silent. Dogman said nothing. Fogbow continued to stare at Penwyn.

Penwyn slapped the rail. "Well, then, here we are, aren't we, these many years later. I'll bring you out some supper in a bit, Dogman, and something for your friend, too. For Fogbow. Would that suit you?"

"There's no need, but it's kind of you. Thank you."

"No bother, none. Until then, sir."

Penwyn headed off to the midship ladders feeling light and content. He hadn't talked to anyone for that long at a time since his drunken, boastful days on the crude settlement wharves along the trade routes. It felt good.

He liked this Dogman, too, though the man hadn't said spit about himself so far. Penwyn felt a strange kinship with him, and it didn't really matter that he didn't know why.

* * *

Early the following day, the Hour of Regrets found Penwyn already awake and immersed in a feeling of deep sadness and anxiety. He could not recall the dream leading to his unease, but was certain the cause of it would come to him sometime during the day. A thought, something seen, something heard, would reveal it. Meanwhile he sorted through memories that matched his mood, or perhaps the memories were brought forth by his mood, he knew not which, but one after another his mistakes, little cruelties, and shames surfaced to inflame his face and cause him to cringe. He was not a bad man, but in the moment thought himself one.

The ship's motion tugged Penwyn from this purposeless punishment by reminding him of the Dogman. The young man knew the water, indeed. Penwyn felt himself rising feet first as the ship scaled a long swell, then his head rose as the ship descended a slope of equal length and grade. *We'll be a bit shorthanded today*, crossed his mind. Such conditions always affected even the most experienced seamen.

He roused himself from the weight of the darkness by lighting his lantern and swinging his legs from his berth. He dressed sitting down as the ship slowly pushed him from side to side.

He emerged from the midshp hatch, lantern in hand, to a dense, wet fog. He felt beads of water form on his cheeks and chin as he moved, as if he were walking through standing rain. The fog smelled metallic and fishy, as if it had been dredged from the bottom of the sea.

"Good morning, Penwyn," Captain Kepper said, close enough to startle him. He didn't see Kepper until the man nearly bumped into him.

"Morning, Cap'n. Salty weather, eh?"

"We're on headings and chains today," Kepper said gruffly.

"Yes, sir," Penwyn said, knowing that for hours now a crewman on either side had been watching the chains hanging overboard; if the chains started stretching sternward, they were hitting bottom and *Lionfish* was drifting to shore.

The fog had thinned somewhat by the time Penwyn had finished his chores and readied the galley for the noon meal. There were few takers, even among the crew, for the morning meal of seafood broth, brown bread and ale. At the cabin of the sequestered family, his invitation to breakfast was met with weak groans and a request for fresh buckets.

When Penwyn made his way forward and the faint shadow of the Dogman emerged from the fog, he noticed that the young man had used the sailcloth bundle on his pack to fashion a cozy, dry tent from the bow rail to the anchor rope capstan. Fogbow lay under it, staring at Penwyn. Dogman stood looking ahead, his hood over his head and water trickling down the surface of his cloak.

"Good morning, Penwyn," he said without turning.

"And the same to you, Dogman," he said cheerfully. "There's plenty of broth and bread left from the morning meal for you, if you wish to have it."

"I've packed my own food, but I might accept your offer, as part of the fare paid."

"Yes, that's the way to think of it, certainly. You've paid for it indeed."

A moment of silence passed before Dogman said, "You said we'll be coming to Eden Isle this morning."

"Yes, soon, but of course we'll not see it. With this fog, perhaps not even smell it as I usually do, its lovely scent's in the air even though it's some twenty lengths to port."

You said you were sent there at nine," Dogman said.

Penwyn looked at him curiously. "Yes, at nine. We lived in Spott's Woods, inland quite a ways, but there was too many of us and my mother sent me off." There was a twinge in Penwyn's chest. Perhaps that was the dream he'd had? "She kept her favorites. Sent the rest of us off."

"My sister was given up," Dogman said quietly. "It must make you sad to know that."

"Oh, it's been so long, you know, so many years in between. And Mr. Florynoyle was a kind man, perhaps because of knowing I'd been given up."

"Have you ever been back? To Eden Isle? You pass by it so often. Have you ever stopped?"

"No, I haven't." The pain near Penwyn's heart was suddenly sharp and deep. *That was it*, he thought. *The dream.* He remembered it now. He had dreamt of Mag. "I have thought of it often, to see if Mag is still there." He started slightly, realizing he'd spoken the thought out loud. He hadn't intended to. He was embarrassed.

"Mag?"

He sighed, committing himself to explaining. "Yes, she was the stonemason's daughter, Mason Nestor was his name. He made the arches and pathways and walls for the climbing vines and bushes. He made the sheds and houses. His wife, Mag's mother, died of the Wet Cough just before I arrived. Mag was my age, but when I was young I rarely saw her. We worked on different parts of the island, and Mr. Florynoyle, my mentor, he kept me close by, teaching me my work, and I suppose protecting me.

"I was fourteen when Mr. Florynoyle allowed me to work and travel Eden Isle on my own. The first time I saw Mag was on the rock beach, the stonemason's garden, you might say, where she was gathering the best of small stones to accent a walkway through the Astor Cottage gardens. Oh, she was lovely, Dogman, such deep brown eyes, such wild, long hair. We talked for a few moments, about nothing, saying our names to each other because that was the most important thing right then, you know, to call each other by name from then on, like a bond.

"Well, Mason Nestor was having none of that, I'll tell you. He was saving Mag for a man of property, certain she would catch the eye of one of Mr. Florynoyle's wealthy friends whom he entertained for walks and tours of Eden Isle. I confess that I would find work somewhere near her just so I could see her, and she never looked lovelier than when Mr. Floynoyle was bringing guests from the mainland for the day. But Mason Nestor would always be there, too, smiling at me, shaking his head and slowly waving that hammer of his, 'No, no, boy. Not for you.'"

Penwyn's throat suddenly closed and tears stung his eyes. He looked about, driving the feelings away.

"So, you see, how I came to join Captain Kepper."

"And here we are, these many years later," Dogman said. "You should stop at Eden Isle, Penwyn. You should find the people in your life. Know where they are, or where they are not."

"Oh, she no doubt is long gone to some respectable person, Dogman. And Mason Nestor, well, he was in middle years when I was a boy, so he's likely passed on by now."

"But you don't know. If you don't visit, you'll never know. How can you bear that?"

Penwyn was suddenly very curious about Dogman. He

seemed to be saying something about himself in what he was saying to Penwyn. But what? Penwyn told himself that he must remember the chat later, and puzzle it out.

"You shame me, Dogman. You prove me to be a man of little courage after all," Penwyn smiled. "Perhaps, next time."

Dogman nodded, looking into the fog.

"Well, things to do, Dogman, things to do. Would you like me to bring you something to eat, then?"

"Don't trouble yourself, Penwyn, please," Dogman said. "I'll come inside for it."

"Good, then. I'll see you in the common hall, perhaps." He nodded. "As always, a pleasure, sir."

Penwyn disappeared into the fog. The bow lines dripped. The glassy green mountains rose out of the mist and passed under them, one, and another, and another.

* * *

By dawn of the following day the water was nearly dead calm and *Lionfish* barely swayed at all. The sky was clear and the sun broke orange over the edge of the sea. Some of the crew and passengers who had been ill finally stirred from their fetid cabins and crept warily out onto the deck. The warm breeze blew away the fusty auras that clung to them and brought color into pale faces. The family of three, in particular, looked much the worse for wear, but sat, exhausted and grateful, against the stern rail relishing the wind that washed over them.

Penwyn bustled about, serving the passengers on deck instead of inside. He was also grateful for the change of location because it had been getting awfully ripe below decks. With most people above, he had quickly opened all the portholes to let fresh air circulate before assembling trays of bread, biscuits, tea and honey to carry up. Soon everyone seemed possessed of a buoyant mood, many making acquaintance for the first time on the voyage. Penwyn noticed that the boy with the squeaky voice was with Dogman, petting the Bear Dog on its broad head.

Mother's Bay and the Province of Swallows were yet two hours away, but for Penwyn there was much to do. He sorted through his passenger parchments to separate the ones who would be continuing on to Riversend—they would need to be assigned sleeping accommodations, for which they had already paid, until midday the next to give the crew time to tidy up the ship. Ferried stock would have to be assessed and any exceptional damages accounted for out of the ship's purse. Galley stores were now being inventoried by the mate for resupply. Pay had to be counted out for one crewmember who was getting off for good at Mother's Bay. And freight to be handed over to the cartage company on the wharf had to be readied for off-loading.

The time passed quickly. When all was attended to and Penwyn emerged on deck again, the air had filled with wheeling, squeaking gulls and *Lionfish* was entering the gentle embrace of Mother's Bay. The passengers were clustered in the warm sunlight chattering excitedly among themselves, eager to step on land once again and get on with the business for which they had made the journey. Dogman and Fogbow stood apart, which did not entirely surprise Penwyn.

As the ship approached the broad wharf with its simple clutter of outbuildings, wagons and knots of people awaiting the passengers, Penwyn helped his deck hand ready the gangplank which would be hauled out by two burly men waiting for them beside the mooring posts. Penwyn felt a presence behind him, and turned to see Dogman.

"An enjoyable voyage, Penwyn," he said. "Now, if you could tell me the way to Gravenwall?"

"Ah, Dogman, yes, certainly, I'm glad you enjoyed the trip." Penwyn looked about for a moment, then pointed to a thin white road that wriggled up the side of a broad, green hill. "There, take that road there. So you've decided to go. That's splendid. It should be quite an affair, and I suspect you'll have company on your way."

"Will you be going? Or doesn't your schedule allow it?"

"No, no, we'll be busy carrying those that are going, you see. It's a rare opportunity for us, all this traffic, so we must take advantage of it while we can. But I hope you have a fine time of it, you and your friend. Fogbow."

Dogman nodded and backed away to give Penwyn more room as the ship glided slowly toward the wharf.

The gangway was dropped, and Penwyn stood at the bottom of it addressing passengers as they disembarked. Those who were going on to Riversend he directed to the Mother's Bay Hotel, and those who were ending their trip here he wished a safe journey and hoped to see them on the return voyage to Storms. The family of three, however, he was assured he would not see again.

"My uncle's estate should provide us with more than enough to purchase overland transport back," the father said. "No fault of yours, sir, but this has been an astonishingly hideous experience, yes indeed, one not to be repeated by any of us, I'm sure, never again, no doubt. But no fault of yours, mind, sir."

"I'm very sorry for your discomfort, " Penwyn said. "Some aren't meant to sail, others take to it. There's no telling which you are until you go. Have a successful time here, at any rate, sir."

The passengers straggled away, and the livestock was brought down and penned. Crew members had the afternoon to themselves, so they too wandered away. The wharf grew quiet except for the creak of ropes and wood. Penwyn went back on deck to join the deck hand who had helped him ready the gangway.

"Most queer thing this is," the deck hand said.

"What? What's queer?"

"Well, I was up night before last to fetch a bucket, and seen that fella there, the one with the dog? I seen him talking to a short, round-ish man by the bow rail. No one else around but them two, talking, but I didn't see no short roundish man get off the ship just now. "

Penwyn frowned. He had not checked in a short, roundish man that he could recall.

"Hmm. Where was the dog? When you were on deck, where was the dog?"

"Didn't see no dog. Just the roundish man. 'Course, the dog could have been hid. But where's the man, is what I don't know. I didn't see him just now."

"Well, there's no one left aboard. At last check all the cabins and rooms were clear. Have another look around, though, won't you?"

"Ayup, sir."

The deck hand left his side, and Penwyn gazed at two small figures, a man with a walking stick and a dog, moving slowly along the Gravenwall road. He liked the fellow, but he was a curious one. Penwyn wondered who Dogman was, where he came from, what was in the life behind him, but couldn't even begin to guess.

All he could do was wish him good fortune.

Chapter Five

DOGMAN

The road under Dogman's legs was flat and hard, leveled over the years by boot and hoof and wagon wheel. During summer what rain fell on Swallows usually came during the night when traffic was lightest, so the Gravenwall road was almost always free of ruts and holes. Though suited for fast traveling, Dogman and his companion walked leisurely, enjoying the warm light and rippling breeze scented by sun and sea.

Once beyond the rise above Mother's Bay, the road gently lowered into great, empty fields of green grass that nodded the direction of the breeze. Above the walkers towering white clouds lumbered like mangonels across a hard blue sky. A tree appeared, then another and another, thick branches casting pools of shifting shadow on the grass while their leaves hissed in the gentle wind.

Dogman paused in the shade of one such tree to remove and roll up his cloak, which he tied to the backpack with lengths of rawhide. He also removed the short sword and scabbard at his side and inserted them into the pack, positioning the sword hilt at an easy reach over his shoulder. He left a dagger in its sheath on his belt.

"Are you hungry yet, Fogbow?" he asked.

The black and white Bear Dog looked away disinterestedly.

"No? Very well. Neither am I just yet. You did well on the voyage, I thought, for one who would much rather be in the water than on it. Even so, firm ground must feel good to you now." Dogman looked out from the shade at the rippling lake of grass across the road and smiled. "It would be nice to spend the day here, don't you think? Just sit and doze off from time to time?"

Fogbow growled and Dogman laughed.

"I'm teasing. Let's be moving on, then." Dogman hoisted the pack onto his back. As he returned to the heat and brightness of the road, he looked back toward Mother's Bay.

"No one comes behind us yet, Fogbow," he said. "Either the carters and carriages must still be loading, or King Harald's fair will be less a success than he expects."

Half an hour's walking without haste took them past a large, well-ordered tomato field and a farmhouse near the road. A dog in the open doorway barked at Fogbow (who immediately ducked behind Dogman for protection) but its yaps seemed to come more from a sense of obligation than aggressiveness. A stout woman with a broom smiled and waved from the gloom behind it.

Soon after passing the tomato farm a carriage rumbled by toward Gravenwall, and four bored, flushed faces peered at Dogman and Fogbow as they went by. Dogman instinctively looked for the family of three that had experienced such a hard crossing, but they were not among the passengers.

Farther on, a man and his son, both with walking staffs, passed on the other side of the road and both raised a hand in greeting, which Dogman returned. He idly wondered if they were going to Mother's Bay, and why, since they had no traveling gear with them.

"What do you think, Fogbow? Do they work afternoons on the docks? Perhaps they tend the stock pens between ferry trips. Or maybe they're visiting the lady at the tomato farm. Or perhaps they are related to the lady at the tomato farm."

Fogbow barked sharply, his irritation clear. Dogman shrugged and fell silent again.

Some minutes later Dogman heard a growing rumble from the road behind him. He turned to see a wagon approaching, pulled by a team of horses. Atop the driver's bench sat a thin man with big hat and a long, thin nose. As they drew closer, Dogman noted that the man was smiling, and seemed to possess the sort of good nature that found a smile in nearly everything.

"Hello, traveler," he hailed as the wagon drew alongside. "Would you care to ride for a while rather than walk? You can tell your dog there I won't bite!" He laughed with a perfectly enunciated "ha ha ha."

Dogman glanced at the contents of the wagon, which was loaded with wooden wagon wheels of different sizes. The driver saw Dogman's glance and slapped his hand against a sign on the wagon's side, which read—

"Rollie Roundtree's Wagon Wheels. We Keep the Wheels of Commerce Turning! Ha ha ha! And how might I address you, sir?"

"Lately, I've been called Dogman," the foreigner said.

Roundtree looked at Fogbow. "As appropriate a name as my own, I expect. Ha ha ha! You are welcome to climb up here, young fellow, unless it's beneath you! Ha ha ha!"

Dogman smiled. "I will gratefully accept your offer, Mister Roundtree. Fogbow? Find a place that suits you."

Fogbow growled and trotted around the wagon looking for the best place to jump up as Dogman climbed aboard, After a moment the dog bounded onto a rear wheel hub, up onto a large toolbox, then over the back of the driver's seat to land next to Dogman on the bench. He barked once, as if to say, "So there." Roundtree watched all this with interest, lightly rubbing his long chin.

"That's one smart fellow there, Dogman. Do you always talk to it like to a person?"

"Yes, I suppose I do."

"Does it always seem to know what you're saying, like that?

"I suppose it looks that way," Dogman smiled. "As you said, smart fellow."

"Well, I mustn't mention anything about me cats, then, mustn't I? He might overhear. Ha ha ha!" He gently snapped the reins and clucked. "Come along, boys."

The wagon creaked into motion. Roundtree glanced at the pack that Dogman had just set in the footwell beside him, noting the sword hilt.

"Would you be a soldier then, Dogman?"

"No, just a traveler. In other lands, an unarmed traveler is a fool, Mister Roundtree."

"That sounds of truth, indeed, though I wouldn't really know, never having been north, south, east, or west of Swallows. Where are you bound now, if I may ask?"

"Gravenwall."

Roundtree brightened. "Oh, to the festival! How splendid! Are you going there to listen, or to tell a tale?"

"I plan to tell a tale, Mister Roundtree."

"Wonderful! Oh, that is exciting. A traveler to other lands like yourself must have quite an interesting story to tell, I'm sure. Now, me? Were I to tell a tale it would have to be about me good old wife or me cats, which would only be of interest to your dog. Ha ha ha! As for the wife, she's a fine, strong woman who has given us four lovely children, a plentiful enough family for us, indeed. When we was younger, I finally had to tell her, 'Heed me, now. Once a king always a king, but once a night's enough.' Ha ha ha! Sorry to say, I cannot take you all the way to Gravenwall, as me house is along the way but short of the castle by half a day. The part I can carry you should help spare your dogs a bit anyway. Ha ha ha!"

"We're happy to ride any distance with you, Mister Roundtree," Dogman smiled. "Has your wagon wheel trade served you well?"

"It has indeed, though sometimes business is flat. Ha ha ha! I have just come from the Mother's Bay docks. Whenever the ferry comes in and the carters gather, I go, because when you're in need of a wheel, nothing else will do, and the carters and carriage services can't afford to miss any ships' business. That's why I can charge a bit more for dock sales than farm sales, you see. However, I know them all and they joyfully dun me back when I must bring in new supplies, so what goes around comes around! Ha ha ha!

"Good wheels are serious business, Dogman, and my wheels are well regarded, I must say. Some put all their efforts into the rims, you see, tricking them up with embellishments and burnishing and exotic woods, but the real secret to the best wheels is the spokes. Crafting great spokes of fine, hard wood and shaping them precisely, I say *precisely*, Dogman, to nest in the hub and rim as if they had grown there from seedlings, that's the key. That's the key. I have done as well making and shipping spokes to other wheel makers as I have selling me own, oh, believe it. Me own wheels are eight-spoke made, and I put a pretty charge on them, you bet, because they will last and last and, you know, my reputation is riding on them. Ha ha ha!"

"Do the children help with your business? Surely you have one child old enough to keep you company on your trip to the docks."

"Oh, I do, yes, my oldest, Raymond, does exactly that from time to time, but the wife and the others have their own enterprise to keep them busy. She grows and sells what we call Plumper's Breeches, a lovely hybrid flower that is quite popular at the florists' fairs. A new crop has matured, you see, and the family are all aflutter with potting and preparing them for sale at the Gravenwall festival next week. This very wagon, Dogman, will look quite different in two days' time, after the wheels come out and the Plumper's Breeches go in. I suppose I shall have to change me signage to 'We Keep Commerce Growing.' Ha ha ha!"

Roundtree playfully poked Dogman on the shoulder.

"Or perhaps, 'Don't Plant A Garden Without Your Breeches.' Ha ha ha!"

"You are certainly an industrious and prosperous lot, Mister Roundtree. Is all of Swallows thriving as well under King Harald's hand?"

"That would depend more on the person than his ruler, I would suppose. King Harald is decent enough, anyone will tell you. He did raise the tariffs quite a bit, and if we don't pay our taxes and tithes precisely to the penny or the pig, he can be, let's say, difficult. But he is an occupier, after all, and we miss our Queen Anelie dearly. She was so lovely, the whole family, all so lovely, King Alfred, Queen Celia, such lovely people." Dogman happened to see a slight tremor cross Roundtree's lips, and thought tears might follow. "Do you know the sad story, Dogman? Have you heard what happened to them all?"

"I have heard of it in my travels. It's a great pity for Swallows to feel so much heartbreak all at once. But perhaps the queen will return one day."

"It is a dream all of us here share, Dogman, but a dream nonetheless. We can only do the best we can."

The silence that followed and the troubled expression on Roundtree's face lasted only a few minutes before his smile returned. Dogman guessed that very few things would dampen Roundtree's jolly spirit for long.

"Tell me you'll join us for supper today, Dogman. You will have to overnight along the road anyway, as you will not reach Gravenwall before dusk tomorrow. Come stay with us and see the glorious Plumper's Breeches harvest for yourself! My wife will welcome the company. Her name is Brenda, but I call her Flora. Ha ha ha! Oh, and I'm sure we can find a bone for your dog to gnaw upon."

Fogbow glanced at Roundtree, grumbled once, and looked away.

"That would be more than kind, Mister Roundtree, but only if it's not too much bother."

"None at all, or I wouldn't have offered. I'll have the children tumble for you! Long ago when they were but mites, they tumbled at Gravenwall for a day. Had a marvelous time and have rolled about from time to time ever since. We're lucky none has cracked a head. What's this now?"

Dogman looked ahead to see a boy of about ten years limping from a woodlot on the right. He appeared to be crying, covering his eyes with the shirtsleeve of one arm. The boy stood in the middle of the road waiting for Roundtree to pull alongside, where Roundtree halted his team.

"What's wrong, son? What's happened?"

"I ga' lost in the woods from Dormley." He sniffled and rubbed his face with his hands. A white blaze ran through the boy's black hair like a scar. Dogman peered at him curiously.

"Dormley? Dormley, you say? Well that's easily fixed, boy, as it's just ahead along this road. Climb aboard now, and we'll get you home."

The boy grasped Roundtree's outstretched hand and clambered up. When the boy's face was uncovered Dogman recognized him as the boy who had passed on the other side of the road hours before. He opened his mouth to speak, but by then the boy was beside Roundtree holding a short knife at his throat.

At that moment the man who had been walking with the boy emerged from the trees with a short sword in his hand, impatiently waving his free hand. He wore a floppy hat and a dusty black patch covered one eye.

"Now, now, now, nobody move, please. This'll be of little bother if we all behave calmly. There's na' murder in our plans today." He eyed Fogbow. "Unless it's for rude dogs."

Fogbow jumped from the seat and ran into the woods. The man watched him go with a surprised look on his face.

"Hmm. Na' much of a fighter, eh? Ya' been wastin' food on 'im, soldier. Now hand me down that pack and your sidearms, too, please."

Dogman smiled slightly and dropped the pack with the sword onto the road. He dropped his dagger beside it.

The man approached, keeping his one watchful eye on Dogman, and pulled the weapons far out of reach.

"Funny, is it? What's funny, soldier?"

"You're clever about this, is all. You fooled me."

The man smiled in turn, flattered. "Ya think so? Well, thank you. Works out nicely to pass walking travelers so we can see their kit, make note of weapons and such so we know what we're up against. Most we halt aren't armed, so it's easier done." He gestured toward Roundtree, who was still under the knife. "This one here was a gift. We was just going to take your purse, but we'll scobber ya' wagon instead. Sell it over by Manley's Gorge."

Roundtree spluttered. "You can't do that. Everyone knows my work and trade. Anyone will know you took this from me."

"All the better, then, wouldna' say? Ain't even a pious man won't take the best goods for a quarter its worth and be quiet about it."

"The king's men, what about them? You know how he hates thieves."

"Got to catch us first. With this haul, we'll be on our way out of Swallows for good. We been tethered here seven cursed years since we got rousted out of the militia. I won't shed a tear puttin' Swallows behind me."

Dogman said, "You're one of Master Turnbolt's men, then?"

It would have been hard to say who was more surprised, the thief or Roundtree.

"What you know of Master Turnbolt?" the one-eyed thief asked.

"I heard of him a while ago. He's said to be on Moon Island in the Faradays."

"You're havin' fun w'me. I'll be damned to dust and back again. What unholy fortune brought that about?"

"It's complicated. But he still thinks of his men."

"Did he say he's comin' back, then?" the thief asked hopefully. "Puttin' together an army, perhaps, and comin' back again?"

Dogman shook his head. "No, I'm afraid he won't be back. He lives alone, mostly starved and raving mad. He's been there for years, eating snails and leaves and talking to himself."

The thief's expression fell with disappointment, which turned to sadness. "Ah, then," he said softly. "That's an end to it. Well, this 'a been a curious crossing indeed, soldier. Now everybody down, and hands high when y'alight."

The boy sprang down, never taking his eyes off Roundtree, who was trembling as he clumsily left the wagon. The man with the patch motioned the two of them together.

"You'll be inconvenienced for a bit, I'm afraid, while we make off. Someone will find you, no doubt, within a day or so." He glanced into the deep woods beside him. "One can hope."

Dogman and Roundtree were marched into the woods for a quarter mile and halted beside a tall, thick tree.

"Backs agin' it, either side," the man with the patch said.

Roundtree backed against one side and Dogman the other. Their arms were pulled backward and their wrists tied together by the boy. Roundtree was muttering to himself in a thin, high voice all the while. He was pale and quite terrified.

"The worst that'll happen, I believe, is you won't be able to scratch your noses. Unless there's a bear come by." He dropped Dogman's pack and knife beside a tree several yards away.

Roundtree whimpered softly.

The man with the patch ordered the boy to give each of the prisoners a long drink of water from the skin at his side. "Drink up, now, so it'll hold you for a while. Stay to the side of their legs, boy."

When each man had drunk, the boy and the one-eyed thief backed away into the gloom of the forest, returning the way they had come.

"Oh, dear. Oh my Flora will be so worried," Roundtree mumbled.

"Patience, Mister Roundtree. We won't be here long."

"No one comes this way, Dogman," he said testily. "And no one can hear us from the road if we halloo."

"Fogbow knows what to do."

"Fogbow? Your dog that ran off?"

"Yes. He's fetching help, I would think. Be patient and relax. Enjoy the birdsong. Enjoy the quiet."

* * *

A couple of hours later, after watching coins of sunlight on the dappled ground slide toward late afternoon, Roundtree heard a faint rumble in the distance. At first he thought it might be a barely perceptible grumble of thunder, but it seemed to be a steady sound that stopped abruptly.

A few minutes later, a portly man with closely cropped white hair and a white goatee appeared, pushing his way through the forest. He looked up at Roundtree and Dogman with a look of surprise, even though he seemed to have come directly to them.

"Howdy, gentlemen, there you are, yes, yes. I hope you haven't suffered too much."

Roundtree watched the man, his eyes wide with wonder.

"Who in the world are you, sir? How did you know where to find us?"

"The name is Starling, from Rampal. Martius Starling, from Rampal, is who I am." He set about removing the rope from their wrists. "A dog alerted me, actually, and led me to a wagon load of wheels." He blinked large, moist blue eyes at Roundtree. "You are Mister Roundtree, I take it? He who keeps the wheels of commerce turning?"

Roundtree nodded, smiling. "Ah, the sign. I am he."

"Great slogan, sir," Starling said, untying the last bindings. Roundtree and Dogman faced the wild-looking man, who was a mite taller than Roundtree had first thought, and of a curiously indeterminate age. Though his hair and beard were pure white, his skin was youthful and bright. And though he seemed to be an older man, he moved with vigor and certainty.

"How did you know where to find us? " Roundtree repeated.

"Oh, the dog led me here, of course."

Roundtree blinked. "Where is it, then? The dog?"

Starling waved a hand vaguely. "Off sniffing something, I suppose. I don't know. Dogs do what they must do."

Dogman was smiling.

"Mister Starling," he said. "What a pleasure to see you again."

"Likewise. What's that unpleasant moniker you adopted? Dogman?"

Roundtree gaped from one to the other.

"You know each other?"

"Mister Starling and I met long ago," Dogman said, retrieving his pack and weapons. "We encounter each other periodically."

"This is most astonishing," Roundtree mumbled. "A most astonishing day."

"Let's be off, then. I parked your wagon on the road. We'll have you home before dark," Starling said.

"Most astonishing," Roundtree whispered to himself. "First a Dogman, then a madman."

The wagon was indeed on the road, as if they had just left it there to go for a stroll. This time, however, there were two cats on board, one small and one large. The smaller one was black with a white blaze on its head. The larger one was gray with a patch of black over one eye. Roundtree stopped and stared. There was something uncomfortably familiar about them.

"Oh, them, yes, they hopped aboard when I started back." Starling looked at them and smiled. "They must have thought it better to serve a kindly master than risk being savaged by other animals or shot with an arrow. Say, Mister Roundtree, would you mind if I rode along with you for a ways? I am off toward Gravenwall."

"You too? Do you have a story to tell as well?"

"No, no, no. I have other matters to attend to. No time for storytelling, no time."

They climbed aboard the wagon, all three sitting on the bench. Roundtree looked around once more for Fogbow, but the dog was nowhere to be seen. Dogman patted Roundtree's shoulder as if reading his mind.

"Don't trouble yourself, Mister Roundtree. Fogbow will show himself again. He has played this trick before."

Roundtree clucked at the horse team, and the wagon grumbled into motion again. The cats curled up on the lid of Roundtree's toolbox and licked their paws.

"Well, Mister Starling, I can only show my appreciation for your rescue of me livelihood by offering you a place to have supper and spend the night, as I've offered Dogman here. It would be a treat for my family if you accepted, sir."

"Then I shall, I shall."

And so, as the sun was casting late-day light as soft and golden as dust over the green fields and swaying trees, they arrived at Roundtree's farm to an excited gathering of children and chickens. In this lively company Starling and Roundtree were shown the modest grounds, admired the beautiful Plumper's Breeches harvest ("Wow," Starling said. "They do resemble fat bottoms!"), and huge berry pie. Several of the children amused themselves by rolling a ball of twine across the floor for the cats to chase. The older ones sat fascinated by Starling's odd manner, occasionally laughing at unfamiliar words that struck them as funny.

Later, as the adults were sitting outside watching the sun slip beneath the horizon, dragging its light behind it like a blanket, Roundtree tapped his forehead.

"Oh! I meant to have the children divert you with a few tumbles. Now it's too late for that, I'm afraid. They might break their necks rolling about in the dark."

Starling jumped to his feet with one hand upraised.

"Ah, no fear, Mister Roundtree. I sometimes deal in entertaining lights. Be right back."

Through the gloom they watched Starling trot over to the wagon, rummage around among the wheels, and saw his hands emerge with a cluster of thin rods about six feet long. He then stuck them one by one into the grass until a large circle was formed. After the last was planted, Starling seemed to snap his fingers and a small flame leapt in his hand. He touched the fire to each of the rods and as he did so they smoked and hissed and bloomed into bright crowns of sparkling light.

Roundtree was again struck dumb by what he was seeing, but soon his awe turned to delight as his children used the bright island in his yard as their stage. They performed simple routines and called out their own names for them, such as "Sheep's Knees" and "Rolling Goats." The adults cheered and applauded until Starling's sparklers began to sputter out.

Mrs. Roundtree clapped her hands and ordered the children off to bed. Starling and Dogman collected the sparklers and tidied up the lawn. Roundtree then led his guests to a comfortable room in small guest quarters near the main house. He bid the gentlemen good night, and, studied each of them in turn before rounding to go home. He wished to remember them as best he could, for he knew he would never see a day such as this one ever again.

* * *

Early the next morning, after a breakfast of coarse bread oatmeal swimming in honey, Starling and Dogman collected their things and prepared to leave. Roundtree accompanied them to the gate at the end of his walkway. The morning air was fresh with dew, and the sun, barely risen, cast their shadows across the road.

After "thank yous" and "no trouble at alls," Roundtree wished the travelers farewell.

"I would very much like to hear your tale, Dogman. We will be along in a few days, after we pull up our Breeches. Ha ha ha!"

"I doubt we will be able to find one another, but it will be comforting to know you are there," Dogman said, grasping Roundtree's hand warmly.

"Oh! Your cats, Mister Starling. Let me find your cats."

"Don't trouble yourself, Mister Roundtree," Starling said. "They seem at home here with your other cats, if you don't mind having them around. They will do a good job of helping to keep pests away and entertaining the children, I promise you that. I told them I'd be back to turn them over to King Harald's Bull Hounds if they misbehaved."

Roundtree laughed, just a bit uneasily. There was something oddly familiar about those cats, and something definitely odd about Mister Starling.

"Well, then, I suppose we have acquired two more cats. Thank you, sir. And Dogman? I do hope you find your friend Fogbow. He seemed a wonderful companion."

"He is, and don't give it another thought. I am very certain he's waiting just up the road."

With goodbye waves, Starling and Dogman walked toward the Gravenwall road, which they rejoined after just a few minutes. As the hours passed, more and more travelers appeared on the road, entering from tributary paths and highways. Some were mounted on horses, some rode in carriages or wagons, but most were walkers talking quietly to companions or not at all.

Atop a hill a few miles from Gravenwall, Dogman and Starling stepped to the side of the road. The weather had grown cooler and cloudy, so Dogman unrolled his hooded cloak and donned it, replacing his short sword on his back and the dagger in his waist cord.

"Well, Dogman, we'll part company here. I'd best backtrack and see to our other business."

"Yes, it's time."

"I know you will be fine, just as you know I will take good care of them."

Dogman smiled and patted Starling's shoulder affectionately.

"I have no doubt of that. Anyhow, we will see each other again soon."

"That will be a grand day. Keep them enthralled."

"I'll do my best, Mister Starling."

With each giving the other a quick wave of the hand, they separated, Dogman moving on toward Gravenwall and Starling returning to an intersecting road a few hundred yards back the way they had come.

By the time the great flanks of Gravenwall appeared, Dogman found himself shoulder to shoulder with people walking toward it. The buzz of voices continued to grow louder and more animated, punctuated by sharp barks of laughter. Dogman heard the sound of trumpets above the sound of voices, hoof beats, and creak of leather, but they seemed to serve no purpose, as if the musicians were merely playing musical scales.

Dogman moved along locked in the dusty, noisy throng until everyone stopped. He stood on tiptoes to see what might be the cause, but saw nothing. He patiently shuffled along for nearly an hour until he saw a small group of soldiers ahead directing people one way or another.

"Merchant, storyteller or audience?" they called out wearily as each person, horseman or wagon confronted them.

When Dogman drew close, he was directed to a small encampment in a field to his right. As he drew abreast of it, a tall, thin man sitting under an umbrella on a collapsible wooden chair looked up at him.

"Find a spot, lad," he said gruffly. "You'll likely be here days before you're heard." He looked around quickly to make sure no soldiers were within earshot. "The king mi' be havin'a grand time, bu' the planning is brainless. Many's given up and gone home a'ready, given no chance. Food and drink is over that way, bu' some costs you dear. Don't pee in the brook; the soldiers'll cuff you sense-less. Not to worry about y'gear. The king slays thieves."

"Thank you for the advice. I had considered it might take a while."

"Smart lad," the man grumbled and turned away.

Dogman wandered among the campers, some of whom looked up at him curiously as he passed, until he found an isolated spot near a stand of trees. He created a small tent using a piece of cloth from his pack, which he draped over the hilt of his sword, which he had stuck into the ground. He gathered a pile of moss and small deadfall for a fire he would light later in the day. After a meal of bread and cheese that Mrs. Roundtree had graciously packed for him, Dogman observed the activity both near and far until his eyes grew tired. He stretched out, his head under the cover of the cloth, and went to sleep.

Strangely enough, it was quiet that awakened him. He opened his eyes to a sky purpled with dusk, and felt a crisp breeze against his cheek. He lifted his head to see that many of the campers had settled into their evening quarters while a number of others had left, returning home, presumably. The susurrus from the main intersection in front of Gravenwall was gone, as was the throng of people and wagons. Dogman smiled, delighting in the peacefulness that had come over the grounds.

He started and stoked his little fire, building it more for company than heat or light, both of which were feeble at best. Luxuriating in the chill, he ate the last of the bread and cheese from his pack, his eyes locked onto the small, darting tongues of his fire.

His mind wandered among the memories that such fires stir.

He recalled faces, places and times burnished and tinted by firelight, and features that darted in and out of flickering shadow; it was not necessary for him to hear the voices, only to know what was said. He remembered a young woman with green eyes and red-gold hair laughing in the light of a guttering torch, and the softness of her lips when he kissed them. He saw a constellation of campfires, a universe of them, and countless children with soulless stares who huddled in their dancing light. On and on they came and went, ghosts and grievers, friends and murderers, passing through the flames.

"You there," a gentle voice said. Dogman looked up directly at the broad-shouldered guard who had spoken to him. There were three other men with him, two standing at his side with their hands resting casually on their sword pommels. The guard in Dogman's sight was smiling. "I know you saw us coming."

Dogman smiled, too, nodding.

"Have y' nowhere to go?"

Dogman shrugged and looked around him.

"I'm here. That's good enough for now."

"Are you here to tell a story?"

"I am."

"Then y' should meet the man who will judge that tale." He stepped aside to allow one of the men behind him to advance. A medium-sized, strongly-built fellow with a lean, hard face stepped into the firelight. He wore gauntlets of slate tied together with rawhide cords. "This be King Harald Stonearm, lad. On yer feet."

Dogman rose and bowed.

"Your Highness."

Harald shook his head. "No 'highness,' please. You appear to be a soldier, as we are. As such, simple civility will do."

"A soldier of sorts, sire," Dogman corrected. "Now just a traveler."

"A traveler. Of Swallows? Or farther?"

"Much farther, sire."

"Tell me then, have you ever been as far as Maurisia?"

"Far past it, to the Faradays. We passed well away from Maurisia. There was no reason to stop there."

"No," Harald said. "No reason to stop. He regarded Dogman closely. "You are a foreigner. From where do you come?"

"Riversend, sire."

Harald reacted with surprise. "Riversend? Here in the Provinces? Really? I've never been there. It is a lovely town I've heard, and has a lovely harbor as well. And many foreigners who come and go. Where are you bound in your travels?"

"Riversend."

Harald smiled. "How poetic. Yes, I suppose all our journeys lead us back to where we began. You say you used to soldier, yet your cloak is that of a holy man. Are you now a holy man?"

"No. I spent time with some from the orders, but I assure you I am no holy man."

"Your name, then. How about a name for us to call you."

"I have had several, sire. The one I am called now is Dogman."

Harald peered around Dogman's small campsite.

"I see no dog."

"I have none with me, sire."

Harald again studied Dogman, his expression amused but hovering dangerously near suspicion that Dogman might be playing him for a fool.

"A foreigner who is from these lands. A soldier, of sorts, dressed like a holy man. A traveler who searches for the place from which he came. A man of many names who is now a Dogman with no dog. You must have an interesting tale to tell, indeed. Over the past several weeks, I have suffered endless, dramatic recreations of finding lost cattle, climbing gigantic trees, and felling entirely purposeless monsters. I had just begun to believe that this whole endeavor was a bad idea. I am becoming desperate to hear a strong tale, Dogman. It would appear that you might have one. I dearly hope so or my eyes will permanently glaze over."

Harald tapped Dogman on the shoulder.

"You are next, then. Tomorrow morning after breakfast. Someone will fetch you, and the stage will be yours."

Dogman bowed. "I hope I do not disappoint you, sire."

"Likewise," Harald said. "Goodnight then, Dogman."

The group turned and left, becoming no more than dark shapes against a darker sky in just a step. Dogman settled back down near his little fire and tossed a few sticks into the flames.

He smiled.

*   *   *

It appeared to the two guards who came for Dogman that he was sitting exactly where they had left him the evening before. The fire was out and lightly scattered, leaving no more than a few small sticks with smoking ends on the damp lawn. Dogman was chewing on a piece of dried beef as he watched the guards approach. As they neared, Dogman stood and retrieved his pack.

Without a word, the guards turned and led Dogman down the grassy slope toward the castle. Although it was early and the sun was just beginning to break over the horizon, some hopefuls were just arriving to join the few remaining campers for the day. They resentfully watched Dogman and the guards pass, but no one dared say anything. Dogman knew they would be muttering angrily among themselves before long.

At the castle wall, they turned down a crushed stone path along the rampart. Some distance down, the path veered outward onto a large square paved with flagstones. A section of the rampart was cordoned off and two soldiers stood guard beside it. Dogman slowed his pace slightly to look up at a tall, narrow expanse of stone that was considerably lighter than those around it. Within the light area were engravings, with the ones at the top an indecipherable group of shapes and gashes. This was the famous graven wall, Dogman knew, on which the names all the province's rulers were carved, beginning with symbols from a time before written language. The earliest names had been chiseled on the capstones of burial cairns, then sawn to size and fitted into the top of the wall by King Zea, whose idea the commemoration was. Inscribed beside the list, which ended some ten feet above the ground leaving room for many more names, were the words: *Forsaking the past condemns the future. Celebrate. Honor. Remember.*

When the group reached the end of the path and turned the corner, Dogman saw that he was approaching the entrance to a large amphitheater. To his left was an open, arched stage on which the King and a few of his staff were already seated. King Harald was reading a parchment and looked up when he heard their footsteps.

"Good morning, Dogman. I trust you slept well out there in the open air?"

Dogman was amazed at the acoustics of the surroundings. He heard Harald as clearly as if the man were standing right next to him.

"Yes, thank you. I am used to it," Dogman said, consciously trying not to shout. His voice carried to the stage as crisply as Harald's had come to him.

"Splendid." Harald turned back to the parchment, pressed his seal onto it, then handed it to a soldier next to him. He then leaned back in his seat after the soldier turned away.

The guards stopped and turned to face Dogman.

"Your weapons, please," one said, holding out a hand while

the other stared at him, his own sword in his grip. Dogman turned over his sword, dagger and pack.

He was then directed to a comfortable chair on the amphitheater floor before the king's stage. The chair was shaded, and beside it was a table with a jug of water and a cup. About a dozen spectators were lying or sitting on the grassy slope surrounding him. Others were arriving carrying baskets and blankets, all looking for the best spots to settle.

"You may sit or pace, whichever you prefer," Harald said. "If you need a latrine break, simply raise a fist for a time out. Your meals will be served twice during the day, if required. Fair warning, though. I have yet to feed a storyteller. Their tales are either told within an hour or two, or I boot them out for boring me. If it happens to storm, we will move into the Great Hall. Are there any questions?"

"No, sire," Dogman said, removing his cloak, folding it, and laying it on the stones beside the chair.

"Good. Then begin." Harald eagerly wiggled deeper into his seat.

Dogman remained standing.

"It is said that in the end of every tale lies the beginning of another. So it is here today, sire. And so it was then on an evening long ago in Riversend, when I was called Benjamin."

Book Two

THE FOREIGNER'S TALE

Part One

BENJAMIN

Chapter One

WATERBORN

Riversend. You said you know of it, but have never been? It lies where the Hours River joins the Sea of Caprice in the Province of Doves. Like most port towns it is never entirely still nor completely quiet. During the day, dust rises from the horses' hooves and wagon wheels and boots of laborers. The air hums with shouts and bangs and rumbles of rolling hogsheads and heavily laden wheelbarrows. Smells change with every step, every turned corner, from the acrid sting of long unwashed bodies to the exotic, almost dizzying scents of cargo from other lands. I'm sure you know such places well, my lord. Many lie between Riversend and where your own journey began.

A broad avenue connects the wharves and docks, the far side of which is lined with liveries, warehouses, mills, smithies and carpentries. Among the shifting throngs are men in leather aprons, thick-armed men with sooty faces, black and red and yellow men from other countries, and the lawmen, those being knights retired by age or injury from their long marches, but still in the service of their kingdom.

From the avenue, crooked, narrow lanes wander like snakes

this way and that. Some are devoted solely to goods and stores, others to physicians and chemists, or inns and public houses. And some are where the permanent residents of Riversend live. The human tide, like the high tide of the sea, washes into these estuaries when the day's light fades.

We lived on Pitcher's Handle Lane, which, as you might expect, curved away from Wharfside Avenue and rejoined it a half mile farther on. Our house was small but made surprisingly spacious by the ingenuity of my father, who was a shipwright. Shipwrights must be as clever with their ideas as they are skilled with iron and wood. Therefore, our home was a cozy wonderland of concealed storage spaces, nesting furniture and cookware, pocket doors and accordion tables and counters embedded in the walls that emerged with a satisfying series of clicks as each perfect oaken slat fell into place.

My sister Marya and I were a year apart in age, and grew up amid the heady smells of wood and freshly baked bread. My mother baked loaves and pastries for both our house and to sell to ship's officers and crew and laborers who passed her stall on the avenue. She was up and at her tasks very early, which meant Marya and I awoke hungry every morning, drawn from our beds to the kitchen by the most exquisite smells. We would rise, wash our faces and hands, dutifully fold and store our bedclothes in bins under our beds, then fold the beds into their spaces in the wall. We each had a chest of drawers for our clothes. Mine resembled a sailor's footlocker, out of which rose three drawers like trays on hinges and springs when the lid was opened. Marya's was fashioned like a dollhouse, with each drawer serving as a floor.

My father would always be seated at the kitchen table before us, with Mother kneading dough or filling pans at one of the counters beside the stove, and always, always, they would both look at us and smile as we came into the room.

Our duty, from as early as each of us can remember, was to help them as best we could at whatever age we happened to be. Marya would fetch pans or fill measuring cups or cut pats of butter until she could help make and knead or knot or roll dough as she grew older. At cock's crow, as the sun edged slowly from the molten surface of the harbor, Mother and Marya would load a small handcart with their work to sell from the family bakery stall on the town side of the wharf, between a leathersmith and a cheese artisan, one Mister Miles. Mister Miles closed his shop every day whenever Mother closed hers (and that was only after the last crumb was sold) so he could see her safely home.

My duty was to accompany Father, whom everyone called Mister Carpenter, to his shop near the wharf. It was a barn-like building with a vast array of chisels and saws and brushes and burrs, all hanging from pegs on the walls. Though it was swept every afternoon, a fine layer of sawdust always covered the floor, which our footsteps stirred into thin clouds that drifted aimlessly through curtains of sunlight. My contributions were mostly theater until I was old enough to identify and lift tools or help carry boards and buckets of pitch, but I was set to tasks anyway to keep me busy. The rough men who often worked with Father all indulged me with patience.

But every morning at breakfast, as we ate our sweets or porridge or sliced fruit, Mother and Father would each announce the day's agenda.

"Oatmeal bread today, Marya, " Mother would say. "Poppyseed muffins and strawberry scones."

"Benjamin, we're fitting the graving pieces for that spice ship from Manuto this morning," Father might say then, knowing full well I could be of no help to him at all. But he enjoyed including me in everything, nonetheless.

When all the preparations were made and the kitchen straightened up we set off on our separate ways. Mother and Marya went right, and Father and I went left, as our destinations were at both ends of Pitcher's Handle Lane. I enjoyed those walks in the early morning. The air was usually cool, damp and smelled of tobacco smoke, cold fires, beer and the sea. Few people were about at that hour, but those who were drifted in and out of the soft, gray light like figures from a fever dream. Here for a instant was a fierce dark man in a feathered skullcap and patchwork robes, or a one-eyed man wearing animal skin breeches and a vest made of tiny bones, or a leering hairless woman wearing more weapons than clothes. I wasn't afraid of them, though, because I was with my father, who always had a small smile or nod for the world, and feared nothing in it.

On days when school was held, a lawman would walk Marya to Father's workshop, and the two of us would set off together for Goatfoot Lane and the cottage of Mistress Nearly. She taught a small group of Riversend children how to read, write and master numbers without counting on their fingers. She was paid in goods from the Riversend School Committee, but was a frail woman who was often ill with a cough or high temperature or weak legs, all of which she attributed to the damp air and vile vapors brought from other lands. When she felt able to receive us, she rang a distinctive, tinkling bell that hung in front of her cottage. The sound carried far, even on foggy days, and was clearly different than the bells aboard the ships. When it sounded, we children immediately set off toward it, not driven by any great love of learning but more because it usually meant getting out of some sort of chore.

Marya was easily our best student. She seemed to inhale information and new skills. She was a beautiful girl with a perfect oval face and piercing, inquisitive eyes. Even as a very young child, she unsettled many of her elders with her steady, appraising gaze.

Compared to her, we other children, including me, seemed to lag, even though we were, in one of Mistress Nearly's more colorful judgments, "quite a shiny bunch of apples."

Although she was small and slender, Marya was strong and not intimidated by much. She might, for example, stand aside thoughtfully watching a new game we were playing, no matter how rough it might be, then, when she was satisfied that she understood what was required, she would come in and often beat us at it. People sometimes mistook her reluctance to join in right away for shyness or fear. It was neither. It was her method.

She could be stubborn and vexing. If reasoned with, she was quite agreeable. If commanded to do something, her small face would seem to gather, and her brows created a furrow between her eyes, and she would look steadily back as she said, "I will not." She was sometimes punished for this, at which point tiny jewels of teardrops spilled over and slid down her reddened cheeks. Some thought they were tears of contrition. I knew they were because she felt she didn't have enough power to fight back. Yet.

Despite this serious portrait, she seemed happy most of the time, chattering away when some subject caught her interest or mischievously watching for an opportunity to say something funny when others talked. No one could resist her laugh, which seemed to ring with the same attractive melody as Mistress Nearly's bell.

I adored her. I was always bigger and stronger than she was, but that never mattered. Whatever attributes each of us possessed, we existed to aid or defend one another. We never competed for anything. We never challenged each other. We faced the world side by side.

* * *

To Marya and me, the most joyous words we ever heard were

when Father, with his customary half-smile, announced at breakfast, "Taking the boat out today, Mother."

That meant a few hours of lessons in Father's small cogboat. These short voyages usually took place after Father's work was done for the day, no matter what the season, and nothing excited us more. If it happened to be a school day, we raced down Goatfoot Lane to Wharfside Avenue bounding over obstacles and darting around pedestrians, horses and carts that dared get in our way. If there was no school, I counted the hours at Father's shop, waiting for Marya to arrive with the lawman after Mother and Mister Miles closed up their shops. Once we were all together in the workshop, Father dismissed whomever might be working with him that day, if anyone, and we swept the floor, replaced tools and tidied up the workbenches. Then we closed and locked the shop doors and walked to the mooring beside Father's building slip where the trusty *River Rose* yawed gently between the piles, its mast moving back and forth like a wearied metronome.

We children clambered aboard first, taking our positions at the halyards while Father loosed the bow and stern lines. He pushed us out, and then rowed us away into the estuary. When we were clear of the docks and the sterns and tenders of whatever ships might be at anchor, Father would ship the oars and take his place at the stern, his arm draped over the tiller, and quietly say, "Set the sail, you two."

We then hauled on the halyards, dragging the spar aloft, and the vertically rectangular sail unfurled, bellying in the breeze. When the rigging was secure, Marya and I could watch the water ahead, faces turned into the damp wind that tossed our hair and crackled through our shirts or coats while sea birds mobbed and wheeled and shrieked above us. We never tired of the sky, sometimes rumpled and dark, sometimes a blinding blue studded with tall white clouds that looked like castle keeps, but always with the low thin band of white on the horizon that marked the path of the warm Boundary Current. Gradually the river smells of mud and shore grass and fish and wood smoke faded and were replaced by the smell of salt and spume. When the estuary broadened to where we could barely see the shores and the *River Rose* began to move like a rocking horse, we were at the edge of the open sea.

Father took us out in every season, during the day and at night. He taught us to swim without fear until we could manage ourselves in the water like otters, able to follow in the boat's wake for miles and swim under water for minutes at a time. We learned how to make judgments based on the water's temperature, the feel of the currents against our bodies and the nature of the waves around us, information we could also use in governing the boat.

We learned to read the stars and moon and to set a course with the starjack, reciting our heading according to the height and position of the North Star and the location of the night sky's brightest guides: the moon, and the Spear Carrier, Fish School, Whirlpool and Bear Cub constellations. Marya, as usual, was the quickest to grasp all this, and was the first to ask, "What if we cannot see the stars? What if there is fog? The starjack is useless then."

That was when we were taught how to read the wind by its sound and feel, the waves by their shape and height and direction and the water by its color, temperature and texture. Father even taught us to reckon our heading and position by the types of fish and birds we saw about, as some fish never left certain regions, and some birds only flew a predictable distance from land.

Our lessons always concluded the same way, with the same phrase that Father used to express his approval and pride in our progress.

"Waterborn, the both of you."

Then either Marya or I would be charged with getting us back to our slip in Riversend by the means we had learned, reciting aloud to Father the reasons we were doing what we were.

One blustery evening as we were returning home in deepening darkness, the time when we felt the most alone and at the mercy of the water, Father must have seen into our minds because he said, "If you are ever at a loss for a decision, children, remember this: persevere. Persevere and an answer will come. It may come slowly or quickly, or even betray you a time or two, but an answer will come."

She and I agree that those were the most wonderful moments of our lives, and even now we can instantly become lost in those times again at the slightest sound of a lapping wave.

On a morning I remember quite well I was a month past fifteen years old and working at Father's building slip, helping him plane the lands on topside strakes for Mister Sharp's fishing boat. The sun was warm but the breeze was cool, almost sharp, signaling the coming of change to the season. The day and the work and our closeness were all so pleasant that we never heard the Harbor Master approach down the gangway from the dock until he said, "*Hala*, Mister Carpenter," using the universal greeting all nationalities spoke and understood in Riversend.

"*Hala*, Master Twining," Father replied. "I hope you weren't kept standing there long."

"Not at all," he said, and went on to remark on how refreshing it was to see people so transfixed by their labors. Too many looked too intently for ways to avoid work these days. He saw slovenliness and lethargy everywhere it seemed, particularly among the peoples from warmer climes. Oddly enough, these same characters often showed an astonishing energy and interest in pick-pocket-ing, brawling, and drinking to excess, and as the duly appointed law of the harbor he, Master Twining, would certainly have personal knowledge about such things. It would be the downfall of human kind if such attitudes were to prevail, but as long as industriousness such as that displayed by Mister Carpenter and his son claimed the high ground, then all might turn out for the better after all, he wanted us to know.

Father listened, smiling as always, and said, "What is it you came for, Master Twining?"

Ah, of course. He had come to tell us that his pilot, Mister Goins, had gone and dropped dead at the Bung and Bollard public house, or rather, he should say, sat dead, since he had just finished his customary supper of batfish almondine with a beaker of beer, belched and smiled, they said, and then perished in his chair. His plate was sniffed by the house dogs, which seemed to detect no hint of poisons insomuch as they promptly destroyed any evidence that remained with their tongues, so it was assumed by all present that Mister Goins died of natural causes, happily, it appeared, which was the most anyone could hope for from this often benighted world.

Father had known Mister Goins for much of his life, and he contemplated this news quietly for a few moments, then gazed off across the bay as if sending his thoughts to Mister Goins, or to The One, or to the sea itself. He then thanked Master Twining for informing him, for Mister Goins had been a fine friend.

Master Twining responded with sympathy, and added that departure services would be held at the Mariner's Bethel on Dory Lane two days hence at noon, and that he was certain he would see the entire Carpenter family there, which was always a pleasure, although regarding the forthcoming event, the circumstances could obviously have been better.

Then the Harbor Master said, "But aside from the somber nature of this occurrence and its very serious impact on all Goinses near and far, I find myself grappling with the absence of a pilot, as with the presence of incoming vessels whose officers and crew do not care one crumb about Mister Goins's unfortunate passing, but need prompt guidance."

Father looked up sharply. Master Twining then proposed that I serve as an interim pilot, under Harbor Master Twining's careful watch, of course, until a permanent pilot could be found among the local population, or until I had both proven myself and expressed an interest in filling that role as my career.

"He's just a boy," was Father's argument, which rankled me a little and sparked a rare feeling of stubbornness.

"Yes, but he's tall and strong and few know these waters better than Benjamin, thanks to your own superior tutelage. In fact, if you yourself want to serve as pilot, I would be more than—"

"I have a business to run," my father interrupted.

Which response, of course, Master Twining expected to hear. Father muttered to himself that well, he could go out with me once or twice just to make sure...

Finally it occurred to both of them to ask me what I thought of the idea. They turned to me in unison and before they could ask, I said, "I can do it."

That quickly and simply, it was settled.

Over supper that evening, Father brought up the news to Mother about Mister Goins and that I would be in training to be Riversend's new harbor pilot. She was alarmed. "It's too dangerous," she said. "He's just a boy," she said.

They went back and forth for a while, Father reasoning and Mother resisting, when suddenly Marya, her face red with annoyance, said, "Why not me too, then? I know as much as Benjamin, and each of us will keep watch for the other."

This idea merited a unanimous "absolutely not." She was too young and lovely, too tempting, to be among such rough men on their own ship, even for such a short time. It was out of the question.

I saw that "I will not" look on her face, and took a sudden interest in my peas. But she was quiet. When I glanced up, those heart-rending pearls of tears were sliding down her face. To see them made me feel like weeping, too, so strongly did I feel her hurt and helplessness. But what her intrusion achieved was to gain agreement from Mother that it was all right for me to try it out under Father's gaze. If it became my livelihood, then I would have an income and a respectable profession on which to build a life.

I agreed that the opportunity was great. But the look I gave Marya told her that once I was in the position for good and had accumulated even a modest amount of authority, I meant to have her join me.

We would bring in the ships together.

* * *

The first vessel I guided in was the *Eastern Dove*, and it was as benign an assignment as I could have wished for. The captain was a friend of Father's, so they chatted happily all the while I was offering cautions and directions to the mate. The *Eastern Dove* was a regular visitor to Riversend; every fortnight she delivered staples, hardware and lumber, and left three days later with the goods our community marketed to other provinces. The day was calm and offered no unusual conditions to overcome. It was a very pleasant passage, and its ease was a relief to my taut nerves.

The captains usually paid five silverins for pilot's services, and often passed along a small sampling of the cargo. Consequently, I wound up contributing honey, salt, ginger, a variety of spices and sometimes even cloth and yarn to Mother's house. Father received more nails, canvas oddments, slightly dented or scarred dowel rods, and two or more sharpening stones than he could use in three lifetimes.

Truthfully, most of the ships I piloted until I was nearly eighteen years old were of the same sort as the *Eastern Dove*. What made the job interesting was the weather, the tides, shifting sandbars and the vagaries of the seasons. I relished the opportunities they offered me to exercise what Father had taught Marya and me, and my own powers of observation and experience.

Once in a while, though, a foreign ship arrived, and these were the most instructive times of my piloting days. I learned bits and pieces of many different languages, and taught bits and pieces of our own to eager, smiling, head-bobbing officers and wheel-deck crew members. Their boats always smelled the most exotic, too, and it was on vessels like these that I first tasted the naturally salty sea wheat, scalding yellow Mustard Peppers, sweet pearl berries and dried, oblong nut pods called Rum Tongues. As often as I could, I lingered on board longer than usual because I enjoyed the company of these men, even though some glowered and sneered with what I can only guess was suspicion and distrust.

One sailor I remember clearly, for reasons you will discover later on, was a short, solidly built young man about my age at the time. He had straight, night-black hair cut close to his scalp, a round, friendly face and dark eyes which never left mine. He was the one who brought me the sea wheat, and he pushed it toward me in the air between us as he nodded and chattered away. He watched me intently as I tasted it, and when I made an expression that reflected how surprised I was at its fine taste, he clapped his hands happily and pointed to somewhere over my shoulder. "Far, far," he said excitedly. Then his eyes followed to where he was pointing, and a heartbreaking wistfulness came over his features. "Far," he said once more, and turned away.

The captain, watching this scene, shook his head and dismissively said, "Tulak," and he too turned away, leaving me with my silverins, a bundle of sea wheat and not much else to do but go ashore.

When I wasn't leading boats to their moorings, I helped Father with his labors as before, and Marya helped Mother with her baking and housekeeping. The subject of marriage came up once or twice during those years, but not with much insistence. The family was getting by modestly well, and neither Marya nor I had any prospects in the offing. In my case, there was little time for such things, and most of the boys enamored of Marya's beautiful face and wild, streaming hair were also intimidated by her directness and strong nature. Sometimes I caught even Father studying her with respectful pride.

On the day everything changed, I was in Father's workshop setting more tool pegs in the wall while Father sharpened wood files. Outside, dark clouds tumbled and cold rain pelted against the windows. It was the type of day when one feels the near rapturous pleasure of being inside, warm and comfortable in one's work.

The door blew open, followed by Harbor Master Twining and his barrel-bodied son Micah, both covered with shining, wet rain slicks. Master Twining directed the pilot boat that took me to ships waiting offshore, and his immensely strong and stolid son did the rowing. Their appearance meant only one thing: that my cozy situation was about to end.

As it turned out, the work to be done was more a rescue than guidance. The ship in question was stranded not by unfamiliarity with the water, although that was certainly a factor, but mainly by a lack of able seamanship. The boat was crewed by ten members of the Brotherhood of Penitents from Islingia, and their abilities had been taxed to the limit just in getting as far as they did.

Harbor Master Twining had come by this information from the Sand Point lightkeeper's wife, who had been sent off to fetch the Harbor Master before the whole foolish bunch of them drowned, in her testy words. Master Twining and Micah were outbound, then, and did the Carpenters want to go along?

We did. Father and I shrugged into our weather shells and donned our boots. Father suggested that the safety of the boat and Riversend were better served if Master Twining stayed ashore. He handed the harbor master two coppers and asked him to send a boy to his house to tell Mother and Marya we were going out. Master Twining agreed, and we followed Micah down to the docks.

By then ragged, silver vents had opened in the clouds, signifying a slackening in weather. The water was chaotic and black, and waves leaped up and fell against the empty wharf. We climbed aboard the tossing, yawing pilot boat and settled in.

Expressionless, Micah rowed against the waves and shifting wind. He seemed not to notice how much effort it took to make headway through the foaming chop until he met the first of the incoming sea swells, and then his neck bulged and his lips stretched wide and taut with every stroke.

I could see Father assessing what we faced with the old boat as it bounced and rocked on the green-black water. While Micah held us close enough to board, several hooded, robed Brothers reached out to help us on. "Thank you, thank you, praise The One," they shouted over the wind.

Father said, "Benjamin?" giving me command over the situation. Like him, I had noticed several things as we got closer to the ship.

"Furl that sail," I said, and two Brothers hauled it down.

"Hoist the stern anchor," I ordered, and then called to Micah, "Back away. She's coming about."

When the anchor was aboard, the boat swung prow first into the wind and waves, but still wallowed. As best we could, Father, a couple of the Brothers, and I quickly redistributed the weight below decks and immediately felt her stabilize.

Once we were topside again, Father took the helm as we drew in the forward anchor, and he steered us around.

"Half mast," I called, and the sail was raised halfway, bellying out with the following wind, but keeping us on an even keel. Micah fell behind, alone in the pilot boat, but the work was easier for him this time, and while we kept a close eye on him, we did not fear for him.

Back in port and after both boats were secured, all of us trooped up to Father's spacious workshop. Mother and Marya were there with bread, cheese, and warm wine. The two of them were also wet, after having trundled the loaded cart through the rain. Harbor Master Twining greeted his son with relieved, affectionate slaps on the back.

Most of the Brothers were exhausted, and some sagged limply against walls in a state of half-sleep. Father got a good fire going in the stove, and the room soon warmed. I cleared a number of tool pegs so the Brothers' sodden, hooded robes could be hung to dry, noticing with some surprise that for being soaking wet they were surprisingly light and seemed to be drying quickly already. The weave was extremely tight, too, so it was unlikely much wind could penetrate them.

A tall, angular, older man with a wan smile approached us and thanked us profusely for helping them gain the shore. He was Brother Gerome, the unofficial spokesperson for the group since part of their credo was that none was of any more worth than the others. Soon, he said, they would return to their humble ship to fetch the black bread and water they had brought with them, and would sleep outside, on the wharf.

"No, you will not," my sister snapped. "You will spend the night in this very place, eat a decent meal and wait for the weather to clear."

Brother Gerome patiently explained that the purpose of their order was to suffer for the sins and excesses of mankind, so hunger and discomfort were part of their daily lives.

"Oh, that will certainly stop the sins of mankind," Marya said, and Mother told her to shush, she was being inexcusably rude. But Marya went on.

"You may resume suffering tomorrow" she said curtly, "and not involve us in it by letting our good food and generously offered shelter go to waste."

I saw that Micah was already quietly dispatching the cheese, which made me think not much of the spread would actually be around long enough to molder, when Brother Gerome relented with a bow, his lean cheeks still furrowed in a smile.

"You are quite right," he said. "It was ungracious of me to belittle your kindness. We will stay here, then, with gratitude."

Marya smiled in her victory, while Mother just shook her head. It was agreed that once we had all warmed up and had a bite to eat and sipped some wine that we would go home, returning again in the morning with breakfast to see them off.

Not many of the Brothers joined us for the food, and none drank wine, but Brother Gerome chatted quietly with us and nibbled at some bread. As darkness settled down, the wind died to a breeze and a three-quarter moon emerged from behind the ragged clouds. The Twinings left first, and as we gathered our baskets and cups, the Brothers gathered to sit in a circle on the floor with their arms interlocked, heads bowed in silence.

We left them there, a ring of unmoving, dark shadows in pale moonlight.

* * *

Morning dawned clear, and Marya and Mother had already prepared loaves of pumpkin bread and a sizable pile of crumble buns. These were put aboard the cart as the first rays of light cast long, black shadows across Riversend.

If the Brothers had ever slept, there was no evidence of it. We found that most of them were huddled on the dock by their boat, so Mother grumpily directed that the cart be wheeled down to them despite the sharp chill, perhaps preempting Marya, who would not let them depart without at least attempting to feed them. As we neared them, their colorless faces raised up from their dark frocks into the light like pale flowers.

"You have been too kind to us," one said. "All the blessings of The One upon you this day and all the days to come, but we will take your offerings with us when we sail."

"And pitch them into the water as soon as you're out of sight, no doubt," Marya said. "The people of Riversend would think themselves blessed indeed if pumpkin loaves suddenly come bobbing in from the sea."

"Marya," Mother warned, but I heard Brother Gerome chuckle beside me.

"You have a marvelous spirit, young lady," he said. "But I can assure you that no such miracle would visit Riversend. We will take what you have made for us gladly."

I helped Mother and Marya unload the food, and heard Father ask, "Well, Brother Gerome, where are you bound?"

"Norwall Island," Gerome answered.

"Norwall! My, that's a lonely part of the world, sir."

"It suits us, I think," Brother Gerome responded.

As I laid the bundles of bread on the dock, I saw Father shake his head and seem to consider his next remarks. "If you cannot negotiate our humble bay," he finally said, "how do you expect to get to Norwall? I must say, from what I've seen I don't have much confidence in your ever arriving there."

Brother Gerome glanced at the gathering of Brothers beside him, and told Father that actually, that very notion had been discussed among them a few hours ago, and that they were very impressed by my piloting abilities, referring to me as "Son Benjamin."

"We would like to hire your boy to guide us to Norwall Island," he said. "We intend to stay. Son Benjamin can use our boat to return home."

As you might expect, the response was instant from Mother, Father, and Marya: "Absolutely not."

Father added, "I would not allow him to turn and just leave you on Norwall. You will die. Sooner or later, that knowledge will come to haunt him."

"If death is what The One means for us, then there is little we can do to change it. But we do not intend to die, sir. We intend to labor and live and pray and earn The One's acceptance. The greater the struggle, the more our efforts will mean. That is why we chose Norwall Island. For its harshness."

Brother Gerome then turned and nodded slightly to his group, from which two Brothers arose and went aboard their boat.

"Along our way from Islingia, we encountered many good hearts like your own, and against our protests have accumulated a modest fortune in silverins, small gems and gold. This is of no use to us, of course, and we had intended to drop it into the sea as an offering to The One upon our arrival at Norwall Island."

"I told you so," Marya snorted, earning her a sharp elbow from Mother.

"It now occurs to me that it would be put to much better use in your hands, to do with as you see fit for your family and your neighbors in Riversend."

At this point, the two Brothers appeared carrying a plain wooden chest between them. It was set on the dock with a thump. All of us stared at it. Brother Gerome waved his hand aimlessly in the air as he said, "I have no idea how much it is."

Marya bent and opened the chest. It was nearly full of treasure, glittering in the early sunlight. My sister stood and backed away as if the gold cords within the box were snakes.

As if in answer to an unspoken question, Brother Gerome said, "Not some of it. All of it."

A wave of dizziness struck me as I thought of the possibilities. Father would have to build a dozen schooners to earn this much, and he had never been offered a contract for even one so far. I knew him. He would indeed use it to benefit Riversend. He would invest in Riversend's commercial future, buy a house to be used as a permanent school, set up relief funds for the sailors and fishermen, repair homes for those who could not do it themselves, and on and on until it was gone, and it would be the greatest joy of his life.

As for me, it would be a great adventure, an exciting foray into the world beyond what I knew so well. I would be helping others while gathering wonderful tales to tell in Father's boat shop when I returned.

I told him he must let me go. I could do it. Such good fortune would never appear again. I knew where Norwall Island was, and I could guide them there, and knew how to rig their boat to sail it back by myself. I knew the stars and the waters and the wind, and Father, my mentor, knew that I knew all this.

I was eighteen, and you, my lord, know how it is when you are eighteen.

My arguments beat against their alarm and tears and protests like waves against the rocks, until they were eroded to silence. I reassured them further with hugs and promises and smiles.

And I got my way.

* * *

Father was hesitant, but the enormity of the opportunity added to his confidence in my skills resulted in his reluctant assent. Once he agreed, he threw himself into making the voyage and my return alone as immune to failure as possible.

He prowled the boat examining every coil of rope, board and fastening. He itemized the stores aboard and ordered more, telling Brother Gerome that "even if you and your brethren decline to eat, my son must and will." He examined the stitching on the sail, and had the spare unfurled on the dock to examine that one, too. He inspected all and replaced several of the leads so that they easily reached the tiller house for my single-handed trip back.

He and I pored over charts, making note of as many details as possible of the conditions and features of the route between Riversend and Norwall. Marya was at my side with a crease of worry between her eyebrows. She studied star charts and composed a chronicle of what I should see above and around me at different points of the journey. News of the adventure brought Harbor Master Twining to our boathouse to help us with information he could recall hearing from sailors experienced in working those waters. Among all of us, we estimated that the voyage should take six days out, five days back with the wind aiding me, and two days unloading and refitting on Norwall.

Mother stayed home to gather what clothes I would need. She was quiet and pale during the two days it took to prepare. One of my most vivid memories is of her sitting in her chair under a halo of lamplight, her fingers trembling as she searched every inch of my weather shell for defects. I carry that image with me like a talisman, for it said more about love that anything I had seen before, or have seen since.

I was not indifferent to feelings of my own, either. I spent two fitful nights, my sleep churned by sudden waves of doubt and fear. What if I made a misjudgment and drowned us all? What if I misread the stars and led us off into the unknown? What if? What if? But when the sun arose and the world took shape in its familiar hard lines, doubt and fear vanished.

As for leaving my family, I easily rationalized my way to calmness by repeating that I would only be gone a fortnight. That thought comforted my parents, too. Only a fortnight.

When it was at last time to leave, Father paced the boat one more time while I hugged and reassured Mother and Marya on the dock. A small group gathered to see us off, crying "Good luck, boy!" and "The One is at your side, son!" and "Safe passage, Benjamin!" After delaying as long as he dared to, my father finally came ashore, gave me a long, quiet look, and embraced me.

"I'll see you by month's end, Benjamin. Stay safe."

"By month's end, Father," I said.

As I took my place on the tiller bench, the Brothers settled into their places. It was a clear day with a fresh offshore breeze that took us smartly over the bay toward the sea, accompanied by a swirling cloud of squalling birds. I felt a surge of joy and excitement, the same as when Marya and I reached the river mouth in Father's boat and saw the vast, open world of restless water before us.

We neared the lighthouse point, and I saw the lightkeeper and his wife on the jetty waving to us. I remember to this day how small they appeared in the bright morning sunlight, and the look of her faded blue dress pleated by the wind. The Brothers waved back in both thanks and farewell. Then we were upon the heaving sea, and the northbound current carried us away.

Chapter Two

THE BLEAK SHOALS

For the first few hours I was overly anxious, very aware of the responsibility I had assumed. It was difficult not to be aware, with that congregation of drawn, pale faces watching either the quickly fading shoreline or me. But soon all my attention turned to what I knew best, and why I was there. My body began to feel the sea through the boat, and my senses began to attune themselves to the clouds, wind, scents and colors of the great ocean.

The sea was kind to us that day, setting out long, gentle swells and a stiff stern-wind. Clouds played shadow games with the sun, which was warm on our heads and hands when it was clear. Gliding shorebirds escorted us for a while, until they realized we were not fishing. Their leaving seemed to magnify the immensity of the waters upon which our tiny boat bobbed along.

The Brothers were silent. When they weren't praying, their heads, now deep inside their cowls, were lifted in the direction of the water or the empty horizon, and their fingers rhythmically walked over rows of knots in their waist cords. Only Brother Gerome showed his face to me from time to time, gracing me with his constant, encouraging smile and regarding me with a fondness I had only ever seen in my father's eyes. Among us all, for most of the day, the only sound was the long, splashing sigh of water against the bow, the creak of timber, and the snap and hum of wind in the sails and lines.

Early on, a couple of the Brothers became seasick, but retched over the side as quietly and discreetly as they were able. No one else paid them any mind. Their discomfort seemed to be expected, and something to be endured alone.

Toward afternoon, Brother Gerome brought me some of the bread and water and dried fish my mother had packed for us, but took none himself. Instead, he and the others ate the rough, hard fare they had brought with them. I ate contentedly, thoroughly enjoying the cool wind and rise and fall of the boat. One couldn't help but breathe deeply of that air, and idly try to unravel the many scents from the pungent richness of the whole. Brine, certainly, and rainwater, but also sweet grasses, fish oils, the sharp odors of sea mats, and the brief, startling smell, once in a while, of spices.

The day slipped away. I held us on course for Norwall Island with the starjack and reckoning, watching the light thin, then turn to an iridescent murk. The water gleamed and chattered against the hull; the wind grew colder and quartered; the clouds stratified and shone pink and blue and gray along the horizon. In this peaceful, quiet, impending gloom, the Brothers gathered close together and their voices came together in a chant that chilled my back. It was a somber sound, measured and in a language I had never heard before, not even among the eclectic crews on the boats I had guided into Riversend. Their voices rose and fell in unison. I had never before listened to anything so transfixing.

When they once again were silent, the Brothers who were not still ill went below to sleep. Brother Gerome approached me out of the near dark carrying a bundle across his outstretched arms. Behind him was one of the Brothers, whose lips were also set in a gentle smile.

"Son Benjamin, you have certainly earned your rest. Where will you sleep?"

I answered that I would sleep in front of the wheel deck so I could better feel the boat and the water, and be able to react quickly to changes.

"What will cover you? What will keep you warm?"

I tapped my weather shell. "This has always done, Brother Gerome."

He then held his bundle out to me.

"Brother Moutin has offered his spare habit for you to wear. You are about the same size. You will find it much more comfortable, I think, and just as warm and dry. Will you accept this from us?"

I hesitated, feeling quite content in my weather shell, but relented out of politeness. Brother Gerome seemed delighted when I removed the stiff jacket I was wearing and slipped the heavy habit over me. The fabric was coarse on the outside but smooth inside, and sat upon my shoulders like a second skin. My face was chilled from the evening breeze, but when I raised the hood over my head, my cheeks warmed almost instantly. The wind did not penetrate anywhere, and I sensed that it never would, no matter how fierce. It was a remarkable garment, and I have worn it ever since.

I expressed my genuine surprise and gratitude to Brother Gerome, and asked him to thank Brother Moutin for his generosity. Brother Gerome seemed very pleased.

"With me is Brother Tom," he said. "He was our helmsman on the voyage to Riversend. With your permission and counsel, he will tend the wheel whenever you wish to give you time to sleep and eat. Though not nearly as skilled as you obviously are, I think you will find his competence acceptable. You need others to help, Son Benjamin," he said. "We have a long way to go."

I surely couldn't deny that fact, and, since I would be sleeping only a few yards away from the wheel, I agreed.

Brother Gerome turned away to go below, and I said, "Brother Gerome, please, what language was that you were singing?"

"Assantic, the original tongue of The Follower's Scrolls. It's very old. No one speaks it now, except in prayer."

"What were you saying? Can you tell me?" I asked.

"I believe so. We sang, 'As you trust in us to dwell without fear in the vault of your darkest night, we trust in you to return us to the embrace of your precious light. So it will be.'"

I commented that if they sang that chant every evening, I would look forward to hearing it, for it sounded wonderful. He said, with his ever-present smile, "It feels wonderful, too," and went below.

Brother Tom stepped closer. With youthful self-importance, I pointed out the North Star, with which Brother Tom was no doubt very familiar, and handed him the starjack, which was aligned with both it and the prow. Our heading, for now, would be directly toward that star. With a graciousness that embarrasses me to recall, Brother Tom took up his position, his smile never wavering, although it seems to me now that it might have changed from one of good nature to one of near laughter.

I was tired. I could feel it pulling me to the deck. I lay down on my side with my face and drawn-up knees toward the below-deck cabin wall. The habit and cowl enveloped me in warmth and stillness, and I fell into sleep like a stone.

* * *

Over the next few days, life on the boat fell into a rhythm, and my anxiety left me. Most of the Brothers did not speak except to pray or trade brief comments among themselves. As I had told

Brother Gerome, I looked forward to evening prayer, and even picked up a few Assantic words from the chant and the loose translation I had been given. Afterward, as Brother Tom took his place at the helm and I sat cross-legged on the deck with my back against the cabin wall eating my supper, the two of us talked.

Brother Tom was born Thomas Green, the son of a green-grower in Lee of the Mount. It is a quiet and gentle art, and he took to it with eagerness because he relished the sense of peace it brought him. Working outside with the saplings, pruning fruit tree branches, and nurturing, feeding and guiding a myriad of shrubs and bushes gave him great satisfaction. He experimented with different fertilizers, engineered surprising hybrids and introduced several new, productive species to the region. He quickly outstripped his father in skill and knowledge, but there was no friction between them. His father was immensely proud of him.

Brother Tom was often called upon to apply his talents to forming hedges, walls and majestic ornamental pathways for the area's farmers and wealthier citizens. His reputation expanded from simply "green-grower" to include "artist."

Thus, it was no accident or surprise that he turned to sculpting plants and bushes into forms by using constraints, trellises, netting, skillful pruning and trimming at various points of growth. He could create the shape of just about any animal or object by knowing the variety and characteristics of the plant, shrub or tree that was best suited for the idea. He found himself being called upon more and more to design signature ornaments — a Heatherwood stag resides outside the Lee of the Mount hunt club; a giant pig stands atop a cluster of Bluetrees at the entrance to a hog farm; a raven in flight rises from a Blackleaf hedgerow outside Fewton Castle.

Then one day the Brotherhood of Penitents contacted him to create a collection of living holy symbols for their seminary in Turim.

Turim was a long way from Lee of the Mount, but Brother Tom was intrigued by the opportunity, and old enough to fend for himself away from home. He packed as lightly as he could, bought a reliable horse from a neighbor, and made the journey.

To hear Brother Tom tell it, he knew at first sight that the Brotherhood was where he belonged. The seminary's vaulted halls and long, arched cloisters brought him a level of peace and serenity even beyond that of his work. Since he had come so far, he was housed on the college grounds in a small room in a dormitory nestled among fragrant trees whose leaves hissed softly in the summer breeze. As he went about his work, he made the acquaintance of many of the Brothers. Slowly and willingly he was led to the lessons and language of The Follower's Scrolls.

The Rite of Brotherhood is to copy The Follower's Scrolls in your own hand, on your own scrolls. The reasons for doing that are three: during the course of transcription, a duplicate is made; the student more quickly learns Assantic while "absorbing" the teachings of the scrolls; and the original language is preserved, remaining uncorrupted by translation.

Brother Tom finished his ornamental work for the seminary in one year, and turned his skills to caretaking the seminary grounds while he worked on his copy of the scrolls, which took another two.

Though he visited often, he never lived at home again, because once a Brother completes his scrolls and accepts a place at the Brothers' Table, he is charged with guiding ten others to write their own duplicates. If that task takes a lifetime, so be it. If it is done with life left to live, then the Brother is released to spend his remaining days in penitence for all those who were not or could not be saved from their sins through the scrolls.

Brother Tom met his obligations within fifteen years. He returned to Turim to await the annual gathering of Completants, who would decide among themselves the site of their penitence.

This was the group I was taking to Norwall Island.

I remember Brother Tom for another reason, too. He was the first to notice the Roanfish that was accompanying us. If you have never seen one, Your Highness, it would not be a surprise. They are rare, solitary creatures, sometimes nearly half the length of a ship, and appear to be more animal than fish. This one was sleek, rust-red and white in color, and surfaced periodically within throwing distance of our boat, with one huge round black eye seeming to look directly into our own. Roanfish are considered good fortune, a sign of the sea's favor, and we were all happy to have it with us. Brother Tom named it Bringer, a messenger from The One.

When I was at the helm I was often joined by Brother Gerome, I discovered over time that his life story was similar to that of Brother Tom. Brother Gerome was the son of a small town chandler who made and sold candles. His customers were such that it was necessary to use tallow rather than the more expensive beeswax. Because of the terrible odor of rendering tallow, his preparation site was a small cabin outside the village.

Brother Gerome never got used to the smell, and his job was mainly to gather wood for the fires, a task that kept him outside more than in. Once, at the age of twelve, he rebelled against the stink that assaulted his nose as he brought in a load of small wood and tinder and angrily hurled a handful of Winetree bark into a batch. By itself, Winetree bark is of no distinction, he said, but its oil, when heated, releases a wonderful, rich floral scent. Those who burned the wood knew this, but no one had ever attempted to use the oil in other ways.

Brother Gerome's father was furious with him, certain that the suet was ruined and would not burn as it usually did, but the process was too far along to waste, so he decided to strain and use the taint-

172

ed tallow anyway. During its many passages through the cheese-cloth, the tallow retained the Winetree scent, and the oil proved to not only burn brightly and evenly, but also perfumed the air.

They continued to make their candles this way, mostly for their own benefit. Their customers enthusiastically received the change as well, and soon his father could not keep up with the demand. The entire family became involved in the enterprise, and a second, larger rendering cabin was built. At this point they could afford to expand their offerings to include beeswax, and experimented with scenting those candles as well. The family grew quite wealthy and well known, and their daily lives became especially comfortable.

For Brother Gerome, that all changed when a candle request was fulfilled for a small, simple school run by the Brotherhood of Penitents.

Brother Gerome delivered the candles on a crisp autumn after-noon and was intrigued by the long tables within the dim, rough building. The master, one Brother Marcus, explained that a candle was placed at each space where a student was writing his own copy of The Follower's Scrolls, and, depending on the student's level of industry, they burned through quite a few candles.

"Something about the smell of wood and ink, the low light and the silence embraced me," Brother Gerome told me. He visited several times more when he wasn't working, learning a little more each time about the Brotherhood, the Assantic language and the teachings of the scrolls. Then he became a student himself, giving up his fine life for the coarse robes and long hours of the Brotherhood apprenticeship.

"My father greeted this news with disbelief," Brother Gerome said. "That turned to pleading, then to disgust, then resignation, and finally he simply waved me out of his life."

After his scrolls were written, Brother Gerome drifted into and out of various hamlets and cities until he found a Follower's School that needed a new master, as its current master was leaving to do his penitence. He remained there for twenty-five years, teaching the scrolls to far more than ten students, before deciding to travel to Turim to join that season's Completants.

And here he was.

"What is in the scrolls?" I asked him once. "Is it all songs and prayers?"

"No," he told me. "They contain stories and hope and infinite peace." I asked to hear one of the stories, and this is what he told me.

"After The One made the world and a sun to light it during the day and a moon and stars to light it at night, he found it to be a very lonely place. So he made innumerable creatures to walk, crawl, swim, and fly on, below and above this place. He took great pleasure in making so many different kinds of things, and it brought him joy to see them so busy in all their colors and forms. But it still seemed like a very lonely place. So he gave each creature a unique voice, a single voice like no other, and now the world was full of innumerable creatures with innumerable voices of their own. We hear them one at a time wherever we wander, but don't know what they say. We enjoy hearing them one at a time, and giving them names, one at a time, but never know what they say. Then, at the very moment when we leave this world to join with and become The One, we are allowed to hear all the voices together, every voice at once, and they all rise together in one unutterably glorious chorus, and they all sing the same song, and we at last know what they say."

*　*　*

Brother Moutin died one night as we were about a week and a half from Riversend. He had been the frailest of them and among the oldest. The Brothers gently placed his scrolls inside his cloak near his silent heart and bound his arms over them. They nestled his head within his hood and sewed it shut over his face. His few possessions filled the pockets of his habit, and they too were sewn shut. Then his ankles were bound together, and in silence the Brothers slipped the body into the water.

It crossed my mind that from now on the habit I wore would be in remembrance of him, whether I wanted it to be or not.

Later I asked Brother Gerome why no songs had been sung, no prayers offered for him. He said that Brother Moutin had already gone on, that he was already part of The One, and anything said here in this world would mean absolutely nothing. Had the Brothers been near him before he left, then they would have prayed aloud so he could hear and be comforted. But now? Now they said silent prayers for themselves because he had left them behind, and it was they who should be pitied.

I also asked why he hadn't kept Brother Moutin's scrolls to pass along to someone else, and he gave me a stern look. Each scroll, he told me, was a life, and one's life cannot be given to another. "You must write your own life," he said.

But he had kept one thin scroll he found among Brother Moutin's things. It was a map, and throughout the daylight hours he and the other Brothers studied it. Brother Gerome seemed to be the focal point of the discussions as he took it to a couple of the Brothers at a time, pointing at the wind-buffeted parchment as they quietly spoke. Sometimes the Brothers nodded their heads.

That evening, when Brother Tom relieved me at the wheel, I asked him what that was all about. He smiled and told me that it was Brother Gerome's charge to answer that question. I admit to being a little upset about this turn of events. I felt I was too much a part of the group for them to have secrets. Then I imagined that they were questioning my navigation and double-checking our course. I didn't sleep well that night.

In the morning I had worked myself into surliness, and did not speak to anyone. I glared at their shuffling and lurching as they emerged from the cabin stairwell into a cold, steel-gray day on a tossing sea. I saw Brother Tom murmur something to Brother Gerome, who glanced at me, then nodded and made his way forward.

What he had to say was that he and the others had studied Brother Moutin's map and saw another destination about which they hadn't known, one that seemed to be better suited for their mission than Norwall Island.

"Have you heard of The Bleak Shoals?" he asked me.

I had, but only in passing, as a mention overheard among the crews of incoming ships. I knew nothing about its location, currents, or nature. I asked Brother Gerome to show me where it was on the map, which he eagerly did.

The Bleak Shoals were far east of Norwall Island, and farther north. It appeared to be a long, curving peninsula attached to some unnamed and empty land, which could have been an island or a country, as it was unfinished on the parchment Brother Gerome held. From its location in relation to Norwall Island, I reckoned it to be directly under the heel of The Spear Carrier constellation.

"Would you, can you take us there instead?" he asked.

I sensed a challenge to my skill in his question, and felt a shiver of excitement from the thought of entering someplace unknown to me. My thoughts sped over the foremost facts: the season was late spring, so there was plenty of time to deliver them there and return home; the sidetrack would take another week or perhaps two, so we would have to ration the food and water we had left, and we would have to do some fishing; and we would have to acquaint another Brother with the wheel to help Brother Tom and me. The largest detraction? I didn't know the water.

Perhaps it was youthful arrogance or an abundance of pride or the mind-quickening attraction of a daunting test, but I said yes, I thought I could take them there.

And with that I reset the starjack to a new course, and turned us into the wind toward The Bleak Shoals, turned us toward the heel of The Spear Carrier, and turned away from my family's sight.

* * *

Where I had just a few days before been lulled into long periods of daydreaming and inattention, I was now fully engaged. There would be new events to deal with, new signs to interpret, and new situations on board. The Brothers were unperturbed by my plan for rationing food and water; they were already used to deprivation. I was the one who would be most affected, and Brother Gerome offered to augment my portion with a small part of each of theirs. I told him not to bother; I would be fine.

On the second day of our new heading, Brother Tom and I introduced Brother Caril to the role of part-time helmsman. He seemed very nervous and uncertain at first, but quickly took to it, and within a few hours we could see contentment in his features. I used my free time to turn our vessel into a fishing boat by arranging lines, fashioning a crude net and constructing a gaff in which I had little confidence should we need it for anything larger than Morningfish. For bait we used whatever the sea offered, from minnows to water grapes, mats of which floated by from time to time and which Morningfish loved to eat. I was aware, too, that all the fish I was used to seeing may not be found in these new waters, and that unfamiliar fish might not rise to my bait. We would have to adapt.

From the beginning, Brother Enoch proved to be the best fisherman. It was apparent that he had some experience from his previous life (exactly what he never told me), so that became his primary task. Catches were infrequent, but he was patient, diligent and committed. I realized that I would feel better about leaving them on The Bleak Shoals with his abilities to help them survive.

The others worked the sail and lines, distributed rations and mended equipment.

On the third day I spotted the magnificent bulk of Bringer again, seeming to watch us with one inky eye before disappearing again. I was relieved to see him. We needed whatever good fortune he could give us.

As the days slipped by, the air grew colder, the sea grew darker and the sky lowered. I thought, *If this is very early summer up here, I would not want to see winter.*

Bringer, however, blessed us with untroubled weather. We encountered no storms or fierce winds. There was wind, to be sure, and it often pushed the water into steep, white-capped hills, but never really threatened us. My confidence grew with every passing hour.

Then, early one morning, we saw the fog.

Seeming to rise out of the ocean as we sailed, the great, gray wall stretched as far as we could see in either direction. I told the Brothers that there was probably a current under that massive cloud because it seemed too still and dense to be temporary. The fog lay between us and The Bleak Shoals, so there was no way to avoid it.

I offered the Brothers a choice: we could continue on and push our way through it, or turn back to Norwall Island.

After a brief meeting out of my hearing, Brother Gerome told me they wished to continue come what may, but that since this voyage was their idea, the final decision belonged to me. I was the one who had to return single-handed, after all.

I should have turned back. Common sense said to turn back.

But I wanted to see what was ahead. Ignorant youthfulness again, I suppose.

I stayed on course.

Everyone aboard was quiet as we approached the cloud during the day, watching it grow higher and higher. Every hum of the wind in the lines, every flutter of the heavy sail, every complaining timber seemed twice as loud as usual. I don't remember anyone eating anything all that day.

In late afternoon, I remember very clearly, my lord, we slid down the back of a long wave into the fog, and into dead calm. We bobbed for a few minutes, and then sat utterly still. All the sounds of the ship silenced. Our sea legs flexed automatically against waves that were not there. The boat was moving, however, but without a breath of wind in the sails.

I admit that I was frightened. I felt desperate. I took a look at the starjack and felt more than saw that we were at least moving in the direction of The Bleak Shoals. The compass wheel within the starjack stayed true, but without the sky our exact location would be unknown unless the fog lifted. The current could very well sweep us right past our destination. I realized I might have to take a guess at which point to break out the oars in an attempt to row us free.

The only certainty I felt at that moment was that I could not make my way back single-handedly. I could not return home against this current. The thought made me ill with fear and regret. I tortured myself with thoughts of how much anguish I would cause my family, and, if Father ever discovered what had happened, how deeply disappointed in me he would be. He trusted me to do what I said I would do, and I had not.

Brother Gerome saw how disturbed I was and did his best to console me, but out of anger at myself, I grew sharp with him, which only added to my self-criticism. I was miserable.

Brother Enoch was catching some strange, dense fish with glossy black bands in addition to batfish, which we hadn't brought in before. Batfish is delicious, but we were wary of the other, smelling and tasting it cautiously. It too was delicious, and made no one sick. I thought to myself that if we were being swept to our deaths, at least we would go well fed.

The silence was unnerving. The usual sigh and chatter of the sea was gone. The boat made only the barest whisper as the current carried us with it. No birds cried, no fish jumped and splashed or cut the waves as they playfully raced beside us. The only sound was the murmuring of prayers from the Brothers.

I had never felt more alone in my life.

When night came, it came with the suddenness of a snuffed lantern flame. First the fog seemed to grow a little sootier, and then it was completely dark. All of us on board were watchful, apprehensive, and no one slept that night.

At some point, we heard the sound of some great beast breaching. It snorted and explosively vented, after which was a sound like falling rain. The thick, metallic smell of the fog briefly gave way to a strong, fishy odor. Whatever it was did this twice, then submerged again, leaving behind a silence even louder than that into which it arose.

Dawn seemed to come days later, but when it did, showing itself only as a whitening of the fog, I felt like I was breathing again. I checked the starjack often; we were still close to being on course. Brother Gerome asked me what I planned to do if the fog did not lift, and I told him my plan to start rowing when I thought we were in the vicinity of The Bleak Shoals, but that it would only be, literally, a stab in the dark. He offered that the Brothers would then turn their prayers to helping the plan succeed.

Despite the tension, or perhaps because of it, we were hungry, and ate hard bread and some of Brother Enoch's black striped fish. Our water supply was still holding out well, which comforted me, because one can survive much longer without food than without water.

A few hours after our meal, a most astonishing thing occurred.

Ahead of us, we heard a very faint splashing and what sounded like mumbling voices. Thinking our ears were deceiving us, we looked at each other to confirm that we all heard it. We stared into the fog toward the sound, straining to see through the shifting gloom. The splashes and voices stopped. Then, like a vision in a dream, the shape of a small, low-sided boat appeared. It was more round than elliptical, and in it sat three men holding fishing lines. They were motionless and blurred by the cloud, but we could see dark faces turned toward us and even darker eyes fixed on ours. They appeared to be bulky men, but I think it was because they wore skin suits with the fur on the inside, for the cord stitching showed clearly. On their heads were round, wide-brimmed hats with droplets of water falling from their edges . . .

"*Hala*," I said, but was so startled it came out as a croak. "*Hala!*" I then shouted. They said nothing, and slowly disappeared back into the mist.

We were shaken by this, and wondered whether, if those people fished this strange current, then perhaps others might be out here too. But where did they come from? Was there land nearby, within the fog? What land? Were we in danger of suddenly running aground? Or were we closer to The Bleak Shoals than I thought we were? Brother Gerome unrolled Brother Moutin's map, and we pored over it, pointing at where we thought we were. If the fishermen had come from land, then it was not on the map, because The Bleak Shoals were still some ways ahead. Or perhaps they were very intrepid seamen and traveled far, but from what we briefly saw of their boat, they were not equipped for a long voyage.

Brother Gerome became concerned with the notion that we

might collide with another such boat. He rummaged around below decks and returned with a bell, which he tied to the prow and swung with a thin line. From then on, the Brothers took turns sitting on the foredeck periodically tugging the line to ring the bell.

On the third day there appeared the first fogbow I had ever seen. It emerged gradually ahead of us, a magnificent, broad-banded arch of unimaginably intense color. We were sailing directly underneath it, and were so enthralled by its vividness and size that we were shocked to find ourselves suddenly bouncing on a choppy sea. It was as if the current simply dove under the surface. Behind us was the towering fog with its enormous bow arching like the mouth of a cave, but everywhere else around us was blue-black water and sunlight with lumbering clouds above. The cold, sharp breeze slapped us awake, and we withdrew into our hoods. I checked the starjack and adjusted our heading directly toward The Bleak Shoals.

The sense of relief aboard our boat was palpable. The Brothers were animated and smiling now that they were again on their way to their destination, and I was grateful that I didn't have to enter that current to return. I would be going home again after all.

The fog and its brilliant bow slowly receded from sight. Brother Enoch tended his fishing lines diligently, but was catching nothing. The wind was cold and strong, and we moved at a good pace over the waves. A couple of the Brothers became seasick again, and clutched the gunwales in misery.

I cannot say for sure when we heard it, but it was on that same day, and it was a sound that seemed to slowly emerge from the wind. It began as a hiss, and grew into a sigh and rattling roar, like the breathing of a giant. On the horizon I could see a thin ribbon of white.

"There they are," I remember saying, feeling both relief and anxiety. We were approaching something about which I knew nothing. The Brothers, too, were anxious, no doubt wondering what they were getting into by choosing this place as their new home. Several of them began chanting softly.

The Bleak Shoals rose as a black band along the horizon with a froth of churning water at its edge. The sound we heard was that of the sea washing back and forth over a seemingly endless beach of fist-sized, smooth black rocks. Waves were breaking in two places: once ahead of us and again at the shore, meaning that I had either a reef or sandbar to cross before landing. Our boat was a shallow-bottomed, short-keeled craft that carried no dinghy to ferry us in from an offshore anchorage. It was meant to ride like a bottle on the sea and be beached near land.

I worked a course just beyond the outermost waves, straining my eyes to find an approach that might allow me to single hand my way back out again. A few miles north, at a point where I could faintly see the vague lump of more substantial land joining the shoal, I saw calmer water. That was where we smoothly breached the reef. Between waves, I saw the shadow of blunt spikes like dragon's teeth rising from the sandy bottom far below.

Ahead, there was not a tree or cliff or any other sign of shelter to be seen other than a low hill with what appeared to be a cave mouth beneath it. This shoal was bleak indeed, and loud with the clatter of rolling rocks.

"Here, Brothers?" I asked. "Are you sure?"

With pale faces and solemn nods, they assented. I felt in the depth of my stomach that I would be leaving them to their deaths. It was sunless and cold, and it was late spring. What would come later, I didn't want to imagine.

"Last chance," I yelled over the wind and roar of stones. "I can still get us out of here, take us to Norwall Island."

"Here will do, Son Benjamin," Brother Gerome smiled. "The One will favor us here."

And so I beached us in the most sheltered place I could find, a short distance south of the hill. With the help of the Brothers, I anchored our boat as securely as I could among the moving stones, digging down through them to find some semblance of earth. With great effort, we crossed over the rocks to a beach of coarse sand, which in fact was more moraine than sand, but at least we could walk on it without stumbling and turning our ankles.

As the Brothers hunched against the wind and gloomily appraised their new surroundings, I looked into the cave beneath the hill. It was surprisingly large and sloped slightly upwards into pitch darkness. I entered a little farther, feeling firm flat ground under my boots. The roar outside subsided. There was no sound from within the cave, no flutter and squeak of bats or sign of other life at all. The cave smelled of dampness, but not of seawater, meaning tides and storms did not enter it. Because the interior was out of the wind, it felt surprisingly warm.

This was a great stroke of fortune for the Brothers.

We spent the rest of the afternoon carrying the most essential stores—food, water, and the Brothers' scrolls—from the boat to the cave, where we piled it near the entrance for them to sort out later. I unloaded what gear and clothing I needed for a few days, and brought in the starjack for a good cleaning before the return trip. Then Brother Gerome and I lit candles and explored the rest of the cave, which did not take long, but revealed another surprise. The smooth floor continued upward for another fifty paces or so, where it tapered to an end just beyond a small, flat area. We heard a soft tinkling sound, and found a natural stone basin into which water dripped from the roof just above it. I dipped a finger into it, and tasted sweet, fresh water.

"Brother Gerome," I said. "The One favors you quite a lot, it seems. This is fresh water, and enough to serve you all, if you are careful with it."

So, the Brothers had water, shelter with plenty of room for all of them (though it could not be called what my mother or Marya might describe as comfortable or cozy), and a fisherman in their number to help gather food. I felt a tension release within me. I could leave them here with a clear conscience.

Therefore, my thoughts turned to how I would make my escape from The Bleak Shoals. I walked along the sand, studying the water and wave patterns. Tides would be the same here as in most places, and judging from the location of the incoming waves to the tide line in the rocks, I should be able to go out in the early afternoon a few days later, with a great deal of luck and a gift from the wind. If the Brothers were properly situated by then, I would attempt it.

The daylight slowly left us. When the Brothers gathered outside the cave and began their haunting evening chant, I clambered up the hillside onto the turf above. The ground was firm and covered with a tough, thin, knee-high grass I could not identify. The wind had dropped to a sharp breeze. The plain on which I was standing stretched endlessly to the north and west.

In the dimming silver light, the grasses obeyed the wind, and pools of purple shadow came and went among them. The sky was an infinite, broken, black and gray presence, seeming to lower to just above the startlingly white waves breaking offshore. The rocks murmured and chattered. I felt a tremendous surge of joy, knowing that at that moment I was looking at the most desolate and beautiful place I would ever see in my life.

The storm came just before dawn.

I sensed it long before it arrived. As the Brothers and I slept in the cave, all of us burrowed into our habits, I felt a tingling against my cheeks and woke instantly. The rocks were silent. Time seemed to hover, and I knew what was happening. I fought the urge to rush outside and race to get on the boat, but did move closer to the cave entrance.

As the wind slowly rose to a furious wail and the sea erupted into thunderous blows against our little beach, I watched foam nibble at the sand just beyond our hole in the ground. Brother Gerome joined me and sat with a comforting hand on my shoulder. Both of us watched and waited for the ocean to find us, to burst into the cave and tear us away.

It did not. As the storm passed over us, a sick, weak light was left behind. I stepped out into the buffeting wind. Brother Gerome followed me down the wet sand to our anchorage.

The boat was gone. Only a few timbers remained of it, dark splinters tapping against the rocks in the retreating sea. Farther out among the breakers, I saw the top of our mast rocking madly near the reef. Brother Gerome turned without a word and left me there.

Guilt overcame me again, the certainty that my family would be saddened, disappointed and above all aggrieved by my vanishing. Shame and loss forced tears down my cheeks.

Whether because of ignorant choices or recklessness or arrogance or just foolishness, I was now a penitent too.

Chapter Three

BENJA

I was as dejected as I have ever been during the first few days after the storm. I wallowed in self-pity, morosely sitting for hours on the sand near the cave or slowly exploring the site of the splintered boat, picking up pieces of wood and turning them in my hands before tossing them aside. I repeatedly conjured up visions of Father, Mother and Marya and others I had known in Riversend, telling myself I would never see them again.

The Brothers indulged me by quietly going about their various tasks and leaving me alone. At some point one of them, a Brother whom I had never before heard speak and whose name I never knew, shook my shoulder and sternly said something that irritated me at the time, but that has become one of the rules guiding my life:

"Never waste time encouraging sadness, Son Benjamin. It will come often enough on its own."

Even Brother Gerome made me angry by trying to be helpful. He suggested that perhaps beginning to learn The Follower's Scrolls would comfort me. While I would not be able to pen my own copy, I could learn by tracing the words of one of theirs with my finger. I recall thinking hotly, *Will tracing Assantic words build me a boat?* but fortunately I did not speak my thoughts or I would be too embarrassed to even mention it here, my lord.

In the end, what broke this pitiful spell was Father. As I was envisioning his face, I heard him say, "Persevere, and an answer will come."

Of course. Persevere and an answer will come. Is there any stronger foundation for hope than that thought? My job was to persevere, not grieve. My purpose was to make the best of my situation until I could find a way to change it.

I awakened to The Bleak Shoals and a community of stranded men.

While I had been sulking, the Brothers had been organizing. They established sleeping spaces along the walls marked with their belongings, leaving a wide aisle to the water basin. With an iciness deep in my stomach, I noticed that they had also made one for me.

Next was the dining area, which was no more than a place where they set their bowls and cups and a bucket of seawater in which to rinse them. After that, the largest area nearest the cave entrance was their meeting and praying place. Just outside the entrance was a large fire pit, a space scooped out of the sand and bordered by stones. Wood from the demolished boat was piled alongside.

Brother Enoch had coiled and stored all the fishing line and fabricated simple, small nets from line he wasn't using for hooks. Usually alone but sometimes assisted by another Brother, he was most often found at the water's edge searching for bait, casting out weighted lines, or cleaning his infrequent catches.

I found Brother Tom in the grassy plain above the beach marking out gardens. He would plant cabbage, squash and bean seeds he had packed for the new colony. He was cutting the grass close to the ground with a small sickle and carefully laying it out in bundles. I asked him what it was, and he said it was called finger grass. It has a strong, interlocking root system that holds the soil in place and protects the plant from being torn up by the wind. The grass it-self is hardy and almost magically flexible. To demonstrate, Brother Tom, with obvious delight, took a strand and quickly tied a series of knots, pulling firmly each time. The grass didn't break.

"I will weave it into mats and covers," he said. "And it's also wonderful fire fuel, so I'll weave it into tapers, too. We can also use it to cook with, if it's bundled correctly."

I offered to help him clear the grass stubble from the gardens, and he told me he would not be doing that. He believed that the grasses, having no nerves as we do, did not feel pain when cut, but that tearing up the roots caused pain to the earth. His cabbages, beans and squash would grow among the grass roots, each helping the other. Under his care, they would both survive and thrive. Even though it meant much more attention and labor on his part to do things this way, he said, it was work that would please The One.

I took the knotted strand of finger grass and pulled it in oppo-site directions. It held. An exciting vision took shape in my mind. Could my answer come so soon?

"Brother Tom," I said. "Would this be strong enough to make a small boat?"

The smile slowly receded from his face, and was replaced by a look of unhappiness.

"Rain water keeps finger grass alive. Seawater kills it, I'm sor-ry, Son Benjamin."

He saw that I was not entirely convinced.

"Bring that along," he said. "I'll show you."

We descended the dune and he led me into the cave, then on to the bucket of seawater in the dining area. I was told to hold the grass strand under the surface, which I did. By five breaths the strand wilted and paled. By ten breaths it simply dissolved in my fingers. Here was irrefutable proof. Oddly enough, I wasn't overwhelmed with disappointment. I simply thought that this was not the answer for me, not yet. Another would come in time.

I threw my efforts into helping the Brothers where I could. While I was helping Brother Tom clear garden spaces and punching holes in the ground with a planter's dowel for the seeds, other Brothers were painstakingly scooping out their sleeping hollows in the cave. They scraped up some earth onto a blanket, and then carried it outside to bank up against the fire pit walls. When my work in the garden was done, I helped Brother Gerome dig the latrine trench farther down the beach. Once it was dug, we piled the black stones up into a low, windward wall along it for privacy and some degree of shelter. After that was done, I helped Brother Tom and several others weave the mats for their sleeping hollows and place mats for their dining hall. In all these things, we made ten, because I had a sleeping hollow and mats, too. They did not yet know I had other plans.

The Brothers did their work slowly and very deliberately, because the work was their penance. They did things the hard way, by hand, whenever they could. After a few days my own hands grew stronger and harder, and though the muscles in my back and arms were sore most of the time, they gradually adapted to the labor.

It took two weeks to make all the preparations. By the time we were finished, we had a well-ordered little commune. It made me happy to look at it, knowing that I had helped, because it seemed to me that the Brothers had a kind of distracted helplessness about them. None of them were young any more, and they were all preoccupied with their prayers and chants.

During that time and our time on the sea, I had learned the words to their evening chant, and had begun joining my voice with theirs as the light faded away each day. The words, the deep intonations around me along with the resonance of my own voice in my chest gave me a deep sense of security and peace. Where earlier

I had looked forward to hearing the evening chant, I now looked forward to being part of the ritual.

But afterward, while the Brothers prepared the tapers for reading their scrolls before going to sleep, I went up into the grass above the cave to sit for a few moments in the chilly evening breeze, watching the last sliver of light close down along the horizon. There was a restless sound in the wash of the waves onto the shore, and the rattle of the rocks as the waves returned home.

I would not be staying with the Brothers. I was satisfied that they were secure. It was time for me to go as I had planned. But if I could not leave by boat, I would see where the bending grasses led.

Brother Gerome was concerned when I first told him what I wanted to do, but nodded his assent. He offered to have one of the Brothers accompany me, but I respectfully told him I was going alone.

On the morning of the first day I left, the Brothers helped me pack food and water for four days into a woven grass basket they had quickly made for me, one that I could carry on my back. Using the starjack, my plan was to go due west to the other side of the shoal from where we were now, then travel south as far as my supplies allowed to see what was there. I would return with any news that could help the Brothers before going north.

Brother Gerome then presented me with three things. One was a walking stick Brother Tom had whittled down from a long piece of boat wood. The second was Brother Moutin's long dagger that I could use for defense, and for cutting and eating food. It has been at my side to this very day, Your Highness, and has served me well.

Then he gave me this, which I have also carried since then. It is a flat piece of one of the black rocks from the beach with an Assantic word carved into it. Do you see it? The word, Brother Gerome told me, as closely as he could translate into our language, is "strength." But there is much in that word, he said. It contains the security that The One is with me every moment; that I don't need to fear anything on this earth; that I can endure anything that doesn't kill me; and that I can always keep going as long as I need to.

Can you make it out, King Harald? You would think the word would have faded away, worn smooth by now, after all these years of my fingers holding and rubbing this comforting stone. But the word has become more pronounced than ever, and the stone even blacker. Curious, isn't it?

Thus armed, I set off. The day was customarily dismal, with low clouds and periodic rain showers, but my habit and hood kept me warm and dry. The ground was even, so walking was easy. I saw no sign of life, not even a bird, nor heard anything other than the wind and the slowly fading susurrus of the stones behind me. Once I looked back, and saw that even the track of my own passing was erased from the grass by the swirling breeze.

Before long I was enveloped by silence. While the feeling was blissful after being in the close company of others for so long, it was also unnerving. With no sun to follow and no trail behind me, it was easy to imagine being stuck alone in that ocean of grass forever. Without the starjack, I could easily have wandered in circles until I dropped.

I continued on, absorbed by a shifting range of thoughts as I mechanically marched along, but still alert for any changes in the smell, feel or sound of the wind. One hour? Two? More? I have no idea. But with a suddenness that stopped me in mid-step, the grass came to an end.

A brown sand beach sloped away, a soft, wide strand that slipped beneath quietly lapping, utterly calm waters. Between this beach and my boots in the grass was a swath of flat, partially submerged flat rocks as far as I could see in both directions. Recalling the map I had seen in Brother Gerome's hands on the boat, I guessed that I was at the edge of a vast gulf. Ceremonially striking my walking stick into the ground, I named the water Marya Sound.

I sat on the edge of the grass, and had some bread and water, studying the wind-wrinkled sea ahead. The contrast was remarkable, and I pictured the fierce currents ramming against the rocky, windward side of the shoal, then rushing around it somewhere to the south, leaving this placid, protected sound in its wake. The message was clear: somewhere south was the end of the shoal, and somewhere north was a cove where a main body of land curved out.

After I rested, I gathered a number of the flat, wide stones and piled them up into a cairn as high as my waist. My intent was to walk south along the beach to find the end of the shoal, then come back to this spot, this cairn, in a few days before returning to the cave.

I set off along the water's edge, noticing the shadows and flashes of fish and the peering eyes of crabs and bottom walkers looking back at me. Brother Enoch would have a much easier and more successful time of it here, I thought. The shoals seemed far less bleak.

I walked for the rest of that day accompanied only by the wind, scudding clouds and a few jumping fish far from shore. As evening fell, I scooped out a comfortable place for my back in the sand against the rise beyond the flat rocks and ate my supper of bread, dried fish, and water. I hummed the evening chant as the light faded, and cocooned in my warm robes, fell deeply asleep.

By midmorning the next day, I came to the end of the shoal. I heard the sound of waves ahead and the water in the sound became choppier. The sun broke free and scattered its light across the sea like countless brilliant coins. My beach ended in the ocean, and where it disappeared was marked by a magnificent grove of giant, black standing stones covered with glistening, bright orange star-fish. It was a lovely, wind-tossed place, and I rested there for a long while. With a smile at my presumptuousness, I struck the sand with my walking stick and named it Starfish Point.

Much later, as I rose to start making my way back, I remember turning my face in the direction of Riversend, now so impossibly far away. Whether in greeting or farewell I do not know, but I lifted my hand and waved.

* * *

It took me a while to find the best flat rock to suit my needs, but I did find it.

On the way to Starfish Point and back, I thought about the best way to help the Brothers and still explore more of the shoal. If Brother Enoch were to fish the calm side and return to the cave, he would need a path to follow. My simply walking through the grass wasn't clear enough, and I could not leave him the starjack. My solution may sound like a fool's plan, my lord, but it worked.

Before crossing the shoal along roughly the same starjack line I used to reach the spot where I built the cairn, I found a wide, flat rock and trussed it with rope I had in my pack. Then I tied a long, single length around my waist and dragged the rock behind me. I'd seen no rocks such as these on the ocean side, so it had to be done on my return walk.

The rock wasn't too heavy to pull, but heavy and rough enough to scrape a clear trail wider than a man straight across The Bleak Shoals. From then on, I guessed, any foot traffic would maintain it.

When I reached the commune, I was met with a truly peculiar sight.

All the Brothers were scattered about among the black rocks.

They appeared to stoop, pick up a rock, cradle it close in intent study, and then gently put it back where they had found it. I sat in the sand beside the cave entrance watching them for quite a long time before anyone saw me.

Brother Tom told me what they were doing. He said they were each scratching one word from The Follower's Scrolls on each smooth stone. They would keep doing this all day, every day until either all the stones were marked or the entire Follower's Scrolls had been transcribed. With a bright shine in his eyes and a big smile, he looked up and down the beach and presumed that they would never run out of writing material.

"But why?" I asked.

His answer was simply, "Each word is every word, Son Benjamin. And every stone is a soul."

I was left to figure out that every rock represented someone, somewhere, and the Brothers were blessing all with the wisdom of the scrolls. They were out to save everyone, whether they were known or unknown to them, in the name of The One.

"This is our work," Brother Tom said. "This is what we came here to do. We would have done the same on Norwall Island. This is what we will do until we die."

I admired their dedication, but it certainly wasn't work I wanted to do, nor was it mine to do. My work was to protect them as best I could, and to save myself as well.

Toward evening, I sat down with Brothers Enoch and Gerome and told them everything I had seen and found. Brother Enoch was excited by the prospect of more productive fishing, though he was not unaware of the irony that he also had to transport the larger catch much, much farther than he did now. He turned his thoughts to how he would do this, and we decided to make the trek when he had a workable answer to test, and he could familiarize himself with the trail and its distance.

For the next day or so I helped out where I could, working in the gardens, bundling tapers and gathering what firewood I could find. One afternoon Brother Enoch found me and led me to see his solution. It was a good one indeed. He had fastened a series of three large baskets to two long poles, curved at one end like sled runners, which ended in a sort of harness he could slip over his head. When he demonstrated it, I saw that the poles were perfectly adjusted to his height and the last basket cleared the ground by just a hand's width, distributing the weight away from him to the ends of the poles. The harness allowed him to comfortably pull the whole contraption.

"Where did you find all this?" I asked.

"A couple of us had already woven the baskets. One can never have too many baskets, you know, to put things in. The poles come from pieces of strake I found on the beach."

He was so eager to try it out that we made plans to make our way to the sound the next morning. I asked if he wanted to take another Brother along as an apprentice, and he shook his head.

"The Brothers must do their work. This is my work. I will do this alone."

We must have made quite a sight the next day, Brother Enoch hauling his sledge and I hauling my flat rock back to the place where I found it. The trail was easy to follow, and the walking easy.

Several hours later we arrived at Marya Sound under a low, dark sky. The waves wore white caps, and a cold wind gusted around us. I don't think Brother Enoch could have been happier. His sledge had held up well, and he was quickly organizing his fishing gear. I sat down at the edge of the grass to watch.

He used chunks of dried fish for bait, affixing them to iron hooks he'd brought with him from Islingia. He had also fashioned a basketful of finger grass bobbers, which held the line near the surface for a few moments before they melted and allowed the line to drift deeper down. It was an effective measure, because he was soon pulling in fish.

As he cleaned the first of his catch and piled the entrails on a rock beside him, something remarkable happened.

Seemingly arising from the sea itself, birds arrived. Their feathers were shimmering black and blue, and their eyes were as yellow as sunlight. They made no sound except for the whisper of their wings. It struck me then that they were the first birds we had seen on the shoal, or animals, either, for that matter, not even mice. Perhaps their absence was part of the overwhelming bleakness of the place. They quickly snatched up Brother Enoch's cleanings, but lingered above us waiting for more. When the offal was gone, the birds vanished too, and I cannot to this day tell you where they went. Although I watched them scatter, they simply grew smaller and disappeared.

"Why do you suppose we haven't seen them before, Brother Enoch?" I asked.

He guessed that it must have been because on the other side he threw the cleanings into the receding waves as he went. Or perhaps it was too windy on that beach.

"Regardless, Son Benjamin, this is becoming an interesting bit of ground, it seems to me."

He fished for another couple of hours, and the birds came and went in their silent way, and when Brother Enoch filled all his baskets, it was time to return to the cave.

This time I walked back carrying nothing more than the rope to which I had trussed my scoring rock, while Brother Enoch pulled his basket sled, apparently with little more effort than he exerted on the first passage.

We did not speak. Brother Enoch was content to be quiet, and I was making plans for the next exploration. This one would be far longer and less certain, so I had to organize with more thoughtfulness.

I was mentally sorting out the things I would need to fit into my backpack when I was utterly distracted, because as we waded through that undulating lake of grass, the clouds above suddenly fragmented and great shafts of silver light streamed down. They danced ahead of our two small, trudging forms like towering, playful spirits, darting this way and that, now here and then there, leading the way.

Brother Enoch and I left together one morning, he to go fishing on the sound side and I to go north from the trail's end. I was freighted down with all the food and water as I could carry, simple fishing gear, a sparking wheel and bundle of tapers for fire and light, and my rolled up shelter cloth lashed to the top of my pack. Brother Gerome's inscribed stone was in my pocket, and the dagger was at my side. I felt the familiar mixture of fear and excitement in the pit of my stomach.

All the Brothers, even the ones to whom I had never spoken a word, filed by to wish me well with muttered blessings, shy smiles and bowed heads. Brothers Tom and Gerome were last, and each clasped my shoulders and affectionately touched their cheeks to mine before hurrying away to their beach of unsaved souls.

The pangs of parting stayed with me for a while, but grew fainter with every step I took. As usual, clouds tumbled overhead and wind rippled our cloaks. I was pleased to see that the path was already worn clear, and would stay that way for some time.

I had grown fond of Brother Enoch. His good humor and patience were comforting. Thus, leaving him was more difficult than to leaving the others. After reciting a traveler's prayer on my behalf, he too embraced me and wished me good fortune until we once again looked into each other's eyes.

My last glimpse of him was that of a distant, frocked figure with one leg slightly lifted behind him as he cast his line into the water. I saw in it a singleness of purpose carried out with an almost childlike joy. I cherish that image, for that truly was the man.

*   *   *

The way north was much as it was in the opposite direction, in the company of lapping water, jumping fish, and occasional thumps of gusting wind. The sand beneath my boots, flat rocks farther up the beachside, and whispering grass stretched on unchanged hour after hour. I stopped to eat and rest for a while, and moved on again. In the evening I set up my shelter cloth over my hiking stick, chanted the evening prayer, and slept soundly.

On the afternoon of the third day, I saw the Roanfish surprisingly close to shore and moving parallel with it. Mostly to hear a voice, even my own, I shouted, "Hala, Bringer! Where are you taking me now?"

It gave me an inscrutable glance with one great, round eye and disappeared.

On the fifth day I saw a smudge that seemed to rise out of the beach ahead, a smudge that soon stretched out into the sea like a dark cloud line. The mainland I had seen on the map and from offshore lay before me. My first concern by then was for water; I had been sparingly drinking what I carried because I saw no other source of it along the way. If I could not find fresh water within the next couple of days, I would have to turn back with what I had left.

The closer I got to the grassland ahead, the higher it rose. I realized I was approaching a plateau that protected a cove with its high, sloping walls of rock and sand. Most curiously, it seemed that part of the grassland had settled on the water itself, and by the time I arrived I realized that what I saw was a vast swath of tall dun stalks tipped with rough green cobs standing majestically in the shallows. To my right was a faint path in the sand that led to a small cave halfway up the slope. It was a glorious, quiet place, and as was my custom there, I struck the ground and named it Carpenter's Cove.

I set down my pack and waded a few steps into the water. I broke off the tip of a plant and saw that the growth resembled a dense cluster of small nuts, so I rubbed them loose and ate them. The flavor was delicious, hearty and filling, though somewhat bitter. As I chewed, I remembered the taste from my days as a pilot in Riversend. This was sea wheat, which only flourished in cold climates. I guessed that its bitterness was because it wasn't yet ripe. Though the air here often turned icy and raw, it was still early summer.

I visited the cave next, because it represented shelter above the reach of storm waters. It wasn't very large—the daylight dimly reached its furthermost wall—but it was deep enough to protect me from the wind and rain. I sat for a moment to look out across the cove, and heard the faint, marvelous sound of dripping water.

Following the slow, clock-like drips, I discovered a cleft in the wall wide enough for me to pass through sideways. Feeling my father's critical gaze to use some of the common sense I was born with, I retrieved and lit a taper before going in. I found the water easily; it dripped from the ceiling near the cleft and fell into the sand below. It was sweet, and I was greatly relieved. Moving the light, I saw that the space was not quite large enough to inhabit, but could offer a little more protection from a direct wind.

All in all, it was a very fortunate find, and I silently thanked the Brothers for any part they might have had in it. I hauled my pack into the cave, spread out my shelter cloth and roughly settled in. I drank the last of one of my remaining containers of water and set the empty vessel under the drip behind the wall. After a quick meal, I went back to the beach and fixed my location on the starjack.

I rested in my snug little hollow for the remainder of the day, feeling secure and content as I watched the clouds tumble past until they were lost in the looming darkness, and softly chanted my evening prayer.

* * *

I met Umjuno the next day on the immense steppe beyond the cove.

I had packed lightly for a daylong walk. The early morning was, as most were in that land, very chilly, but as I pressed on through the coarse, knee-high grass, a hint of warmth came to the air, even though the sun would not show itself. Instead, great bruised white clouds rose up from the horizon and lumbered lazily overhead.

It seemed a remarkably empty plain. The wind was too stiff for there to be flying insects, and I saw no birds or small animals scurrying out of my way. There were no trees or shrubs to break the endless rippling prairie.

Near midday I suddenly found myself standing on a path worn into the earth. It was fairly wide, rough, and didn't appear to have been recently used. The ground was pocked with timeworn impressions of hooves the size of my hand, and the trail snaked away from north to west. This was the first sign of animal life I had seen so far, and seemed to be the migration path of some herding beast. The cloven prints reminded me of deer tracks, but were larger and broader.

With my dagger I cut a large circle of grass to mark the spot at which I should turn back to the cave. My starjack would lead me the rest of the way. Then I set off to see where the tracks led.

An hour or so later I noticed an unmoving dark shape far

ahead. It looked like a black rock, and was certainly not an animal. Intrigued, I marched on, keeping it in my sight.

As I drew closer and closer, I realized with a profound shock that it was a human form, one that had seen me long before I saw it and was watching me approach. A man about my height stood relaxed and still, his hands covering the butt of a spear, its point on the ground. He wore a black skin vest, fur covered trousers and skin boots. His hair was ink black and a brilliant white smile showed against shiny dark skin. He raised a hand and shouted, "*Hala!*" Then he patted his chest. "Umjuno!" Pointing toward the west he said "Tulak!" Nodding vigorously, the smile never wavering, he repeated himself.

I patted my own chest. "Benjamin!" I yelled back. "Benjamin!"

He laughed and stamped one boot on the ground. Pointing at me he said, "Benja!" then pointed past me. "Min! *Hala* Benja Min!"

I had heard the word Tulak before but could not remember where. I knew, however, that he was telling me his name and that his people were the Tulak. Which meant he thought my people were the Min. There was no profit in trying to correct him. To him, I would be Benja.

"*Hala* Umjuno Tulak!" I called back, raising my hand and smiling.

He laughed and stamped his foot down again. Then he started to turn away, pointing at me and waving his arm to follow him. He waved several more times, then made an eating motion, and waved again, nodding his head.

There was really no way to refuse his invitation, and I did not, even though it almost surely meant not being able to return to the cove until the following day. With my heart pounding, I followed.

Umjuno was a deceptively fast walker, so I had to quicken my step to stay within a few yards of him. He did not use his spear as a walking stick, but rather carried it on his shoulder as if prepared to hurl it at any moment. I was glad for my own walking stick because the dirt path was uneven and often rocky, but Umjuno never faltered or slowed.

The sky ahead was bright, and I smelled water long before we reached the source. Clouds of the mysterious birds I had seen on the shoal appeared and swirled and disappeared above the plain. Umjuno stopped and turned to me with his bright smile, pointing ahead.

"Tulak," he said, and then something that sounded like "Modo."

As I drew abreast of him, I was met with a breathtaking sight. Before and below me lay a lake, but one so large it looked more like an inland sea. The still water that stretched out of sight in every direction was pale green with a thick band of tan rushes along its edge. On the shore was an encampment of several dozen domed huts. Farther on a herd of shaggy bovine animals grazed in the grass.

A group of men were working in water up to their chests, dragging a dark net toward a small beach. Some women and children were bundling rushes. Others carried baskets toward the gathering of huts. One by one they stopped what they were doing to look up at us.

Umjuno slapped me on the back and strode down the slope toward the lake with me in tow. As we drew closer to his people, I saw that they were all smiling too.

"Benja!" he shouted to them while pointing at me. "Min!"

Those nearest us nodded and repeated my new name. A couple of children, showing no hesitancy or fear at all, rushed up and began tugging on my cloak, feeling its coarse fabric while one child stooped down and lifted the bottom of it up to get a closer look at my boots.

Umjuno walked up to a woman only a little bit shorter than he was, laid down his spear, interlocked his fingers over the top of her head and rested his forehead upon hers. She also locked her fingers over his black hair. They remained in this pose for several seconds, and I thought it a very touching show of affection.

When they separated, he said something to the woman and she walked toward one of the huts. Umjuno pointed at my cloak and pantomimed that I should take it off if I was going to help them fish in the water. I was surprised, but not the least bit insulted because his ever-present smile was so ingenuous. The woman returned carrying a skin vest like the one Umjuno wore, something that looked like a wineskin and a woven tray of long, gray, wrinkled strips of dried fish. It was the most unappealing fare I'd ever set eyes on.

Umjuno pantomimed that I should take off my hooded Brotherhood cloak, and both he and the small gathering around me seemed very interested to see what I was wearing underneath it. I removed the cloak, and they all appeared a bit disappointed that I wore a light tunic and woolen trousers which, truth be told, were growing a bit thin with wear.

I had not been out of my robe very often. The cold air seeped through my shirt instantly, raising goose bumps on my arms. Umjuno held out the skin vest and motioned for me to put it on. I started to pull it over my other shirt and Umjuno motioned for me to take that off too. The vest was soft and snug and warmed my torso instantly. I smiled and nodded and there were smiles and nodding heads from the Tulaks around me. Umjuno was holding my habit and an inspiration struck me: I signaled that he should put it on himself. He looked a little uncertain, but the others urged him on.

He let it drop over him, held out his arms and, encouraged by the crowd, began to striding around with long, exaggerated steps. All of them roared with laughter.

When he tired of this, Umjuno stood before me again and clapped his hands together, then pointed at the fish. I took a breath, broke off a piece and before I had time to think about it, popped it into my mouth. I was pleasantly surprised. The meat was very succulent for something that looked and felt like a dried fillet. I helped myself to seconds, which met with great approval from the Tulaks. Umjuno then held out the bladder and pointed at the hairy cows in the distance. Milk I was familiar with, so I took a mouthful.

It was horrible. I barely was able to keep from spewing it out. I managed to get it down, then shuddered violently.

This was apparently one of the funniest things the Tulak had ever seen. They laughed until they were breathless, wiping their eyes and slapping their thighs. Umjuno was reeling around in my cloak, unable to even stand up straight. One young man mimicked me, widening his eyes and puffing out his cheeks, which made the others laugh even harder. They were infectious. I was laughing too.

When things calmed down, Umjuno took off my robe and had the woman he had greeted earlier take it to the hut. He motioned me to the edge of the water and pointed to the group working the net, nodding and making gathering gestures with his arms. It wasn't done as a command, but rather as an invitation, which I appreciated.

The water was freezing and of course soaked my pants, but the vest kept my torso warm and dry, preventing me from getting chilled to the core. The group had stopped to watch me approach. They were all smiling. One handed me an edge of the net, and I realized with a shock that I was looking at a very lovely young girl about my age. She too wore one of the skin vests and her hair was cut as short as that of the men. Through the water I could see that they all wore tight fitting pants of the same material as the vests. I guessed they could work in that water all day and never get cold.

They walked away from the shore very slowly, floating the net on top of the water. Soon I found myself wading through a huge pool of the long, thin fish I had just eaten. They barely moved away from my legs.

The girl pointed at them and said, "*Gobu.*"

We lowered an edge of the net down among them, and then pulled it back to shore. Once there, a group of women and children plucked the fish from the net and tossed them onto a large mat, where they lay gasping, but hardly moving.

We repeated this several times until the fish on the mat had formed a sizable pile. Then everyone left the water and formed a circle around the mat. The girl I had been working beside pulled me gently into the circle and held my hand in hers. Someone grasped my other hand, and we all bowed our heads. After a few moments everyone tipped back their head and raised their arms in what seemed obvious to me to be some sort of thanksgiving or honoring ceremony.

Then everyone knelt on the ground and pulled forth snow-white knives from sheaths at their waists. Cleaning the fish was very easy, requiring only one cut down their length. All the innards came out neatly in a tight string. This was then thrown into the air for the yellow-eyed birds, which seemed to always be hovering above us even though we could not see or hear them. Cleaned and washed, the fish looked like bundles of kindling wood.

The girl recruited me to carry one corner of the mat and four of us hauled the fish to one of the huts. Inside was a stack of racks on which to lay our catch.

When the daylight started to weaken, the work stopped. Children scurried around with bundles of sticks, and I learned then that the Tulak had an ingenious method for starting fires: they brought it with them. One of the men carried out what looked like large tureens, inside of which were glowing, hot stones. They lit their equivalent of tapers from them, and the stones were sealed up again. I never learned where the stones came from or what kept them hot.

There were two fire circles, one large one and a smaller one a few paces away. Among the Tulak, it seemed that everyone shared every duty. Two men were cooking something at the smaller circle, and I loitered at the large one watching a couple of women settle a large, thin stone bowl over the coals and fill it with water. A tall woman approached us holding a child on one hip while steadying a wide woven tray on her head. They were chattering to each other as one lifted the tray down. It was covered with *Gobu*, the fish we had been netting. The woman who had brought the tray out walked over to me and shoved the child into my arms with scarcely a glance and without interrupting her conversation. The women broke up the fish and dropped it into the water, which was soon steaming. Ground up grasses and slivers of something red were added. I glanced down at the child, whose dark round eyes were staring up at me curiously, completely unafraid. When the chowder was complete, the child's mother wiped her hands on her fur trousers and retrieved it from me, still talking to the others.

Umjuno appeared carrying my habit and shirt, which I put on after returning his vest. He wandered off again. My own robe felt good to me, as my pants were still wet, but my legs warmed quickly under cover. The men at the other fire brought over a big pot filled with what looked like spongy bread and set it down beside the chowder. The group assembled. I was handed a long handled bone spoon, and everyone started dipping in.

The chowder was delicious, and the hot food felt as if it flowed through my limbs. Someone pressed a chunk of the bread into my hand and I cautiously took a bite. It had a strange texture and unidentifiable taste, as if it was made of the fluff from cattails. I didn't care for it much, but it was tolerable when eaten with the soup.

When the food was gone, the community bowl was carried away and washed in the lake, but the group remained around the low burning fire. Umjuno started talking as if addressing the flames, but he was telling a story and everyone listened quietly, their eyes also on the fire. He talked for some time in a lilting, gentle voice that lulled me half to sleep.

Then I heard, "Benja? Benja."

Umjuno mimed that I should talk now. Slowly at first, I told them where I came from and how I got to these waters. I saw that not understanding a word I said made no difference to them. They listened, staring into the fire, as if they did understand. I'm afraid I went on for a while, but none of the Tulak seemed to care. When I fell silent, Umjuno rose to his feet, a signal that it was bedtime for everyone else, too.

He motioned for me to go to the huts, but I shook my head and signaled that I preferred to sleep outside by the fire. He smiled and nodded. A young man appeared shortly thereafter and handed me my back basket. A quick search showed that everything was still there, including three containers of water, which meant I would not have to drink their vile cow's milk any more. I used the pack for a pillow, wishing I'd brought along my shelter cloth.

The camp was utterly still within minutes. I watched the fire for a while, but before too long I fell soundly asleep.

* * *

The next day after breakfast, Umjuno ushered me to the cattle herd. Each of us carried two of the big bladders. As we walked, Umjuno casually pointed to various things and said the Tulak word for them. I tried a few of them, but if I mispronounced it, he repeated the word only once before moving on to the next one. I gave up quickly. He didn't seem to mind.

The cows were short and squat, coated with long, coarse fur that smelled quite rank. They had only one teat on their swollen udders, and Umjuno showed me how to affix the bladder to it. They were milked by squeezing the udder between the thumbs and fingers. The first time I tried it the beast swung its short-horned head around and gave me such a baleful look I was prepared to run. But I eventually filled both my skins to Umjuno's satisfaction.

Before we went back to the camp, Umjuno pointed to the dagger at my waist. I withdrew it and handed it to him. He turned it over in his hands, studied the carving on its handle and hefted it a few times before testing the edge with his thumb. After he handed it back to me, he offered me his own: a slightly longer, wider-bladed version of the gutting knives we had used on the fish. This one was pure white and delicately etched. What sort of bone it was I never found out, but it was both extraordinarily sharp and light to hold. I had seen no iron items among the Tulak and understood why Umjuno seemed unimpressed by my stark, heavy dagger. His was the most beautiful knife I had ever seen.

Later that day I found myself cutting rushes beside the girl I had fished with the day before. Her name, she told me, was Natana. We exchanged smiles and nods of the head, after which she looked me up and down and pointed at my habit, shaking her head and wrinkling her nose. I laughed and took it off, mostly because it was easier to do this type of work in shirtsleeves. The way these plants were harvested was to grab a bunch of them just below the seed crowns and then slice through the stems at water level. The bunch was then taken to shore and laid down, where another person beat the stalks with a flat wooden paddle. The seed crown was cut off and stripped into a basket. The stalks were laid out to dry for weaving into more trays, mats and baskets.

I enjoyed the work and was only scolded once. I gathered up a bundle of the rushes in my arms instead of grasping the ends and carrying them upright to be beaten with the paddles, which I assumed was to soften them enough to weave. Natana shook her head fiercely and said what sounded like "*irriku*" several times while miming the right way to do it. I nodded that I understood, and carried them the way she wanted me to.

Following a simple midday meal of some sort of earthy tasting root vegetable and nuts, the names of which Unjuno spoke in a bored tone while he ate. I was set to work learning how to weave the rushes into usable items. Thus I passed the afternoon sitting cross-legged with a mixed group of Tulaks, weaving, knotting, and listening to them talk to each other.

While the experience was pleasantly novel, I wondered why they were including me in all this, unless they assumed that I would be staying with them indefinitely. The notion seemed logical in one way, as I was a stranger wandering alone in the endless plain, but illogical in another way, because Umjuno did acknowledge that I was from another tribe he called the Min, to which, ultimately, I would return.

In the end, I decided that this was simply an embracing form of hospitality. Where my own society made a show of welcoming others as guests, deferring to and serving them, the Tulak welcomed their visitors as no less or more than one of their own. This seemed to me a much warmer way to demonstrate trust, tolerance and respect.

Nonetheless, I had begun making plans to return to the Brothers within the next few days to share what I had found. There was no mutually beneficial reason to introduce the Tulak to the Brothers even if it were possible, so my plans involved only myself. As I sat clumsily and badly weaving a small square mat, I was again mentally preparing for a long walk.

As the day started to fade and the hot stone urns were brought out, I signaled to Umjuno that I wanted to show him something. I brought my sparking wheel, gathered together some dry grass, and sparked and blew and sparked and blew until the small pile caught, smoked, and finally caught fire. I pushed the pile toward the fuel in the fire pit and puffed it into life. I stood up, proudly watching my little struggling fire.

Umjuno watched all this with curiosity and smiled at me. Then he stuck a taper into the urn, withdrew a flame and had the cooking fire crackling into hot coals within a few seconds. My sparking wheel immediately went back into my back basket and I sat quietly watching my hosts go about their business.

While we were eating, Umjuno talked again, but this time it didn't appear to be a story. Those around him nodded, smiled and became excited about whatever he was saying. A couple of the younger men trotted off to one of the huts. They returned with a big bundle of rushes and a long stick. They tied the rushes around the stick with vine cords and stuck it into the ground a few feet from the fire circle.

The young men then brought out two short flutes and sat down again. Umjuno wiped his hands on his vest and rose. He stood before the barrel shaped rush pillar and withdrew two of the exquisite white knives. He held them so that the dull sides of the blades rested against his forearms.

The onlookers began to hum a single note while the flutes played a wonderful, drifting melody. Umjuno danced in fluid movements that looked to me like the motions of cats and snakes. The blades periodically snapped out against the rush effigy as he passed it, sometimes crouching, sometimes turning quickly around, sometimes sweeping his arms as if clearing away smoke. Deep slashes appeared as if by magic and the loose ends of severed rushes lifted up.

It was such a graceful series of motions, smooth and unhurried, but astonishingly lethal. I had never seen anything like it before. Umjuno finished and passed the knives to Natana, who commenced her own nimble dance, which included more quick steps and darting motions than Umjuno's, but had the same effect on the rushes. When she was done, I had to restrain myself from cheering.

Then, in a moment of horror I'll never forget, she smiled slyly and brought the knives to me.

The music never stopped, but everyone watched me with obvious amusement. I held the knives the way I had seen them do it, and taking a deep breath tried to emulate some of their movements. They laughed, of course, but I kept moving, experimenting with flicking the knife blades out like serpent's fangs. Soon I was perspiring and breathing heavily. I stopped and everyone applauded, laughing and chattering. When I returned the knives to Umjuno, I thanked him by pressing my palms together and bowing, and tried to indicate that I wanted to learn more, that I wanted to know how to do this.

Umjuno nodded.

As I said earlier, I had planned to leave the following morning, but ended up staying another four days. Between chores and meals, in which I was always involved and given a variety of tasks, Umjuno taught me a number of moves and techniques such as thrusting the knives behind me when I turned or springing from a crouch while holding both knives out at arm's length with the blades pointed downward. It seemed my muscles were always sore, but the motions were so satisfying, I practiced on my own each day until long after dark. Umjuno seemed surprised and pleased that I was so taken with this exercise.

On the fourth day I told myself that I had to take leave of the Tulaks the next morning. I had been gone from the Brothers too long already, and they were probably starting to fret. After the last lesson, I awkwardly pantomimed to Umjuno that I was going back, and thanked him. He swept his arm to include the whole encampment, pointed at my chest and said, "modo," which I took to mean his "home," and that I could consider it mine too. I thanked him again.

That afternoon I was again cutting and gathering rushes. I was imagining a series of movements to practice later and instead of grasping the tops of a bunch of rushes, I embraced them as I cut them. I took a few steps on shore and felt a sharp, burning pain in my forearm. I dropped the reeds and yelped. Natana was instantly by my side, but was intent on the rushes I had dropped, spreading them out with one of the paddles, and then pounding the ground with it. Umjuno appeared in front of me and looked at my arm. Before I could protest, he deftly cut a cross in my skin and squeezed so that blood welled up and dripped to the ground.

That was when I found out what an *irriku* is.

It is an emerald green spider no larger than a thumbnail. The Tulak were obviously afraid of it, and my stomach grew queasy seeing their concern for me. Umjuno let me bleed for a few moments, his dark face grim, and wrapped my arm with strips of some brown cloth-like material that looked like tree bark. Natana angrily swatted my shoulder and made a choking motion, which meant to grab the rushes at the top. Then she clasped her hands over my head and pressed her forehead against mine.

Weakness came within an hour. My limbs gradually grew heavy as iron. My breathing became shallower. It's hard to describe, Your Highness, the otherworldliness of these things. My mind was as clear as it had been all along, but as the symptoms worsened, my body felt detached from me. I was led to a hut where a pallet had been laid out for me. My habit was removed and I was covered with a soft, skin blanket. Even though the inside of the hut was gloomy, my vision filled with sparkling lights. I remember looking all around the inside of the hut, feeling a deep sense of dread. I remember very little of the following days and nights.

I was caught in an eternity of sleep and near sleep and recurring images. Over and over I saw the Brothers pass before me to wish me well; over and over I saw myself walking toward a herd of bright green Irrikus at pasture, their glittering eyes watching me approach; over and over I saw Natana or Umjuno or Umjuno's wife lifting my head to feed me or give me something to drink or wash my chest and face with cool water. Although I thrashed and tried to get away, I could not escape seeing the same things a thousand times.

Then the fog gradually began to clear and I slowly returned to my body and my senses. I held up an arm to see that it was shockingly thin. When I felt my face, my fingers traced hollow cheeks. Natana and Umjuno were smiling again at last, and the images stopped coming at night, but time still dragged like an anchor. Ever so slowly I gained strength and was able to sit up, then stand, then take a few steps. Finally the day came when Umjuno half carried me outside for the first time since I had been bitten.

I was appalled to see that the summer was nearly gone. The air was sharp; the rushes had begun to curl and turn brown; flags of vapor streamed form the nostrils of the cattle.

I was younger then. I recovered quickly, driven by a fierce need to return to the Brothers, to let them see that I was alive. As I took longer and longer walks, the Tulaks were busy packing up the camp. Umjuno signed that they would be moving on far to the west soon. By pointing at the lake, knocking on a rock and spreading his hands apart, he told me that the lake would freeze all the way to the bottom. There could be no staying here through the coming winter. He wanted me to go with them.

I shook my head no, and pointed back toward the shoal. He nodded sadly, pointed to each of us and mimed that he would walk with me to the point at which we'd met.

Day by day the camp diminished into rolls and baskets and

bundles the cattle would haul or carry. Day by day I built more endurance. Though the Tulak milk was hideous stuff to drink, it was a powerful medicine.

The hut in which I had lain for so long was the last to be taken down, rolled up and tied. My own basket was packed, too. I said my goodbyes among the Tulak, some of whom, including Natana, pressed their foreheads against mine. They almost all spoke to me but I didn't understand what they said.

Umjuno and I set off along the trail, striding up the low slope back onto the steppe. The grass was now brittle and brown. We walked in silence for some time until Umjuno suddenly stopped. He pointed at the ground and then ahead. This was where he had been standing when I arrived.

From his fur jacket he withdrew two white knives encased in plain, woven sheaths. Through some inventive pantomiming and chattering he communicated that they were made while I was under the fever. His brilliant smile returned and he pointed to some delicate glyphs on the handle of one knife handle and pointed at me. The glyphs on the other handle represented him. He proudly held them out for me to take.

Still smiling and nodding, he pointed down the trail toward the shoal.

"*Ke modo*, Benja," he said, as we touched foreheads. "*Ke a Min.*"

I started walking, and glanced back once or twice. He hadn't moved. He stood there just as he had when I first saw him, like a dark rock. I studied the trail to see if any trace of my circle was left, even though the starjack would lead me back regardless. I finally located it, a faint shape in the longer grass.

Relieved, I turned and raised my hand as high as I could into the blustering wind, but the dark rock was gone.

Chapter Four

WULFKIN

It took most of the day to reach the cove because I had to rest often. Between the weight of the distended basket on my back and my weakened body, I grew lightheaded more easily than before and needed to catch my breath. I had not needed all the provisions in my pack for the return to the cove, but did need it to prepare for the long walk back to the cave on the shoal.

A great source of strength was imagining being back among the Brothers. Winter would be coming in force within a month or two and I had no idea what it would bring, other than to guess that it would be fierce. The thought of the company of the Brothers, the shelter of the cave and even my little sleeping depression within it were very appealing to me then. It would be a tolerable way to weather the coldest months. Perhaps the answer I awaited would come in the spring.

My little hollow in the hillside was just as I had left it. I did some housekeeping by shaking out my shelter cloth, setting a new container under the water drips behind the rock wall and organizing the contents of my pack, paying special attention to my invaluable starjack.

I had enough dried fish to eat well for several days, but I

would have to gather more food to make it all the way back to the Brothers' commune, five days away. The sea wheat outside my door had ripened in the time I'd been gone, and was now tall and golden. When I rubbed the ends of the stalks into my palm, the nuggets tasted more like small, tender beans than hard nuts. They had a rich, satisfying flavor, and the crop at my disposal was large enough to feed a village for a year.

For the next three days I ate often, drank as much water as I could hold and slept whenever I felt tired. I fished with good results, and this was the bulk of my diet for those three days for I was saving the dried *Gobu* fish for the journey back. I also gathered sea wheat, both to eat and to store for the trip.

I regained the strength I had lost, and felt confident that it was time to move on. On the evening of the third day, I packed to leave. My basket pack was heavy and distended, but so well woven that though it sagged, it showed no signs of weakness.

I was so eager to be on my way that I lay with one hand on the pack and barely slept at all. I was up, fed and had the pack on my back by the time the darkness paled to blue-gray.

The journey was unremarkable, except for one exceptional day when a storm rolled over the shoal from Marya Sound. Lightning forked into the sea and thunder shook the ground. Rain gushed over me, and I was forced to cocoon myself against the bank in my shelter cloth. By late afternoon, a sharp, clean breeze picked up and the Marya Sound glowed a brilliant rosy pink as I traveled on.

Your Highness, try to imagine the joy I felt when at last I saw the faintest dark speck on the horizon of the beach, a tiny dot that could only mean Brother Enoch was fishing. A dozen steps more and I saw the wink of a few yellow-eyed birds in the air. And as I marched on, my eyes fixed on that spot, you cannot comprehend the dread that crept into my heart and belly as I realized that the spot was not moving, was not upright.

Brother Enoch had become entangled in his line as he was backing up to haul in a fish, and fell. The line was still wrapped around his ankles and around his hand, and the bones of the fish rocked gently in the wavelets. Brother Enoch's head had broken on the rocks; a flag of faded blood lay beside him. He had perished a long time before, and the birds had done their work on him; he was little more than a skull with a few tufts of hair that lifted in the breeze.

I felt sadness, but no repulsion. To my mind, Brother Enoch was no longer there. These bones were just bones. The Brother Enoch I knew was on another beach I could not see.

As I gathered his habit tightly around his frame and closed the hood over his ruined face, I recited the evening prayer in Assantic.

"As you trust in us to dwell alone in your darkened house without fear or faltering, we trust in you to return us to the peace and safety with your light. So it will be."

Not very fitting perhaps, but it was all I knew.

The fish baskets on his sled were empty, so I did not have to cut them loose. I untangled Brother Enoch's hands and leg from the line, freed it from the fish in the shallows, and spooled it around my hand before tucking it into my pocket. I laid his surprisingly light body on the sled along with my pack. The trail was still visible, although mostly grown over again. I decided it would be clear enough to follow without the starjack.

I sat on the bank in the silence, drinking water and eating some dried fish while I wondered how Brother Enoch's departure would affect the others. I was certain that they probably had concluded that something was wrong, yet no one had come to find him. Were they so preoccupied with etching stones that they didn't notice his absence or couldn't take the time to cross the shoal? That would be devotion I could not understand.

After my long walk to Carpenter's Cove and back, crossing the shoal was an easy matter, even hauling the sled behind me.

I suppose my mind already knew what I would find, based on what I knew of the Brothers and reviewing memories of them in the boat and along the shoal. I could see them accepting their dwindling food as a matter of their fate and faith, and growing weaker every day as they stumbled among the rocks, trying to save as many souls as possible. Certainly they knew in their hearts that neither Brother Enoch nor I would be coming back, and that this was the way it was meant to be.

Having such thoughts along the way was why I was not surprised to find the commune silent and Brother Tom's garden gone back to grass. The wind and thumping surf exaggerated the loneliness I felt as I surveyed the beach and the cave.

Brother Gerome's desiccated frame rested in a sitting position outside the cave entrance, his scroll in his skeletal fingers. Inside, the others were lying neatly in their sleeping hollows, their hands holding their scrolls in their chests. All their hoods had been sewn closed over their faces.

I placed Brother Enoch in his bed beside them. Then I brought Brother Gerome in to join them, laying his scroll on top of him. I found the needle and cord close by and sewed his hood shut, as well. There was one hollow left beside him, the one meant for me.

I sat outside pondering what to do next. Winter was nearer now, and I could not spend it sheltered in a grave. The only option I had was to make the trek back to Carpenter's Cove and try to survive the winter there. If I could do that, then I would await Umjuno's return to the lake in the spring, and travel with him from then on to see where it led me.

There was no food in the commune, so I would have to fish and make what I had left last as long as possible. The thought of going back all that way, especially with uncertain weather coming, made me feel both weary and afraid. I had to resist the thought, the reality, that everyone was gone. Everyone. I was utterly alone.

Persevere. I heard my father's voice again, and clutched the smooth stone Brother Gerome had given me. They both gave me strength.

I spent the remainder of the day walling up the entrance to the cave with black rocks, including all the etched stones I could find. Let someone else decipher them. In the meantime, prayers would guard the Brothers.

I spent the night outside the cave next to a good, rumbling fire. I slept in short naps, and stared into the fire or at the night sky when I was awake. A fog moved in before daylight, dampening the stones and the outside of my habit. When there was enough light to see, I gathered my pack and walking stick and once again began the long, last hike to Carpenter's Cove.

At the fishing site, I acknowledged the red stain on the rock with a short bow, and turned north. My tracks were still visible in the sand, but grew fainter the farther I walked. Day followed day with little but darkness to separate them. I ate sparingly and made my plans for using what good weather was left for harvesting sea wheat. I hoped the sound did not freeze over during the winter, but vowed to fish through ice holes if it did. There was little choice. If my water trickle in the little cave froze too, the fish and melted ice would be my only source of fluid.

Once again, on the fifth day, the distant smudge of the bluff lifted slowly from the beach, and then the sea. I was relieved to see it. I was exhausted, downhearted and hungry. I kept my gaze on that part of the smudge where the hollow would be and kept planting one foot in front of the other.

My weariness was probably why it took so long for the spot

of white at the far end of the sea wheat field to register in my mind. I was far enough away for it to be very small, like a seagull on a far shore. My focus shifted from the bluff straight ahead of me to the pinpoint of white much farther away. Another hour of walking brought it clearer to my straining eyes.

Furled sails.

There was a ship out there.

Both apprehension and excitement leapt up in my chest. I had to consciously pace my steps to keep from trotting. By the time I reached the bluff, I saw a small boat leave the larger one, and it was coming my way.

I had no idea what to expect, so I decided to err on the side of suspicion. I set down my pack. The two bone knives Umjuno had given me were at my waist under my robes, reachable through openings in the tops of my side pockets. I drew them out and held them as Umjuno had taught me, with the dull sides of the blades back against my forearms. To burn off nervous energy as they approached, I paced back and forth along the beach.

There were four men in the boat. Two in particular caught my eye. One was tall, very lean, had long black hair and held a broadsword. The other was older, stocky and had a long beard. His hair was tied tight against his head, and a shoulder-length reddish white mare's tail swung in the wind behind him. He was smiling.

I continued to pace even as the prow of the boat scraped onto the beach. I was mentally rehearsing defensive and offensive moves, and my heart was pounding. After all, I was young and had never seriously fought anyone before.

The man with the broadsword stepped out of the boat, the wide blade resting on his shoulder. He regarded me warily.

"Du Kinish," he said over his shoulder. "I believe he means to gut the gang of us."

Du Kinish turned out to be the smiling, bearded man. He wore a half-sword at his waist, but did not reach for it as he came forward.

"Hala, Wulfkin. Calm yourself, there, son. We mean and bring you no harm, *yeh*? We're just farmers and coppersmiths and occasional sailors, not marauders. We've been watching you for some while, Wulfkin. It's not an ordinary day when one sees a holy man armed to the eyeballs out for a stroll in the middle of nowhere." He chuckled.

"My name is Benjamin," I replied, "and I did not expect to see a ship full of men in this cove before winter. Pardon my caution. You are Du Kinish?"

He nodded, his smile never wavering. "Kinish Ard's Son is my name. We use 'Du' to address all the elders. I have been quick enough to become an elder, as you can see." He chuckled. "And you are smart to be cautious, but you are no Benjamin. You are a Wulfkin, pacing, pacing, young, fierce and fanged, am I right, fellows? A Wulfkin?"

The others good-naturedly agreed.

"If that entertains you, then so be it," I said. "Where do you come from?"

"Gylgova," Kinish answered. "It lies up by...it's near..." he waved his hand impatiently past me to the east. "...over that way." His eyes rested on the knives in my hands. "Say now, what are those? Never seen weapons like them before."

"They're Tulak knives. They were a gift."

"Tulak? And gifts, you say? You traded with them? Hmm. You can use them then, can you?"

"Yes, I can use them," I said. "I lived with them for most of the summer."

Kinish leaned back in surprise. "Really, now? How interesting. We must talk about that later." He stroked his beard thoughtfully.

"You're quite a ferocious looking figure, Wulfkin. Quite. What on earth are you doing here? Are there others about somewhere?" His gaze drifted to the top of the bluff and then back to me.

I told him briefly about my guiding the Brothers here from Riversend, and that they died of starvation and I had just buried them.

Kinish leaned back in surprise again. "You mean to say you came here on *purpose*? My, my. I want to hear more about that, too."

I mentioned that the Brothers came here on purpose. I never meant to stay, but my boat was crushed in a storm. I told him about the mysterious fog bank, and that I had intended to stay clear of it on the return.

"Yes, yes, very wise of you. That's Ranulf's Slide, we call it," he said. "It's a wicked current, roams the ocean like a snake. You're lucky you didn't wind up on the other side of the world, Wulfkin. "He waved a hand at the beach and bluff and asked me what I planned on doing in this particular place. I told him I planned to survive the winter and rejoin the Tulak the following season.

"Not to doubt your abilities, my friend, but that would be an unlikely event. The winters are very hard here. And the *gracka* get hungry." My questioning look prompted him to keep speaking as he stirred the air with an upraised finger. "The birds? You've seen them? Yellow eyes? *Gracka*. They would find you, I'm afraid."

I asked him what they were doing here, then. Winter was quickly coming, so why were they in the cove? He said they were there to harvest several ship's holds of sea wheat, which they use to trade for beaten copper sheets in the southern lands. He said they visited several market ports every other year, and they were very rough places indeed.

"You look like a fighter," he said. He told me I could be very useful to him.

"I have never actually fought anyone," I admitted. "I've only battled straw bales and air."

He laughed loudly. "You would be quite remarkable if you were an experienced warrior at your age. I said you *look* like a fighter. That's my interest in you, Wulfkin." He waved his arm to include the men with him, who were all smiling now, and said, "Look at us! We are farmers and artisans, not fighters! We dress and rehearse and play roles so we won't stand out among the real thieves and thugs in the south. They would take our heads along with our copper in an instant if they did not think we were more risk than reward." He laughed loudly and slapped his palms on his thighs. "We're actors, son. We're all very good actors. But you, you can wield those knives like a Tulak, you say. You need no special role, no training. What a precious gift that will be to us."

I was both amused and unsettled by this strange confession. It seemed like a very dangerous ruse to me, and told him so.

"I suppose so," he said, "but I think you'll find us very competent, and quite convincing if need be." He motioned toward my pack. "So, come along, Wulfkin. We have a lot of harvesting to do very quickly. We are late arriving this year. Young Snod here is a new father to twins, and we wanted to be sure they were safely among us before we left home."

Snod was the dark haired man with the broadsword. He smiled proudly and nodded. I suppose I must have hesitated, still trying to digest what I had been told, because Du Kinish then said, "Unless you prefer to stay here awhile longer?"

Once again, there was no choice. But at least I would not be among, as he said, marauders.

I returned Benja and Umjuno to their sheaths inside my habit, picked up my pack and stepped into the boat.

*   *   *

A mate named Porcee rowed us along the edge of the sea wheat field to the ship, and by the time we arrived it seemed that most of Kinish's crew were waiting along the spar deck railing. The boat was steadied fore and aft by Snod and another young fellow named Rogie, who was not much older than I. I followed Kinish aboard up a rope ladder.

I was introduced as a castaway who would be joining the crew on the voyage to the islands. The others were curious but very shy, and some were clearly suspicious of me. A short, feral-looking man of middle age sidled up to me and quietly said, "You're not going to preach at me all the time, are you? I hate people preaching at me." I told him what I told you, my lord; I am no holy man, and have no right to preach to anyone. He slipped away again.

Over the coming days and weeks I would get to know most of them as simple, hardworking men who had grown up together in the cottages and farms of Gylgova. The hamlet's main industry was metal craftwork, the making of ornate cups, plates, spoons and knives, decorative shields, jewelry and religious items. The area's copper ore resources were depleted long ago, so they were driven to the copper markets far south of their homeland. They did not like having to do that, but the Gylvga coppersmiths were renowned for their elegant work and superb quality. Such a distinction could not just be abandoned, nor could the heavy riches that came with it. In fact, several of the crew members, including Du Kinish himself, were very wealthy men.

Kinish told me I was actually in luck that year, because they were short two crew members—one had fallen ill at the last moment and another had broken his arm in a tree trimming accident—which meant I had an available hammock in the crew's quarters and there was even a little extra space around it. I was led below decks and left my pack in the hammock assigned to me.

"The next order of business," Kinish said when I went back on deck, "is to give your garments and you a good washing."

It turned out that they were obsessive about cleanliness, and even had bathing cubicles aboard, in which seawater was funneled from a large wooden tank through several layers of cheesecloth to strain out most of the salt. The captured salt was used in the galley and to scrub the deck.

Thus, I found myself in an unexpected near-paradise. I would work for it, of course, but I was clean and shaven, had clean clothes and I ate like royalty. Meat, bread, cheese, soup, wine—it was set before me every day. I could not imagine greater good fortune.

From dawn to twilight, they had me working in the galley, fetching water, brushing down the deck, helping with the harvesting and storing, greasing the chains and oarlocks and hinges and redistributing barrels in the hold. I did it all willingly and almost with joy. I was stronger than I had ever been before, and I was getting off The Bleak Shoals. I did not know where I was bound, but at least I would not be in that cold, implacable place much longer.

My evenings were mostly spent in the company of Du Kinish, Du Magram, the second officer, and a bottle of *spinrok,* a clear, strong liquor that I quickly learned to treat with great respect. They were endlessly interested in what stories I had to tell and pressed me for every detail. They told stories of their own, too, which I will relate later. Du Kinish often fondly mentioned his younger wife Leeni and their daughter, a precocious, wide-eyed child with superior intelligence. Her name was Abbe.

Kinish was also quite interested in my starjack, even though he had an instrument much like it aboard. Because of my familiarity with the starjack and skill in reading water, I was given the task of sharing navigational duties on the voyage south.

And that voyage was announced one late afternoon. Kinish was on deck, looking into a freshening wind that carried stray snowflakes into his hair and eyebrows. He suddenly and very loudly said, "We sail in the morning." This was the cue for everyone aboard to immediately begin making ready. Lamps were lit. Conversation lapsed. I was given quiet commands to do this and that or help here and there, while everyone else seemed to have a specific job to do. We worked until long after dark.

There was no comradely drinking and laughter that night. I was summoned by Kinish to the quarterdeck and his cabin, wherein he and second officer Magram outlined the voyage on a table-sized map. I, of course, had never been in those waters, and noticed with a pang the outline of the provinces and, on the coast, Riversend. We would pass far from them, around the far side of Welland, and travel south from there. On a map, however, home looked close and possible to reach. In reality, it was neither.

Our first resupply point was Port Char on Broom Island, a speck all by itself in the middle of the sea. I set the coordinates on my starjack and then went topside to reconcile our destination with the North Star. We were bound on a course under the eye of The Whirlpool constellation, the third point at which the starjack was set. My duties would be to back up Kinish's own reckoning, stand watch every other night, and be available all the time.

First, though, Kinish would take us west along the plateau's edge for three days to enter the Scimitar Current, which rushed south and west from the coast of that massive rock. I was too excited to sleep well, and so was on deck the morning when dawn rose to reveal the dark shape of the steppe sloping down to the sea. The air was warmer there, and I wondered if that was where Umjuno and the Tulak wintered, and if they had arrived there yet.

The sea birds were starting to stir, wheeling above our wake to feed on the minnows our passage churned to the surface. The smell of the water and feel of the breeze on my face exhilarated me.

Then Bringer surfaced to regard me with one huge eye for a long moment before submerging again. A couple of other crew members that happened to catch sight of the great, rare Roanfish pointed and chattered excitedly. I did not tell them that Bringer was a longtime companion, nearby, it seemed, since I left Riversend. His presence was reassuring.

As our ship slowly cleared the headland, the appearance of Bringer brought thoughts of the Brothers to mind. They would remain behind forever. I recalled what I could of their faces and voices. I imagined them lying in that dark, close cave and wondered if at the end they heard the voices of all the birds and animals in the world rising together in one glorious chorus, and they at last knew what they said.

Or if all they heard was silence.

Interlude

THE FIRST MEAL

DOGMAN'S REST

Dogman gradually returned from the ship and the shoal to the amphitheatre at Gravenwall. He blinked and looked up from middle distance. The perimeter of the arena was lined with standing and sitting soldiers, and the grassy hillsides beyond were now carpeted with listeners. They were all watching him.

Most of the day had gone. The yard lay completely in the shadow of the castle.

King Harald rose from his seat on the stage and nimbly trotted down the steps. As he advanced toward Dogman, he clapped his hands and the audience followed suit. Applause rose around Dogman to a soft roar that died away when Harald stopped in front of him.

"Bravo, Foreigner," Harald said. "You have earned the first meal of my little competition." He glanced at the table beside Dogman's seat. "Or the second, if you count the bread and cheese that were set out for you earlier. Of which you have eaten exactly nothing, I see."

Harald helped himself to both, and spoke as he chewed.

"Come. We'll have the table set for the two of us and find you a bed somewhere to spend the night."

Harald turned to the onlookers, who were standing now.

"Soldiers, return to your posts. All the rest of you, go home and tend to your children and your gardens and whatever else you do. Dogman deserves a rest. We will begin again tomorrow morning on the ninth chime." Harald seemed suddenly stricken by a thought, and turned to Dogman. "You do have more to tell?" It sounded less like a question than a command.

"Yes, sire," Dogman said, nodding slowly. "More to tell."

"The ninth bell, then," Harald shouted. "Good night."

Dogman picked up his habit and a soldier returned his pack.

"If you don't mind, we'll keep the sword and dagger awhile longer," Harald said. "It makes me nervous to have armed guests in my halls."

Dogman followed the king indoors, walking in the company of several guards. Harald led them into a spacious private dining room, not the banquet room as Dogman had expected. Its walls were cloaked in tapestries, banners, and shields. A blaze burned in the fireplace, and a long wooden table stretched under two chandeliers of burning candles. The room smelled of smoke and wood and leather. Dogman breathed it in deeply and sighed.

The two men rinsed their faces and hands over wide basins of water near the door, and toweled dry.

"Sit wherever you like, Dogman," Harald smiled. "Or Benjamin, or Wulfkin, or whomever you really are."

Wine was brought first, and Harald drained his cup and had it refilled before the servant even turned from the table.

"I commend you, Foreigner. This is a story that interests me. You are not only the first to receive supper here, you also hold a commanding lead in the possible possession of some very pretty land nearby. I'm quite pleased, because as I think I mentioned before, you have no idea of the tedium to which I have been subjected thus far. Stories of sprites with squeaky voices who live under toadstools, babies snatched up by eagles, grandfathers who fought valiantly in this or that great battle, the history of villages, and so forth. I have caught up on a lot of sleep since this event began. Frankly, I expected more from the whole thing, but to be fair, these are simple people living simple lives.

"But we have come a long way, you and I. A long way indeed. When you finish your tale, I will tell you mine. Would that suit you?"

"Very much so, Your Highness. I would love to hear it."

"Good, good. There will be no reason to rush. You most likely will be close by. We can pass the winter nights with wine and stories, the way winter nights are meant to be passed."

Food was brought in and a very rich table was set. Dogman was tired and ate slowly. He had paced through most of the telling, and unconsciously acted out the hauling of sails and the Tulak fighting moves and the burying of the Brothers as if he saw it all clearly before him.

Harald watched him thoughtfully.

"Tell me. Do you still have those Tulak knives?"

Dogman nodded. "I do."

"I should love to see them sometime."

Dogman stood, retrieved his pack, and sat down with it in his lap. He withdrew the two bone knives in their sheaths.

Harald smiled in surprise. "Well, well, look at this. Disarmament seems not to mean what I thought it did. I can name a guard or two who will be busy washing all the castle dishes tonight."

Dogman smiled in return. "They are very light and easy to overlook. It's not their fault."

Harald's eyes suddenly glittered. "In this castle, fault is what and where I say it is," he said quietly, and then softened. "May I?"

Dogman passed him the knives, handles first. Harald unsheathed both. He held them gently, tested their weight by bouncing them in the palms of his hands and studied the carvings on the handles carefully.

"This is you?" he smiled, holding out one bearing a triangle, a circle, and a rectangle over two short scratches, all bracketed by two rows of slender, gracefully curved vertical lines. "Your habit, the spider, a cow and the rushes?"

"Yes, that's me."

Harald smiled with admiration.

"They are remarkable. Quite remarkable. What treasures."

There was a silence. "Do you mean to keep them?"

Harald looked at Dogman and saw a different man than the one who had been wearily eating his supper. This one was alert and his gaze was hard. Harald felt a new respect for him that bordered on affection.

"No, Dogman, I don't steal memories. And I don't fear you, either."

He sheathed Benja and Umjuno and handed them back.

"You have no need to even mention threat, sire. I have no reason to think badly of you." Dogman slipped the knives back into his pack and set it down.

"Have you any other surprises in your bag, Dogman? Anything else I should know about?"

"Just my father's journal, written while I was gone. You'll hear from it at length tomorrow."

"Ah. A journal, you say? To help tell your story? Well, you certainly came prepared to stay awhile, didn't you?"

"Not really. I merely thought that if you elected to hear my tale, you might as well hear all of it."

Harald considered this, regarding Dogman thoughtfully for a moment before continuing brightly, "You know, I used to be good with a knife too, when I was a boy and a young man. I had experience in gutting and skinning animals from the forest where we lived. The same techniques also work exceptionally well on people, I discovered. And I also have a spider story for you, as a matter of fact. But we'll save that for another day. You must be tired, and the wine is making me sleepy."

They rose together. Harald clapped a hand on Dogman's shoulder.

"Good night, then, Foreigner, until tomorrow. A servant will take you to your room and bring you breakfast in the morning."

Harald strode out of the room, and true to his word, a servant silently came for him shortly afterward. He was led down a long, stone hallway through pools of torchlight and shown a small room intended, Dogman assumed, for another servant, perhaps even this one. The bed's head and foot each touched a wall.

He set down his pack, laid his habit over it, and stretched out on the straw mattress. He had certainly had less comfortable accommodations, so he sighed with contentment.

He closed his eyes and slipped into the comfortable rest that comes before sleep and dreams. His smile remained as his thoughts drifted, flying far away to alight on Bear Cape in the Province of Doves, and into the midst of anchored ships, the din of shouting men and nervous horses milling in a fog of dust, and the roil of shimmering color he imagined was converging there — the singular tumult of a gathering army.

Part Two

THE OVERSEER'S
DAUGHTER

Chapter One

NORWALL

Good morning, sire, and to all those present. If Your Highness agrees and if it does not compromise the integrity of your competition, I would like to turn this telling over to another for a short while. Be assured that it is all part of the same tale, but seen through different eyes.

The day I sailed with the Brotherhood, my father began writing a journal. His intention was to use it as a record of his plans for the treasure the Brotherhood left behind and of his dealings with the Riversend Town Council, on which he had occupied a seat for many years. But, as happens with most diaries and journals, it quickly became his confidante during those days, and later became his truest memory of them.

Here, then, is the record of Mister Carpenter of Riversend.

✳   ✳   ✳

Benjamin raised sail with his crew of seekers this morning, bound for Norwall. Watched until his craft cleared the headlands. He handled her well.

Mother is quite tight-lipped. She never approved of the idea. It will be awhile before she speaks more than one word at a time to me. Knowing Marya, she is as envious of her brother as she is fearful for him.

The rather raucous crowd dispersed quickly after Benjamin was out of sight. Marya and I returned to the shop to assess the contents of the Brothers' chest. I had secured it in my vault below two false bottoms for safekeeping. No one would ever find what I keep there unless they were told exactly where it is. And its contents would still remain recoverable even if the place burned down.

After two hours of separating coins, gems, strands and bands, we were still left with no idea of the collection's total worth, although it was certainly enough to transform Riversend.

What I will propose to the Council:

1. *A dedicated schoolhouse with two large classrooms, one each for the youngest and older students. The upstairs would become Riversend's first library, open to all in the town. We should accept all maps, drawings, logbooks, memoirs and fictions we are offered, in whatever language they are created. Perhaps we will be able to teach the more common foreign languages downstairs one day.*

   We would of course need at least two more teachers, who would be chosen by Mistress Nearly and the Riversend School Committee. I suggest that Mistress Nearly and the new teachers no longer be paid in goods but in coin. This would not only help invigorate our own economy but might also improve the quality of our candidates. For Mistress Nearly, such rewards would be just, and long overdue.

2. *Riversend would benefit from improving its waterfront commercial frontage. At present we have a tidy but rath-er ramshackle collection of stalls and shops. More uniform sizes and appearances for our sellers and services would*

be much more appealing and more secure against damage from foul weather.

3. *We should increase the number and skill of our lawmen. As Riversend looks and becomes more prosperous, its safety should increase as well. Care must be taken that while we want to appear far more well-policed, we must also feel welcoming to traders and crewmen.*

That will be ambitious enough for now.

Benjamin has been gone three days now. I am plotting his approximate course on a map in my shop. I have confidence in his abilities and in having fair weather for the coming month.

Nighttime seems to be best for making these entries. The candlelight and quiet are soothing. Mother pretends to sleep, but I know she will neither smile nor truly sleep until Benjamin is back at our table excitedly telling stories of his adventures.

Met with H. M. Twining today. He came by my shop, invited me to join him for a beaker at the Bung and Bollard. This put me on alert, the old saying goes, "Reach an agreement at the B & B, but seal it at the Rose and Thorn."

Sure enough, Master Twining had a suggestion to offer.

In his sometimes (but not always) delightfully long-winded way, he said that he found himself in need of a harbor pilot again. He himself had assumed these duties when Benjamin left, but had to apply himself to other matters requiring a Harbor Master's attention. Therefore, he would like Marya to serve as pilot until a permanent replacement could be found.

I immediately refused, of course. There wasn't any way I would allow her aboard some of the vessels that appeared in our waters.

He understood and agreed. What he proposed was that his son Micah serve as co-pilot. While Micah knew the harbor, too, he was not as quick to notice changes as Marya was, which is why Master Twining had not installed Micah as the interim pilot in the first place. Marya would make the decisions; Micah, with all his stone-faced bulk and strength, would be at her side to act as both assistant and deterrent. My daughter would be safe, and the ships safer, too.

Again I refused. The idea made me heartsick. I allowed my young son to ferry inexpert holy men to a far island, and now I was being asked to allow my young daughter to board foreign ships in the harbor? Mother would surely be unable to tolerate such a situation.

Master Twining nodded and said he understood completely, but I had never seen him more crestfallen and weary. He fell silent as we finished our beer, and remained silent as we returned to the shop, except for one brief encounter on the street walk with Mistress Lynch, the milliner's assistant. She drew up stiffly as we approached and snapped at me, "Mister Carpenter, I am forced to wonder what kind of father you are to jeopardize your own son for money."

Master Twining spoke up then, all right. He said, "Mistress Lynch, it was young Benjamin who offered his all for the good of Riversend. Should the opportunity arise, may I expect the same from you?"

Her cheeks turned rose red and she marched away. I commented to Master Twining that I thought his response was entertaining, but rather harsh.

He said, "Ah, the mistress of my house will no doubt burn my supper when she hears of that, but the boy is doing a remarkable thing, in my humble opinion."

By the time we reached my shop doorway, I had decided that I would assume the pilot's duties myself until Master Twining could permanently resolve the issue. He was delighted to hear this, and promised to find someone else as quickly as possible so as not to hamper my business any more than necessary, since my enterprise was also of great value and need to our fair town's fortunes, etcetera, etcetera. He then set off in a much brighter mood than when he arrived.

Later, I made the mistake of revealing this arrangement to Mother and Marya. Not a mistake, really, as there was no way to keep such a thing unnoticed. I saw the hot spark in Marya's eyes and braced for her objection.

She did not explode, however, as I expected. She did something much smarter. She quietly picked the request and my decision apart point by point, like a barrister. Was Benjamin deemed knowledgeable enough to pilot? Did he prove out his knowledge? Was she not given the same training at the same time by the same experienced mentor? Did her performance suffice, in my opinion? If her safety was the issue, did Micah's presence not count for anything? If there was confidence enough in Micah's physical power to merit his presence as a solution, then what was the reason for my not allowing her to serve as interim pilot?

She led me to my own gallows. I had to admit that her skill was not in question. It was simply the fact that she was a girl.

I was pinned by Marya's heated stare and Mother's implacable silence.

There was really no other choice to make. I told Marya that I would inform Master Twining in the morning that she would serve as Riversend's harbor pilot until another could be found.

Very lively Council meeting tonight.

For openers, I suggested that the chest of valuables be put into the care of the Town Council Committee and a trustworthy treasury committee be appointed. Marya and I had itemized the contents to the last coin, and upon transfer, the items should be counted once more against our list.

Mister Carver, the butcher, said that since none of them were present at the initial tallying, how did they know it was all there that was supposed to be there?

I told him that if he saw me with a fancy new hat and carriage he'd have his answer, wouldn't he?

The next round of discussions concerned securing the valuables. It was agreed that ironmongers be consulted for the acquisition of a vault.

I then presented my proposals for a schoolhouse and waterfront renovation. Much excited discussion followed. The school issue was tabled until the School Committee could be brought in. A number of suggestions and thoughts, all penned by the meeting secretary, concerned the waterfront renovation and corresponding increase in a peacekeeping force. One idea was to require a modest rental fee from vendors to help support the expansion of law enforcement. It was noted that vendors currently pay nothing, so why should they agree to start now? Mister Carver offered that payment of fees be voluntary; paying vendors could count on higher security and periodic cost-free improvements to their stalls, and those who refused to pay would be responsible for improving their own stalls, and if they were found lacking, then we should heavily fine the cheap numbskulls.

A motion was made to not call people names, as it would sound bad in the reading of the meeting minutes, to which the secretary said he did not write down name-calling anyway, so have at it.

It was then offered that a committee to monitor and oversee vendor stall compliance be formed, which would of course require the writing of a manual of standards with which to comply.

The group also decided to appoint a committee to study the issue of fees, including a list of ways the proposed improvements would increase individual income enough to warrant paying in the first place, but the members of that committee would be voted upon at the next meeting. It was unanimous, however, that the only certain member of all these committees so far was me.

According to my charts, Benjamin should be more than halfway to Norwall. The weather has remained benign.

I have a headache, and am going to bed.

Marya has brought in three ships in the past week. The first was The Crosswind, a frequent visitor to our port. I was told that Captain Knowles and our Marya had a spirited conversation while she was on board, and that he was delighted to see her in her present duties. He presented her with one of the small, gold ship's wheel shirt pins he awards to crew members who demonstrate exceptional effort. She accepted it graciously, but found the whole thing aggravatingly condescending and dropped the pin into a kitchen drawer as soon as she got home.

The other two were a packet boat from South Doves and a small, rude freighter requiring some service to its rudder. Those on board were a rough lot, but seem decent enough fellows. I was nonetheless relieved to have Marya and Micah safely on shore again. My confidence in their unique partnership grows by the hour. As for the rudder, I immediately hired and assigned a work gang to the task, under my direction.

Riversend is a busy place these days. That is good. It keeps our minds off other things.

My shop has become a sort of alternate council chamber.

First, Mister Gaines came by to tell me that the ironmongers happened to have a safe on hand with double locks requiring different keys so that two council members would have to be present to open it. The council officers were asking for my approval to procure it, which I uncomfortably gave, since they do not have to consult me at all.

Next came Mistress Billings, inviting me to the next school council meeting three days hence. She and the others had heard that I had some exciting things to discuss with them, and how much they looked forward to hearing my proposals. She never stopped smiling.

I have also been asked to accompany a small group that will survey the waterfront market district in order to begin a list of specific renovation measures to recommend. In addition, my help would be appreciated in drafting a manual of construction standards to assure uniform quality; these sessions would, for my convenience, take place in my shop at times of my choosing.

And arriving almost daily since word got out about the Brothers' treasure chest are members of the community requesting an astonishing variety of civic actions from upgrading boat slips to hanging flower baskets on the street signs.

To avoid making the same error twice, I have enlisted Marya to help me at those times when the baking is done and no ships need her attention. She helps me keep track of meetings and the status of activities, and greets whoever arrives unexpectedly. Marya is a confident, capable young woman who can anticipate what needs to be said or done and say or do it.

Sometimes I watch her and marvel that she is my daughter, until I remember that she isn't.

Mother is suffering. I know she keenly feels the loss of her family. It all happened to her so suddenly. Benjamin is at sea, Marya is fully occupied with other duties, and my time is in demand until late in the evening. I see her loneliness in the way she moves.

In quiet moments, Marya and I study the maps in the shop. Benjamin should be on Norwall and getting the Brothers settled in to meet their suicidal obligations. He should be restocking dried fish and storing water for the return trip. He should be re-rigging the boat for solo handling. He should be on his way within two days.

I tell Mother this, and she studies my face as if trying to remember who I am.

Time to catch up. Have been so tired at day's end, I have no will to keep up my journal.

The chest has been transferred. Safe delivered and installed, with much effort, in a corner of the council house. Misters Carver and Pounds elected keepers of the keys. The contents were tallied once again and compared to our original list with nothing found amiss. The coin will be spent first while the others are appraised. Coin alone will keep the council busy for some time.

The waterfront committee completed its survey. Many ideas came forth. In vigorous discussion now is the striking notion of putting all the vendor stations under one, long roof. Sharing common walls would make a much tidier appearance and allow most to increase their interior space. Proponents argue that such a plan would ease the idea of establishing fees and present a more prosperous image. Detractors contend that vendors would lose all their individuality and charm.

The school committee meeting went well. Mistresses Billings and Nearly expressed sincere gratitude to the Town Council for its thoughtfulness. It was suggested that because it was my suggestion, the proposed building be called "Carpenter Schoolhouse." Thanking them for their kindness, I said I thought not, because the school should belong to Riversend, not to me, and therefore should not have my name on it.

The school committee members, numbering only three, will begin looking for a suitable property forthwith.

Thankfully, the waterfront renovation manual of standards has been tabled until we decide just what it is we're standardizing.

Mother, Marya, and I grow more animated every day in anticipation of seeing Benjamin again. He should be home soon.

A ship came in from north of Storms today. Marya asked the captain if he had seen a boat bound in the same direction along the way. He had not. The weather in those waters has been calm for weeks, too, with fair winds for sailing.

The Sea of Caprice is vast, and the chances of seeing a small boat, even one on the same heading, are slim, particularly if one is not looking for it. Also, preparations on Norwall may have taken longer than expected. We all know these things, but each of us begins to feel uneasy nonetheless. We do not mention it.

The school planning has been a tonic to Mistress Nearly. She has color in her cheeks and moves with a vigor not seen before. Her transformation is so noticeable as to cause comment among the townspeople.

She busies herself with the applications of teacher candidates. The news of there being salaried positions available traveled quickly and elicited interest from some very qualified prospects. The children of Riversend cannot help but benefit.

The renovation committee has split along predictable lines: those favoring progress and those who want to hang on to the way things have always been done. The futurists outnumber the others, however, so the path is inevitable. There will be common roof construction, and there will be modest vendor fees. It's only a matter of time.

Benjamin is a week overdue. The weather still holds, but the shoulder season will begin soon to make a passage more unpredictable.

Many townspeople are also mindful of Benjamin. Day fishermen drop by my shop and lean inside to say, "No sign today," or, "Didn't see a boat," or, "Not a thing so far." Other friends take a sudden interest in the healthy benefits of daily walks to the lighthouse point, where they picnic and scan the horizon. Mother, Marya, and I are moved by their concern, but feel worry constrict us a little tighter with every passing day.

I imagine he's broken a leg and hasn't even left yet. Or perhaps he is trying to sail alone with a damaged rudder. Or he misjudged his landing and grounded the craft. Or he became ill.

I see all these possibilities and many others clearly in my mind. And with every grim "what if," I become angrier with myself for letting him attempt the voyage. His confidence infected me. My own judgment of his abilities lulled me. My pride in him clouded my thinking. Whatever the reason, this looks more and more like a very bad decision.

Rightly, Mother blames me too, though she also blames herself for not forcefully squelching the misadventure when she had the chance. Sometimes I look up during our silent suppers to catch her watching me coldly. I don't want to know what she is thinking.

Marya, on the other hand, has no second thoughts about Benja-

min going. Of course he should have. She would have gone, too, had anyone thought to ask. Her main concern now is not finding fault, but finding him.

And of course, she is right.

Two weeks late.

Marya asks anyone who has been on the water if they have seen anything, even flotsam. No one has. We go over and over the charts, discussing different possibilities, but arrive at no conclusion.

They have stopped asking me to council meetings, and members have stopped visiting my shop. In fact, to my knowledge, council meetings themselves have been postponed. Our worrying seems to affect them, too. Mother, Marya, and I try to hide our feelings, but do a poor job of it. The tension within us is almost crippling. We feel as if we are sleepwalking through the hours.

Sometimes I have to stop what I am doing and sit down. I have to drag air into my lungs. There is pressure in my chest. I am close to the point of taking some action, any action, if only to save myself.

Today brought an extraordinary occurrence I will never forget nor ever be able to repay.

A boat came into the harbor without announcement or need of Marya's guidance. It simply appeared offshore and slowly approached the docks, riding low on the water but pulling a shallow draft. I had never seen one of them before, but knew what it was.

I watched it pull up to the slip nearest my shop. A tall, tough-looking man with long hair and in need of shave hopped out. A second man sat in the stern regarding me impassively.

They were guardsmen from Bear Cape, at the far reaches of Doves, and their boat was Dove Arrow 3, a long, sleek wavecutter craft designed to knife through the water with astonishing speed. The three Dove Arrows and their crews were legendary for their relief and rescue missions to distressed vessels in the Rampal Strait and cape region.

The tall man extended his hand and introduced himself as Mister Lorr Burnside. In the boat was his nephew Rand, who nodded to me. Their superiors, who had heard of Benjamin's situation, had given them loan of the Dove Arrow 3 and some time off from their duties. This is exactly what Mister Burnside said next:

"Let's go look for your boy, Mister Carpenter."

Both men shared our table this evening, and sleep in Benjamin's room as I write. Their reticence borders on the laughable. As they spooned Mother's wonderful, rich fish stew into their mouths during supper, we asked innocent questions to encourage conversation and received replies with just the number of words required to form a sentence. An example: Marya asked what was the most extreme rescue they ever had to perform at sea. Lorr pondered for a second or two, answered, "That would be The Rum Cloud," and continued eating.

Speaking of Marya, she offers no resistance to being left out of this undertaking. Even she can see the impossibility of her coming along with three men in a very fast, cramped, open boat.

This one will be all business. Fine with me. The sooner we locate Benjamin, the better.

No more entries until I return.

I arrived home two days ago, exhausted and feeling much older than I am. Have since been resting most of the waking hours, but am unable to sleep at night. Lorr and Rand left for Bear Cape early this morning.

We made Norwall Island in three and a half days. The Dove Arrow seemed more like a flying fish than a boat, skimming over the water so fast it sometimes left the sea entirely for a second or two. The speed took its toll on each of us, but on me most of all. I felt battered and bruised, and my face was wind burned raw. Lorr and Rand are as tough as rope, but the journey wore them down, too.

We shared all tasks equally and slept as best we could in two-hour shifts. There was very little talk, mostly because it was so hard to be heard above the cracking of the sail and our weather shells as well as the drumming of the wind past our ears. You will never hear a complaint from me, however. What those men did for our family is incalculable.

Norwall is an ugly, black edifice with only one approachable side. When we entered calmer waters, we dropped sail and took turns at the oars. For half a day we floated parallel to the island, searching every bit of beach for a settlement or fire smoke or any sign of a ship. We saw none of them. We found a good, safe landing spot and took the Dove Arrow in to the rocky shore so we could do some exploring on foot. Our legs were wobbly and our ears still rang, but we went in separate directions, arranging to meet back at the boat by late day.

I followed the gravelly beach to the south, constantly shifting my gaze from the shoreline to the path ahead and then inland to the ragged, black rock wall. The grinding of my steps on the stones, the low thump of the wind pierced by the cries of swirling seabirds high above and the wash of the incoming surf seemed to me the loneliest chorus on earth.

I followed the beach until it ran out. Ahead were only wave-battered boulders at the foot of the towering cliffs. I returned to await the Burnsides, whom I saw approaching our meeting site from a distance, Lorr from the north and Rand from inland. None of us had seen anything, not even a splinter of wood.

Lorr said, "Mister Carpenter, they was never here."

I felt fear and desperation descend like a weight. Oddly enough, I did not think of Benjamin just then, but of Mother. In my mind, I clearly saw Mother's face, every crease and pore. Breaking her heart would truly break my own. I could not imagine what I would say to her, how I would console her. Every comfort would be refused, every excuse unheard. In a flash, I saw nothing throughout the remainder of my days but despair. Then, more oddly still, this bottomless sadness turned to bright hope in the next few seconds.

"*So you think they've sunk,*" *I said.*

"*All I said is they wasn't here,*" *Lorr responded.* "*Doesn't mean they're not somewhere else.*"

The notion stunned me. I had not considered that possibility. Might Benjamin have changed course? Might he have sailed the Brothers to another place?

"*Where else could he have gone, Mister Burnside?*"

He shrugged. "*I don't know the Sea of Caprice, sir,*" *he said.* "*Know parts of the Great Western, and all of the Strait, but not the Caprice. Too big and cold for me.*"

My overwhelming need to roll out the maps on my shop's big cutting table carried me through the voyage back to Riversend. Little was said among the three of us, but the quiet was welcome for it allowed me to think and plan and extend my plans into imagined scenarios, all of which ended with Benjamin back in our arms.

Even though we three were tired when we stepped ashore, we almost immediately made way to my shop. Mother and Marya greeted us at the dock with a small group of townspeople, all at first fearful of what we might say, and then dazed by what we did say. Our eagerness overshadowed the fact that we returned without either Benjamin or any idea of where he might be.

The conclusion that he had changed course was supported by logic, if nothing else. He was a skilled sailor. The weather had been calm. They had provisions enough for a long voyage. There was no sign that they had set foot on Norwall Island. There was no sign of wreckage. There had been no sightings of them in the area. In the absence of tangible proof that they had met with disaster, there was reason to continue the search.

Even Mother joined us in the shop as we unrolled my largest chart. A kindly neighbor arrived with a basket of bread and a jug of water. The Burnsides chewed thoughtfully as my finger skimmed over the water from

Riversend, north toward Norwall Island, then east into the reaches of the Sea of Caprice, stopping at every speck. They were all too small, too barren to consider as destinations.

West, then. My finger traveled west from Norwall into the gaping mouth of Lostman's Bay with its miles of jagged interior coastline and turbulent winds. I told the others that Benjamin and I had discussed the dangers of Lostman's Bay while we studied his route to Norwall Island. To my mind, he would never have consented to taking the Brothers there if they changed their minds and asked him turn that way. He was young, daring, and brave, but not a fool. There had been no storm to carry him that way. After examining every possibility that occurred to us, we all agreed that Lostman's Bay was not where they would go.

Marya said, "North?" The map at which we looked showed Norwall Island just below its northernmost edge. I unrolled another chart. And another.

The fourth map was old and crudely marked. We identified what we knew from the shapes that had been drawn. We found Norwall Island near the center by a rough circle that was intended to be Lostman's Bay. Above were ragged lines meant to represent coastlines. Far north and east of Norwall Island was a larger island with the name "Gylvga" written on it. We all judged it much too far for Benjamin's small craft and store of provisions to reach. After all, the ragged lines to Gylvga's east represented the sparsely populated highlands of the Eastern Continent. Such a voyage would be senseless for the Brothers to make.

Marya traced the waters back from Gylvga to the west. A thin line squiggled down from the map's top edge, and dipped down into a long, curving tail. In the expanse of the map, it was barely noticeable, but the long tail lay halfway between Gylvga and Norwall Island. She peered at the tiny letters written along its side: "Bleak Shoals," she read.

Lorr Burnside stepped over. He triangulated the positions and said that while they would run low on provisions by turning to that destina-

tion, the return voyage to Riversend would be only slightly longer than the outward bound one to Norwall Island. If Benjamin restored his supplies at Bleak Shoals, he could easily have made it back, even single-handed, before the weather turned.

Unless something happened there to damage the boat. In which case, they would all be stranded. Mother pointed out in a most heart-breaking whisper, that if they were all together, they would help each other. They would work together. They would survive.

Rand, who had hardly said a dozen words in two weeks, said, "And there's land above, see? Where there's land, there's shelter. The sea will feed them."

Marya and I scoured the map again, looking for other questions to ask. We saw none in any direction. If Benjamin had triangulated their positions on his starjack, he would have seen what we did, and might have gone that way.

So here I sit tonight, sleepless again, in candlelight that plays hide and seek with shadows, writing this down for a purpose I've forgotten. I decided even before the Burnsides left that I would be going to Bleak Shoals in the spring. To go now would be suicide, with the weather beginning to turn, and our suicide would not help Benjamin at all. We must wait, and use the time to prepare. The work, planning, organizing and gathering will help keep our anxiety in check. All that must be done in the next few months will give us reason to rise before the sun, and go to sleep long after it sets. But I am not young anymore. For the time being, I will stumble between sleep and waking until I fully recover from the mad dash to Norwall Island. That recovery will be soon, I'm sure, because there is a great deal to do.

Therefore, I will not be jotting down any more thoughts or events. For now, this journal is done. There may be a postscript at some later time. How much later, I have no way of knowing. I will have Benjamin make the last entry. I will have him write it in his own hand for me to look at over and over.

"I am home."

Chapter Two

THE EMISSARY

Let me show you, Your Highness. Can you see them? Those words, in my own hand, just below my father's. Both the possession of the journal and my signature in it are proof that I did indeed rejoin my family. How that joyful reunion came about is a tale for tomorrow.

For now, however, we will remain in Riversend, where my mother, father, and Marya experienced a few remarkable events.

The season was turning colder and the days shorter when my father set aside his book. Even though Riversend is far farther south, winter still comes, as do the ships and boats. Marya continued to guide them in for a few more weeks, until Harbor Master Twining announced that a replacement had been found at last. The new pilot was a local man whose reticence had long hidden a formidable history on the sea. When his fortunes fell, he came out of his self-imposed shadows to seek the position.

My sister then joined Father in his shop to prepare for the spring journey to the Bleak Shoals. The old map was on permanent display on his cutting table, and was often consulted. They could not foretell exact distances or changing conditions between Riversend and the Shoals, so every item on the supply list was considered and reconsidered. A topic of considerable discussion was whether or not to return to Norwall first, and go to the Shoals from there. Perhaps something had been overlooked on Norwall's rocky fringe. But Father retraced every second of his time there, and concluded that they should follow as straight a line as possible to their goal.

Late one blustery, gloomy afternoon, the shop door swung open and a man stepped in, quickly closing the door behind him to keep the wind from following him in. He was of medium height and wore a long coat that was well tailored to his slim frame. In fact, everything about him spoke of privilege. Father thought, *This is no ordinary ship's captain looking for work to be done to his boat. This was more like one who owned a fleet.*

He was a handsome fellow, which my sister noticed immediately, and appeared to be not much older than she was, but it quickly became clear that he was older than he looked.

The stranger surveyed the room with casual self-assurance before settling his eyes upon Father and my sister. He was smiling pleasantly the whole time, which everyone would come to learn was his usual expression.

"Mister Carpenter," he said as more of a statement than a question. "And you are Marya." At which point he removed his hat and bowed deeply toward her.

"And who might you be?" my sister asked, unimpressed.

The gentleman then crossed the room while withdrawing a parchment envelope from his coat pocket. After asking for permission to introduce himself, he handed the paper to Marya, and bowed again.

This peculiar behavior puzzled them both, but Marya kept her questions to herself and opened the envelope.

The document within identified the man as Darwen Avellone,

Special Counsel to the Sovereign Lord and Lady of Rampal, Indus, and the Isle of Provinces. Below was the official seal of its origin, the legendary fortress castle of Red Cliffs.

Father and Marya, quite naturally, were surprised to suddenly find themselves in such august company. Almost everyone had heard of the Sovereign Lord and Lady Freehold, who had assumed rule within the past few years after a long, bitter quarrel among the children of Rampal's despotic Sovereign Lord Angus, who had abruptly dropped dead during a minuet. The successors were said to be energetic, fair and of good nature.

"How on earth did you get here?" Father asked. A ship hadn't arrived in Riversend in more than a week.

It turned out that the stranger had come up by coach from lower Doves. "I have never visited this province before," he said. "I wanted to see a little of the country."

The errand on which he had been sent, Mister Avellone went on, was that he had been instructed by the Sovereign Lord to offer Mister Carpenter a proposition of some magnitude. Would he care to speak in private?

Your Highness, I can see my sister's eyes narrow when she heard that, and hear my father say, "If such a proposition affects my family, then my family will be part of the conversation."

Mister Avellone must have noticed Mary's expression because he quickly asked forgiveness, told her he meant no slight, and bowed again. He would gladly do as they wished.

Father invited Mister Avellone to have supper at our house where they could all talk further, an offer that was graciously accepted. After making certain that the Special Counsel had comfortable and trustworthy lodging during his stay, Father sent Marya on ahead to alert Mother. Then he and Mister Avellone dawdled in Father's shop for awhile.

By the time the two men arrived home, the table was set and the house was filled with delicious scents. Introductions were made, and after glancing at Marya, Mister Avellone bowed to my mother.

Glasses of wine and small talk preceded what was one of Mother's typically exceptional meals, during which Mister Avellone revealed a little about himself.

His parents were co-Ministers of Reception for Red Cliffs, responsible for planning and implementing every aspect of hospitality and security for visiting dignitaries. Preparations began months before an arrival, with the initial stages being influenced by length of stay, itinerary, size of the visitor's retinue, and so forth. Darwen's father usually established the protocol for diplomatic protection services, and Darwen's mother structured the daily calendar. Both coordinated the myriad details involved with lodging, banquets, entertainment, and, of course, meetings.

Thus, Darwen grew up absorbing the languages, cultural backgrounds, manners, and politics of a number of countries. This fundamental education was furthered by university instruction, so that Darwen eventfully became fluent in five different languages. Under his father's tutelage, he also became well acquainted with the art of self-defense. Lord Freehold thought the young man's cumulative skills formed the basis for an ideal emissary, and groomed Darwen to be his Special Counsel.

Father saw an opportunity to ask what could possibly bring his Lordship's emissary to Riversend?

Mister Avellone responded that the Sovereign Lord had long been aware of Father's exceptional workmanship and inventiveness with sailing vessels, and an idea gradually took shape as to how his Lordship could utilize such talent.

Therefore, Sovereign Lord Freehold wished to have a flagship built; a flagship of far more artistry than opulence; a ship that pleased the hand as much as it did the eye. He wished Mister Carpenter to design and oversee its construction. The compensation suggested for these services was a sum that exceeded the value of The Brotherhood's treasure.

During their utter speechlessness, Mister Avellone continued.

"His Lordship estimates a term of two to three years from the laying of the keel to commissioning," he said. "You and your family will be housed in spacious quarters within the perimeter of Red Cliffs. You will be afforded every comfort, and given whatever you need for the ship.

"A vessel will arrive here at Riversend from Rampal in three months to transport you, your family and your belongings to Rampal."

Try to imagine their astonishment, Your Highness. For a few moments, none of them could form a coherent thought. Finally, Father asked why on earth was his Lordship doing this? Surely he could find other equally qualified shipwrights in Rampal. Why all this bother for a ship, no matter how well crafted it was to be? Father did not understand.

Mister Avellone paused for a moment, and said that there were many reasons, which would become clear once they arrived at Red Cliffs.

All Mother had to do was look sternly at Father for the answer he had to give. Father quietly apologized, but had to refuse. Their son was missing at sea, and as soon as spring came, they would spend as much time as it took to either find him, or some trace of him.

Mister Avellone looked at each of them in turn as if judging their expressions for consensus, his pleasant smile never wavering.

"His Lordship does not wish you to suffer any further worry. He has instructed me to tell you that Benjamin is safe, and we know where he is."

Mother nearly fainted and Marya nearly wept, but when this moment passed they were all asking questions at once.

His Lordship had cooperatives in Riversend who kept him informed of ship traffic, goods transfers and civic activities. He had been told of the arrival of the Brotherhood and the bargain made for their treasure. All was well until their son did change course for the Bleak Shoals, and lost his ship to a storm not long after they arrived.

He spent the summer in the area, and then boarded a ship that happened by.

Father wanted to know how they could possibly know all this. It sounded like a fabrication.

The answer was that Lord Freehold had a singularly talented agent named Mister Starling, who performed surveillance duties for him, among other tasks.

Then, if Lord Freehold knew, why didn't he tell the Carpenters before they went thrashing across the Sea of Caprice looking for Benjamin?

Because Rampal was a very long way from The Bleak Shoals. Word did not arrive to Red Cliffs in time to halt the flying trip to Norwall Island.

Mother wanted to know more motherly details — when could she see me? When would I be home? Was I unhurt? Was I eating?

Mister Avellone suggested that she get the answers to those questions from my own lips. I would be at Red Cliffs by the time they arrived.

They were stunned, of course, and probably would have left within the hour if they could, but the enormity of all this information had to be sorted out.

At first, the idea of leaving Riversend and all their friends for perhaps three years was daunting, but it didn't seem that long at all when they considered the extraordinary opportunity for Father to create the ship of a lifetime, the riches with which they would return—enough to turn Riversend into a thriving city— and, most important of all, reclaiming their son.

There was a brief discussion among my family as to which decision was the most sensible, but all knew that there was really only one decision to make.

They would go to Rampal.

Mister Avellone did not seem the least bit surprised.

Two copies of a legal agreement were produced. One was given to Father for review, and the other lay on the table in front of Mister Avellone. After Father read it, he passed it to Marya.

She read it carefully, and then began to pick it apart. She thought it vague in several places.

One, she wanted the clause "provide comfortable quarters" to read "provide comfortable quarters for four." Since I would be staying there too, she wanted to be certain there would be space enough for all of us.

Two, she wanted to add the condition that there be a shop for Father either newly built or an available property near the shipyard. If possible, it should resemble his Riversend shop for the sake of his comfort and efficiency.

Three, the clause "the keel shall be laid by the first day of summer" imposed a deadline that might do a great disservice to both his Lordship and Mister Carpenter by rushing the all-important planning stage. That clause should read, "the keel shall be laid upon the Sovereign Lord's final approval of both the ship's design and its construction timetable." If the deadline had to remain, then the ship from Rampal had to arrive in Riversend to pick them up in two months' time, not three.

She also had comments to make in a few areas concerning Father's responsibilities in the project.

Mister Avellone, according to my mother, at first beamed at Marya like a proud uncle, but then began making notations on his copy of the agreement. These notations wee also put on the first document. All present initialed each of the amendments, then signed at the bottom, with the understanding that his Lordship had the final say.

Therefore, Marya asked, should they wait for a response to the agreement before proceeding?

Mister Avellone saw no reason why Lord Freehold would object to any part of the agreement. Acting on his behalf, Mister Avellone urged them begin preparations to leave in three months. The emissary would return to Rampal the way he came, and be on his way within a day or so. He would be aboard the returning ship to accompany them to Red Cliffs.

Thus, the deal was made, and the future looked much different for everyone than when the day began.

* * *

There was no way such news could or should be kept from the community that had shared in the concern caused by my disappearance. But how best to do it? Mary was the one who came up with the perfect way to inform everyone in the town very nearly all at once.

They would tell Master Twining.

This they did after Mister Avellone had boarded his coach for the return to lower Doves, in order to spare him from being besieged with questions. In the meantime, my family enjoyed several meals with the emissary, and Father toured Riversend with him. If an acquaintance approached, Father introduced Mister Avellone as a prospective customer.

Warm farewells were made on a clear, cold morning. The Special Counsel again bowed to Marya before climbing into the coach.

Master Twining was asked to visit my father in his shop not long after the coach had faded from view, and he was told the news that I, Benjamin, was found and well. The news spread quickly, as expected, and the shop was soon full of jubilant, congratulatory townspeople.

The buoyant feeling of relief spilled over into a party. City Council spent some of its Brotherhood treasure on a public cele-bration, which they coined the Riversend Winterfair. The event was boisterous and well attended.

The news of Mister Avellone's identity and Father's extraordi-nary appointment were revealed afterward, and greeted with both happiness for Father, and concern about losing such an influential family. The City Council board was slightly miffed that they had not had a chance to formulate a list of issues for Mister Avellone to carry back to Red Cliffs, but this feeling was overwhelmed by the possi-bilities when Father returned to Riversend after three years with an even greater fortune than he had already invested in the town.

Master Twining's main concern was how to replace Father's skills as a shipwright. Such work by Father and his crews was a major source of income for Riversend businesses, which profited from the presence of the sailors during repairs.

Father was asked if he could recommend anyone he felt could do a serviceable job in his absence, and Father obliged, though he knew of only two that he respected for both in ability and character.

My family turned its full attention to preparing for their big adventure, and counting the days until they were able to look me in the eye again.

The first few weeks after the hullabaloo died down were spent with each carefully considering what they actually needed and wanted to take with them, keeping in mind that they would be returning. What could they do without for three years? What did they require that would affect their day-to-day life in Rampal? Each was preparing for homesickness, too, which is why Mother included her most versatile cookware and utensils, Marya set aside her favorite books and a few essential tools with which she helped her father in the shop, and Mister Carpenter planned to take a box of custom-made tools he used to make little wooden toys and puzzles for anyone who might enjoy them. Beloved chairs, tables and Marya's and my clever chest of drawers would also be part of the move, since they were traveling by ship and had room for it all.

The packing was pretty much done by the end of the first month. The last items would be those they needed to endure the long two months until spring and the return of Mister Avellone.

Early in the second month, a special session of City Council was called, with our whole family invited to attend. The meeting was memorable for its energy, enthusiasm and unexpected joys.

After the meeting was called to order and opening prayers, an announcement was made that one of the individuals Mister Carpenter had recommended to replace him had agreed to the idea. My father then advised council members to part with some of the town treasure to make the relocation worth the shipwright's while. This was to be resolved in a private discussion with Father.

Next, it was revealed that the plans for a complete renovation of Miss Nearly's school had been approved and would commence as soon as the weather turned more reliable. Then, as a complete surprise to Father, an architectural drawing of an institution of higher learning was unveiled. A mention was made that while Father had requested that the children's school not be named after him, he had said nothing about an edifice devoted to higher learning. Therefore, the new building would be named "Carpenter College."

After other official business, a group of children came forth to sing a couple of touching songs, including an original one titled "When Springtime Comes." Then the children presented my family with a beautiful chessboard-sized diorama of Riversend, to remind them of their friends and home. The walk back to Pitcher's Handle Lane that evening was a quiet one.

Then they waited.

The cold season was usually slow for Father in Riversend, as the ship traffic slowed to only a few a month, but that winter seemed torturously long for them all. Mother and Marya cleaned the house until it was nearly sterile, continued to bake bread and rolls for the neighbors, and made busy work of preparing the packing. Father was often asked to attend this meeting or that to be part of the events that would occur during the time he was gone. Day after day, they felt as though they were walking in their sleep.

Gradually, warmth began creeping into the breezes. Daffodils raised their yellow trumpets. Ships became more frequent.

Then came the morning when a neighborhood boy ran into Father's shop, his face red from excitement and the still-chilly air.

"A ship, Mister Carpenter!" he said. "She flies royal colors!"

Father and Marya both said their stomachs became nervous at the news. Marya wordlessly left the shop to go fetch Mother, who came bustling down to the dock where Father stood watching a speck at the mouth of the harbor. The three of them linked arms with Mother in the middle, their faces solemn.

"We will see Benjamin soon," Mother said. And with that, all their anxiety and doubt left them.

They were smiling as the *Red Moon* from Rampal, its royal pennants cracking like whips in the wind, sailed toward them.

Chapter Three

TWO GIRLS FROM RED CLIFFS

By the time the *Red Moon* had berthed, it seemed as if half of Riversend had joined the Carpenters on the quay. When the crew had all made ready, the first to disembark was Darwen Avellone, dressed in casual but finely made clothes. His smile broadened when he saw my family, and he warmly shook my father's hand before bowing to both Marya and my mother.

When people weren't staring at the Special Counsel, they were staring at the ship. Its proud lines and exquisite wood humbled those on shore. Her copper-colored strakes gleamed as if coated with ice, and just past midship there was a large, circular, rose-tinted window. Crew members were dressed more like officers than laborers, and a strikingly tall fellow with silver hair moved unhurriedly about directing them with quiet authority.

Father recognized the wood as Bronzewood, which flourished in only a few places in the world. One of those places was Indus, a large island off the west coast of Rampal where cool currents were in constant contact with the region's sun-warmed air. A nearly perpetual fog drifts along the coast, enabling the water-hungry Bronzewood trees to reach spectacular heights. Father knew that the wonderful, straight-grained wood, if patiently oiled again and again, would never rot and would glow when it was polished.

When Father remarked that it was very expensive wood, Mister Avellone laughed and said, "Not if you have sovereignty over it." Father was promised all the Bronzewood he needed if he chose to use it for his project because of a long-standing requirement that for every such tree harvested, two others were to be planted.

Mister Avellone mentioned that Indus is also notable for its vast herd of wild ponies. No one is sure how the ponies got there to begin with—whether by a now-sunken land bridge or long ago shipwreck—but they are unique in the world. They are not much taller than an average person's shoulder, and have only a short ridge of mane along their necks. The ponies are smart, quick and agile, and their hides have evolved into an astonishing variety of colors, stripes and spots. They are too small to be of much use as working or ware horses, but until Indus was taken under the protection of the old royal houses of Rampal, the ponies were taken as pets, used as bait by hunters, and even kept as food for the crews of long open water voyages. But now they lived in peace on Indus's endless prairie.

The tall, silver-haired man was introduced as Captain Treer, and Mister Avellone insisted that my family call him Darwen, since they would all be in each other's company quite often from then on. At that point, Father became Rodger Carpenter to the Special Counsel.

Then began the procession of my family's belongings from the shop to the ship. The onlookers made a wide, clear path for the crew, and watched in solemn silence as furniture, trunks and boxes, tools, and the precious Riversend diorama passed by. Everyone, my family included, realized the enormity of what was happening.

There would be no delay in leaving once supplies and my family's possessions were loaded. There were embraces, good wishes passed back and forth, promises made, and a few tears as the Carpenters left their home and neighbors.

But under it all there was joy, too, because Benjamin would be coming home.

*　*　*

Inside, the *Red Moon* was as dazzling as its outside.

On the cabin deck, the hallways were paneled with Bronzewood, and elegant lantern sconces lit the way. Four cabins flanked the hallway. One, very simple, close quarters, was Darwen's. Two others were handsome, comfortable rooms appointed with large beds, wardrobes and writing tables. The last was spacious and ornate, with a round bed, private water closet, washstand and a porthole for light and view.

Beyond there was a sitting area outside a large dining room suffused in soft light from a circular, rose-tinted window on both port and starboard sides. A round Bronzewood table gleamed in the center. Discreetly positioned stairwells fore and aft led below decks to Captain Treer's and the crew's cabins.

Darwen led Father and Mother to their cabin, which Father immediately began inspecting for its excellent craftsmanship. Mother, I'm told, sat on the edge of the bed in stunned silence.

Darwen then led my sister to the cabin with the round bed.

My sister turned on him with suspicion and no small amount of anger.

"Why are you doing this?" she demanded. "What is your meaning? If anyone stays here it should be my parents, not me."

Darwen told here there was much to be explained, and it would be at dinner the following evening. In the meantime, he begged her to trust him.

She looked around the chambers and said, "I will not stay here. I will not."

Her tone and sharp gaze were so direct that Darwen was forced to accede. My sister was moved to the cabin across the hall from our parent's quarters.

As the *Red Moon* turned about in the harbor and entered open water, they explored the deck, supported each other. Darwen had left them alone, excusing himself to attend to other duties. The voyage to Red Cliffs would take ten days, because the vessel had to sail against the Boundary Current. My family found more than enough diversion among the ship's books, games and extensive map collection to keep them occupied.

During the evening meal, Captain Treer and Darwen kept their guests entertained with a wild assortment of tales and facts gathered from their respective careers. My sister did a good job of pretending to be an attentive audience, but her thoughts, and often her eyes, were on Darwen Avellone. She found him very attractive, but regarded him with caution. She told me that she could tell he was drawn to her too, but remained steadfastly distant.

Before making any judgment, she would wait to hear what he had to say the next day.

They all slept late. Everyone was exhausted from months of tension and doubt, and their deck was almost unnaturally quiet. They could hear nothing from above, and no boards creaked or groaned from the nudging of the waves. This combination of factors allowed them a deep, untroubled sleep.

As soon as they began to stir, there was a soft knock on their cabin doors and someone said, "Good morning. Breakfast will be served whenever you wish."

The morning table was set for three, and my sister found herself feeling disappointed. Mother was revived by a good night's rest and wanted to explore the galley, where she and the cook had a pleasant chat about the nuances of mixing bread dough.

Afterward, Father sat down to study the Rampal tide charts and Marya went up on deck. Though the air was still chilly, she could feel warmth rising within it. Darwen was prowling the deck with a spyglass, occasionally pausing to study the distant coast of Doves. He and Captain Treer conferred about something Darwen had seen, but the conversation was casual, with no hint of alarm. When Captain Treer had left, my sister approached Darwen. He smiled and seemed pleased to see her, but quickly averted his eyes.

With her customary directness, Marya pointed out that while she had learned quite a bit about Darwen along the way, he had not asked Marya anything about her. To Marya, this meant he must already know all about her or had no interest in knowing. Instead of being put off by her challenge, he appeared to be delighted, and said he did know quite a bit about Miss Marya through the Sovereign Lord's study of Mister Carpenter's business and career, but he himself did indeed want to hear more of Miss Marya's thoughts and opinions. He was glad they had the better part of ten days to talk.

The day passed in a very relaxed manner for my family. Now that they were finally on their way, the thoughts of what they were leaving behind fell away, and anticipation of their new adventure energized them. Father and Marya explored the ship, talked to crew members and spent time on deck. Mother was invited to help the cook in the galley, if she wished to, an offer she happily accepted.

For that reason, the evening meal—a wonderful seafood stew in fresh bread bowls as the main entrée—was no surprise to my mother. But the rest of it certainly was.

When the dishes had been cleared except for small glasses of dessert wine, Darwen spoke, not as Darwen Avellone but as Special Counsel.

"The Lord and Lady Freehold instructed me to inform you all of a few things early in the voyage, so that you would have time to consider them before arriving in Red Cliffs.

"The last Sovereign Lord of Rampal and its nation wards was Lord Angus, the founder of the House of Freehold. He fathered more than a dozen children, most, but not all, with his wife, the Lady Ermine. She died during her last childbirth, along with the infant.

"For the next thirty years, Lord Angus continued his rule alone. Among his many children, he most favored a son named Tryon. In this young man Lord Angus saw many admirable traits he himself did not possess, but recognized some of his own characteristics that he felt were essential in a strong governor. Although Tryon was not the eldest child, he was the one Lord Angus favored to succeed him, knowing that this would be a very unpopular notion with the other children. His thinking was that he would transfer authority to Tryon while he was still alive to assure a peaceful transition.

"In the meantime, Tryon married, and his wife Alyssa had two children in quick succession. They were both girls whom he adored.

"About twenty years ago, Lord Angus died quite unexpectedly, thus upsetting his grand plan. Almost immediately after Lord Angus's funeral, a battle began for the vacant lordship. This became known in Rampal as the Conflict of the Siblings.

"Because there were so many children, the war unfolded as a sort of bloody chess game. Those deemed most likely to seize power were isolated and in some cases slain. Of course, those deemed most likely to seize power were not going to go away gently, and engaged in their own maneuvers against their brothers and sisters.

"The major protagonists in all of this were, unsurprisingly,

Tryon and his family. Lord Angus's judgment was sound — Tryon proved to be very capable of playing this game. But he and Alyssa both knew that their beloved girls were in serious danger. The thought of their infant children being taken hostage or worse was unbearable to them both. But they also knew that for the good of Rampal, Tryon should lead. Besides, this was Lord Angus's wish, and Tryon was determined to honor it.

"Their solution was a painful one. They decided to remove their children from harm's way until the conflict was resolved. Anonymity was crucial to the survival of the infants.

"Tryon sent his most trusted friends to scout for safe havens far from trouble. Two impeccable places were found where the girls would be loved, protected and most of all, invisible to everyone else. Tryon and Alyssa formed a group they called The Witnesses, who were appointed to keep the girls under surveillance and thus, indirectly, always in the eyes of their parents.

"Now that the conflict has finally ended and the lordship stabilized, the girls are being called home to meet their true mother and father, and assume their roles in the royal houses of Rampal.

"The youngest daughter, Sofia, was left with a large but obscure family in the Province of Swallows.

"The eldest, Lilea, became the daughter of the Carpenters of Riversend."

Then Special Counsel Darwen Avellone rose from his chair and bowed deeply toward Marya.

"Your Highness," he said.

Interlude

THE SECOND MEAL

QUESTION

"What's this?" Harald's voice rang clearly. "Your sister? Your Highness? You are spinning quite a tale here, Dogman."

Harald left his perch and was next seen entering the amphitheater. He strode toward Dogman with two guards in tow.

"Bring me a chair," he commanded them. "Some food for our storyteller, and a cup of wine for me."

Harald held out his hand. "Let me see this book of yours."

Harald's eyes skimmed over the pages of Mister Carpenter's journal. He looked curiously at Dogman just as his chair arrived. Wine and a meal of bread and dried fish arrived close behind, carried by two servants who were practically running.

Harald sat.

"You certainly appear to be the adventurous Benjamin Carpenter. You showed me proof of your brief time among the Tulak. And now you are acquainted with the Sovereign Lord of these parts? Being a backwoods boy from Maurisia, I was not aware of such a presence. Indeed, in seven years I have not had a word or a visit from the Sovereign Lord of such and such, who would, I am sure, object to my being here. You understand my doubt."

Dogman smiled. "Every story is both true and untrue. We are the ones who decide which is which according to our nature. Some will gladly believe everything they hear. Others will be too cynical to believe anything at all. Even proof can be doubted. That journal? How do you know I did not write it myself? My Tulak knives? Are they the work of an artist in some hamlet in Doves? You choose to believe my father wrote the journal and the Tulak made the knives."

"And?"

"You would be correct," Dogman said.

"Unless you are lying," and both men laughed.

"Assuming the true has trumped the untrue in this case," Harald said, "what of your sister, who is not really your sister? How did you discover this?"

"When we were old enough to understand such things, Father and Mother explained it all to both of us. Marya was a foundling, although Mother always referred to her as a gift. Neither of us knew she meant it literally. One afternoon when Mother was closing her bakeshop on the waterfront, she turned to pick up her breadbasket and found it already filled. A little girl of about eighteen months sat in it watching her. So many people come and go along the wharf, she did not even know where to look for someone who might have left the infant. A parchment also lay in the basket, one that read, "Love and protect this child," written in a firm, woman's hand. The commanding tone seemed to speak to her directly, so she never really considered doing otherwise. This was a girl, a sister to grow up with me, and a help to her in the kitchen. A gift."

"After you both knew, how did you feel?"

"No different."

"How about your sister?"

"She felt no different, really."

"Oh, come now. This young lady finds out she was abandoned, stuffed into a bread basket no less, and she blithely goes on with her life?"

"She did. She reasoned that if someone she did not know sent her away, and all her remembered days were among these people who loved her and whom she loved, then that is all there was."

"She never wanted to find out who her real parents were?"

"She was curious for awhile, of course. We even played a game, off and on. Depending on her mood or behavior at the time, she would ask me: 'Whose child am I?' And I would answer, 'Dragons. Or explorers. Or a town mayor.' And so forth. Eventually the game was forgotten. Even if she did want to find out, there was no place to begin the search."

"I would guess she was a mite less cavalier when she found out she was sailing into the arms of her birth parents after all those years. There must have been quite an introduction when she arrived. You said you were there. Tell me about it."

"Lord Freehold was smart to have Darwen tell her long before she reached Red Cliffs. The time gave her a chance to assimilate her new reality. Darwen helped her adjust by spending the rest of the voyage answering all Marya's questions describing the Lord and Lady and Red Cliffs, and giving her examples of their natures. I think she recognized some of her own characteristics from theirs. By the time they met, I believe the Lord and Lady already felt somewhat familiar to her. The Lord and Lady were there to welcome them rather than having them brought to the castle, and the greetings were warm, friendly, as if this was a gathering of close relatives who had not seen each other in awhile."

Harald slowly shook his head in wonder.

"Remarkable. You mentioned another child, her sister, Sofia. She was left here in Swallows, you said. Where? With whom?"

"She was left with a chicken farmer and a seamstress in Nodding Elms."

Harald snorted. "Forgive me if I don't send a detail galloping off toward Nodding Elms to interrogate the townspeople. First of all, I don't care that much. And second, this is probably one of those untruths you talked about, as I cannot imagine a royal child being left with a chicken farmer. "

Harald, never taking his eyes off the foreigner, finished his wine while Dogman ate the last of his bread and cheese.

"That brings us to you, Dogman," Harald said. "You were waiting for your family at Red Cliffs. How did you end up there?"

"That is a story unto itself."

"I'm sure it is." Harald looked up at the sky, noting the location of the sun. "You have most of the afternoon left. Take some time to relieve yourself, wash up, doze for a bit."

He stood to address the hundreds of listeners around them. It seemed to Harald that most of his men and half of Swallows were there listening. "You too, all of you. Stretch your legs. Relieve yourselves as well, but not on my lawn. We will begin again within two hours."

Part Three

BENJAMIN AGAIN

Chapter One

THE *ABBE* GLEN

After being so cold and getting even colder whenever I tried to wash myself on the Bleak Shoals, the warm sun and cleanliness of Du Kinish's boat were pleasures you cannot imagine. Du Kinish even insisted that my precious Brotherhood cloak be cleaned as well, which certainly did it no harm. The material fascinated the crew, because it was lightweight, warm when the air was cold, cool when the air was hot, and windproof. Du Kinish studied it intently, but could not identify the fibers from which it was woven.

"If I could discover how to make this cloth," he once told me, "we would never have to sail from home again."

The lazy Scimitar Current and fair weather made this voyage seem like a pleasure cruise, even though there was always work to do. When we weren't cleaning or polishing something, we were attending to our assigned tasks. Mine was to help Porcee turn the sea wheat.

The sea wheat was stored in four rectangular bins as tall as a man's shoulder. Across the top of each bin was a wooden bar connected to four devices that looked like vertical plowshares, each facing opposite directions. With Porcee on one side and me on the other, we pushed the bar from end to end. Six round trips at each bin brought the sea wheat from the bottom of the bin to the top, keeping the entire cargo fresh and dry. We did this once every day. At first my arms and shoulders ached fiercely, but I got used to it quickly. Porcee and I had many enjoyable conversations during this process. Porcee called me "Preacher," even though I had laid away my cloak after its washing and wore a loose shirt instead. It was he who told me that when the sea wheat was removed, the bays would hold copper sheets. In each case, the cargo also served as ballast.

The ship was the *Abbe Glen*, and was named after a quiet, lovely little valley near Gylgova on whose gentle slopes Kinish had walked for many peaceful hours. He had given this valley his daughter's name when she was born.

"Little Abbe grew up to be quite a creature," Kinish laughed proudly. "A tall, smart, resilient soul. She can out-walk most of the people in Gylgova, and she's pleasant as springtime to everyone. She can be stubborn sometimes, though."

Gylgova is a village of simple homes with attached workshops, which also serve as stores. Everyone works, whether to support the village and its residents or to manufacture goods to sell. Walk through the town and you will find a woodworker, building sup-plies, a toolmaker, a weaver, and so on. On the outskirts are the saw-yer, blacksmith, farmers and herders, livestock and wagon masters.

Kinish Ard's Son is one of the coppersmiths, and his specialty is creating lanterns and candlesticks in a number of different designs.

His wife, Leeni Gron's Dahtter, tends to the house and Abbe, and occasionally helps Kinish in his shop. But Leeni's main role in Gylgova is to educate the children.

When Abbe was born, Leeni vowed to expand Abbe's knowl-edge of the world beyond Gylgova, whether she ever left the village or not. For those lessons, Leeni drew upon her own good fortune.

As a youngster, Leeni had sometimes traveled with her father, who took collections of the town's products to markets throughout the region. Being exposed to the teeming marketplaces showed Leeni how many different languages, appearances, and customs existed outside her own home fields. She also relished the thrill of approaching new places; they invariably proved to be full of mysteries and surprises.

Trundling along by horse and wagon during the dry season, her father helped pass the time by telling Leeni stories of his past travels and adventures. Her active imagination vividly recreated the spires, towers, dazzling white cities sprawling down mountainsides, and endless hard sand deserts that turned purple in the late day sun. Her mind heard brilliantly colored birds whose cries sounded like mad laughter, the indescribable thunder of a waterfall so wide the other side could not be seen, and the mournful bellow of sacred horns high above a valley hidden in mist. She locked every word and image in her memory, because the more she saw, the more she wanted to see, and knew she would never leave Gylgova.

In every market town, her father would at some point always barter one item for a souvenir that would remind Leeni of the places they visited together. The gift might be an odd stone, wooden figure, a unique feather or colorful hair ornament. She treasured every one, and the stories each one told.

One particular day, her father approached her with his hands behind his back. "I have something special for you," he said, and placed a simple woven crown on her head. "There. Now you are a princess. You can command armies now."

Leeni studied her crown with a smile. "Did you ever meet a princess?"

"Yes, actually, I did, once."

"What was she like?"

"No different than you."

One day when Abbe was still a child, Leeni set the braided crown on Abbe's head, and told her the story of how she came to have it. "This is what I was to someone else", she said, "and this is what you are to us. Because a princess is no different than you."

Leeni never intended to found a school, but when she began teaching Abbe about her curios and where they came from, her stories attracted other children to her as if by invisible strings.

The townspeople saw the value in this situation, and encouraged Leeni to continue as their teacher. Soon she was guiding the children into reading, writing, crafting, and developing the skills they would need to manage in their lifetimes.

Her favorite time, however, was telling the tales of exotic places and people she had seen or heard about. She watched all of her students as she spoke, recognizing in a very few, or perhaps only one, a certain rapture in their expression and distance in their eyes, and knowing a traveler had been born.

* * *

While I was standing at the starboard rail one morning, Kinish appeared at my side.

"Do you feel it?" he asked.

I said that I did. There was a subtle change in the air, a faltering of the wind, a difference in the behavior of the water. A storm was coming.

"Yes," he said, "and Southern Ocean storms can be fierce. Help Porcee cover the wheat."

By the time I reached the hatch to go below, the rest of the crew was already tending to their storm preparation tasks. Everyone moved very deliberately, almost as if in a trance, because Kinish had drilled into all of us that to move slowly is to make fewer mistakes that require time to correct; therefore, moving slowly completes the job more quickly. Slow is fast.

Porcee was wrestling with the sailcloth bin covers when I arrived. Together, with each of us at either end of each bin, we unrolled the tarps over the top. The stirring mechanism stood just high enough to form a peak that allowed water to roll off the cover instead of pooling in the middle. By the time we covered each bin and tightly lashed down each tarp, we were sweating like horses, and the *Abbe Glen* had begun to pitch and roll.

Over a mounting rumble and creak of timbers, I asked Porcee if we were to stay below with the wheat.

He grinned at me and said, "If you fancy bouncing like a ball off a wall, we do."

With a calmness we did not feel, we made our way back to the hold ladder, plucking each lashing rope like a violin string on the way to make sure they were tight. As we emerged on the crew deck, Rogie handed us weather shells and pointed his thumb upward, motioning us to get up on deck.

Outside, heavy clouds darkened the sky, but there was a metallic sheen over the water's surface. The wind was blowing hard and increasing, pushing long, steep swells ahead of it. Porcee and I fought the ship's roll and pelting rain to reach Snod, who was directing men while Kinish fought the wheel against the waves. Snod sent Porcee to help Kinish, and yelled at me to deploy the rescue ropes from the bow.

The rescue ropes trailed in the water on each side of the ship along its entire length, giving any man who went overboard a chance of salvation. The coils are heavy, but if half of it could be fed over the side, the moving water helps haul out the rest of it. The larboard rope went over perfectly, but the starboard rope, with the help of a freak wave, took me with it. The rope was in my hand, but was jerked away as I landed on my back and was immediately pulled under.

Righting myself took a few seconds, because I was being pushed and pulled back and forth in the turbulence. When my head finally cleared the surface, I saw that the *Abbe Glen* was already nearly past me, and that I was too far away to reach the rope.

The stern passed, pulling me into its wake, but I was not taken under again. I saw Porcee and Kinish looking forward from the wheel. No one had seen me fall.

Sire, try to imagine my state of mind — adrift in that heaving sea with wave crests breaking over my head. I am a strong swimmer, but it was all I could do to keep my head high enough to breathe. I was very aware of the void below me, and cold was already stiffening my arms and legs. Many thoughts crowded into my mind, each in a hurry to be seen before every one was gone: regrets, apologies, my family, a realization of coming to an end. I could feel my legs begin to slow their kicks, and my head lowering into the sea.

Then I felt a bulk underneath me. My numb feet set down on firmness, and suddenly there was a dorsal fin in front of me. I grabbed it with both hands and locked my fingers over the front.

The bulk below me was orange. I was holding onto Bringer, the Roanfish.

Slowly, Bringer moved toward the ship, keeping me high enough to breathe. Gently rising and falling, he took me through that maelstrom to the rescue rope. Rogie had noticed the big fish and watched it carry me in, so he was already hauling in the rope and belaying the slack around a capstan. Joined by Snod, the two of them pulled me back aboard the *Abbe Glen*.

By the time I could look back, the Roanfish's reddish shape was already submerged.

"Never seen anything like that before," Snod bellowed over

the wind. "You're a lucky sailor to have friends in the sea!"

There was no respite. Within minutes I was put back to work with the others until the storm abated, the sea calmed, and sunlight spilled through cracks in the clouds.

The Gylgovans glanced at me curiously at supper that evening, making wondering comments and promising to turn the event into a fine tale for the rest of the villagers. Kinish was looking forward to showing me off, if I chose to return with them, a notion for which I had no alternative at the moment.

I could not explain what had happened, but knew one thing for certain.

I had been followed ever since I left Riversend.

* * *

One evening a few days later, Kinish invited me for a glass of *spinrok* in the galley. His purpose was to tell me how the rest of the voyage was going to unfold.

He said we were bound for Grand Reef, the largest of the Faraday Islands.

Grand Reef was one of the few places in the world that mined and smelted copper, silver and gold. The port town sprawled in a warren of narrow lanes and alleys, along which were shops and dens selling every conceivable item and service from tankards of rum and pipes of opium to slaves and assassins. Through these channels flowed multi-cultural streams of buyers, sellers, thieves, kidnappers, extortionists and opportunists from all over the world.

Beyond the town of Grand Reef was the hardpan leading to the mines, inside which legions of poorly paid workers, prisoners and slaves worked, fought each other, and died digging out the ores that fueled the economy. Scattered over the hardpan were tall chimney furnaces, mounds of charcoal and piles of slag. The air reeked, and a choking haze lay over most of Grand Reef, a byproduct of the smelters which poured out heavy smoke and ash throughout the day and night.

When Kinish was a much younger man and the small copper mine three days from Gylgova ran dry, the villagers gathered to decide if the danger of traveling the great distance to Grand Reef for copper was worth the risk. The answer was yes; because of the rare quality and consequent profitability of Gylgovans copper work. For trade, the most valuable commodity they could think of was the equally uncommon sea wheat that grew near the Bleak Shoals of Vastland. Kinish's merchant ship was converted for long voyages and renamed the *Abbe Glen*.

The first time the Gylgovan crew went to Grand Reef, they discovered that their naïve farmer ways and appearance drew far too much attention from swindlers and thieves. They struggled through their first transaction for copper, only to have it stolen on route to the ship. After days of searching, the furious Gylgovans recovered their cargo, but several men suffered wounds and two lives were lost in the process.

Kinish reasoned that Gylgova could not afford such a high price for copper each time, but had to have it for the sake of the town's prosperity. They were not fighters by nature, and realized that becoming fighters only led to more trouble and loss. So they became performers instead.

"If you are good enough actors," Kinish laughed, "others believe you are what you appear to be. We can fight if we have to, but we don't want to. The idea is to repel the same types who took advantage of us the first time. And by the time we arrive in Grand Reef, you will see that we can be a very imposing lot."

They all had costumes of different kinds. Though varied, all the clothing was well worn, almost tattered in some cases, and none had been washed in years. Kinish laughed again and told me, "We stink, Wulfkin, so we fit right in."

Then his attention turned to what role I might play in their drama. Kinish eyed me carefully, and announced: "You are a former soldier. I have a rather rank old tunic bearing a symbol that Leeni designed. If we tuck your cowl inside, and you wear your cloak open and loose with your weapons visible, you will look very soldierly indeed. I expect your Tulak skills will serve you well in a pinch."

Our first stop, however, would be Port Char on Broom Island, where we resupplied our water. We did not have to wear our Grand Reef clothes there, but we would have to be on our guard nonetheless.

Before we staggered off to our hammocks, Kinish told me an interesting story. He said that the first island of the Faraday chain is a place called Moon Island. This is a long, thickly jungled piece of rock and sand on which a madman has lived alone for years. Stark naked and burned dark by the sun, he marches up and down the beach as if it were a parade ground, shouts and points at invisible troops, flaps his arms, and periodically gallops along hunkered over like an ape. The first time Kinish saw him, he was astounded. The man had obviously been there a long time already; his hair was nearly waist length.

After watching this madman's peculiar dance, Kinish took pity on him and ordered a boat to be lowered. He intended to pick him up and take him, for better or worse, to Grand Reef, where the poor fellow would at least be among other people. Kinish wondered, in fact, why no one had already done so, but quickly had an answer. As soon as the savage saw what was happening, he bolted into the jungle. It appeared that he did not want to be rescued; he wanted to stay, even though, Kinish said, there was little to eat there other than leaves, bitter berries, and whatever fish and birds the man could catch. The story goes that by strange circumstances he was abandoned there by a passing ship. His name is Master Turnbolt, and he hails from somewhere in the Isle of Provinces.

Ah! I see you know the name, sire. You say you sent him there? Really? How remarkable. I would like to know more about him, if it pleases you. Yes. Over the evening meal, then, yes, with pleasure.

* * *

Port Char on Broom Island is misnamed on two counts.

First, its name would imply a place of searing heat and land burned black. In fact, it is a truncation of "Charlotte," the name of the wife of a sailor who visited the island and stayed. Poor Charlotte never saw her husband again. The island is anything but the victim of flames, but rather is a temperate, breezy paradise in the middle of nowhere.

Second, the "port" is really a beautiful harbor within a crescent of fine, white sand. The water is more green than blue, clear, and calm. The beach is fringed with tall palm trees. Kinish told me that inland, at the end of a path through scrub grass and prickly bushes, is a series of three waterfalls which feed five pools of clear, cold water. It is this water that supports the *Abbe Glen* with extra ballast and drinking water for the rest of its journey to Grand Reef.

As we dropped anchor offshore, I saw a group of people gathering on the beach, but saw no other boats. Kinish rubbed his jaw and said, "It appears we have a welcoming committee." We lowered our longboat, and spent an hour filling the inside of its hull with empty water casks. Then Kinish, Snod, with his broadsword, the blacksmith, Porcee, two others and I climbed in amongst them.

The closer we got, the more fearsome the group on the beach became. One big fellow leaned casually on the upturned hilt of an executioner's axe, and another carried a whip. I felt uneasy.

They made no move toward us as we beached. Kinish jumped out onto the sand, and we others followed. The leader of this group was a man of medium height, slim, and sported a puffy scar that ran over his right eye from forehead to jaw. Kinish approached him, with all of us close by.

"What have we here?" Kinish asked cheerfully. "Who are you?"

"Port authority," Scarface said. "There's a port tax to be paid for your anchorage."

"Really? I've been stopping here for many years, and there has never been any such thing before. What is this port tax of yours?"

"A third of your cargo if you're going to market, or three measured pounds of silver."

Kinish was incredulous. "A third of our cargo? Three *pounds* of silver?"

"Aye," Scarface said. "And we'll do the checking to help you stay honest."

Kinish was quiet for a moment, and then said, "Wulfkin. What do you think of this port tax? Should we pay it?"

This was obviously a cue for me to act, not answer. I took a couple of steps forward. Scarface and the man with the axe tensed, watching me. My arms hung relaxed alongside my dagger and short sword. I hoped I had not lost too much hand speed since Umjuno's training sessions. While their eyes were on the weapons, I took one more long stride, Tulak style, and in the time it took them to blink with surprise, *Umjuno* and *Benja* were on either side of Scarface's throat, crossed like a scissors. The blades were so sharp that even resting lightly on his skin was enough to start thin strings of blood working down.

Kinish said, "Well, now. It appears our Wulfkin wants to make a bargain. Do we have a bargain?"

Scarface smiled slightly and said, "We do."

Kinish said I could let him go.

Scarface touched his neck and smiled even more.

"My, my, Kinish," he said. "Where did you find this one?"

Kinish told him I was a stray they found marching around on the Bleak Shoals. I looked back and forth at them with wonder while the crew of the *Abbe Glen* and the thugs on the beach laughed, clasped hands and slapped each other on the back. Smiling native women and children emerged from the shadows.

"How did we look, Rowen?" Kinish asked.

"Good enough," Scarface answered. "And you have added some bite with this Wulfkin fellow."

"Pray we don't have to use him," Kinish said. Then he turned to me and introduced me to Rowen, an old friend from Gylgova. Many years before, Rowen had asked to be left on Broom Island with the native people. Rowen had little family left in Gylgova, and his loss did not harm the industry of the village, so Kinish agreed. Since then, others asked Kinish for passage to Broom, with Rowen's approval, to take up permanent residence among the natives.

This arrangement proved to be convenient for everyone. The *Abbe Glen* needed a safe place to restock water for the last weeks before reaching Grand Reef. Broom had plenty of it, and the expatriates protected it for their countrymen. They, as former members of the "Gylgova Players," as Kinish called them, also allowed a good rehearsal for the odd illusions of the sea wheat merchants. And Broom was a pleasant midway respite.

The *Abbe Glen* also stopped at Broom on the way back to deliver any items the islanders needed from the marketplaces, and pick up letters and gifts the expats wanted taken to friends back home. It would be two years before they saw each other again.

After these enthusiastic greetings, we all walked through a

sun-dappled maze of palm trees and giant ferns until we reached a clearing occupied by a dozen or more grass huts on stilts. Chickens, children, dogs, and small pigs ran about in comical confusion.

The villagers, young and old alike, all came forward with smiles and touches of welcome. A couple of children played hide and seek around my legs, and our hosts, the former Gylgovans, brought out gourd jugs of coconut wine. The old friends and village families sat on grass mats and chattered away, catching up on news from home. Since most of the references were lost on me, I played games with the children. We played tag for a while, then booted around a ball made of palm leaves tied with thin vines. At one point, a lovely girl with a bright, white smile came to me and gently led me back to the group, handing me a wine gourd after I sat down cross-legged on the mat. I began to understand why some did not want to return to ice, sleet, and long nights.

Awhile later, two big native fellows, Rogie, and I were sent to transport our water casks to the pools outside the village. I was grateful for the diversion, because between the wine and the soft breeze, I was sinking into sleep.

A separate path led to the waterfalls, and the walk was easy with empty casks. The four of us made three trips, leaving the longboat empty. As we set down the last casks, Rogie told me that we wouldn't be filling them right then, and to leave them where they were.

We spent two glorious days on Broom, chatting with the villagers and the families of the expatriates, getting to know the children by name, lolling in the cool, clear pools, and telling stories until well after sunset. Nighttime was never truly dark there, because the sky replaced the sun with great swaths of bright stars and moonlight.

All things must end, of course, and the morning came when Kinish said it was time to fill the casks. The whole crew, followed by downcast villagers, trooped off to the waterfalls. The casks filled quickly, and with so many strong shoulders available, the casks were soon back in their places in the bottom of the longboat.

The goodbyes were next, and it didn't take long for them to resemble the greetings. I was in the process of hugging the pretty, smiling girl when I noticed Porcee and Kinish looking out to sea. One by one, all of us turned.

"We have visitors," Kinish said.

As we watched, a ship slowly came into view from behind one of the jungle-covered points of the crescent beach — a splendid copper-colored ship with a large, rose-tinted round window in its side.

Chapter Two

STARLING

The figure in the prow of the approaching tender certainly didn't seem to present a threat. He was a stout man with short white hair and white goatee. As the boat touched the sand, the portly man nimbly hopped out onto the beach.

"Hello, all," he said, instead of the usual "*hala.*" "The name is Martius Starling, from Rampal, a long ways from here, I can tell you, a long ways. But fortunately we travel fast when I am aboard."

Everyone in the group onshore was gawking as much at the others in the boat as at Starling. The crew was dressed in very crisp, clean casual clothes that appeared to be freshly made.

"Welcome, Mister Starling," Rowen said. "Did you come for water? Food, perhaps? Pardon my saying so, but you look in want of neither."

Starling slapped his stomach and laughed. "No pardon required, because the proof is abundant. No, actually, we have come for this young fellow here," gesturing with his head toward me.

Everyone turned to look at me, as people will do, to see if there was something about me they had missed.

Starling approached me and gently touched my arm.

"May I speak to you in private for a moment, Benjamin?"

Hearing my name for the first time since my days with the Brotherhood startled me, and definitely awakened my curiosity. I nodded.

We walked down the beach until we were well beyond the hearing of the others, with Starling talking the whole time: "Wonderful spot here, absolutely wonderful, sand as fine as powder, intoxicating breeze, it's a wonder the place hasn't been overrun by pleasure seekers yet." When we stopped, Starling withdrew a parchment from his shirt pocket.

"This will introduce me as one in the service of the Sovereign Lord Freehold of Rampal. He invites you to Red Cliffs for an audience. You will, of course, travel aboard our own ship, the *Red Moon*."

He noticed my distrustful expression.

"Your mother, father, and sister Marya, as you call her, will be meeting you there in a couple of months. Your Mister Carpenter has been commissioned by His Lordship to oversee the design and building of a vessel for the Sovereigns. Special Counsel Avellone, a lovely fellow, you will like him, has already visited Riversend with the offer."

The shock of all this unexpected news made me lightheaded, and I must have tipped enough for Mister Starling to quickly support me by grasping an arm. I had been prepared to dismiss his parchment—after all, even if it were festooned with official-looking seals, how would I know it was genuine?—but using the names of my family and me was proof enough. These were certainly not people who would sell me into the mines of Grand Reef.

"Those are marvelous words to hear, Mister Starling," I told him. "Of course I will join you."

Holding the unread parchment in my hand, we both rejoined the curious onlookers.

I announced that I would be returning to Rampal with Mister Starling. There was silence among the crew of the *Abbe Glen*.

Kinish stepped forward and placed his hands on my shoulders. He told me that he had enjoyed my company, and had been hoping that I would go back to Gylgova with them. "You would love Leeni and Abbe," he said, and I told him I was certain I would.

Now all the hugs and goodbyes were for me alone. Mister Starling and I gradually disengaged ourselves from those who seemed not to want to release us.

While our boat turned from the shore, I studied the *Red Moon*, surely the most unusual ship I'd ever seen. Then I happened to look over the gunwale into the clear, green water below us. A horseshoe crab was following in our shadow, gliding over white sand under a shimmering net of sunlight. As the water deepened, I watched the crab follow the sand sloping down, and I thought that all ships and people must look like that to those being left behind, figures slowly diminishing as distance increased, fading, fading, and gone.

We returned to the *Red Moon* by way of Kinish's ship. As we came alongside, rising and falling with the gentle swells, I called up to a crewmember to fetch my belongings, that I was going with the other ship. This he did, dropping my cloak and pack down to me with a smile and wishes for good luck.

By the time the *Red Moon* weighed anchor, Kinish's longboat, now carrying full casks of water, sluggishly began its trip back to the *Abbe Glen*. I would not see them again.

Mister Starling gave me a short tour of the ship, all the while apologizing by saying, "Not much to see here, really, not much," but of course there was. The Master Cabin, reserved for his lordship and family, was spectacular. I dropped my possessions in one of the two guest cabins, and was led into the dining room with its big rose windows.

The cook brought us plates of cold food and tankards of beer. As Starling poked around on his plate to see what was there, he said, "Well, Benjamin, I imagine you have some questions for me."

I laughed and said, "Only a few dozen."

"Ask away, then. We have some time."

My first question was that if he was sent to take me to Red Cliffs, how in the world did he find me out there in the middle of the Southern Ocean?

He gave me an impish glance and said, "I've been keeping an eye on you ever since you left Riversend. A rather large eye, actually."

My blank expression caused him to smile.

He asked me how I got back on board the *Abbe Glen* after I fell overboard during the storm.

You cannot imagine my amazement, sire. I said, that Bringer, the Roanfish, took me to the rescue rope, and he could not possibly mean the Roanfish was him.

But that is exactly what he meant. This is what he told me.

Starling's father was a city planner in Central Rampal, and his mother was a sorceress. He liked to tell people that he got his unusual gifts from his mother, but he got his good looks from his father.

These gifts of his were discovered when Starling was about four years old. A boy in the next town had gotten lost in the woods. Dozens of townspeople searched and called out for an entire day without finding him. That night, Starling had a dream in which he was floating over those woods and with extraordinary clarity saw the boy huddling against a tree near a creek.

He told his mother the next morning. She asked him if he could find the boy, and Starling said he could. Off they went to the town, which lay some miles away. When his mother located the mayor and told him that her four-year-old knew where the lostling was, the mayor got angry and told them that this was no joke, and they should go home.

"We looked all day yesterday," he said. "If he were nearby, we would have found him."

Starling and his mother then went to the parents of the lost boy, and his mother told them her child had second sight and knew where their child was. They also told the parents that they had gone to the mayor, and he threw them out. The parents were more desperate than dubious, and the father agreed to go with them.

Starling marched off with absolute confidence, picking his way through the underbrush. He led them straight to the boy, and an astonished reunion took place. When they returned to the town, there was great relief and commotion. The mayor defended his actions by saying, "Wait, now. How was I supposed to know?" but he was removed from office anyway.

Starling's mother had a sneaking suspicion that her son had gifts beyond second sight, so one day she led Starling to a high cave where they could be alone. The sorceress told Starling what she was going to do, which was voice an incantation dedicated to the air, and see what happened. After taking a deep breath, she laid her hands on her son's head and chanted an arcane phrase. What followed was a rather unsightly transformation from little Starling into a Gray-Barred hawk that awkwardly stumbled around the cave floor. His mother laughed with sheer joy at their good fortune. Then she held out an arm, and her new hawk hopped onto it. At the mouth of the cave, she swept her hawk into the air, and watched her son fly away.

At last, there was a shape shifter in the family!

She watched her hawk swoop and soar for a while before she called Starling back and returned him to his earthly self.

Sire, the way shape shifting works in Starling's world is that when they return to human form there is a slight shift in time, so that shifters arrive exactly as they were at the moment of the first transformation. If Starling had flown around for an hour, he would return as he was an hour earlier — but the hawk would be an hour older.

As for what shape shifters become, each is unique, but is capable of transforming into only one being from the air, the earth and the sea. Starling's air form was the Gray-Barred hawk, and the hawk is the only bird he could become. Over time, his mother brought forth his earthly alteration — a huge black and white Bear Dog — and his water form, the Roanfish. He could be no other than these three, and at some point, he would be called by the author of his gifts to choose one to be until the end of its — and consequently his own — life in this world.

I asked him which he would choose, and he stroked his goatee for a moment, and then said he would know when the time came, but there were benefits to recommend each of them.

He enjoyed his time following me around as the Roanfish, particularly gliding along in the dim stratum between the milky blue and darkness. Here, he traveled with the shadows of deep-water fish above and mysterious lights in the eternal blackness below. Once he saw the dark expanse of a leviathan of nearly impossible size cross in front of him, and waited a long time for it to pass by. Another time he saw a sprawl of tiny lights below arranged in rows and curves, and the lights never flickered or moved. Most of all, he enjoyed the thrill of approaching big islands or continents, when the sea bottom slowly rose to meet him and he found himself in a dazzling new world teeming with life, color, and light.

As a Bear Dog, he found life curious and often dangerous. Humans were afraid of him, and fear drove some to try to kill him. Some larger animals also did their best to get him, but his size and speed worked well for him. On the other hand, the experience of being brushed and petted was wonderful, and he liked the delighted romping of children on and around him.

As a hawk, he gloried in the imperial solitude of soaring high above, but still being able to see a mouse on the ground. The hawk's extraordinarily sharp vision enabled Starling to help others either find their way, or find something lost. The freedom of the air was almost dreamlike.

He was both happy and lucky to have been granted three such interesting forms to represent the air, land and sea. After all, he could have been a goldfish, a pocket dog and a buzzard.

Starling much preferred his present, portly, human form, he said. The food was much better.

After Starling's mother died, as all mortals eventually do no matter how magical they may be, he wandered Rampal in one form or another helping humans. As the Roanfish, he herded schools of fish (with apologies) into the nets of fishermen. (Since the Roanfish is sizable and rare, he sometimes had to dodge attempts to snare him, too.) As a Bear Dog, he defended others against mad or carnivorous beasts and highway robbers. As a hawk, he could travel vast distances quickly, and do his work on a broad scale.

One day, as Starling sat on the veranda of his infrequently occupied little house, a courier came to him. The courier delivered a letter from the newly anointed Sovereign Lord of Rampal, Indus and the Isle of Provinces. The letter read that the Sovereign Lord of Rampal, etc., had heard of Starling's unusual abilities and requested a visit from him to discuss permanent position with the House of Freehold. The Sovereign Lord of Rampal, etc., had been aware of

Starling's shape shifting for some time, but had not bothered with trying to employ those skills to secure the leadership position more quickly during the Conflict of the Siblings because he knew Starling wouldn't do it anyway.

The offer was to become an agent for the Freeholds, tasked with more of the helpfulness for which Starling was known.

Starling flew to Red Cliffs for his interview, and stayed. A few years later, Starling found himself with the job of helping to bring together the royal family, the Carpenters, and me.

Also, Starling said, in his official role at Red Cliffs, the food got even better.

Nothing of consequence occurred during the rest of our journey to Red Cliffs, and the reason for that was, as Starling said, that he was aboard. Walking on deck not long after we set sail, I looked forward from the prow, and laughed out loud. Even though the sea was agitated that day and the waves broke and danced every which way, an utterly smooth path as wide as a coach road preceded us. We sailed fast, as if on a lake, across the Southern Ocean.

Mister Starling told many more tales of his adventures, but I will spare you the details and the time it would take to tell them. As you might imagine, they were strange and fantastic, and made the time pass quickly.

Then, of course, came the day when the red mountains of eastern Rampal began to rise from the sea. I had never seen anything like it before. The town and fortress castle of Red Cliffs lay in a jumble of dazzlingly white walls with rooftops the same color as the high, red cliffs beyond, all framed by a pale blue sky above and deep blue water at its shore.

During our approach, Starling assured me that I would like the Sovereign Lord and Lady. They were always in good humor, he said, and active, bustling about from one project to another with relentless energy. The Sovereign Lord Tryon was a figurehead and possessed a kingly manner, but could sometimes be found working alongside laborers building a new house or harvesting crops. He also frequently appeared in the kitchen, where he minced and diced and experimented with soups and stews. Since his ascension, even the population of Red Cliffs seemed happier and livelier. These days, Starling said, one could hear laughter in the streets.

The quay was busy, but most of the people were watching the ship come in to see who would emerge. Everyone recognized the *Red Moon*, and knew that it only sailed for dignitaries. For that reason, eyebrows rose in surprise after the gangplank was secured and Starling disembarked with a young man wearing a holy cloak and weapons at his waist.

A well-dressed, confident man with a friendly smile stepped forward to grasp my hand. Starling introduced him as Special Counsel Darwen Avellone, who would escort me to the castle. Avellone asked Starling to join them for the coach ride, but Starling declined.

"Errands to run, many errands," Starling said in his distinctive way. "And cleaning, my, my, the cleaning. I've been away for a long time and imagine my quarters are cobwebbed and airless and altogether unlovely." He told me he would be joining His Lordship and Lady, Mister Avellone and me for dinner that evening, and went on his way through the shifting crowd.

As I looked out the coach window to see as much as I could of this extraordinary place, Mister Avellone told me of his trip to Riversend, and the meeting with my father and family. He described the conditions up there at this time of year. Surrounded by so much warmth, brightness and color, it was hard for me to imagine the cold dampness and blustering wind that I knew so well. He assured me that everyone was well, and that they would be guests at Red Cliffs until Father's commission was completed. He assumed I would also stay, but I was, naturally, free to go where I pleased, with His Lordship's blessing and support.

Really, sire. Where else would I go, besides Gylgova or Broom Island? Back to Vastland to share Umjuno's nomadic life? None of these destinations were more appealing than being with my family.

Mister Avellone said that he and the *Red Moon* would return to Riversend in two months to pick up my father, mother and sister. In the meantime, I would occupy what would be our family home for the next three years.

The castle of Red Cliffs is grand, beautiful, and interesting for its oddness. Gravenwall is majestic and proud, but Red Cliffs is flooded with light and energy. Its hallways are as broad as streets, gleaming with marble and silver, and its walls showcase large paintings and vivid tapestries. There is even a complete bedchamber right in the main hallway, mostly screened by potted plants and a couple of small trees. I have no idea why it is there or who would use it.

As I would discover later, beneath the main hallway is a jousting list surrounded by dining tables. The floor is red sand, taken from the mountains, and the tilts were ornate, carved panels depicting various pivotal battles in the history of Red Cliffs. The most dramatic feature of the upper floor, above the main hallway, is a library of only one shelf near eye level that runs the length of that long hall, broken only by the entrances to all the royal and guest quarters. Below this shelf are sculptures, artifacts, shields and totems. The juxtaposition of these elements is almost dizzying. However, balance is restored above. Along the length of the hall, on its high walls, is a collection of unique doors and gates from other countries, most painted in vivid colors or designs intended to protect the dwelling from superstitions.

A curiosity I found fascinating was a collection of images of Gravenwall painted by one Queen Anelie.

But I'm rambling.

Mister Avellone led me down the broad main floor hallway, identifying rooms as we passed them, until we came to the Chair Chamber, in which was an elegant, throne-like chair for his lordship. Along the walls on either side were a number of straight-backed chairs for ministers or other officials. Mister Avellone gestured with a sweep of his arm that I could sit anywhere I pleased, except for the obvious, and he would tell the Sovereign Lord that I was present. I did not sit. I studied the paintings on the chamber walls instead.

After a short while, in came Lord Freehold, walking quickly and smiling at me. He is a tall fellow with the kind of face people like instantly, because he seems to like them. He marched up to me and clapped both hands on the sides of my shoulders.

"Benjamin," he said cheerfully. "Here at last. I hope you are feeling well and not too exhausted from your journey. Mister Starling no doubt kept you entertained along the way."

He led us to a couple of chairs, and pulled one away from the wall so he could face me.

He said that I had experienced quite the time trying to get back home, but all would work out well in the end. Then he related the same information to me that Mister Avellone had passed on to my father, about Marya really being Lilea, Princess Freehold, and how she had a sister named Sofia. I told him that my parents had rightly told us some time ago that she was not my birth sister.

Lord Freehold laughed and said, "Which is strange indeed, because I have heard so much about you, I feel as though you are the son I never had."

He spent some time reviewing my father's new responsibilities and how delighted his lordship was to have his inimitable skills here at Red Cliffs.

An hour or more later, he stood and prepared to leave the room. As if on cue, Mister Avellone entered. Plans were made for me to join the royal couple for dinner that evening, and Mister Avellone was to take me to the new Carpenter house nearby.

The house turned out to be simple, but spacious and splashed with sunlight from windows all around. The space would shrink somewhat when my family's furniture and other belongings were moved in, but there was more than enough room for all of us and any guests we might invite.

Mister Avellone said he would come back in the late afternoon to escort me to the banquet hall, but in the meantime, I should rest. There would be time enough for him to show me the rest of the castle, walk me around the town and down to the docks where an exact replica of Father's shop now stood. He then excused himself, and I was alone. Muffled sounds from outside drifted in. Shadows from the windows lay across the floor. I wandered for a few minutes, testing chair cushions and peeking into rooms, until I came to the bedroom, which would be mine until my family arrived. The bed was made, and looked cool and comfortable.

I lay down, and soon fell into the deepest sleep I had known in years.

There is much more to tell, certainly. Of my days in Red Cliffs until my family arrived, more of the adventures of Mister Starling, of the joyful reunion with my family and my reattachment to the one who was now Lilea, Princess Freehold, and of two more journeys I would make: one with Lilea and Mister Starling to Sloedon Castle, where we retrieved Sofia and her eminent guardian, and the other to this place, here, to Gravenwall.

But those are really part of a story already told. A new story begins from here.

The sun is lowering, King Harald. The crowd is restless and growing hungry. Time, for now, has run out.

We have finished.

The tale is done.

Epilogue

A Season Of Welcomes And Farewells

ANELIE

The crowd was indeed restless. In fact, the crowd was rising to its collective feet. Some were pointing. Some held their faces in their hands. The murmur swelled to full voice.

Harald felt a presence on either side of him, and the unmistakable pressure of two sword points against his upper back.

"Easy, now, Harald. Keep still," a voice said.

Harald heard footsteps in the hallway below his balcony, and watched in wonder as a tall woman dressed in riding clothes emerged onto the amphitheater floor. She was flanked and followed by nine soldiers, who, he was to find out later, represented the elite guard of the Sovereign Lord Tryon Freehold. When the woman stopped and turned to face Harald, the guard formed at her back, alert but not anxious. One went to Benjamin and slapped him on the back affectionately. The volume from the crowd increased, broken by scattered applause.

"Now, that is what I call an entrance," Harald said. "Who might you be?"

"Anelie, Queen of Swallows, Harald. You are in my house, and I want you out."

"Ah, the queen. I'm sorry I never got to meet you. How in the world did you get in here with your entourage and not be seen?"

"The same way I was forced to leave," Anelie said. "The Siege Stairs."

"Siege Stairs? I never heard of them. Where are those? How does one get to them without being spotted?"

"You would have to be shown, Harald. And you won't be. They lead to hidden passages throughout the castle. You and your guards were so taken with Benjamin's tale, I could have brought my army in with me."

"You have an army, do you?"

"Of course, in case we were noticed in time for you to put up a defense. They follow half a day behind. Only three hundred, but enough."

Harald knew this to be true. Over the preceding years, about half his men had assimilated into the Swallows population through marriage or employment. Many had families now, and homes of their own.

"Much too late for a defense, or even a retreat," Harald said. "Well done, Dogman."

Benjamin nodded his appreciation.

"So, what now, Anelie?"

"Your Highness," she said.

Harald smiled and tipped his head. "Your Highness. Do you plan to relieve me of my head, or make me a permanent guest in your dungeon?"

"Neither. You were given Gravenwall by Master Turnbolt. You did not seize it. And you have done no harm in the time since. Here is what will happen: you will assemble whatever men are still loyal to you, and you all will be escorted to Fugitive Bridge. You will go back where you came from, and if you are lucky and no one along the way recognizes you, you may even make it safely."

"Very gracious of you, Your Highness. I am grateful for not having to anticipate the sting of an axe. Should I begin preparing for my leave?"

"Yes. I don't think you will try to escape by hiding in this crowd. These are my people. You would not last long. The rest of the troops should arrive by dawn, and some of them will lead you and your followers out."

Harald sighed and rose slowly, so as not to alarm the two behind him.

"You have a wonderful province here, Your Highness. I have enjoyed my stay here. And you, Dogman. I have enjoyed these past two days in your company. You had won this event by the end of the first day, and I was looking forward to having you as a neighbor. But we all must move on. Now I need to decide if I should go back, as Her Majesty said, to where I came from, or try to make a new life somewhere in Welland. I'm sure the answer will come to me at some point."

Harald bowed, a bow meant for both the queen and the crowd.

When he turned, one of the guards said, "If you don't mind, we'll come with you."

Harald laughed. "To make sure I don't steal the silverware?"

The guard shrugged his shoulders.

The word went out that those who wished to accompany Harald should be at Gravenwall's main gate at dawn or risk being left behind. During the night, several of Harald's closest friends visited him to tell him they were staying in Swallows. None had any desire to make the trek back, or to chance being hanged by some townspeople who years earlier had been in Harald's path. Harald wished them well.

As expected, the main body of Anelie's force arrived in the pre-dawn murk. They were told to rest and eat for a few hours before a small contingent was chosen to return Harald to Fugitive Bridge.

As Harald sat in a chair near the main gate, thoughtfully chewing pieces of hard bread, a grand total of six of his men arrived to accompany him. They all lived in various places throughout Welland, and wanted to go home. There was no chatter, no relief or joy. They sat quietly and waited.

When the sun was high enough to cast long shadows across the grass and set the dew alight, a group of mounted soldiers arrived, leading seven horses, one of which was Harald's old companion Typhoon. As he affectionately stroked Typhoon's soft, white muzzle, Harald was again grateful for the queen's kindness.

A small crowd had gathered to watch them leave. The queen was above, at the window of her throne room, looking down at the procession as it moved slowly away into the shadow of Gravenwall on the ground, then out of it into the sunlight. Benjamin was near her, watching from a different window.

"Well, Benjamin," she said. "I am back. There is much to catch up with, and many things to do. I want you to stay with me. I want you to be my ambassador to Riversend and Red Cliffs."

Benjamin looked pleased, and bowed slightly. "It will be my pleasure to serve you, Your Highness."

"Not serve. Help."

"Yes. I will gladly help, then."

In the weeks and months that followed, Gravenwall was host to many happy occasions. The first was the reunion of Ma Guen with all her girls except Hanna, now Sofia, Princess Freehold. The fabulous traveling tumbling show was disbanded, and the girls either found work in the castle, or married, or relocated to other towns in Swallows. Ma Guen retired as seamstress to Queen Anelie and hostess for the entertainment of local children. She lived quietly in her spacious chambers, doting on a yappy and altogether overly spoiled little dog she named Mister.

Near fall, several nearby towns got together and staged a rollicking lawn fair of their own to welcome their queen back to Gravenwall. There was dancing, music, food in abundance, and a special performance by three of Ma Guen's girls, who had certainly not lost their edge, thrilling the crowd to applause.

The affection that sparked the moment Anelie and Benjamin saw each other at Sloedon Castle just before she was freed, only grew stronger during their time together at Red Cliffs before the mission to reclaim Gravenwall. Anelie, fascinated by Benjamin's anecdotes, was the one who suggested that Benjamin enter the storytelling competition to distract Harald long enough for her to enact a bloodless coup.

The affection turned to love at Gravenwall, but a love founded on respect as they formed a new administration, and worked through the myriad details of regaining oversight of provincial affairs. Benjamin had assumed the advisory role once held by Thomas Chancellor, whom the queen named Minister of Ministerial Activities—meaning that Chancellor made appointments and issued reminders for the other ministers.

One day, as they walked through the rose garden outside the castle discussing the Agriculture Minister's recommendation for an irrigation system, Anelie suddenly turned to Benjamin.

"Benjamin," she said, "this has gone on long enough. We should marry and be done with it. Soon."

"Is that a command, Your Highness?"

"Yes."

A few days later, in the same garden, surrounded by red and white and pink and yellow blossoms, they talked about plans for a wedding in the same Gravenwall chapel where her parents were married. This would be quite an affair, involving the heads of state who had given Anelie their support and encouragement while she was in exile. As they were talking, a shadow passed over them. Then again. And again.

"What was that?" she asked.

Benjamin smiled. "A Gray-Barred hawk, I believe. Mister Starling must have made his choice. If so, this bird will be our guardian for a long time."

"If that is true," Anelie said, "then this bird must be Gravenwall's guardian for *all* time. Its image should be carved into the Gravenwall crest."

Benjamin thought this a fine idea.

And they made it so.

SOFIA

Ma Guen died at Gravenwall, where she wanted to be — in the room where all the children ramped and yelled and tumbled. She was quite mad by then, but happy in her madness. Her attendants and even the guard at the door smiled to watch her hands embroider invisible cloth, tapping her feet, and chuckling at a joyful tumult no one else could hear. Beaming, she would say, "They're 'ere. Heverybody's 'ere."

Queen Anelie declared the day of her passing a holiday. Not for mourning, she insisted, but for celebrating their good fortune in having known such a fine, selfless person.

Sofia was in Red Cliffs, having stayed behind with Lilea while the queen regained control of her province. During the dreary years in Sloedon Castle, Anelie and Hanna had grown apart. Anelie's continual preoccupation with her loss and her absorption with painting created a growing distance between them. More and more, Hanna found herself tending to Ma Guen, who was often ill from the never-ending chill and dampness that filled Sloedon. The Baron did his best to dispel the gloom and discomfort; there was a fireplace in every room, and he ordered his groundskeepers to keep them all burning brightly morning and night.

As Hanna grew older, she became increasingly self-reliant. There was a touching resignation about the way she found things to do, and ways to amuse herself. The Sloedon staff became accustomed to her visits in the kitchens, the gardens and the stables, where she helped feed and groom the horses. She had no fear of the big animals, one of which was a scarred, unpredictable old warhorse named Dorian. The stable hands were impressed by her absolute ease in talking to all the horses, stroking their muzzles and foreheads, and leading them out to the paddock while the stalls were cleaned. The stable hands said she had a special gift with the animals.

On the afternoon Hanna discovered she was Sofia, Princess Freehold, she was a little less than presentable when she was summoned to the queen's quarters, having come from feeding time in the barn. She carried the smell of hay and manure in her clothes, which she found very pleasant, but others sometimes found startling.

She entered, and found herself staring at a girl about her age who was looking back at her with a smile. A young man, also near her age, was there too, along with a big dog. She felt herself go numb as she was told that she was a royal from Rampal, and that the girl was her sister. Sofia was told to prepare to go home to meet her real mother and father. All of them were going, including the queen, because the Sovereign Lord intended to return Anelie to her rightful position in Swallows.

Ma Guen clapped her hands with delight when Sofia told her the news that her Hanna was actually a princess. Ma Guen was thrilled, but Sofia didn't feel like a princess, and did not want to leave Ma Guen. Anelie vowed to return Ma Guen to Gravenwall, and look after her as if she were her own mother.

She and Lilea grew closer the longer they were together. Lilea was irrepressible, and loved to refer to themselves as Lileamarya and Sofiahanna.

To Sofia, the confusion grew even more absurd when she saw the way her friend, the queen, looked at Benjamin, who was Marya's brother, but not Lilea's, and that as Marya, she had, in effect, lost her mother, father and brother, but as Lilea, she had gained a sister and a new set of parents.

Even though they had never known each other, their blood remembered, and they were soon chattering and laughing at each other's stories.

When it came time to leave Sloedon and take their places on the ship to Rampal, Lilea and Sofia walked aboard hand in hand.

* * *

Sofia's first days in Red Cliffs overwhelmed her. The bright, bustling town, a huge castle with an almost infinite number of corners in which to peek, a mother and father she had never known, and a sister who was quickly replacing Queen Anelie as her best friend all disoriented her.

She liked the lord and lady. They were energetic and treated both young women with an almost comradely familiarity that bore not even a hint of condescension. Because the girls were older, they judged the lord and lady from a more mature perspective. Both Lilea and Sofia looked for and noticed similarities among them all in mood, wit, interests, opinions and even in the way they walked. There was no doubt, after a week or so, that they were all of the same family.

Unlike Lilea, Sofia accepted the circumstances of her separations. She understood the lord's and lady's reasoning, and from what she heard of the Conflict of the Siblings, there was a real possibility of some vile retribution. To her, all that was far in the past. She'd had a good life with the queen and Ma Guen and the girls. But this was her life now.

When the strain of all this newness weighed her down, she sought the solace of the stables. The smell of the horses, hay and oats, manure and leather comforted her. Both Lilea and Lord Tryon learned early on that if Sofia was absent, she could be found in the stables.

One day, Lord Tryon said to her, "Sofia, how would you like to take a trip with me? We have to check our tree crops and I'd like you to come along. This might be one of your responsibilities later on."

How could she refuse? He was the Sovereign Lord and he was her father.

They began preparing for a journey to Indus.

They arrived less than a day after leaving Red Cliffs. Lord Tryon had with him two of his foremen, one of whom was an arborist. They were met at the little dock by a couple of the caretakers, who stayed on Indus for a month at a time on a rotating schedule. Sofia was embarrassed when the caretakers bowed to her.

The group had come ashore on the forest side of the island. Lord Tryon and his arborists preferred to emulate natural regeneration by planting new Bronzewood saplings in among the more mature trees. Periodically, Lord Tryon and his foremen surveyed and assessed different sectors of the forest for growth status, leaf diseases, exposed roots, and foliage quality. In his conversation room, Lord Tryon kept a wall-sized map reflecting each sector of the Bronzewood forest and the date on which it was surveyed. By studying his map, Lord Tryon could best judge which trees could be cut down, and the status of its nearest replacement. Bronzewood generated a lot of income for Red Cliffs.

The crew spent their time on Sector Six on the day Sofia went along. They walked most of it, watching where their boots set down, and kept records in parchment notebooks.

After a few hours, the group, its work completed, turned to make their way back out. Lord Tryon said he and Sofia would catch up to them in a little while. With a smile, he said, "Come with me, Sofia. I have something I want to show you."

As they walked, Lord Tryon told her a little of the history of Indus and its uniqueness. He mentioned the generosity of the currents that allowed these rare species to flourish, and the early days when plunderers and thieves came, and then of the royal house taking Indus under its protection. Through the trees, the light was growing ahead of them, and they emerged at the top of a long, grassy slope.

Below her, Sofia saw an immense herd of ponies grazing in the rich, green grass. Their variety of colors and patterns made it look as if paint had been splashed over the valley.

Lord Tryon heard her laugh quietly to herself. She started walking down the slope. His lordship said, "Remember, they are wild, Sofia. They are still wild animals." He wasn't concerned, because he knew from experience that the herd would shift and move away as soon as they saw a human coming toward them. Her blond hair glowing in the sunlight, Sofia kept walking unhurriedly, closer and closer.

To Lord Tryon's amazement, the herd looked up, but did not back away. Sofia approached with her hand raised, talking to them as if she were greeting acquaintances at a summer gathering. With a serenity that allowed no room for anyone else, she walked among them, touching each pony she passed lightly on the head or neck or back with her fingers, and where she went, they followed.

* * *

A month or so later, the Lady Freehold and both girls visited her brother in his large but modest house a day's ride from Red Cliffs. Lady Freehold's purpose was to introduce her now-grown daughters to her brother's family. The house easily accommodated them all, while the royal bodyguards camped comfortably on the lawn. They stayed three days, trading lifetimes of experiences and thoughts. While becoming more familiar with their uncle, the girls became much more familiar with each other. Lady Freehold declared the time well spent.

By the time the three of them returned to Red Cliffs, Sofia had long since run out of patience with talking and company. Lord Freehold met them at the top of the stairs to the second floor apartments. After welcoming hugs and assurances that his brother-in-law was in fine fettle, Lord Tryon took Sofia aside and said, as if reading her mind:

"We did some work in the stables while you were gone. I want you to see it before you go there."

When they reached the main stable, the stable hands were waiting for them, and smiled when they saw Sofia.

"We have altered the rear stalls," Lord Tryon said, "which might have confused you if you happened upon them without warning. I think you will like the improvements."

The improvements turned out to be six brand new, smaller stalls, each containing an Indus pony.

Afterward, Sofia blamed her exhaustion from the visit for her sudden tears, but that didn't explain the breathlessness which accompanied them. Her father explained that there were six ponies because they were such handsome animals, and they were on the small side, so one didn't look like enough. If there were any she did not want to keep, he would return them to the herd on the next tree survey trip.

Sofia shook her head. No.

Anticipating her thoughts again, Lord Tryon said, "They were very comfortable and well cared for on their way here."

He did not need words of gratitude or a hug to know how Sofia felt, so, still smiling, he laid a hand on her shoulder and said he would see her again at dinner.

The ponies became her obsession. She spent most of every day brushing, walking, feeding them and cleaning their stalls—when it came to this particular chore, she was grateful the ponies were small, but then again, there were six of them.

As for feeding them, Sofia was not happy that she had to fill their feed boxes one at a time. That meant that one had to be first and one had to be last. To her, there was no first or last among them. She loved them all equally.

Therefore, with the help of a stable hand, she created a device involving a crossbar with a lever in the middle, six buckets and a simple system of ropes. The ponies watched with interest the first time she filled the buckets one at a time, then pulled the lever. The buckets tipped all at once and filled every feed box at the same time.

The ponies were smart and devoted to her. Like dogs, evidence of their strong bond was in the way they watched every move Sofia made. She quickly trained each of them to stop when she held up her hand, and lie down when she lowered her palm toward the ground. This led her to wonder if she could train them to do things as a team.

Lord Tryon listened to her progress with the ponies with pride and contentment. To help her with her experiment, he ordered the tilts taken out of the jousting arena so that Sofia could have all six ponies with her at once. This was no hardship for anyone—there hadn't been a jousting contest at Red Cliffs in fifty years.

In late mid-summer, plans were made for a state visit from Queen Anelie and Prince Benjamin sometime in the fall, after the heat of the southern sun had waned. There would be another reunion of the Carpenter family, which gladdened Lilea.

Sofia had missed Anelie, her girlhood friend. She knew that Anelie as queen was extremely preoccupied, but the distance between them hurt. Sofia wanted to do something special during their visit, something to remind the queen of the companionship they used to have.

Throughout the rest of the summer, Sofia was busy with her ponies and seldom seen in the castle halls. In fact, the only way Lilea could spend time with her was to join her in the stables or in the jousting arena, even though Lilea did not share Sofia's consuming passion for ponies.

The royal couple arrived on an ideal, cool fall day that appeared planned for them. The noise level in the Red Cliffs conversation room was high with excited laughter and loud greetings and news from Riversend and Gravenwall. An afternoon luncheon was no less raucous, but once the meal was over, things calmed down and short naps were next.

Wine was served on a veranda as the daylight turned golden. Lord Tryon announced that dinner would be enjoyed downstairs, in the former jousting list, because Sofia had a special welcoming gift planned for them all.

They trooped down a winding stair and took assigned places along the barrier, with the queen and prince in the center.

Rather than a horn fanfare to quiet the crowd, Sofia had decided that a couple of large hand bells were more appropriate. As the last notes echoed away, she entered the list with her six ponies, each a different color or pattern, all gleaming from their last minute brushing.

Sofia tipped her head toward the gathering.

"As a welcoming gift to Her Majesty the Queen and a tribute to someone very dear to me, we will perform a few unique exercises I learned a long time ago, in a big room in Gravenwall. We hope you all enjoy them."

She turned to the ponies, raised her arms, and brought her hands together over her head. The ponies formed a single line.

Then Sofia called out, "Chainstitch!" with the command's hand signal. The ponies began weaving in and out among each other.

"Running stitch!"

"Blanket stitch!"

"Basket stitch!"

The ponies executed a different formation for each call, moving flawlessly in unison, and although they certainly did not tumble as Ma Guen's girls had, they nevertheless presented a colorful and thrilling sight.

Anelie's cheeks were bright with tears when the show ended and the applause began. Everyone rose to his or her feet with shouts of praise, surprise and amazement.

There were three ponies on either side of Sofia when she turned to face the dinner guests, and all seven bowed.

LILEA

By the time the *Red Moon* reached Rampal, Darwen had given Lilea as much information about her biological parents as was wise. Lilea listened patiently, but Darwen could see her mind at work. He just didn't know what she was thinking.

He did know, however, that he found her lovely, sharp and interesting, but kept these opinions as well hidden as possible. She was the Sovereign Lord's daughter, after all, and although Lord Tryon was an affable man, he was not one to provoke without expecting memorable consequences.

The Carpenters found themselves in an unexpected emotional limbo. The foundling that had become as much their daughter as Benjamin was their son had suddenly become someone else. They had never thought of her that way, because it never crossed their minds that her real parents might come for her. Now they noticed mannerisms in her that they themselves did not have. Their confusion was not lost on Marya—pardon, Lilea—who did her best to reassure them. She hugged them more often and sat with them when they were alone.

"I don't know these people," she told her father. "Nothing has really changed at all."

But of course, it had. For a little more than twenty years the Carpenters had a daughter, and now they didn't.

The closer the *Red Moon* drew to Red Cliffs, the more anxious the Carpenters became. Darwen did as much as he could to ease their tension by continuing his soft chatter, telling them of all the interesting sights to see in and near Red Cliffs.

The gangplank could not be lowered fast enough to suit the Carpenters, because Benjamin was waiting for them, along with the Lord and Lady Freehold. The presence of Benjamin made all the difference in the world when it came to meeting the Freeholds for the first time. Had he not been there, the Carpenters, not yet knowing the protocol for meeting the Sovereign Lord and Lady, would have felt very uncomfortable and awkward. Seeing Benjamin again put them all in high spirits.

The Freeholds helped by welcoming them all one at a time with smiles, laughter and genuine happiness that they were there. Lord Tryon did not hug Lilea, but took both her hands in his and brightly told her how happy he was to finally have her at Red Cliffs.

Amid the raucousness and affection, Lilea watched Lord Tryon's handsome face and realized with a shiver of fear what an alien new life she had just entered.

After all the Carpenters, including Lilea for the time being, had a few days to settle in, get reacquainted, and explore a little bit of Red Cliffs, Lord Tryon asked for Lilea to meet him in the Conversation Room at the castle.

She entered warily, and sat where Lord Tryon motioned she should sit.

"Do you understand how you came to be a Carpenter child?" he asked.

"Mister Avellone explained everything very well, thank you."

Lord Tryon, just to make certain, recapped the long, often brutal Conflict of the Siblings, and the removal of the girls from harm's way. Lilea sat quietly until he was finished.

"Why didn't you leave us with families in Rampal?" Lilea said. "That would make more sense than going to all this trouble."

Lord Tryon smiled. "Darwen warned me about you," he said. "The reason is that if you two were anywhere in Rampal, you would have been found and sold to the highest bidder among our enemies."

"Then why the Provinces? Why not some pleasant, balmy little island in the Southern Ocean? That would have been nice, I think."

"The Provinces were easier to reach, and accessible by ship along the coast or by clipper across the Rampal Strait, where we could go overland if the coast was not feasible.

"We also had people from Rampal and, in your case, in Riversend to watch over you. We could have moved quickly if any trouble came to you. Sofia was a different circumstance. We had been aware of Harald Stonearm's advance, but did not anticipate Gravenwall being handed over to him. Because of the speed of the surrender and the ongoing conflict here, we could not respond in time."

"I have no idea what you just said."

Lord Tryon laughed. "I suppose you don't. You will soon. I want you to go with Benjamin and Mister Starling to bring Sofia back. I'll explain everything before then."

"Mister Starling?"

"You will enjoy him. He's a man full of surprises."

"He's not alone, then," Lilea said. "These families you left us with: are you going to compensate them for raising us?"

Lord Tryon stared. "What?"

"Will the Carpenters and Sofia's guardians be compensated for raising us? They worked for years and years, and used their own money for our well-being."

Lord Tryon sat back in his chair and studied her with wonder for a moment before, saying, "You were there when Mister Avellone presented the letter of agreement to Mister Carpenter. In fact, you challenged parts of it, which I admire. You already know that Mister Carpenter will be more than adequately compensated."

"I believe that agreement was for the design and building of a ship. I heard nothing about child-rearing."

"Well, well, well. We must correct that that oversight, mustn't we? And we shall. I will have Mister Avellone draw up a contract to fairly reward your guardians and Ma Guen, Sofia's guardian. You may read it over with an eye toward closing any loopholes and clarifying its intent. Consider it the first of your new duties.

"Also, you will be moved into your rooms here at the castle in a day or so. The Carpenters are nearby. You can visit any time you like."

"They are my family," Lilea said.

"You are a Freehold. Your first obligation is to your people, the people of Rampal. The Carpenters certainly understand. And so will you, in time. For now, you are excused. I would like to see you again tomorrow, and often afterward, Lilea. You are a splendid addition to Red Cliffs."

She did not try to stretch her luck. She rose, tipped her head, and left the room.

✳ ✳ ✳

By the time Mister Carpenter's seagoing masterpiece was

completed and the Carpenters were faced with preparing to return to Riversend, Lilea was fully reconciled with her transition. She had quickly become a devoted and loving sister to Sofia, and gradually became a joyful and affectionate daughter to the Lord and Lady Freehold. She never neglected the Carpenters, but slowly — because of a procession of events and new responsibilities — estranged herself enough to make the eventual Carpenter leave-taking far less difficult than it might have been. Also, in this particular case, promises to see each other often were easily kept. As Ambassador to Riversend and Rampal, Benjamin made scheduled visits to see his parents, then sailed on to Red Cliffs for time with Lilea.

By then, Lilea's quick and creative mind had proved her to be a perfect complement to the Special Counsel office of Darwen Avellone, and the two of them soon became the most formidable diplomatic negotiators and treaty advisors of their time. They were always professional and focused on their duties, but their emotional closeness was not lost on the Lord and Lady. Because there was no need for a politically brokered union — which Lilea would not have tolerated anyway — the way was clear for their eventual marriage.

Sofia enjoyed her beloved ponies, but was haunted by the fact that they, too, were far from the home they had known. One day, with a heart as heavy as lead, she went to Lord Freehold and told him she wanted to return her ponies to their herd. That was, she said, the only right thing to do.

Lord Tryon was proud of her decision, knowing how difficult it had been for her to make it, and how much courage she had shown in telling him of it. Lord Freehold had come to a decision of his own along the way that resolved several issues at once, and considerably lightened Sofia's spirits.

He gave her the island of Indus.

The Bronzewood forests were hers to routinely survey and

nurture, with the help of the caretakers and foremen. The pony herd was her charge, too, and she monitored their health, diet, foaling, and general well being with tireless commitment and pleasure.

To make these tasks easier to achieve, Lord Tryon had a house built for her on Indus, at a location from which she could see both the forests and the herd just by stepping outside onto her veranda. Sofia took up residence there for two weeks of every month, returning to Red Cliffs for the remaining two weeks in order to administrate the logistical side of caring for the herd, and to facilitate the culling, marketing and sale of small batches of mature Bronzewood to the world at large. Lilea always found time to spend at least a week with her sister in the Indus house every month or so, and they agreed, as did most visitors—which sometimes included Queen Anelie—that sunset over the Indus valley was one of the most beautiful sights in the world.

Mister Carpenter's ship was, too, in the estimation of many. The Freehold commission was a glorious creation, inside and out. Its sleek lines, tasteful adornments, and flawless, copper-colored strakes arrested attention every time they were seen. Inside, dramatic touches such as stairways that could be raised to become part of the ceiling and easily lowered when needed, and cabin bunks that folded up against the bulkhead to create more space were meticulously finished and mechanically perfect. He had even kept the distinctive *Red Moon* porthole concept, installing two round windows with leaded blue glass designs depicting ocean waves. When guests were seated in the dining room, the windows cast a wonderful blue tint over all, one that subtly changed with the lowering of the sun.

Lord Tryon had given a lot of thought as to what name this marvelous creation should carry. He was searching for a name that would unite the families and offer a small tribute to Mister Carpenter's inimitable involvement. He wanted a name that was distinctive and graceful. Finally, after hours of pacing and consideration, he remembered something from a story Lilea told him of Benjamin and her learning to sail and swim under Mister Carpenter's watchful eye.

And so it was that one splendid spring morning, to rowdy cheers and hurrahs from a sizable throng on the dock at Red Cliffs, the Freehold flagship *Waterborn* first raised her sails.

ABBE

By the time the *Abbe Glen* returned to Gylgova with her worn and weakened crew, seventeen-year-old Abbe had a plan in mind to keep them home for good.

The idea came to her slowly while she was thinking about the risks the Gylgova men took to acquire the copper sheets. Grand Reef was one of the few places where the ore could be found, so the mining and smelting consortium had the market to itself. Over the years, they kept nudging the prices up until a point was reached at which sales dropped because few would pay what was asked and the rest could not afford it at all. Even though prices were lowered, they were still exorbitant when compared to the cost of creating the product.

Abbe knew this. She had overheard her father complaining about the situation for years, but the town was cornered. Its copper items and skill in making them were the source of Gylgova's wealth. The sea wheat they harvested was likewise found in few places, so its worth was high enough to barter for what they needed.

In mulling all this over while the men were gone, Abbe reasoned that when the cost of the voyage to Grand Reef was added to the cost of the copper, Gylgova was paying almost twice as much as they should. But the copper was in Grand Reef. The sea wheat was relatively nearby, just on the other side of the Bleak Shoals. If they could keep the sea wheat, they could start a whole new industry in Gylgova: sea wheat flour and baked goods.

Would those be enough to replace the copper business? Probably not. Their copper products were obviously more durable for taking to far-flung markets and would always generate more income than flour and bread. Those things she envisioned being sold right in Gylgova.

The copper business had to stay. The only way around the risk and cost of getting it was to make it themselves. But the ore was in Grand Reef.

Then a thought struck her. They didn't need the ore. They just needed the copper.

She went to the Gylgova blacksmith who had remained behind and asked what would be needed to make a crucible. Fire clay, he said. That could be made hard enough. Was fire clay here, in Gylgova? He believed it was, in the hillsides near Abbe Glen.

"Can you make one?"

"Yes. But why would you want a crucible?"

"I was just wondering," she said.

But in her mind, with surprising clarity, Abbe's plan came together.

One day after Kinish and the others had been home for a while, she went to her father with her thoughts. He listened carefully, and then assembled some of Gylgova's other leaders. Abbe was asked to present her ideas to them as well.

The elders agreed that if it worked, Gylgova would be transformed.

Testing the concept was, fortunately, simple and did not require a lot of initial investment. The next time the wagons rumbled away to distribute their products in the marketplaces throughout the mainland, they also carried and left behind on parchment notices a slightly different message than usual:

We buy and sell copper goods.

Once the word got out, the Gylgova men found customers waiting for them with their used, brittle or broken copper objects, utterly worthless in their current condition. The Gylgovans certainly did not pay much for them, but they didn't have to. To the sellers, something was better than nothing.

Once back in Gylgova, the best copper was separated from the collection and set aside. The junk was melted in the blacksmiths' crucible and poured into uncomplicated molds for simple artifacts like measuring cups, bowls and cooking pans. While the quality wasn't what they were used to, the items it made could be manufactured much more easily and sold for much less than their handmade creations.

The blacksmiths and coppersmiths experimented with the higher quality stock. Again, the quality wasn't quite what the Grand Reef sheets produced, but getting close was an extraordinary achievement.

Soon, the junk was coming to them.

People began gathering valueless pieces of copper and making the trip to Gylgova to sell them. Abbe, Leeni, and Kinish set the prices, and they were fair enough prices to encourage more business.

The best copper was made into ingots and stored. Some of the Grand Reef copper sheets were set aside to mix with the ingots in forming new sheets almost as good as those from Grand Reef. Everyone agreed that they had a sustainable industry growing before their eyes.

But Abbe's idea wasn't yet played out.

The following fall, the *Abbe Glen* sailed to the Bleak Shoals and filled her holding bins with prime sea wheat. Then, instead of facing the arduous journey to Grand Reef, they headed home.

The Gylgovan bakers gloried in being able to use the inimitable taste and versatility of the sea wheat for their own purposes. What the villagers did not enthusiastically consume, the visiting copper sellers and area townspeople bought, often as much as they could carry, to re-sell in their own towns.

Gylgova flourished.

Abbe had one more clever suggestion: that Broom Island become Gylgova's official protectorate. As such, Gylgovans could visit their mid-ocean paradise for a month or two any time the crew of the *Abbe Glen* chose to sail there.

Abbe was happy that everything worked out so well, and even happier that her father could disband the Grand Reef "Gylgova Players." She was not happy, however, to see travelers camp in the woods and fields beyond the edge of town.

Making yet another presentation to Gylgova's elders, she received approval to build a two-story, five-sleeping-room inn with a small restaurant on the ground floor. Abbe would become its sole proprietor after repaying the town treasury for the cost of its construction. She vowed that the inn would become known for its sea wheat blackberry muffins.

She named it *The Braided Crown*.

HARALD

As the column of Harald's men and their escorts traveled slowly along the road from Gravenwall to Westo'n, field hands stopped to watch them go by, and occasionally children ran alongside, careful not to get too close to the big war horses.

In Westo'n, the road was lined with townspeople who mostly stood in silence as they passed, but a few waved goodbye and a few others cursed them. One man stepped forward to throw a rock at Harald, and was kicked backward by a soldier from Rampal who was too tired to bother with any restraint.

Beyond Westo'n, and as the day grew warmer, they did not encounter anyone at all. The column was silent, except for the creak of leather and clink of metal. They did not stop to eat, but ate what few rations they all carried while on horseback.

In this way, they spent the day crossing the Province of Swallows, until they arrived at the garrison post near Fugitive Bridge. The post was unmanned, as per Harald's orders, which he gave to preclude a repeat of the same sort of duplicity that Master Turnbolt had engineered. The system of nets and stakes installed in the place of a garrison had to be dismantled by the escorts so Harald's group could file on through.

"Good luck to you, Harald," one soldier grinned at him. "We ran a little late with this bit, so you'll have to ride smartly to beat the tide."

In the gathering gloom that followed nightfall, Harald and his six companions alternated galloping and walking their horses across the bridge. The way was dimly illuminated by a weak moon, but they all considered it providential. The crossing was made in time, and they rested on the Welland end of the bridge watching the water close over it.

The men made their way through Welland cautiously, staying on wagon roads and under the cover of forests. One by one, Harald's Welland men left the column for towns and farms nearby, returning to their abandoned families and previous lives. The farewells were brief, but painful, and those who remained rode in thoughtful silence afterward.

At a meal of gathered greens and berries and grilled venison from a deer unable to outrun a hardened bowman, Harald asked the three who were still with him if they thought he had a chance of finding a new life in a small corner of Welland.

"Yes," one said. "For awhile. For a big country, Welland is small. Word travels fast and far. You would be found, eventually. Then your new life would depend on who found you."

When the great, blue mountains of Maurisia began to rise ahead of them, only two riders remained. When the mountains were high, Harald's last soldier stopped.

"Here is where I turn, Harald," he said. "I am afraid we must part here."

Harald had given some thought to this moment, and dismounted. He handed Typhoon's reins to the rider.

"A forest is no place for Typhoon. You take him. He's a good horse. Give him good pasturage and talk to him now and then."

"You can trust that I will, Harald. Good fortune to you."

"And you, old friend."

Harald untied his saddlebag and hung it over his shoulder. With a last stroke of Typhoon's muzzle, he turned and walked quickly away from the sound of Typhoon's alarmed stamping and whinnying.

Few people occupied this part of Welland, so Harald walked alone and in silence for two more days, with the ground growing steadily steeper. On the third day, he searched the mountain wall for the tight pass he knew was there, but it was nearly impossible to see. Finding the pass took some time, which occupied his thoughts and shielded him from an approaching feeling of dread.

He stared at the cleft in the rock for nearly an hour before finding the courage to enter it. The pass was wide enough for a horse to get through, but not much wider. When he emerged from the blue shadow of the pass into sunlight, he took a deep breath.

He was surprised to see a few inches of water in the moraine below, thinking all along that it was eternally dry. Beyond was the stone spider, the petrified roots of some gigantic ancient tree. Thoughts tumbled in his mind, memories of the small band of marauders, the tall man who killed Sundor and whom Harald killed in return. Old Paulus, long dead, a good friend from that day on. The first horse he ever mounted.

Finally, Harald began to walk again, descending the steep trail into the rocky river bottom. He patted a spider leg on his way by, smiling at the memory of how fearful the villagers were of this hunk of stone.

At the edge of the woods, he paused again, hoping he remembered the way back and wouldn't wind up lost among the trees. He passed the site of Sundor's makeshift grave, but would not look at it.

For hours he made his way through the forest, his steps far more uncertain than they were when he was a boy. A strange mixture of feelings roiled inside him: excitement, a little fear, sadness, resignation. Smells became more familiar, the hiss of the leaves and chatter of birds seemed to help guide him.

He came upon a young man gathering kindling. The young man dropped all his sticks but one, which he held like a club.

"Who are you?"

"I might ask the same, but your answer would mean nothing. Relax. I am from this village. I have been gone a long time."

"From this village? I know everyone in this village, but I do not know you."

"My name is Harald. My father was Edvar. I left many seasons ago with a hunter named Sundor."

The young man dropped the stick in surprise. If he did not know Harald, he knew the names Harald spoke.

"Who is your father?" Harald asked.

"Jovar."

Harald smiled. "Let me guess. Your mother is Sigrit."

The young man laughed with delight. "Yes, yes. Here, let me walk you in."

When they cleared the trees into the village, the young man could not contain his excitement. "Look! Look who has come back! Look who is here!"

The village was bigger, Harald noticed. There were many new houses and more fire pits. People turned. He did not recognize most of the first ones he saw, and they did not recognize him. But then he saw Sigrit, who was holding the hand of young girl. He felt a sharp pain in his chest.

Much to Harald's surprise, she ran to him, her face beaming, and hugged him. Jovar followed, smiling his wide, handsome smile. Others he had known as children came forward. There was much chattering and touching to make sure he was not a ghost. He heard some telling others who he was, and how long ago he had vanished.

They led him to Edvar's old hut, which was being used as a storehouse. A team of people busily emptied it of its contents, scattering the stores among other houses. Someone else brought a thick bag of leaves to serve as a bed.

The flurry of promises to build furniture and improve the house, questions, news of new vagabond families that had joined them, and references to the death of his parents assaulted his senses. He swayed.

Jovar, who appeared to now be the village elder, said, "Everyone, out. Harald is tired. Let him rest."

Jovar turned to Harald and said, "Will you tell us your story, Harald? This evening? Or is it too soon?"

"I will try."

He was left alone. He laid down his saddlebag and used it as a pillow, breathing in the smell of Typhoon from its leather. He could not sleep. He listened to voices outside, the high-pitched squeals of children, and the distant crack of an axe on wood.

Harald remained immersed in thoughts and conflicting emotions until the light began to dim. He heard the sounds of the evening meal being prepared, but still did not move. He had no idea how to even begin telling his story.

"Harald?" someone said. "Come for dinner, if you're hungry."

He was. He dragged himself to his feet.

Everything was almost shockingly familiar. The scene he watched, the voices and woodsmoke and laughter.

He was subdued during the meal, despite a barrage of introductions and information about changes in the village since he'd been gone — who had died, who had married who, how many children so-and-so now had. As the darkness descended, Harald was absorbed by the circle of eager faces he saw illuminated by the darting flames in front of him. *These are my people*, he thought. *I will leave them only one more time.*

"Tell us about everything, Harald. Please," Sigrit said.

He felt crushed by the reality of where he was. All that had happened before seemed to fade, and everything between the time he left and this moment seemed to mean nothing more than a story to be told beside a fire.

And with that thought, Harald found his words.

In a firm, clear voice he said:

"This is the story of a boy who set out to find the place where the world ended, and instead found the place where the world began."

Additional work by John Scott Brinkerhoff:

All in Time (1973)
Dinosaurs (1980)
The Cloud Fisher (2018)

www.ingramcontent.com/pod-product-compliance
Lightning Source LLC
Chambersburg PA
CBHW051948240626
47153CB00005B/1678